Angela Arney was born in Hampshire, where she still
lives. She has been a teacher, a hospital administrator
and a cabaret singer.

Light Me The Moon

Angela Arney

PAN BOOKS

First published 1994 by Corgi Books

This edition published 2002 by Pan Books
an imprint of Pan Macmillan Ltd
Pan Macmillan, 20 New Wharf Road, London N1 9RR
Basingstoke and Oxford
Associated companies throughout the world
www.panmacmillan.com

ISBN 0 330 40060 6

1 3 5 7 9 8 6 4 2

A CIP catalogue record for this book is available from
the British Library.

Printed and bound in Great Britain by
Mackays of Chatham plc, Chatham, Kent

Prologue

The summer night was clear and still. Evening primroses, growing in chaotic yellow profusion around the walls of the house, filled the air with their heavy incense. Mottisley Abbey's square tower flared black and squat against the unearthly luminosity of the sky; and yet it was dark. Dark and silent. Not a sound anywhere, save for a faint scuffling emanating from the bedroom window of the ancient stone house facing the abbey.

'Keep still.'

'I *am* still.' Wriggling impatiently, Diana was anything but still. She leaned further out of the window, an effort which proved too much for the rotten elastic of her pyjama bottoms. They spiralled down, eventually billowing out around her ankles, concertina fashion.

She sighed, and then was suddenly filled with rage at her mother who was never at home. Why couldn't *she* have a mother who mended things? So that her pyjamas were mended with stitches all neatly sewn in rows like little marching soldiers. Like Amanda, whose pyjamas would never fall down through lack of new elastic or stitching. Why couldn't she have a mother like Amanda Hughes's mother? who was at home all the time, doing the cooking and mending, instead of a mother who was always in London. A recent weekend spent with Amanda had opened Diana's eyes. Amanda Hughes's mother even helped Amanda with her homework. Not that she herself needed any help, Diana was quite confident in her own ability on that score, but she knew her sister, Susan, could do with some assistance. Poor Susan who found spelling and arithmetic such a problem. Diana sighed again and looked up at her elder sister standing beside her.

What a pity Susan isn't clever like me. The thought was ingenuous, without conceit. Although not quite five years old, Diana knew she was clever. Schoolwork was easy, she was way ahead of everyone else, including Susan, who, at fourteen, still found everything difficult. It puzzled Diana that people should think it so important. What did it matter if Susan was bottom of her class? It didn't stop her being the kindest, most loving sister in the world, and she was a marvellous cook. If it wasn't for her they'd starve during their mother's long absences. Mrs Loveday, their housekeeper, was lazy, and her cooking unappetizingly watery, tasting of nothing much at all, so it was always Susan's job to do something useful in the kitchen. In spite of her youthful years, Diana knew very well that without Susan life at Abbey House would grind to a juddering halt. Of course Mummy and Daddy loved Susan, and were grateful for all the work she did in the house, but they forgot to say so.

Of Diana herself, their mother was always saying, 'Of course, Diana takes after me.' Another thing which mystified her.

Too young to understand much about her mother's political career, all she knew was that they had a mother who never had time to be at home, never had time for any of them, and that included darling daddy. Sometimes Diana worried that her parents didn't love each other at all. It was the one worry she didn't tell Susan, the thought being too awful even to contemplate putting into words. She'd heard stories at school of other children's parents splitting up because they didn't love each other, and knew that splitting up meant that the children could only live with either the mummy or the daddy. To Diana it was a terrifying thought. So convincing herself that if she didn't talk about it, it couldn't possibly happen, she kept silent. Now, she sighed lustily and tried, unsuccessfully, to pull up the pyjama bottoms.

Susan, hearing the second sigh, looked down. Seeing her sister's bare pink bottom, she hitched up the offending pyjamas and tied them in a knot at the top.

'How long now?' asked Diana, switching her mind on to more comfortable thoughts. The object of their waiting.

'Just over four minutes.'

'Good, it'll come before Nancy comes up to bed. I don't want her to see. It belongs to me.'

Susan laughed. 'Don't be silly. You can't stop her looking at the moon. Anyway it belongs to everybody.'

'It doesn't. It's special for me. And I don't want *her* to see it.' Diana pushed out her bottom lip mutinously at the thought of cousin Nancy. 'I hate her,' she said. 'Why couldn't she have died in India too? Then we wouldn't have her here with us.'

'You mustn't wish people dead. And we should feel sorry for her. It must have been awful when her parents died.' Susan tried to be fair.

'I heard Mummy say that it was ridiculous for people to die on holiday, and that they should have been more careful.' Diana imitated their mother's hard clipped tones to perfection, making Susan laugh. 'And she said that Nancy arrived from India looking like the cat who'd swallowed the canary, and not at all like a heartbroken orphan.'

'How on earth did you hear that?'

'I listened at the library door when Mummy and Daddy were having one of their rows,' said Diana airily, as if it had been a game. Not for one moment would she have admitted to Susan that it hadn't been a game at all. It was one of their worst rows, and not in the least bit funny. Frightened at the ferocity of their voices she hadn't intended to listen, and had wanted to run away, but her feet had seemed anchored to the spot with invisible chains, giving her no choice but to remain. Recalling it now, she could hear the argument as if it was happening all over again.

'It's no good Geoffrey. I have two children already, and God alone knows *they're* burden enough for me. I do not, repeat, do not, intend to have a third child in the house.'

9

'But we have to take her in. She's my brother's only child. It's our duty and I don't intend to shirk it. Besides I feel as if she's part of the family already. I can hardly prise her from my side. You'd think we'd known each other all our lives. She's a charming girl.'

'Yes, I have noticed her attachment to you.' Diana remembered being alarmed at the strange, harsher than normal note in her mother's voice. 'You're a fool, Geoffrey Leigh. Always have been and always will be. Charming girl indeed. In my opinion Nancy is a nasty, precocious child, determined to get what she wants.'

'Don't you dare call me a fool, Rosemary. And as for being nasty! Well, I must say that's priceless coming from you. All Nancy wants is a home, and I shall see that she has one.'

'I've nothing against her having a home. But not here.'

'Yes, here, Rosemary. Here in Abbey House, which may I remind you is mine, not yours. If you don't like my decision then you can move out and stay in London. You might as well anyway. You're hardly ever here.'

'If I stay in London permanently, I'll take the girls with me.'

Diana had stiffened with terror at that. Was that what splitting up meant? Were her parents going to split up over Nancy?

'You try and take the girls, and I'll fight you in every court in the land.' Her father sounded fierce, quite unlike his usual self. 'I'll tell them what sort of mother you really are. An absentee one. Imagine what that would do to your precious parliamentary career.'

'I suppose that's when Mummy said yes,' said Susan with a bitter laugh. 'She wouldn't want anything to ruin her political image.'

'Well, yes, but it was quite a long time after that.' Diana didn't understand Susan's comments about political images and why it should be important to her mother, but she did remember her mother's eventual capitulation to her father's wishes. 'I can't remember everything they said,' she told Susan, 'because they argued on and on. But Daddy really wanted Nancy to stay and in the end he won.' Diana paused, shivering suddenly at the memory. 'It was a horrible, horrible quarrel,' she said, then added fretfully, 'I wonder why Daddy likes Nancy so much?'

'Because she's our cousin, I suppose,' said Susan matter of factly. 'But don't worry. He'll never love her more than you or me. Especially you.'

'Sure?' asked Diana.

That was another thing she worried about. There was something oddly menacing about their cousin Nancy. In Diana's imagination she loomed as a large threatening figure, in spite of the fact that in reality Nancy was small, dark and slim. An elfin girl, always smiling. But in spite of the sweet smile Diana didn't like her, although she could never find the right words to explain why.

'Quite sure,' said Susan firmly.

But she too had her worries which she had no intention of communicating to Diana. In spite of her firm denial, she also worried about Nancy usurping them in their father's favour. Susan had no difficulty in finding the right words whenever she saw Nancy managing to manipulate every little event to her own advantage. Nancy was a fawning, deceitful, little bitch. For once in her life Susan found herself agreeing with her mother. Nancy should have been sent somewhere else, anywhere else. Abbey House would have been much better without her.

But it was too late now, Nancy had stayed, attaching herself to the household with limpet-like tenacity. The decision having been made, Rosemary Leigh had then acted in character. Never a woman to miss an opportunity she used the event as advantageous publicity. All the newspapers descended upon Abbey House, and Susan remembered the family standing in the garden, smiling sweetly as they presented a united front for the benefit of the photographers. *The Junior Minister For Health Who Really Cares, Rosemary Leigh Takes An Orphan Under*

Her Wing. Those were the headlines. All fiction of course. Rosemary Leigh forgot about all of them once she returned to London the next day. The affairs of state were far more important to her than three children or her husband. It was their father, Geoffrey Leigh, the shadowy, ineffectual man always lagging behind the flamboyant Rosemary, who looked after the children, and ran the farm attached to Abbey House in a haphazard, desultory manner, and they'd always been happy enough. But since Nancy's arrival he had changed. He was still loving and caring and did his best, but to Susan a dark shadow seemed to envelop him. As if he always had something else on his mind. But like Diana, Susan kept her thoughts to herself. The two sisters worried separately, and in silence.

An impatient voice jerked Susan's thoughts back to the present moment. Diana had grown tired of the subject of Nancy. 'How long, Susan? How long?'

Susan looked at her watch. 'Another three and a half minutes.'

'And then Daddy will light me the moon.' Diana had the ability of the very young to swing with mercurial swiftness from one mood to another. Nancy was now completely forgotten as she stretched out her arms, and leaned even further out of the window.

Susan thought her sister looked like a young frog about to take the plunge into a pond. 'You'll plop right out, over into the garden in a minute.'

Diana giggled, spreading her fingers wide until her hands looked like two starfish against the rough stones of the old house. Bubbling with happiness, she stared out into the ever darkening garden, fixing her eyes intently on the silhouette of the yew tree, over the top of which she knew the moon would soon appear. 'He's a very clever Daddy isn't he? And he never forgets a promise, because when he says it will, the moon always comes. It's magic, and it's especially for me. I'm his moon princess.' Diana had been told the story of Diana, the moon goddess, who hunted across the cloudless sky at night in her silver chariot, and she now regarded the moon as her own special property.

But a cynicism born of fourteen years' experience blighted Susan's sight. Magic indeed! It was only because he knew what time the moon would rise and whether or not there would be clouds. Only then did he ever promise Diana. 'I don't believe in magic,' she muttered, suddenly feeling very grown up and irritable.

Diana turned and stared at her sister in shocked horror. For all her cleverness, she was only a little girl, and to her a world without magic was unthinkable. 'But you must believe,' she pleaded. 'How can you live without magic? Say you do, Susan, *please.*'

The confused emotions of adolescence made Susan long to say she'd outgrown such childish beliefs, but now, looking at Diana beside her, eyes shining in expectation, Susan knew disillusionment would be cruel. So she said grudgingly, 'All right. I believe.'

Content to have Susan included in her enchanted world, Diana turned back to the open window and leaned out again. In her mind the moon, her father and she herself were irrevocably bound together; he sailed as high in her sky as the real moon did above the dark earth. 'And he *is* clever,' she said, wanting confirmation from Susan.

'Yes,' Susan agreed. 'He's very clever.' Let Diana believe now if that was what she wanted. She would find out one day that magic didn't exist, and that would be the day she grew up.

'How long now?'

'Two minutes,' said Susan, feeling irritated again. If her little sister was so clever, why hadn't she worked out the rising of the moon for herself? Why couldn't she see through their father's subterfuge? How was it he could pull the wool over her eyes so easily? But she already knew the answer, it was there beside her, showing in Diana's rapt face and lambent grey eyes. She adored her father, and nothing in the world was going to shake her faith in him. She didn't *want* to find out there was no such thing as magic.

'I shall never leave Abbey House,' Diana said suddenly and very determinedly. As if to reinforce her comment, she spread her arms even wider over the wall beneath the window sill, clasping her home to her. 'Feel the house,' she whispered softly. 'It's breathing.'

Susan looked at the small blonde head hanging out of the window, thinking it was impossible to feel irritated with Diana for long. Obediently, she too spread her arms over the walls to feel the house. The ancient stones were warm to the touch. Soaking up the sun all day, the house gave it back now, dark sunlight flowing out into the night through their fingers. Diana was right, it did almost feel as if it were breathing. But as for Diana never leaving, that was silly. Of the two of them, Susan knew it was most likely that she would end up stuck in Abbey House as some sort of unpaid housekeeper, although it was she who longed to escape and explore the world. But Diana's future was sure to be much more exciting.

'You'll change your mind when you grow up, and want to leave,' she said.

'No I won't,' Diana cried. 'I shall always, always live here.'

Susan was silent. It was inevitable that Diana would leave. She would go on to university when she was old enough, and then out into the big wide world, and end up doing something important. Diana's future was the one thing father and mother always agreed about.

Susan's thoughts drifted on to their parents. She knew the people in the village gossiped about Geoffrey and Rosemary Leigh's strangely remote marriage. They were almost always apart, and when they were together they bickered viciously and constantly, unless there was any-one outside the family present. Then, they presented a harmonious, if somewhat strained, performance of marital bliss. Susan often wondered what her father thought. But their parents' happiness, or lack of it, was another thing she didn't talk about to Diana; considering she was far too young to understand the complexities of adult relationships. Even for Susan herself it was a hazy, amorphous area. All she knew for certain was that all was not well, and that the arrival of Nancy had done nothing to improve matters. Her thoughts switched to cousin Nancy. Why was it she could wind their father around her little finger with such apparent ease?

'I suppose you could always stay. If you really wanted to,' said Susan after a long interval of silence. 'You could stay here with me. And then, when we're grown up, we'll stop growing boring things like kale and cabbages and turn the farm back into a vineyard. We could make it just as it was when the Cistercian monks lived in the abbey.'

A warm mellow glow sharpened the dark fringed edge of the yew tree seconds before the rounded edge of a pink harvest moon peeped a clear wink of light over the top of the tree. The square edge of the abbey's tower now stood out sharp and clear in the warm moonlight.

'There it is,' cried Diana in triumph, forgetting everything else. 'My moon has come. Just like Daddy promised.'

Susan didn't answer. A small movement down below, in the thickness of the rhododendron bushes which smothered the lower part of the garden, caught her attention. A gap, a relic of the previous winter's storms, in the branches of the ancient yew, suddenly allowed a beam of clear moonlight to flood the garden, and Susan saw the disturbance was caused by two people. They were making their way silently, down between the overhanging bushes, towards the rickety wooden gate hanging lopsidedly on broken hinges at the bottom of the garden. It was a man and a woman.

Leaning further out, and straining her eyes into the darkness, Susan realized with a jolt of surprise that one of the figures was not a woman at all, it was a girl. It was cousin Nancy, and she was with a man. The couple moved quickly out of the beam of light, and in spite of straining and straining her eyes, Susan found it impossible to see the man clearly. She watched in puzzled silence. Diana, totally absorbed with her beloved moon, chattered on happily, but Susan wasn't listening. Her gaze was fixed on the two figures, moving hurriedly, furtively, as if not wanting to be seen. A few seconds later they had disappeared altogether into the darkness of the alleyway which ran alongside the flintstone wall of the abbey churchyard.

PART ONE

AMBITION

Chapter One

'Oh, Susan. How can you be happy, being so poor?'

At eighteen, Diana looked back with amused contempt at the little girl who'd made the vehement declaration that she'd never leave Abbey House.

'Only poor money wise,' Susan corrected her. 'I have other riches. Love, for instance.'

'Love!' Diana scoffed. 'Is that really enough? Tom is nice, but he has no ambition, and no prospects. He's always going to be stuck here in Mottisley. What sort of life is that? Always the village school teacher. And you, for ever his wife.'

'Not only a wife, a mother soon,' said Susan with a serene smile.

Diana was exasperated. She loved Susan dearly, and because of that she wanted her to have a better life than the one she saw on offer for her at the moment. It couldn't be good to stagnate in the place of one's birth. People had to pull up their roots and move on. That was what progress was all about.

'But that's just it, Susan. Once the baby comes you'll have even less money. And God knows you paid enough for this place.' She flung her arms wide encompassing the tiny cottage which was Tom and Susan's home. She was glad Susan was happy, but for the life of her she found it utterly incomprehensible.

'It doesn't matter.' Susan took a fruit cake from the oven in her cluttered, but homely, little kitchen. 'I know this cottage is small, and was expensive, but we can manage. Are you sure you won't stay for tea and cake? Tom should be home any moment now.'

'No, I . . .' Diana hesitated. She was meeting Joe, but

no-one, not even Susan, knew that she and Joe Kelly were lovers. It was a secret she and Joe had both agreed to keep, feeling there was no need to feed the village grapevine with unnecessary gossip, so that tongues could wag, minds slyly deduce, inevitably reaching erroneous conclusions. 'I promised to ride over to May and Bert's and take some of our Victoria plums. She's jam making tonight.' It wasn't a lie. She had the plums with her, and she *was* going to Aunt May's, and then she was meeting Joe.

'Off you go then.' Susan gave her sister an affectionate peck on the cheek, 'and give my love to May.'

'Of course.'

Weighted down by the bag of plums Diana pedalled furiously through the winding lanes towards Willow Farm and her great Aunt May. Face pink from the effort of the last steep slope up towards the farm, she grinned as she thought of her aunt and Bert. '*May's common-law husband*,' as her mother insisted on calling him, in a tone of voice that always reeked of disapproval. Not that the disapproval mattered to May, it bounced off her like water off a duck's back. Where matters of so-called morality and convention were concerned, May and Bert were light years ahead of their time. They loved each other, were faithful to each other and had lived together for as long as anyone could remember; as far as they were concerned marriage was an unnecessary complication. Diana glanced at her watch as she finally struggled into the yard of Willow Farm, and promptly forgot about May's lifestyle. There wasn't much time. Not if she was to meet Joe at 5.30 p.m. as she had promised.

Plums delivered she set off once more on her bicycle. 'You young people are all the same,' grumbled her aunt. 'Always in a rush. Soon you'll be off to that university of yours, and I won't be seeing you at all.'

Diana laughed. 'For someone who spends a good part of her life charging around the countryside on a motor-bike, usually breaking the speed limit, you're a fine one to talk about rushing! But I'll come tomorrow.' The last words were shouted over her shoulder as she sped through the farmyard gate. 'I'll collect some of that jam you're making and I promise I'll stay to tea.' Joe was away tomorrow. She could stay.

The track to Winterbourne Thicket was overgrown and deeply rutted. Hardly anyone ever came this way now. No gamekeepers were employed on the manor house estate, everything was falling into decay and nature was claiming back the land for its own. It was their perfect secret place, hers and Joe's, well away from prying eyes.

Diana rode as far as she could, then dismounted and pushed the bicycle. Already late, she hurried, put her foot down an extra deep rut and would have fallen but for a large pair of hands which clamped tight around her waist. A second later she felt Joe's mouth nuzzle at her neck. Turning, she instinctively raised her face to his, welcoming his sweet warm mouth closing on hers in a slow, deeply pleasurable kiss. He has a way of turning my bones to water, thought Diana, giving herself up to the bliss of the moment. The bicycle, forgotten, slid sideways into a clump of blackberry brambles.

At last Joe raised his head, pausing to take a breath. 'Come on. Let's get off the main path.' He led the way into their favourite leafy hollow, where the thick green moss provided a soft, springy bed.

'I shall always remember this smell,' said Diana, stretching luxuriously, and turning her face towards the fragrant moss. 'This lovely mixture of wood, leaves and earth.'

'The perfume of eternal life,' said Joe seriously. 'A place where things grow, die and grow again. Our small hollow encapsulates the perfect circle of life. What better place could there be to make love?'

'Nowhere,' said Diana, drawing the outline of his dark face with her forefinger. Oh, but he's handsome, she thought. Those blue eyes, so blue and so penetrating; and the faint laughter lines around his firm lips. It will be hard to give him up. She put the thought away. No need to

21

worry about that just yet. 'I didn't know you were so poetic, Joe.'

'There's a lot you don't know about me. Or I you, Diana' he said softly. 'But given time we'll find out, won't we, darling?'

'Kiss me again, Joe.' She didn't want to talk, or even think about time, because it was running out. The swallows were already preparing to leave their summer nests beneath the eaves of the cottages and barns, lining up on the telephone wires, jostling for position, the little ones still precarious in flight and balance; but one morning soon they would all be gone. And then she too would be leaving. Anxious not to talk, she drew Joe down towards her, and found forgetfulness in the enchantment of his body.

Their lovemaking was gentle and innocently erotic. Mutual inexperience had proved no barrier, rather it led them into paths of secret pleasure. Having no guidelines meant nothing was taboo. Together they explored the depths of intimacy and sensuality. Until at last the urge to finish what they had begun was so great, they clung to one another as if willing their very bones to fuse.

Then all was peace. They lay together in silence. Her lips in the hollow of his shoulder, his lips against the softness of her hair.

At last Joe spoke. He too had been thinking of their impending separation. 'Do you really have to go to university?'

Diana raised herself up on one elbow. 'You know I do. What can I do here?'

'You could always marry me.'

'We've already discussed that.' Diana sighed. It was one of the few things she found irritating about Joe. His stubborn persistence. 'I can't marry anyone. Not until I've got my degree, and got a career under way.'

'And then you'll marry me?'

Diana laughed. Even his persistence could sometimes be endearing, but she had no intention of letting herself

22

get boxed into a corner. 'Oh, Joe,' she teased, 'by then you will have probably forgotten all about me.'

'How could I? I'll still see you when you come back to Mottisley.'

Diana was silent. In spite of loving Joe, she was practical to the core of her being. A characteristic she had acquired over the years. She and Joe were so different in their basic outlook on life that it stood to reason that their lives were not destined to run in parallel. But Joe couldn't, or wouldn't, see that. Evasive, she gave an ambiguous answer. 'Of course I'll see you sometimes. But you'll be busy too. There won't be much time.'

'I'll never be busy,' said Joe stubbornly, refusing to be side-tracked.

'Of course you will. You'll have to do *something* with your life. You can't just hang around here for ever.'

'Why not? I'm perfectly happy as I am. I buy a few cars, do them up, make some money. Play the piano in the local pubs. That's always a good little earner.'

Although she knew it was useless, Diana couldn't resist trying to push him into being more ambitious. 'That's the whole point. It's a *little* earner. Wouldn't you like to have a lot of money?'

'Why? My ma and pa haven't a penny to bless themselves with. They're happy enough, in their own odd way. Probably happier than your parents who have plenty of money.'

Diana snorted crossly. Joe's parents were Irish tinkers, living in a picturesque Romany caravan with an assortment of dogs and horses. Odd was the right description. Joe's father did odd jobs, when he was sober, which wasn't often, and his mother made pegs and told fortunes. They moved whenever the whim took them, but Diana had to admit from what little she'd seen of them, they did seem contented enough.

'My parents have not got plenty of money,' she said. It was difficult to argue with Joe, he was too easy going.

'How can that be? Your father has the farm.'

23

'Inefficient,' said Diana.

'And your mother is a well-known politician. Is that what you want to do? Go into politics?'

'Certainly not. A vastly overrated career. Long hours, hard work and a pittance of a salary compared to industry. No, I want a secure source of wealth.'

'Supposing you fail and don't make it.'

'Not make it!' Diana was indignant at the mere suggestion. 'Of course I'm going to make it. I'm going to be wealthy and powerful. I'll have you know, Joe Kelly, that failure is not a word in my vocabulary.'

Joe laughed, and pulled her back into his arms. 'You're crazy,' he said, 'but I love you.'

As they kissed, Diana knew that she'd feel more than a little twinge of sadness when the time came for the inevitable parting with Joe. But it would have to be, it was part of life's pattern, following the choices she'd mapped out for herself. Loving Joe was not enough to forgo reaching out for the fruits of her ambition. All within her grasp. But to grasp them needed dedication and determination. Other girls might let their hearts rule their heads, but not Diana. Her analytical mind had pigeon-holed love and ambition into two quite separate compartments, each to be balanced, one against the other, and the scales were tipped heavily in favour of ambition. In the final analysis, Joe didn't stand a chance. When the time came, Diana knew she would say goodbye and walk away from him. She'd already made her choice, there was no going back.

Dr Evans confirmed what Diana already suspected.

'You are pregnant, my dear.' He hesitated, used to his patients being deferential to the point of humility, young Diana Leigh's self-assurance always unnerved him. She was so different from her sister, Susan. But now he pitied the girl before him. An unwanted pregnancy, never a very happy state of affairs. 'Would you like to talk about it?' he asked gently.

'No.' The answer was abrupt to the point of rudeness. Diana saw no point in talking. Not to Dr Evans or anyone else. She had to think, then make a decision. 'Thank you,' she added, remembering her manners as she reached the door of his surgery. 'I'll come back to you when I've decided what to do, and please don't tell my parents. I'll do that myself.'

'Every word uttered in this surgery is confidential, Diana. You should know that.' Dr Evans was exasperated. It was very difficult to stay feeling sorry for a girl who showed so sign of emotion.

Once away from Dr Evans's surgery, Diana's rigid self control deserted her. The news numbed her mind, making coherent thought impossible. Everything had become jumbled, confused. Logic telling her what she ought to do, get rid of it and get on with her life; then suddenly long submerged morality, in direct conflict with logic, was rearing its head, and all the things she'd read and thought in earlier years returned in full flood. Opposing principles clashed, battling for supremacy, until her head ached, and her mind was in turmoil as the contrary points of view fought for dominion. It's wrong. It's murder. How can you take away the life of an unborn child? But it's wrong to bring an unwanted child into the world. And it's wrong to waste a precious talent, and I have talent. But is that a good enough reason for killing a baby? No, having a termination is not killing anything. It is the only sensible choice.

Having made the decision, Diana told her parents.

'Who is the father?' That was her mother's first question.

'Joe Kelly.'

'Oh my God. That settles it. She can't marry him, Geoffrey. He's not suitable at all.'

'I have no intention of marrying Joe,' said Diana.

Her father wasn't listening. 'If only you'd had a liaison with someone from a good family,' he grumbled. 'Someone like Tony Evans would have done. At least he'll end up being a doctor one day. A respectable profession, medicine.'

'Not much money in it though,' said Rosemary Leigh. 'Diana can do better than that.'

'I am going to do better, and I'm not marrying anyone,' said Diana impatiently. 'It's this pregnancy we're supposed to be talking about.'

That concentrated their minds and they were united. 'There's only one decision possible,' said her mother. 'It has to be an abortion.' Geoffrey Leigh agreed.

'You don't think it's wrong?' In spite of having made up her mind Diana had to ask. They were saying what she wanted to hear. She didn't want the baby, and an abortion was the solution. But the guilt factor was stronger than Diana had at first imagined. 'Is it wrong,' she repeated, 'killing a baby?'

'Nonsense,' her mother was brisk, businesslike. 'It isn't a baby. Don't even think of it like that. It's just a little lump of jelly. A few cells stuck together.'

'And you definitely don't want it, do you?'

Diana shook her head. 'I can't see my future with Joe.'

'Good,' said her mother crisply. 'Joe Kelly is a nothing. No breeding, no brains, no money and definitely no future.' Her voice was razor sharp with contempt. 'Your father and I have not brought you up to have you throw yourself away on a man like that.'

'The place at university is already waiting for you, and a brilliant future beckons.' Her father was saying exactly what she wanted to hear, soothing balm to the remnants of her conscience. 'It's what you've worked for, what *we've* worked for. You've always wanted to spread your wings and taste the real world. You don't want to end up like Susan.'

'No,' said Diana, 'I don't.' That was the truth. The prospect of early motherhood and a dull life in the country was terrifying.

'Then you can see that there is only one decision,' said

her mother. 'It has to be an abortion. There is no alternative.'

'Does Joe know anything about this?' Geoffrey Leigh wanted to know. 'I'd never put anything past that family. Joe and his parents might cause problems.'

'Not yet.' Instinct had made Diana keep the news from Joe.

Her father nodded in approval. 'Good. Now, make quite sure that he never does find out. If he's anything like his father, his reaction is likely to be unpredictable. And although I doubt that he's seen the inside of a church since the day he was christened, he might have a sudden upsurge of faith, and try to persuade you to keep it.'

'Oh yes, of course, they're Catholics.' Her mother was disapproving. 'Such an uncompromising religion I always think.'

'I don't think Joe is particularly religious.' Diana felt an unexpected rush of loyalty towards him. Just because she was pregnant there was no need for her parents to criticize everything about him.

'Evidently not,' was her mother's sarcastic reply. 'If he'd been religious, he would not have indulged in fornication with such enthusiasm.'

'I was enthusiastic too,' said Diana truthfully.

'That much is evident by the fact that you are now pregnant, my dear. Now, don't let's waste time arguing. We must decide how to do what has to be done.'

'First things first,' said her father. 'You must see Joe as soon as possible, and tell him that the affair is finished, and that you are leaving Mottisley earlier than originally planned. Tell him that it won't be possible to see him again.'

'It will be difficult,' said Diana slowly. 'Do I have to say goodbye so soon?'

'The sooner the better, surely you can see that?' said her mother irritably. She looked at her watch. 'I'll get on the 'phone now, and make all the arrangements with a very discreet private clinic I know. You'll leave here tomorrow, and you won't return until the end of your first term at university. By then, all this will be forgotten.'

Geoffrey Leigh was admiring. 'One thing I'll say for you, Rosemary, and that is, when you make up your mind, you're a marvellous organizer.'

'A great pity you haven't always let me do all the organizing,' said his wife acidly. 'Then perhaps our lives might have turned out quite differently.'

There was an awkward silence. Oh please, thought Diana, don't let them quarrel, not *now*!

'When will you get rid of Joe?' said her father to Diana.

Diana felt another pang. It sounded so cold-blooded, talking about getting rid of Joe in that tone of voice. He wasn't bad, just unsuitable. She sighed, but of course they were right. It had to be an abortion, and she had to say goodbye to Joe. The sooner it was done, the better.

'I'll say goodbye to him tonight,' she said. 'I'll tell him I have to leave Mottisley earlier than planned, and I'll also say that it's unlikely that I'll see him again.'

'Good,' said her mother. 'Just make sure that he understands that. And also make sure that he never knows about this pregnancy.'

Joe made his way towards her. He was late, as usual, but didn't hurry. Tall, lean, and athletic, he ambled with an animal like grace through the densely wooded copse of Winterbourne Thicket. He fits in here, Diana found herself thinking, unable to stop the familiar stirring of her body. She pulled herself up sharply. I haven't come to make love. Only to say goodbye.

'Diana.' The sound of his voice unexpectedly caught at her throat, and Diana realized with an uneasy qualm that the parting was perhaps going to be more difficult than she'd envisaged. It was all very well her parents telling her to get rid of Joe; they didn't have to do it.

'You're late,' she accused, anxiety making her acerbic.

Joe grinned, wholly unrepentant. 'You've never held that against me before.'

Without waiting for a reply, he pulled her against him, his fingers already busy with the buttons of her summer dress.

Diana opened her mouth to protest, only to find that Joe's tongue got in the way of words. There's no harm in one last kiss, she told herself, savouring the sweetness of his mouth. But knew she was being less than honest. One kiss was not enough. She wanted him, all of him. The fierce, animal vitality Joe exuded made him irresistible. Forgetting all her good resolutions of keeping the meeting short and to the point, she began kissing him back with increasing fervour. I'll tell him I'm leaving later. Making love one more time doesn't matter. Of course it did, she knew it did. She was cheating.

'I want you so much.' Conscience blew away on the breeze as Diana wound her arms around his neck.

The familiar bed of moss was kind to their naked bodies. Joe lay on top of her, caressing her breasts until the nipples became rock hard and tingled unbearably. Arms around his neck, hugging him tightly to her, Diana rotated her hips invitingly, longing for the feel of Joe inside her.

'One day, my darling. I'll make love to you all night in a bed, not in this damp wood,' said Joe.

Diana didn't answer. She was too busy luxuriating in the exquisite sensation of Joe. It felt so good when their bodies were welded together like this. Utter, utter bliss, and she wished it could last for ever. But rapture was always fleeting. Soon it would end in a mystical explosion. The colours of the rainbow would separate and fade, and then, still locked together, they'd float back down to reality. Rocking her hips, Diana matched Joe's rhythm as they accelerated towards a climax.

Two hours later Diana rolled away out of Joe's embrace. She had to go, it was time to return to Abbey House, and still she had not told him she was leaving. Now, suddenly, and with unexpected force, guilt struck deep within her. I should have been stronger, and said no. Too late, she realized that she'd let her own desire divert her from the real purpose of meeting Joe. She'd made the task harder, for herself and Joe. But it had to be done. She must say goodbye, now, this minute.

Sitting up, and struggling to put on her bra, she began, battling to find the right words. 'Joe, there's something I've got to tell you.'

Joe lay on his back in the grass, and ran a lazy finger down her bare back. 'Don't get dressed yet, darling. I want you again.'

'No, Joe . . . I . . .'

Laughing, he pulled her back into his arms. His mouth searching for hers. 'Are you telling me that I've got to wait until tomorrow night?'

This time Diana dodged his kisses, leaning her arms on his chest to keep them apart. 'I won't be with you tomorrow night, Joe.'

Joe reluctantly released her and Diana sat up. 'Ah well,' he said philosophically, 'the next night then.'

'No, nor the next night. In fact, what I'm trying to say is – goodbye.'

There, she'd said it. A little baldly perhaps, but at least she'd said it.

She had his full attention now. He sat up abruptly, and grasped her arm. 'Goodbye?'

Diana averted her eyes, unprepared for the look of incredulous pain she suddenly glimpsed in Joe's. 'You knew I was going to university at the end of the summer,' she mumbled unhappily. 'I'm leaving three weeks early, that's all.' It's a lie her conscience shrieked at her. *You're leaving to kill his baby.*

'But I'll see you when you come home. It doesn't have to be goodbye does it?'

Suddenly Diana had a vision of herself excavating an enormous dark pit at Joe's feet, and now she was just about to push him into it. She took a deep breath, it had to be done, her survival depended upon it. 'Yes it does, Joe. I think it's better to finish it.'

'Better for whom?' His voice was harsh with hurt anger.

Diana flinched. 'For both of us.' This isn't the way it should be at all, she thought in panic. In my plans it was all so clear cut, and painless. I was sensible, and so was Joe. But the reality was perversely the opposite, not at all well-ordered, and Joe was being stubborn and emotionally untidy. Not making any effort at all to be reasonable.

'I don't see why.'

'Oh, Joe, for God's sake be practical.' The rising tide of guilt made Diana snap sharply. 'I'm going to university and when I've finished there, I shall be going on to somewhere else. I'll never live here in Mottisley again. So there's no point in prolonging our affair because I won't be here. I thought you knew that.'

'And I thought you loved me.'

'I do. No, I mean, I did. But, Joe, you've always known it was not the sort of love that lasts for ever.' She fumbled for the right words, and knowing she was making a mess of it, took refuge in anger, flying at him, her voice trembling in fury. 'Oh Hell! Why on earth do you have to make it so difficult?' Suddenly she realized that his feelings for her were much more intense than her own. He wouldn't have had a moment's doubt. With blinding certainty she knew that if he found out about the baby he'd want to keep it, and would do his utmost to try and prevent her from having an abortion.

By now Joe was struggling into his clothes, anger making him clumsy with the buttons and zips. 'Why the hell should I make it easy for you, just because you've decided it's time for ambition to take over.' Diana started to protest but Joe cut her short. 'Oh yes you have. You've decided to draw a neat little box around this part of your life. The time has come to move on. So you're going. I'm the disposable, the unimportant, forgettable part of your life. You've *used* me, Diana Leigh, and I'll always remember that.' He turned and strode away.

'Joe, I . . .' The denial died on her lips. What was the

31

point in calling after him. It was true, she *had* used him. She deserved those bitter words. Only now did Diana realize that she should have thought more about the end at the beginning. Intent only on her own immediate pleasure and absorbed with her own plans for the future, she had never stopped to consider how much she might hurt Joe. But it was too late for regrets now, the damage was done.

How cold the breeze was whispering through the trees. How lonely this place. Shoulders hunched, Diana watched miserably as Joe left their secret trysting place. Gone was the grace of the young man who'd entered the copse. The undergrowth snapped and crackled noisily as he blundered and crashed his way blindly through the copse. A pair of magpies, disturbed by the racket, swooped down, scolding harshly. Diana bent and picked up her shoes. At least he didn't know about the baby.

Chapter Two

Ten years later, when making one of her rare visits to Mottisley to see her father, the one person, apart from Susan and Aunt May, with whom Diana kept in regular touch, she found to her surprise that Susan had moved back to Abbey House. The whole family had come with her, Tom her husband, and the two children, Clementina and Simon.

Diana questioned Susan about the move. Now a sophisticated woman of twenty-eight, she'd cultivated a reputation for being blunt and straight to the point during her years in business, and saw no reason to act differently with her immediate family.

'Susan, why on earth are you here? I thought you didn't get on with Mother and Father. Or has everything changed?'

Susan pulled a rueful face. 'If you mean has anything changed viz. Mum and Dad, the answer is no. Nothing has changed. But I must admit they have been very good to us, allowing us to move in like this. Believe me if there had been any other way we would not have come, but we had no choice. We can't afford to keep up the mortgage payments on the cottage. Tom's illness has been going on for so long. It's a disaster, and has scuppered everything.'

Privately Diana had always thought Tom a disaster from the word go, but wisely had kept her own counsel. So proud herself, she hated thinking of Susan having to go on her bended knees asking for a place to live. Even now, when she didn't see her often, and the years apart had put, what Diana thought, an unbridgeable distance beween the woman she herself had become and the two little girls they'd once been in Mottisley, Susan still held a very special place in her heart. Just as she had when she was a little girl, Diana still felt that Susan's lovable nature was undervalued by her parents, and it saddened her that now her sister had the added burden of Tom. All the same, she felt a prickle of hurt because Susan hadn't asked her for help first.

'But surely Tom will be able to teach again once he's well? You know I'd have helped you with the mortgage until then. You needn't have taken the drastic step of moving back into Abbey House.'

'He will never get well, Diana.' Susan hesitated, fiddling about with the vase of flowers she was arranging. Then she turned to face Diana. 'Tom has motor neurone disease. He only has a little time left.'

Diana's elegant facade momentarily vanished as she swore like a trooper. God in heaven. Why was there no justice in this world? Her own opinion of Tom was irrelevant. Susan loved him, that was all that mattered; and now she was about to lose him. 'When did you know this?'

'I've known for some time. But I've not told anyone. Now I have to.'

'Oh, Susan, you poor thing.' Diana flung her arms around her sister. Then a thought struck her. 'Hell! And you are just about to produce another wretched child.'

'Don't call it wretched. I want the baby.'

'I'm surprised Tom had the strength to get you pregnant.'

Susan flushed, and her mouth tightened angrily. 'How dare you say that. My sex life has nothing to do with you.'

Diana sighed, chastened. Susan was right, it was none of her business. 'Sorry, that was wrong of me. But you must admit it is an additional problem. How on earth are you going to support it, or the rest of the family come to that? You'll have to let me help.'

Susan looked determined. When it came to stubbornness the two sisters were alike. 'We shall manage. One of the reasons for moving back here is so that I can tend the vines Dad let us plant. Last year's harvest was quite good, and this one should be a very profitable one for Abbey House wines. You wait and see, Diana, you'll be surprised. And Dad has promised me that as soon as we've totted up the sums, he'll set up a proper business account for the vineyard in my name. Then I'll be self-sufficient.'

In spite of Susan's determination and enthusiasm, Diana wasn't impressed. A hazardous, unpredictable venture in her opinion. 'You'll never make much money. Agriculture in any form is subject to the vagaries of the weather.'

'Not much money by your standards, Diana,' Susan agreed. 'But enough for us.'

Diana sighed, the gap between her means and those of Susan yawned as wide and deep as the Grand Canyon. It was ridiculous feeling guilty because she had earned herself a fortune, but when she was with Susan she always did. Maybe it was Susan's silent disapproval of her continual quest for wealth. Money attracted more money, once on the merry-go-round, one had to stay on. Susan didn't understand that. A BSc in estate management had led Diana to a career as a development surveyor with a firm of property developers. Then she took the plunge and became freelance. Now she was hired for her ruthless ability for rapid decision-making, and had moved into the area of regeneration development. She worked hard, and hustled for new clients with all the nerve and daring of a seasoned con man.

Diana looked at her sister and felt the usual mixture of exasperation and admiration sweep through her. 'I'll never understand you, Susan. Not if I live to be a hundred. You're content with so little, and more than that you remain cheerful when one problem after another piles on top of you.'

For once Susan's ready smile faltered. 'Don't be fooled,' she said quietly. 'I'm not always cheerful. And sometimes I get angry with Tom. He can't help being ill, but he doesn't understand how much his illness affects me. I need a shoulder to cry on sometimes, and then I go to Joe Kelly.'

'Joe Kelly!' After so many years Diana was disturbed to find the name still had the power to cause an unpleasant jolt.

'Of course, I forget.' Susan smiled. 'You're here so little you wouldn't know. Joe has moved back and bought the derelict manor house. He's going to renovate it.'

'Really! I'm surprised he has the money, he never had a bean before.'

Susan looked cross. 'For God's sake don't look so disapproving, Diana. Like the rest of us Joe has changed, and I like him. Sometimes I think it's only Joe who keeps me sane.'

Diana was silent. This was a Susan she'd never seen before. Admitting to needing a shoulder to cry on, and Joe Kelly keeping her sane. But if it was me, she thought, I wouldn't be weeping, I'd be suicidal.

'Look, Susan,' she said. 'Don't be too proud to let me help. You know I'm not short of a penny or two. In fact, I've just had a huge fat fee for my work in Cardiff. And soon I'm off to Paris on another consultancy. I've been invited by a French company to survey an area around the Sacré Coeur for redevelopment potential.

'Oh dear,' interrupted Susan. 'Please promise me that you won't pull down *all* the old buildings.'

'Susan! I'll have you know that although I'm renowned for my policies of away with the old and on with the new, I am also known for my good taste.'

'From what I've heard, you specialize in pulling things down and erecting huge concrete buildings. Sometimes I think all the architects you employ must have shares in multi-national concrete companies.' Susan was very concerned with ecology and heritage, and Diana's apparent lack of regard for both worried her. Then she laughed, adding with a twinkle in her eye, 'whoever would have thought that my own sister would turn out to be an environmental hooligan.'

'Never mind all that,' she said. 'What I'm trying to get into your thick head, Susan, is that you needn't go short of anything. You know I'll help. Promise you'll tell me if you really need anything.' Susan nodded agreement, and Diana sighed in relief. 'After all,' she added, 'I've nothing much else to spend my money on. Only myself.'

'You ought to get married,' said Susan.

'When I meet the right man.' But Susan's words struck a chord. She'd been so busy making money that she hadn't had time even to consider slotting a man into her life. 'Yes,' she added thoughtfully. 'The right man would be a definite asset, particularly when socializing with clients. Perhaps it is time I got married.'

'And have a family?'

Diana froze. Why was it whenever she came to Mottisley some careless, casually uttered words always triggered off memories of events she would prefer to forget.

'No, I'll never do that. I don't want children.'

And that was true. She didn't even particularly like children. Unruly thoughts threatened to rush in, but Diana was ready for them. With an expertise born of practice, she snapped her mind shut. Concentrating only on what she wanted to think.

'I still think you ought to get married, children or no children,' said Susan.

'I'll start looking for a suitable man.'

'I believe you mean it,' Susan teased.

'Of course I do.' Diana was serious. 'You've reminded me that the years are passing by. It is about time I did something about a husband.' She checked her watch. Plenty of time before she need return to London. 'Now, I know mother isn't here. I saw her on TV last night, rabbiting on about AIDS. So I'm off for a long talk with father. You know how he likes to keep tabs on me.'

'And you on him,' replied Susan, smiling. She knew Diana still adored their father, and didn't begrudge the strong bond of affection between them. 'He'll always be here. Waiting for news of your latest triumph.'

'Always be here.'

Two short months ago Susan had said that, and how wrong she had been. Diana sat holding her head erect. Elegantly coiffured, not a blonde hair out of place, her beautiful face composed and expressionless. Only her hands, twisting the fragile lace handkerchief in her lap into a rag, betrayed the emotion she was feeling.

Susan, sitting beside Diana, could see the twisting hands. She knew the cold composure masked a deep intensity of grief. Diana had always been a daddy's girl, and Susan knew she must be feeling devastated. Her generous heart went out to her sister. Reaching across, she held Diana's hands, stilling the tormented movements. 'He wouldn't want you to grieve too much,' she whispered. 'Neither would mother.'

'I know,' said Diana, but it didn't stop the incredulous pain. She still couldn't believe that her father was dead. Strange, really, that I should only think of him. Mother was never that important. Always so busy, so distant. Whereas daddy. Fractured memories of the past scuttered through her brain, restless fragments in a dark tunnel. He always said whatever I wanted to hear, he never disappointed. But did I do everything he wanted? Did I grow into the woman he dreamed I'd be? Questions that would now forever remain unanswered. Her guiding light and mentor was dead.

'I wrote to Nancy,' whispered Susan. 'I thought I ought to, even though we haven't seen her for years; not since she was sent to boarding school.'

'Yes,' said Diana, hardly listening.

'My letter was forwarded on to New York where she's working as a model. She can't come to the funeral, but sent this card.' Susan fished in her handbag and drew out a large card with 'Sympathy' spelt across it in violets. 'She says she's thinking of us.'

Diana didn't reply. Their childhood years when she'd disliked Nancy so much seemed remote and distant now. Unimportant. She concentrated on the two coffins, side by side on trestles before the altar. How cruelly ironic life was. Geoffrey and Rosemary Leigh, always separated in life, had been united in death. What freakish dictate of fate had decided that on one of the rare occasions they had travelled together, a motorway pile-up should cut short both their lives? Diana sighed restlessly. All she wanted was to get the funeral over and done with, and then get away from Mottisley as soon as it was decently possible to do so.

Two hours later it was nearly over. Because Rosemary Leigh had been a politician, the funeral had been well attended and afterwards numerous people came back to Abbey House to offer their condolences to the two sisters. Susan had organized the obligatory food and drink for their guests, and Diana had settled the bill.

'Buy whatever you like,' she said when Susan had raised the matter. 'I know you haven't much money, so put it on my account.'

'Thanks, Diana,' said Susan, wondering how and when she should tell Diana the true state of her impecunious situation.

In the event, Mr Grimble, of Grimble, Wiggins and Peat, long established solicitors in Mottisley, and a friend of the departed Geoffrey and Rosemary Leigh, took Diana aside.

'I must point out to you, dear girl,' he said, 'that as your parents didn't leave a will.'

'Yes, why didn't they?' Diana interrupted. 'I'm surprised that you didn't remind them, Mr Grimble. They *were* friends of yours.'

'I did, often. But they always procrastinated. I understand they didn't see eye-to-eye on who the benefactors should be.'

Diana sighed. 'Hardly surprising I suppose. As you

knew my parents so well, I'm sure you know that they hardly ever saw eye-to-eye on anything.'

'Ahem . . . well . . . quite.' Mr Grimble was embarrassed and fidgeted about.

Diana put him out of his misery. 'Well, is there another problem, apart from the non-existence of a will?'

'Yes, your sister Susan is in a very difficult position. She does have a little money of her own, but the bulk of it is money she had made from the sale of wine from Abbey Vineyard. It's not a lot of money, and I know your father did intend to open up a separate business account for Susan, but unfortunately he didn't do it before . . .'

'He was killed.' Diana finished the sentence for him.

'Yes, so you see Susan's money is in your father's bank account, to which she has no access.'

'Then please sort out the estate as soon as possible, and in the meantime I'll make sure that Susan has sufficient funds to meet her family's needs.' And that, had thought Diana, was that.

Three months later her patience snapped.

'Oh dear,' said Susan when she heard of Diana's plans. 'Do you think we ought?'

'It isn't a question of whether or not we ought. We are damn well going to.'

'But Grimble, Wiggins and Peat have been solicitors in Mottisley for over one hundred and fifty years.'

'And are one hundred and fifty years behind the times as far as I can see. Just because old Mr Grimble has had a heart attack,' Diana raised her voice to stop Susan protesting again, 'shouldn't mean that all work on our case grinds to a complete and utter halt.'

'But you don't know anything about this Hugh Stratton.'

'I do. He's a barrister with one of the most reputable firms in the City, and he's coming over to Paris to see me next week.'

'Paris!' Susan gasped when she thought of how much the trip would cost. 'It seems an awfully expensive way of seeing one's lawyer.'

'Susan, I haven't got time to see him any other way. In the long run it will save money. The sooner we get the estate sorted out, the sooner we can invest what money there is, and the more secure you'll be.'

'I hope you're right Diana, and that this Hugh Stratton will be more successful than poor old Mr Grimble.'

'Well, one thing is certain. He can't be any less successful. And if he's no good, or I don't like him, I shall fire him.'

'Poor Hugh Stratton,' said Susan. 'I feel sorry for him. He doesn't know what he's let himself in for.'

Diana laughed. 'He soon will.'

Chapter Three

The clean lines of the ivory and ebony striped knitted jacket flared out behind her. Diana looked stunning and knew it. She felt good as she swept through Charles de Gaulle airport, a gaggle of admiring porters bustling after her with the luggage. Her blonde, ice-cold beauty ensured that she never had any difficulty in finding a willing porter, no matter wherever she went in the world.

'Hotel George V, please.'

The taxi sped away from the airport and into the heart of Paris. Diana relaxed, she enjoyed Paris, although her visits were always working ones. But she loved the bustle of the city. It thrilled her senses and usually spurred her on to work even harder. Susan called her a workaholic and a philistine to boot, when she found out that Diana never bothered to go sightseeing. But Diana maintained that she didn't need to. Just the smell of Paris was enough to stimulate her, and what little time off she did have was spent in the fashion salons of Le Marais. Now, she contentedly watched Paris flash past the taxi windows. First the Bois de Boulogne and on to the Avenue de la Grande Armée, through the frenetic traffic swirling around the Arc de Triomphe and on to the Champs Elysées, then a right turn into Avenue George V and the taxi stopped in front of the entrance to the best hotel in Paris. Diana knew the way by heart. The French consortium employing her as their consultant were very generous with expenses.

'Madame Leigh.' The frock coated doorman opened the taxi door for Diana. 'A pleasure to have you in Paris again.'

Diana smiled at the use of *Madame*. It always amused

her, a subtle reference to her status and the fact that she was obviously over twenty-one. 'A pleasure to be here,' she replied, sailing through into the baroque splendour of the foyer, secure in the knowledge that her luggage would be dealt with.

Once settled in her suite she picked up the house 'phone.

'Oui, Madame.'

'I'll be joined at dinner by a guest tonight, a Monsieur Stratton. You should have a reservation for him.'

'Monsieur Stratton has already checked in.'

'Good. Could you tell him that I'll dine at eight-thirty, and please arrange a secluded table. We have business to discuss.'

'*Un cadre traditionnel et un accueil personnalise, peut-être?*'

A traditional setting and a personalized welcome? Diana thought a moment. 'Yes, why not. That would be nice.' Might as well impress this Hugh Stratton. Oil the wheels, so that he got his finger out and settled the outstanding legal matter of her parents' estate quickly.

At exactly eight-twenty Diana went down in the elevator to the ground floor, making her way past the objets d'art, antique furniture and priceless wall tapestries that were integral to the George V. Hugh Stratton should be waiting for her in the cocktail bar next to the Salon de la Paix.

He was. The man who came towards her was tall, dark, and incredibly good looking. He stood head and shoulders above all the other men in the room, and for the first time since her love affair with Joe Kelly, Diana found herself strongly attracted to a man.

He bent low over her outstretched hand, brushing it briefly with his lips. 'A pleasure to meet you, Madame Leigh.'

The old world courtesy of his greeting charmed Diana, but she was puzzled. 'How were you so sure I was Diana

Leigh? You could have been kissing the hand of the wrong woman.'

He laughed, and Diana noticed how dark his eyes were, although she found it impossible to read their expression. 'I had my secretary search out a photograph of you. I wanted to see what my new client looked like. I must admit that I wasn't all that keen on coming to Paris at first, but once I'd seen your photograph, the prospect seemed infinitely more attractive.'

Diana found herself blushing. Something she hadn't done for years. Hugh Stratton was making her feel ultra feminine, something else she hadn't felt for years. And she liked the feeling. Suddenly she could hear Susan's voice saying, 'You ought to get married.' She wondered whether the attractive man before her was married, and wasted no time in finding out.

'Your wife didn't mind you rushing off to Paris at the drop of a hat?'

'I don't have a wife. And before you jump to conclusions, I am not divorced, neither am I gay. I have not yet found the woman with whom I want to spend the rest of my life, therefore I am not married. How about you? I know you're not married, but do you have a relationship? a partner?'

Diana shook her head, smiling, sensing his interest in her. 'No relationship, no partner,' she said.

'Then we have no-one to worry about but ourselves,' he said. Before releasing her hand his thumb momentarily caressed the palm of her hand, and Diana felt herself respond. This is like something out of a romantic novel, she thought, and almost laughed out loud. How amused Susan would be if she knew that after only a few minutes in the company of Hugh Stratton, she was already mentally trying him on for size as a prospective husband. Diana knew Susan would urge caution, but Diana didn't feel cautious. She felt reckless, and thought she recognized what, in all the best romantic novels, was described as *love at first sight*.

Hugh returned from the bar. 'I've ordered us champagne cocktails as aperitifs. I hope you like them.'

'Perfect,' said Diana, she had forgotten how nice it was to feel cosseted by a man. An illusion she knew, but a nice one nevertheless.

Hugh Stratton had a very definite aura of charisma, and Diana was aware that, together, they were a striking couple. I've been alone too long, she thought, Susan was quite right, I need a man at my side. It was not usually her custom to defer to a male companion. Not something she even thought much about, so used had she become to fending for herself, making up her own mind on everything, but this evening was an exception. Hugh Stratton was obviously knowledgeable about food and wine, and Diana felt quite happy to sit back and let him order.

'Crudités, then Rougets à la Nicoise, followed by Gigot de Pre-Sale, Farci with Pommes Lyonaise. A bottle of Chateau Thieuley and a bottle of Chateau Dauzac.'

'Oui, Monsieur.' The waiter withdrew respectfully.

'How did you know I'd like red mullet followed by lamb?'

Hugh smiled. His deep black eyes crinkled attractively at the corners but, try as she might, Diana still found herself unable to read his thoughts. It made him an enigma, intriguing, heightening her interest.

'Because you look a sensual woman,' he said.

The remark surprised Diana. 'What has sensuality got to do with food?'

'Sensual people like the good things in life, and that includes a varied and exotic diet as well as,' he hesitated fractionally, then added softly, 'all the other good things.' The words were innocent, the tone pruriently explicit.

'I never think about food when I'm alone.'

'A woman like you should never be alone,' said Hugh.

After dinner they started to go through the details of Geoffrey and Rosemary Leigh's estate. They retired to Diana's suite to sort out the papers.

'I see from the papers passed to me by Grimble, Wiggins and Peat that you wish to relinquish your share of the estate and make it over to your sister, Susan.'

'Yes.'

'As your lawyer I must advise you that I do not think that is a wise move.'

'Why not?'

'You never know when you may need extra money. If the estate was sold, it could realize quite a respectable sum.'

'But that would leave my sister and her family homeless and unemployed.'

'I'm sure she and her husband are quite capable of fending for themselves.'

'No, they're not,' said Diana. 'They need a helping hand. And with what I'm earning, I don't need the money. It's only fair that I help.'

When Diana told him her average annual income, Hugh Stratton changed his mind. 'Perhaps you don't need any extra cash after all,' he agreed. 'But,' he reached forward and laid his hand on Diana's, 'I must tell you that I think it is an extraordinarily generous thing that you are doing.' He smiled slowly. 'But I sense that you are perhaps an extraordinarily generous woman in all respects.'

Diana felt a delicious moment of panic. His dark eyes were hypnotic, and she felt desire stir within her. If he suggests that we go to bed in a moment, I might be weak willed enough to say yes, she thought. But strong as the attraction was, Diana was unwilling to give into an emotion tainted by weakness on her part. The desire to be in control of every facet of her life was dominant, too well ingrained to be tossed aside. She stood up. 'Perhaps, Mr Stratton,' she said. 'I think, we will leave it there. We can finish sorting it out tomorrow. I'm tired now. I have an early meeting in the morning.'

'Of course.' Hugh was on his feet in an instant, looking contrite. 'I'm sorry to have kept you up so late. I shall go through all this tomorrow with a fine toothcomb, while you are at your meeting.'

'Thank you.' Diana escorted him to the door.

Hugh paused in the doorway. 'Do you know Paris well?'

'Not really,' Diana admitted. 'I never have time for sightseeing.'

'A pity. I was going to suggest that if you finished your meeting in time, we could explore the bouqinistes on the banks of the Seine, and perhaps even picnic in the garden at the tip of the Île de la Cité. It's an enchanting spot.'

'I could probably be finished by eleven,' Diana heard herself saying.

'Then you'll let me show you the sights?'

'Why not? It seems a pity to waste Paris.'

'My sentiments exactly,' said Hugh.

Diana closed the door behind him and leaned against it smiling thoughtfully. She knew as well as Hugh, that in fact they could have sorted out everything that needed to be done that evening. But Hugh had said he had three days to spare, and she wanted him to stay. The necessary business could easily be spun out to last three days. Diana had no intention of letting such a gorgeous man walk out of her life without finding out all there was to know about him.

For the first time in her life, Diana rushed through her meeting the next morning, and was finished by eleven just as she had told Hugh she would be. He was waiting, and soon they were walking arm in arm in the spring sunshine along the banks of the Seine.

The trees had the misty green haze of early spring, and in the pure halcyon light, the arches of the many bridges stood out sharp and clear above the sparkling water. Happy, carefree crowds thronged the sidewalks of the Seine, soaking up the balmy sunshine.

'This is better than looking at it from a hotel or taxi window,' said Diana.

Hugh stopped by an old woman selling flowers. Her

rows of enamel pails were stocked with flowers of every size, colour and variety. 'What would you like?' he asked Diana.

Looking at the massed array of blue, white, pink, yellow and red, Diana couldn't decide. 'You choose,' she said.

Hugh spoke in rapid French, and the black clad woman smiled at Diana. She picked out a bunch of irises, then white narcissi, then daffodils and finally one single long stemmed red rose. Hugh paid for them and handed them to Diana. 'Irises for the blue of your eyes, narcissi for the colour of your skin, daffodils for your hair, and a red rose as a special gift from me to you.'

Diana buried her nose in the fragrant bouquet. 'They're lovely.'

'And so are you,' said Hugh seriously. Then he laughed. 'Come on, you said you wanted to buy your sister some books. There are always bargains to be had in the bouqinistes.'

Diana spent a happy hour foraging amongst the second-hand books in the little bouqinistes that lined the sides of the pathways of the Seine, and bought two books for Susan. Both books on art, one on French impressionists, and the other devoted exclusively to Picasso. 'She'll love them,' she told Hugh. 'Plenty of colour plates, and not too much reading to wade through.'

They had their picnic in the tiny garden at the tip of the Île de la Cité, and the next day visited Paris's most famous cemetery, Père Lachaise. That night they dined in a tiny bistro near the Sacré Coeur, and afterwards when they returned to the George V hotel Diana knew for certain that she wanted Hugh to make love to her. So when he escorted her to the suite, she asked him in for a drink then let him kiss her. After that it seemed the most natural thing in the world to progress to bed, and Diana was happy knowing she had made the decision.

'You are the most beautiful woman I've ever seen.' Hugh had the extraordinary skill of removing her clothes swiftly, and yet at the same time seeming to take his time.

Cupping her small breasts in his hands, he kissed them reverently.

'You've seen a lot of women like this?' A faint barb of jealousy jangled.

Hugh laughed softly. 'Not many. But Diana, darling, surely you don't expect a man of my age to be completely celibate? Are you a virgin?'

'No.'

'Well then, don't let jealousy spoil this wonderful moment. Forget about anyone else. We are the only people who matter now.' Kissing his way down her body his mouth began to work a compulsive sorcery and Diana capitulated in ecstasy.

'Hugh,' her desire was so great she could hardly breathe, 'I want you.'

'I love you,' he said.

She cried out as he took her. In contrast to his gentle foreplay he was rough. He made her his own in no uncertain manner. He was in control now. After only a fractional hesitation, Diana let him mould her body the way he wanted.

The hesitation had been when, quite unexpectedly, she had suddenly thought of Joe Kelly. Their lovemaking had been innocent and instinctive, and sometimes they'd fumbled in their haste to possess one another. But there was nothing fumbling about making love with Hugh. He knew exactly what he wanted and he took it. Every touch of his hand was a calculated movement to give her pleasure, every kiss teased and tantalized, raising her to unexpected heights of sensuality. Hugh's hands and mouth transported her body to realms she had never dreamed existed. Joe and I were mere children, she thought, how naive we were. She didn't allow herself to remember the delicate innocence. Instead she gave herself up to Hugh's finely honed eroticism which left her shuddering with pleasure.

It was only when he'd left her bed that she wondered how he had become such an expert lover. He had loved other women, of course he had, but where sex was concerned he appeared to be a virtuoso. Then she immediately dismissed the thought as unworthy. When people loved one another the expertise came naturally. And Hugh loved her, he had said so, not only in words but in actions too.

On Hugh's last day, after another blissful night together in bed, they got up early to watch the sunrise over the Pont de Tolbiac. Side by side they leaned on the railings at the side of the Seine. The first rays of sunlight slid along the smooth surface of the river, gleaming pearls of light, bathing the buildings on each side in a reflected golden glow.

Diana drew a breath of sheer delight. 'I shall always remember this moment,' she said.

'I should hope.' Hugh pulled her around to face him. 'A woman should always remember when and where she received her proposal of marriage.'

'Are you . . . ?' By now, sure that she was in love with Hugh, it was what Diana wanted to hear. But everything had happened so fast that she had hardly dared hope Hugh would feel the same.

'Proposing? Yes. Would you like me to go down on one knee?'

Smiling broadly, Diana shook her head. 'Of course not, silly.'

'Of course not silly, don't go down on one knee? Or, of course not, I can't possibly marry you?'

Sliding her arms around his neck, Diana pulled his head down towards her. 'I'll marry you,' she whispered. 'Now, this minute if it were possible.'

They kissed, long and slowly, and an early morning band of road sweepers stopped their motorized cart and whistled appreciatively. 'You'd think they'd be used to seeing lovers,' said Hugh. 'After all, this is Paris.'

Sitting amidst the workmen in the famous *Le Depanneur* cafe, the only cafe in Paris which never closes, Diana gazed dreamily at Hugh over a steaming bowl of coffee. 'We can be married in Mottisley Abbey,' she said, 'I know Susan will do the reception at Abbey House.'

'Oh,' Hugh seemed momentarily put out. 'I thought we could have a quite registry office wedding.'

'It will be quiet.' Diana assured him. 'I don't have that many relations. But why get married in an ordinary registry office when we can be married in a seven-hundred-year-old abbey with all the trimmings?'

Hugh groaned. 'All the trimmings! Diana, I thought you were a hard-headed business woman, not a hopeless romantic.'

'I'm both,' said Diana. 'You don't mind do you?'

Hugh gave in with a good grace. 'Of course not. If you wanted the Band of the Royal Marines I'd say yes.'

Diana laughed. 'I won't be wanting that. But I do want one of those delicious croissants that have just been piled up on the counter. The smell is making me drool, they must have come straight out of the oven.'

'Easily done,' said Hugh, kissing the tip of her nose. He waved his hand and called out. A tray of buttery croissants and a pot of apricot jam materialized!

'I always think May is such a lovely time of year for a wedding,' said Susan. 'Do stand still, Diana, how can I arrange your veil if you will wriggle.'

'Just looking to see if Bert has arrived yet.'

Susan pursed her lips. 'I wonder if we did the right thing, asking him to give you away? I do hope May can persuade him to wear those new shoes.'

'Be practical, who else was there?' said Diana. 'There's a dearth of male relatives on our side of the family.'

'There's a dearth of relatives of any kind on Hugh's side. His guest list is made up of friends and colleagues.' Susan fixed the veil to her satisfaction.

Diana looked at her reflection in the bedroom mirror. Was this vision in cream-coloured lace really herself? The saying must be true, a bride in love is always beautiful. She was glad she'd persuaded Hugh that they should

51

marry in the abbey, so much better than some impersonal registry office. She turned to Susan. 'You do approve of Hugh, don't you? I do so want everyone to like him. He has no family of his own.'

'Darling, you love him. That's good enough for me.'

'May and the children don't like him.'

Susan dismissed that idea with an airy 'Poof! Even if it was the Prince of Wales himself, May wouldn't think him good enough for you. And the children do like Hugh. They're just being difficult. They're finding it hard to cope with their father being in a nursing home, and knowing that he'll never come out. So they take out their sadness and frustration on everyone around them.'

Diana was suddenly stricken with guilt. Susan had prepared everything for the wedding, besides coping with a sick husband, two young children, and a three-month-old baby. 'I shouldn't have let you do all this,' she said. 'You've enough on your plate without a wedding as well.'

Susan smiled. 'Nothing would have stopped me. You are my only sister, and this is your home. I've enjoyed the preparations.' For a second her face clouded. 'Being busy stops me thinking. Next week is going to be the difficult time. But now, I'm going to enjoy the rest of today.' There was a sound of a car drawing up outside on the gravelled drive. Susan looked out. 'That's Bert arriving. And you'll be relieved to know that he is wearing the new shoes.' Diving under Diana's veil she gave her a quick kiss. 'Good luck, darling. Now, I must dash across to the abbey and hope that the children are behaving themselves, and that Griselda has managed to hold on to baby Timothy, and not dropped him on his head. See you in church.'

Hugh and Diana emerged from the dimness of the abbey into the dazzling May sunshine. Hawthorn blazed pink and white at the far end of the churchyard, and a slight breeze caused the chestnut trees to dip their luxuriant white candles in salute to the bridal pair. Daisies drifted like snow between the lichen covered gravestones, and in the shadows, clumps of celandines shone, yellow stars lighting up the dark green of the damp grass.

All their London friends raved to Hugh and Diana about the rustic beauty of the scene. 'How wonderful to get married in a place like this.'

'I'd love to live here. It must be idyllic.'

'It's so peaceful.'

'How could you bear to leave it, Diana?'

For a moment as she looked about her, the beauty caught at her throat, and Diana wondered how she had managed to leave it all for the grime of the city of London.

'The sun doesn't shine all the time,' said Hugh. 'When it rains it's probably ankle deep in mud.'

Diana laughed. 'Hugh is right. The sun doesn't shine all the time. And for me it was *too* peaceful.'

'All the Bride's relations, please,' shouted the official photographer.

Susan rounded up the children, slung baby Timothy on one hip, and stood on Hugh's right-hand side. May and Bert stood on Diana's left. The photographer fiddled about with the focus.

'Diana,' Susan leaned across and hissed at her sister. 'Do you see who I see over there. I'm sure it's Nancy.'

'Where?' Diana craned her head in the direction Susan was nodding.

'There. I'm sure it is.'

Diana was certain too, although it had been twelve years since she had last seen Nancy. 'Did you invite her?'

'Of course not. I don't even know where she's living these days.'

'I suppose she ought to be in the photograph.'

'Over my dead body,' hissed May, who'd picked up the conversation.

'May, we ought to be charitable. I know we didn't get on as kids, but we're all grown up now. And Mum and Dad are dead.' Always generous, Susan was anxious to include her.

'I'm not dead,' said May fiercely. 'And I don't want her here.'

'Smile,' shouted the photographer at precisely the same moment as Timothy opened his mouth and let out a blood curdling howl.

'I think he's filled his nappy,' said Susan.

'Bloody babies, should be banned from weddings,' muttered the photographer. He took another exposure.

'I'll make a point of talking to Nancy at the reception,' said Diana to Susan. 'We can't be mean and ignore her altogether.'

'Who?' asked Hugh, who had gathered that they were talking about the gorgeous looking dark-haired woman in red standing on the edge of the crowd. 'Who is Nancy?'

'Our cousin.' Diana told him. 'We don't see much of her. I'll introduce you later.' She looked at Nancy standing beneath the yew tree at the far end of the churchyard. The blackness of the yew's branches threw her red dress into relief, making her seem like a shaft of fire blazing there. For reasons which she couldn't explain, Diana felt uneasy, and didn't want to introduce her to Hugh. Half remembered ghosts from the past came back to haunt her. Nancy, always laughing. Nancy, always getting her own way. Their parents always quarrelling, and in the background, always, always Nancy. Until the day she had left so suddenly.

But she need not have worried. When she looked for her at the reception, Diana couldn't find her.

She asked Susan. 'What has happened to Nancy?'

'Gone, thank God,' said Susan. 'May was getting most uptight, I was afraid she might make a scene. You know what she's like when she's had a glass or two.'

'Gone, where?'

'Back to her husband. Apparently she's married to some rich American. Said something about flying off to Monaco, and disappeared. She saw the notice of the marriage in *The Times*, and decided to come on the spur of the moment.'

Diana laughed with relief. 'Sounds like Nancy's landed on her feet.'

'Nancy will always land on her feet.' May joined them, her ruddy complexion even ruddier than usual, a direct result of several glasses of Susan's wine. 'The devil always looks after his own,' she added darkly.

Chapter Four

From the apartment high above the river the Thames looked dark and forbidding, and Diana shivered although the room was warm. Snow was forecast. Across the river a banked mass of leaden cloud, looming in on a sharp north-easterly wind, looked chillingly ominous. Far below a stick-like figure of a woman struggled along the embankment with her dog, bent double against the wind; the dog, a large shaggy-haired specimen of indeterminate breed, seemed oblivious to the elements. He hung back, cocking his leg nonchalantly against one of the elaborate Victorian wrought iron lampposts which studded Chelsea embankment. The dog reminded Diana of Galahad, the dog at Mottisley. Susan had written saying that he had died and the children were heartbroken. That had been three weeks ago. I really must reply thought Diana, guiltily remembering that she hadn't been down to Mottisley for nearly a year.

It was 1987, and four years of marriage to Hugh had flown by. Always busy Diana had, without meaning to, relegated Susan and Mottisley to the bottom of her list of priorities. But now, she resolved, if all my plotting and scheming comes to fruition tomorrow, then I can afford to relax a little. I'll write to Susan, and then perhaps I'll persuade Hugh to come with me to Mottisley. She smiled at the thought of Hugh's last disastrous visit, remembering the vision of him squelching through the wintery mud. How he hated the country. As far as he was concerned it was a totally alien world. But he can suffer it for just a couple of days, Diana decided. I will write to Susan, this weekend.

Suddenly the moon burst forth, vigorously piercing the

scudding clouds, blazing a silver path across the water. Diana watched as the hurrying Thames shattered the fragile brilliance of the moonlight, scattering it into a million pieces of silver to be borne away on the quickening waters of the ebb tide. She smiled, Susan forgotten. The moon always made her think of her father. She could almost hear him saying, 'never doubt your own ability,' and thought of the next day. Tomorrow morning could be the turning point in her career. No, not could, *would* be. She hadn't clawed her way this far to fail now.

'Darling.' Hugh joined her at the window. He placed his strong fingers on her shoulders, flexing her taut muscles. Diana sighed contentedly and relaxed against him. Without looking she could picture exactly the way his hands looked. Long, slender, almost feminine fingers, with immaculately manicured nails. But there was nothing feminine about the strengh or touch of his hands. Hugh slowly nibbled the back of her neck. 'Stop staring out of the window all uptight and tense,' he commanded. 'You'll get your heart's desire tomorrow because you have the talent to do anything. That's what you told me your father always said.'

Diana turned away from the window and looked into the darkly handsome face of her husband. After four years of marriage she loved him passionately, still marvelling at the stroke of luck which had caused their paths to cross. Indirectly it had been her father who'd caused the meeting, because if he'd made a will she would never have needed Hugh's services. Their meeting was decreed by fate, it was meant to be. But after four years she was still never quite sure what to read in the dark depths of his eyes. It was all part of his fascination. Now, his eyes were crinkled with silent laughter as he examined her in a quizzical fashion. His hard sensual mouth curving into a crooked smile, a smile which always filled Diana with a thrill of longing. He had the power of making her go deliciously weak at the knees, as well as the power of adding fuel to the fire of her ambition. Strange that Hugh should mention her father when she'd been thinking of him herself. But in many ways, Hugh was like her father. Always encouraging, always urging her on, never jealous because she was more successful than him. He was an exceptional man.

'Yes, Daddy did say that.' Her voice became muffled as Hugh kissed her. 'But I wonder,' she added between kisses, 'if even he envisaged me as a Deputy Managing Director with a salary almost twice that of the Prime Minister.' Hugh's kisses, Hugh's fingers gently massaging her spine were having a disastrous effect on her concentration. Laughing, Diana pushed him away. She wanted to look at him, marvel yet again that this man with the film star looks, coveted by all women who met him, should love her and have no eyes for any other woman. Reaching up, she kissed the taut line of his jaw. 'You know, Hugh,' she said reflectively, 'sometimes I think how like my father you are.'

'I'm not at all sure that I like being regarded as a father figure.' He grinned, and began unbuttoning her blouse. 'But on the other hand,' he slid a hand inside her bra, cupping a small firm breast, 'maybe an incestuous relationship is just what I need for a change.'

'Not yet, Hugh.' Diana firmly removed his hand and rebuttoned the blouse. 'I want to talk.' She always needed to psych herself up before important interviews. 'Suppose when I get there tomorrow all the other directors are against me? They've never had a woman on the board before, and I've been quite brutal with them in the past, cutting the ground from beneath their feet on more than one occasion. In fact, they've no particular reason to like me, and quite a few very good reasons not to.' In spite of her words, and appearing to need reassurance, Diana was confident that she'd succeed at the interview. This was her way of plugging any potential chinks in her carefully assembled shield of armour. She never left anything to chance.

Unfazed by her physical rebuff, Hugh kissed the top of

her head. 'Exactly, my darling,' he said softly. 'You've hit the nail right on the head. You've proved often enough that you're smart enough to outwit them, and that's the reason they know they need you on their team as Deputy MD. They need a tough negotiator. And anyway you know too that Alan Sinclair is determined to have you on the board. The other members might make dissenting noises but it won't mean anything.'

Diana laughed. 'Yes, I suppose they've got to apply a little balm to their egos. Giving me a rough ride will do that.'

'Of course,' said Hugh. 'And remember they've already interviewed four other possible contenders for the post and given all of them the cold shoulder. You're the only one left in the running, and Alan Sinclair has told me he's already put the champagne on ice. So, my darling, it's in the bag if you play his game. *Brainy, Beautiful and Ruthless, the Ideal Woman of the Eighties*, that magazine article really put you in the headlines, and Alan Sinclair wants to parade your talent in front of his rivals. God knows he needs to, he's got little enough of his own.'

A shadow crossed Diana's face. 'Damn! I really can't stand that man. Slimy, cheating little bastard.' She sighed, 'there's always one fly in the ointment, and this time it's Alan Sinclair. I've never enjoyed working with him, and I never will.'

'It doesn't worry you does it? I'd have thought that you of all people are professional enough not to let personal prejudices get in the way of a working relationship.'

'Of course I'm not worried,' said Diana sharply. 'Surely you don't think that I'm going to throw away the chance of a lifetime because of one oily little creep.'

Hugh laughed. 'Glad to hear it. You had me worried there for a moment, sweetheart.'

'You worried?' He must be joking. A lock of his dark hair had fallen, as it always did, across his forehead, and she brushed it back, her fingers lingering in a gentle caress. 'I didn't think you ever worried.'

'Only about you, darling. Only about you,' said Hugh, kissing her fingers. 'You don't have to like Alan Sinclair, just pretend you do and be nice to him.'

'Of course I'll be nice to the wretched little man. But I insist that I'm allowed to loathe him in private.'

'Good girl.' Hugh pulled her back into his arms and kissed her long and hard. 'You can call him whatever you like when you're here,' he said, when he came up for air.

Diana kissed him back, conscious of his hands inside her blouse again, hot and dry, never clammy like some men she'd known. She moved closer, waiting for his familiar caress down the length of her body. She wanted him. He was the only man she ever wanted now, and it would be the same for the rest of her life.

Her mind slid back remembering that first meeting with Hugh in Paris. How right her instincts had been. They made a perfect couple. Their aims and desires complemented each other perfectly, and their sex life was utter bliss.

Now, she looked into his dark eyes and seeing the desire felt an answering leap of fever. 'Kiss me again,' she said. 'You know I'll do anything when you kiss me.' She longed to rub herself, slow and feline, against the length of his body, before relishing the moment of submission to Hugh's will.

'Anything?' Hugh teased. He held her a tantalizing fraction away.

'Anything, darling, anything.' Aroused now, Diana pushed hard against him, her hands sliding into his pockets. Her fingers closed around a crumpled ball of paper in one pocket. 'What's this?' she asked, holding it up.

'What do you think?' Hugh laughed. 'Rubbish of course.' Taking the paper he flicked it with neat precision into the ceramic jar used as a waste paper bin. Then bending his head to hers, he captured her mouth with a sudden roughness. 'I'll hold you to that promise of anything.'

'Let's go to bed,' whispered Diana.

'No. I want you here, in front of the window.' Discarding his jacket, he threw it across the back of a nearby chair and turned once more towards Diana. She stood quite still, the touch of his gentle hands making her tremble.

He began to undress her, unhurriedly fastening his mouth to first one pale pink nipple and then the other before letting his tongue trail down the smooth line of her slender, almost boyish body. Diana shivered, she knew that Hugh enjoyed arousing her then teased and tantalized until she was ready to go on her knees for the release only he could give. Four years of marriage had enhanced his erotic skills, not diminished them.

Impatient now, Diana tugged at the belt of his trousers. Together they slid down on to the softness of the silk kilim spread before the window. 'I want you, Hugh,' she whispered. 'Oh, darling. I want you so much.' The last words came out with a gasp as Hugh entered her, jerking the breath from her body.

Later they lay still, arms and legs twined around each other, pleasurably exhausted. 'This time tomorrow I'll know whether or not I'm married to the Deputy Managing Director of Wycombe and Yatton,' said Hugh.

'You will be.' Diana was confident now. 'Just think of what we can do with all that extra money.' The mere thought of their future life together sent a thrilling shiver through her, and suddenly Diana wanted Hugh again. Stretching voluptuously, her fingers began to massage, feather light and infinitely persuasive.

Hugh groaned with pleasure and rolled Diana on to her back. 'Once more,' he said, breathless with need.

'Didn't get held up by the snow then?' Alan Sinclair's secretary minced, yes, thought Diana watching her distastefully, minced, that's the word, down the corridor and flung open the boardroom door. 'Follow me, Mrs Stratton,' she said breathily, not waiting for a reply to her first remark. Diana followed the well-endowed hips wiggling suggestively in front of her as Kelly gave the assembled men the benefit of a toothy simpering smile.

'Thank you, Kelly.'

Irritably Diana noted the smile. She also noted the shortness and tightness of her skirt. Another millimetre smaller and she'd be bursting out of it. Where did Alan find these girls? And was there something about chubby bare legs, mottled blue by the cold, that she ought to know? Alan Sinclair was obviously fascinated by them.

When it came to choosing secretaries, Diana decided, Alan Sinclair's true character rose, like gas in a fetid swamp, to the surface. They were all similar, and Kelly Riley was the last in a long line of incompetent secretaries he'd employed. A shapely, overweight, twenty-year-old, her over backcombed hair looked as if it could happily harbour a whole colony of rooks. Her appearance was matched only by a complete inability to spell correctly, even with the assistance of a wordprocessor wordcheck.

Diana took her seat.

'Thank you, Kelly,' beamed Alan Sinclair, his eyes fixed on Kelly's breasts jostling for position within the close confines of her V-necked tee-shirt.

She'll soon be getting her marching orders, thought Diana, arranging her papers, and smoothing an imaginary crease from the skirt of her severely expensive suit. As soon as I'm Deputy MD I'll recruit some literate secretaries. That should improve company efficiency by 25 per cent at one single stroke.

Diana settled down and dispassionately observed the assembled company of men now ostentatiously shuffling their papers, and clearing their throats with self-important thoroughness. They had risen to their feet to greet her when she entered, and she had rewarded them with a smile of suitable sweetness with just a hint of demure humility. She had learned the psychology of working with men the hard way. It was irksome having to act out a part, pandering to their combined egos, but it never did to start off by appearing too aggressive. The game had to be played by the rules made up and laid down by men, and one was that whereas a positive attitude was a healthy bonus in a male, in a female it was viewed with distaste as domineering and aggressive. When I reach the top I can afford to be different, then I'll make a few of them jump and there'll be no need to resort to feminine wiles. A faint smile curved her lips in pleasurable anticipation of such a day.

The interview commenced. Alan Sinclair kicked off the questioning. 'What do you think you've got to offer Wycombe and Yatton if we appoint you as full-time Deputy MD?'

Diana had already rehearsed the answer to that. The trick lay in not sounding over confident. Again the demure smile flickered. 'I hope that I've already proved some of what I've got to offer the company during my year here as a development consultant.'

From her position at the table, Diana could see stiff, prejudicial opposition in almost every face. In fact the whole boardroom reeked of prejudice and nepotism, from the stilted portraits of self-satisfied looking past Managing Directors which lined the oak panelled walls, to the dark brown-studded leather chairs and the intimidatingly huge mahogany table. It was an exclusive male club, the like of which were scattered throughout London, where the right old school tie and suitable patronage were usually the only means of gaining access to the establishment; but today, Diana was breaking the hallowed tradition of Wycombe and Yatton by putting a foot in through the front door. They wanted her, in fact they needed her, she knew that. But she also guessed that it was with some fear and trembling that they were reluctantly being dragged into an era where women could compete on equal terms with men. In a way Diana felt sorry for them, their previously well-ordered structure was shifting, and she knew she mustn't frighten them too much. It was still possible to blow it.

'Of course, I know you have interviewed other candidates, and that I'm the only woman. But,' leaning forward and resting her slender hands on the table she flashed them her most beguiling smile, unashamedly using every ounce of femininity to win them over, 'as a woman, it can sometimes be quite an advantage when negotiating a deal.'

The questions followed thick and fast, Diana parrying each one successfully. Her spirits rose, she found the inquisition intoxicating. Gradually she sensed that one by one she had them in the palm of her hand. Her keen eye for detail missed nothing and she could see in their faces that she was very nearly there. The consensus was that Diana Stratton would be an asset to the company.

'Well, Diana. I think we may call you that now.' Diana turned to look at Gerald Marshall. A bumbling idiot of a man, the type who could truly be called a 'sleeping' partner, no use to anyone apart from his money which was why Alan kept him on the board. It was his only merit. Stacked to the eyebrows with inherited cash, he seemed to have missed the boat when the brains were being dished out. Amused at his pompousness, she watched him now as he officiously fished out a newspaper from his briefcase. 'Alan has said that I can have the last question, my dear. Don't be nervous.'

'I'll try not to be,' said Diana, demurely modest, although she wanted to laugh out loud. Gerald Marshall, an inquisitor to be afraid of? It was pathetic. Anyway, nothing could rattle her now. Not once she was in her swing.

'Tell us what you think about this firm's performance, and whether or not it's ripe for a take-over.' He pushed the business section of *The Times* across the boardroom table towards Diana.

Diana took the paper. Gerald had highlighted an article in fluorescent yellow, but for a split second Diana didn't see it. She only saw the headline of the paper screaming at her. Then the room reeled, the walls slipped in, catapulting her to another place, another time, and suddenly she felt very sick.

But as forcefully as it had come, so it went. I haven't battled all this way, almost to the top, to be undermined by a memory that should have been forgotten long ago, she thought angrily.

Picking up *The Times*, she concentrated on the high-lighted article.

'Just give me a moment, Gerald,' she said coolly. 'I've already read their annual report of course, but I'd like to see if this article throws any fresh light on the firm's activities.'

It was a ploy. But a very necessary tactic, one which bought her a few precious minutes in which fully to collect her wits and still the uneasy thudding of her heart.

Outside the office windows the sun had broken through the clouds. The freshly fallen snow sparkled and glittered in the pale January sunshine, pristine white for the moment, although the traffic of central London would soon churn it into ugly grey slush. The gleaming length of the mahogany table in the boardroom reflected the dazzling white light on to the faces of the men surrounding it, and suddenly Diana thought of her father with grati-tude. How right he'd been about her future. Without the encumbrance of children or domesticity she was forging the way to the top of her chosen profession. Directorships in prestigious companies like Wycombe and Yatton didn't come easily. It took years of grim determination battling against entrenched discrimination, and a determination to hold on to her ambition no matter what the cost. The ambition was eventually to attain the ultimate prize, a Managing Directorship. For one brief moment she wondered why she wanted it so badly, but then im-mediately answered her own question. It was for the joy of winning, the pleasure of grabbing the prize from beneath the nose of someone else, and for her father because it was he who had shaped her future. Except that he was no longer a part of her life, only a memory. Now, instead, she had Hugh to be proud of her achievements. Vaguely she was aware that in some nebulous way she had grown very dependent on Hugh in the years since their marriage. The thought was oddly disquieting.

Diana heard Alan cough discreetly and hastily slotted her mind back into its accustomed executive role. The future was all that mattered. No need for self-analysis.

The article Gerald Marshall had highlighted concerned a well-known leisure company, and Diana gave it her full attention. Then turning towards Alan Sinclair, and donning her most charming smile as easily as a familiar coat to hide her monumental dislike of the man, she began to speak.

'Yes, I do consider this firm absolutely ripe for a take-over,' her voice was sharp with confidence. 'This article confirms the conclusions I'd already reached after reading their annual report. Sloppy management, bad financial planning, reduced profits, but some very useful assets. Perfect material for a hostile take-over. The management will never get their act together quickly enough to fight off a bid. My advice is to buy it, strip it, and sell it.'

'Goddamn it, Diana! Just what we wanted to hear.' Alan Sinclair was pleased and Diana knew with a stab of triumphant pleasure that she had the Deputy Directorship in her pocket.

After the official confirmation, there was the congratulatory champagne lunch. Alan, as usual, got belligerently drunk. Not drunk enough to lose control, but enough to be unpleasant. Diana watched the other directors with scorn, not one of them man enough to put him in his place. Instead, they stood, smiling meekly, taking his thinly veiled insults.

Alan put his arm around Diana. 'I think we are to be congratulated for obtaining the services of the most talented woman in the City. Here's to Diana Stratton.'

'Here, here. Here, here.' Silly old fools, thought Diana, bleeting like a lot of inebriated sheep.

She smiled at Alan. 'Flattery will get you everywhere,' she said, watching him flush with inflated gratification at the supposed compliment. Climbing to the top of any ladder meant one could not afford to be squeamish, and as she smiled into Alan's red, perspiring face, Diana wondered how long it would be before she was powerful enough to do without him. The moment that happened she would jettison him without a moment's hesitation. All garbage went overboard sooner or later and, in Diana's considered opinion, Alan Sinclair was garbage.

It was difficult, but finally she managed to escape the prolonged luncheon. The rest of them were obviously going to stay until every bottle was empty, and they were welcome. Diana made her way to the downstairs ladies' cloakroom. It was now 4.30 in the afternoon, and the rest of the staff had already left, using the snow as a perfect excuse for making a quick getaway for the weekend.

Peace and quiet, thank God, after the bumble of noise in the boardroom. A moment to freshen up, and then she'd go home too. Opening her handbag Diana took out her make-up bag, the copy of *The Times* Gerald Marshall had highlighted fell out at the same time. She felt her face flush first hot, then icy cold with anger. What on earth had possessed her to pick that up? Then quite suddenly, without warning, Diana felt her iron self-control deserting her. She didn't give in without a struggle, but it was no use, her will was submerged and memories of the past came back, crowding in on her, suffocating, devastating. Several glasses of expensive Bollinger '82 were wasted as she vomited into the sink. The present slipped away and as it did so the past took over.

Cold winter sunlight bouncing off shiny white walls and ceilings, sterile and dazzling. Window after window flashing past as the trolley sped down an endless corridor. An ever-present fear. Sickening, icy fear.

'Nothing to worry about. All over in a few minutes. You'll be home by this afternoon.' A bosomy nurse with a fiercely cheerful but offhand voice didn't look at her as she gave the still figure on the trolley a cursory, automatic pat. Her mind was already in the canteen wondering what was on for lunch that day. The words were intended kindly. That was her job, what she'd been trained to do. To be kind and caring. But although she said the right thing to the girl on the trolley, the words couldn't hide her disapproval.

The nurses didn't like doing terminations. Diana knew that. Lying on the narrow trolley, trussed up in a white theatre gown, awaiting her turn to be wheeled down to the operating theatre, she'd heard them talking. S.T.O.P. Suction Termination of Pregnancy. S.T.O.P. Stop! What an appropriate word. Diana wondered uneasily if someone had thought it up on purpose? A play on words, some sort of malicious joke.

Home by this afternoon the nurse had said. That was another joke. She wasn't going home. By this afternoon she'd be in the coldly impersonal clinic chosen for her recuperation. Diana had chosen it herself. It was spartan in the extreme, and cheap, and fitted the need perfectly. Without realizing it, Diana was punishing herself by not allowing herself the luxury of a better nursing home in which to convalesce, it was her way of paying for her mistake. After a few days convalescence she'd go straight on to the hall of residence at the university. Her mother had used her influence and a room was already waiting for her. The plan was to ensure that no-one, not even Susan, would ever know that a baby had existed. It was to be expunged from the world before it had a chance to draw a breath. A baby, Diana's mind jerked sharply. No, no it was not a baby. Not a real child. She had used the word baby, but it was just a word, she was sure that the reality was a tiny lump of nothing. But now, quite suddenly, the nothing inside her assumed a life, a personality of its own, and Diana changed her mind.

'S.T.O.P. Stop! I don't want it done. I want to keep the baby. I want . . .' but the words bounced silently, aimlessly around inside her head, without form or ordered meaning, before drifting away out of reach. The bosomy nurse, engrossed with her own thoughts, didn't even glance again in Diana's direction. If she had, she might have seen the desperate anguish on her patient's face. But she didn't, and Diana had no option but to remain silent. Premedication drugs had stolen away the power of coherent speech.

Jumbled memories came crowding in, flashing through her brain as quickly as the windows in the corridor flashed past.

'Joe is a nothing. No breeding, no brains, no money and definitely no future.' Her mother's carefully manicured voice, sharp as a razor blade with contempt.

'And you do have a future, my darling.' That was her father. And because of the future the decision was right. Getting rid of a nothing was right. But it wasn't a nothing, it was a child. Her child. Why oh why wouldn't the nurse look at her? But the trolley rattled on remorselessly, and the guilt grew with each turn of the wheels.

The images blurred, became distant, and disappeared as suddenly as they'd come. The white light was the reflection of the snow on the lights outside the window not a hospital corridor. Diana looked at herself in the cloakroom mirror. Fearful, she almost expected to see the plump teenager of thirteen years ago, but was relieved to find her familiar self reflected in the plastic framed mirror. It was the Diana she recognized, the Diana she'd groomed herself to be. The understated but expensive, superbly cut suit, the matching Gucci accessories, the blonde hair, shining and immaculate, all exactly as she should be. Except for one thing. She looked out of place in the slightly vulgar pink and maroon plastic vanity unit of the downstairs ladies' cloakroom. It jarred her ascetic sensitivity.

'I'll have the storeroom next to my office converted into a suitable cloakroom for myself. That can be the first thing I organize on Monday.' The thought was comforting. A reminder of her new status and power. A touch of blusher to her cheeks, some more lipstick, and she was ready to face the world.

'Mrs Diana Stratton, Deputy Managing Director of Wycombe and Yatton.' Diana repeated the words softly to herself as she went down to the basement of the building in the executive lift. The title sounded impressive. The doors slid open silently on reaching the basement, and Diana stepped out to claim her latest acquisition. The ultimate signal to the outside world that she had arrived. A large black, chauffeur-driven Bentley which was now at her permanent disposal.

Bryant, the chauffeur, stepped forward and touched the peak of his cap. 'Mr Sinclair told me that I'm your permanent chauffeur now, Mrs Stratton,' he said.

'I hope you are pleased.'

'Yes, Ma'am. No more the courtesy car chauffeur at everyone's beck and call.'

Diana allowed herself a discreet smile of triumph. 'Yes, you're on my staff now, and I'm sure we shall get on well.'

In fact, she hadn't expected a personal chauffeur-driven car quite so quickly, but during the luncheon, and when well imbued with champagne, Alan had insisted. As no-one else raised any objection, Diana had seen no reason to dissuade him and had accepted the offer graciously.

Now, settling down comfortably in the back, she was composed enough mentally to toss the past out of the darkened windows of the Bentley. The past was history, it had no bearing on her present life. Diana agreed with Henry Ford's verdict, *history was more or less bunk*.

Composed though she was, a flicker of uneasiness still existed. She needed to purge it, and there was nothing like spending money for lifting the spirits.

Diana pressed the button to slide back the glass partition between herself and the chauffeur. 'Oh, Bryant. A small detour before you take me home. The Armani shop in Bond Street.'

'Yes, Ma'am.' The glass partition slid back, shutting Diana into her own world of luxury. A new dress for the theatre this evening, thought Diana. I deserve it.

The shop assistants watched the large black Bentley gently manoeuvring to park without getting bogged down in the deep slush of the gutters. A chauffeur emerged, and opened the rear door. The tall blonde woman who emerged looked haughty and determined, and it was obvious she was in a hurry.

'A sale I think, girls,' said the manageress gliding smoothly towards the door of the Armani boutique. 'And *only* get out our most expensive models, she looks as if she can afford them. Welcome to Armani, Madam,' she inclined her head graciously towards Diana as she opened the door and ushered her into the boutique. 'How can we help?'

'A dress for the theatre.'

The manageress snapped her fingers. 'Size 10,' she said eyeing Diana's figure. Three junior assistants scurried away to collect a selection of dresses.

It didn't take Diana long to make a decision. Once she had seen the dark green crushed velvet dress edged with silver and gold lace, the choice was made. The softly feminine dress fitted her perfectly. The delicate filigree of silver and gold lace around the low cut neck emphasizing the delicate sheen of her hair and skin.

'The lace is a copy of a traditional Venetian design and the threads are real gold and silver.'

'I should hope so,' said Diana wryly when told the price. She swirled once more and looked at herself in the mirror. It was hellishly expensive, but damn it, she looked wonderful. 'I'll have it,' she said, 'and take it now.'

'Has Madam an account?'

'I don't bother with accounts,' said Diana who had always balked at the idea of being on anyone's mailing list, believing opening unwanted envelopes to be a waste of time. 'This should do.' She handed over an American Express Gold card.

The manageress smiled. 'Yes, Madam, it certainly will.'

She sounds like the television advert, thought Diana, I wonder if she knows. Then she tapped her foot impatiently, waiting for the girls to wrap the dress in miles of tissue paper before carefully sliding it into the distinctive sleek carrier of the Armani boutique.

'I wish we had more customers like her,' said the manageress after Diana had left. 'Not many customers come into the shop, spend a fortune in five minutes, and actually pay for it.'

'Very toffee-nosed though,' said the youngest assistant.

'My dear. With that sort of money at her fingertips, she can afford to be!'

The enormous Armani bag crackled opulently by her side on the back seat, and Diana relaxed. No more hassles with tubes or taxis, now Bryant could take the strain. Because of the heavy fall of snow, London, in the rush hour, was more chaotic than usual, but Bryant was a good driver and Diana closed her eyes. Bryant could do the worrying, that was what he was paid for.

She thought of Hugh and smiled. He didn't know about the Bentley yet. When she'd rung him to tell of her success, she'd saved that piece of information for later, wanting to tell him in person. Already, in her imagination, she was savouring the moment, knowing he would be delighted. Like her, he relished the trappings of luxury.

'What time do you want me to come back for you this evening, Mrs Stratton?'

The car purred to a smooth halt in the thick snow. Bryant, opening the door of the Bentley for his new mistress, looked up at the elegant eighteenth century house in Cheyne Walk, Chelsea. Bit different from my bedsit in Earls Court, he thought enviously.

Before the war, the house in Cheyne Walk had been the London home for a fashionable and wealthy family. Now, it was converted into luxury apartments. Hugh and Diana had bought the penthouse suite because, not only was it the most luxuriously appointed as well as being the largest, but it had the best views of the River Thames. Diana was happy there, even although initially she'd thought it a little pricey. But now, taking her inflated new salary into account, it seemed ridiculously cheap. They could afford to be as extravagant as they wanted. It was a deliciously decadent feeling.

'Ma'am?' Bryant's quiet, deferential voice reminded Diana that she hadn't answered his question.

'Oh, yes, tonight. About 6.30 p.m. please, Bryant. Then we'll need picking up from the National Theatre at 11.15 p.m. I've already checked when the performance ends. I do hope that's not too late for you. I know you've had a long day.' Feeling totally relaxed and happy now, Diana flashed him one of her rare smiles, which illuminated her face, making her grey eyes take on a warm, almost topaz hue. 'Mrs Bryant must get very fed up with you working such long hours,' she added.

'There isn't a Mrs Bryant. Only an ex, and she lives up in Luton. So long as I send her the maintenance money regular, she doesn't give a tinker's cuss what I do. Home is a bedsit in Earls Court, and to tell you the truth the Bentley is more comfortable.'

'Oh!' Embarrassed at his frankness, Diana hesitated, then said, because she could think of nothing else more adequate, 'I'm sorry.'

'Nothing to be sorry about, Ma'am,' said Bryant philosophically. 'Just one of life's rum dos. You never know what's going to hit you next, do you?'

'Well . . . no. I suppose not.' Diana turned to go. Thank God her life wasn't like that. Never knowing what was going to happen next. She always knew exactly what was going to happen, because her life was planned with painstaking care. Poor Bryant, a bedsit in Earls Court. Diana couldn't imagine a worse fate.

'Oh, Mrs Stratton.' She turned back. 'You've forgotten this.' It was the business section of *The Times*. God Almighty, not that thing again! What the hell was the matter with her today? She didn't usually go around

73

carrying newspapers, and she couldn't even remember picking it up. 'Mrs Stratton?' Bryant held out the paper.

Resisting the temptation to tell him to throw it in the gutter, Diana said, 'Thank you, Bryant,' and, taking the paper from his outstretched hand, bolted through the snow into the warmth of the house.

Once alone in the apartment, Diana clutched the paper against her chest and remembered her momentary lapse in the cloakroom. For the second time that day she cursed herself for being a fool. Why unearth long buried memories when they didn't matter a damn?

Even so, against her better judgement, Diana found herself slowly smoothing out the creases in the paper. She began to read. *Joe Kelly, of Shamrock Enterprises, now in the multi-millionaire bracket, will soon be a billionaire if his entry into the property market goes as well as all his other ventures.* She raised her eyebrows. For a man who'd had no ambition he'd done well. Now entering the property market, that was a bloody nuisance. Her mouth tightened into a straight, determined line. Joe Kelly's movements would need to be monitored carefully. Susan could see him if she wished, but the last thing Diana wanted was for the past and present to draw level.

Screwing up the paper she threw it into the waste bin. Out of sight, out of mind. But Bryant's words uttered only a few minutes before came back with disquieting clarity. 'You never know what's going to hit you next, do you?'

Chapter Five

Lawyers mingled with business men and journalists, all hurrying to escape the piercing fingers of the icy wind whistling through Wine Office Court, all battling their way into the *Old Cheshire Cheese* for a snatched lunch. The Fleet Street pub was crowded as usual, and seeing an empty place Hugh claimed it by slamming down his pint of beer and plate of shepherd's pie on to the scrubbed wooden table.

'Hugh Stratton! How are you, and how's Diana? Good God, man, where have you been? I haven't seen you in ages. And what a coinicidence, today of all days.' The voice belonged to Ben Rose. A university contemporary of Hugh's, although not a particular friend. Ben was a barrister with a firm in Gray's Inn.

Slightly surprised at Ben's enthusiastic greeting, Hugh gave a curt nod. Ben had never seemed particularly keen on him before, and he certainly didn't feature on Hugh's list of acquaintances to be cultivated. 'I'm fine,' he said abruptly, 'and Diana's fine too.' Then he relented, and allowing himself a superior smile was unable to resist the opportunity to boast. 'In fact she's got an interview today for the post of Deputy MD at Wycombe and Yatton.'

Ben whistled. 'In the big money then.' He sounded envious. 'I wish my wife worked.'

'She probably would if you didn't keep her busy producing babies,' said Hugh, knowing that Ben had four children.

Ben flushed, reflecting that Hugh hadn't improved with the years, still as sarcastically venomous as ever. How the hell had he ever managed to marry a woman as gorgeous as Diana? 'My wife's not as clever as yours,' he said, thinking how unfair it was that Diana should be brilliant as well as gorgeous.

'Why did you say today of all days?'

Hugh asked not really wanting to know, because Ben was a bore. All men who talked about their families were bores to Hugh, his interest only extended to two things, women and money. Any other time he would have found an excuse to move and leave Ben to his own devices, but today he was interested in the woman sitting beside Ben. She had the most wonderfully long legs, and was sitting with them crossed, her short skirt showing a tempting expanse of thigh.

Although not looking directly at her, Hugh was acutely aware of her presence. Jesus! but the woman oozed the most appallingly attractive sex appeal. He could almost smell it. A rippling against the dark material of his trousers made him jump. Holy shit! he'd got an erection. Hastily pulling in his chair closer so that the table shielded the bulge in the area of his flies, he swallowed hard. God! It was a long time since this had happened. Uncontrollable sexual arousal was something he thought he'd learned to restrain. Something that had disappeared with adolescence and acne. Intrigued, he switched his gaze from her legs and stared into the eyes of the woman opposite who was having such a devastating effect on him. Immediately he felt that there was something familiar about her. She certainly wasn't one of his casual sexual acquaintances. There was nothing casual about this woman, and Hugh knew he would have remembered her. Where had he seen her before?

Ben's face, hot and shiny from the curry he was eating, creased into a triumphant smile; pleased at the fact that he knew something Hugh did not. It was a small triumph, but any advantage over Hugh Stratton was enough to give a fillip to Ben's malnourished ego. 'Why today? I'll tell you why, old man. This gorgeous creature sitting beside me is none other than your equally gorgeous wife's cousin. Nancy Morris, Hugh Stratton, Diana's husband.' Ben made the introductions, then added, 'but it's strange that you haven't met before.'

The memory clicked into place. 'We haven't formally met,' Hugh said. What lazy, lustful dark eyes she had. 'But I remember now, we did catch a brief glimpse of each other at my wedding.'

'What a marvellous memory. I didn't think you'd even noticed me skulking in the background.' Lighting a cigarette and inhaling slowly, Nancy smiled at Hugh. 'A pity I couldn't stay that day, but I was due in Monte Carlo that night; a party with some very boring friends of my husband. But when I saw the notice in *The Times* I was determined to come to the wedding because I was curious to see what kind of man Diana had finally caught for herself. She'd been alone for so long I was wondering if she was a lesbian.'

Ben looked embarrassed.

Hugh smiled. 'I can assure you she is not.'

'Of course. I realize that now. But how is it we've never met properly before? Tell me, where does Diana keep you? At home on a leash?'

'I'm a free man,' said Hugh. 'I regard my marriage as a very,' he hesitated fractionally to emphasize the word, '*liberal* contract.'

'And does Diana think in the same way?'

'You must ask her,' said Hugh, knowing very well she would never bother.

Nancy Morris had porcelain white skin, brown, almost black eyes and blue black hair. Her beauty was quite outstanding. She was not a woman who could be overlooked. Smiling slowly back at Hugh, the vivid scarlet of her lips formed a predatory curve, and Hugh noticed that the colour of her lips exactly matched the colour of her long nails on the end of finely tapering milk-white fingers.

'Maybe I will.' Nancy's voice was as fascinating as her appearance, low and sexily husky. 'But on the other hand, maybe it isn't that important.'

She leaned her elbows on the table, giving him a heart stopping view of her cleavage. The smart black suit she wore was made of clinging wool, and the swell of her breasts made Hugh long to reach out and touch them. He could see the sharp points of her nipples through the soft wool material of her jacket, and the libidinous heat increased in the area of his groin. God! but his trousers felt tight. Keeping his eyes fixed on hers, Hugh made a great show of kissing the slender hand Nancy extended across the table, letting his lips linger far longer than necessary. Nancy wouldn't bore him. Of that, he was certain.

'It was very remiss of Diana not to have introduced us properly four years ago,' he said softly.

'Wasn't it. But then as I recall she always was a possessive little girl, and old habits die hard. Never mind, now that we have met again, we must make certain that we keep in touch.'

'I'd like to make sure we're in touch as often as possible,' said Hugh, wondering if her bush was the same blue black colour as her hair.

A wickedly amused smile curved her full lips, and her eyes were saying bed, bed, bed.

'I've been engaged by Mrs Morris,' interrupted Ben, 'to sort out her divorce. It's going to be a complicated settlement.' He mopped up the last of his curry with a piece of Nan bread.

'Good old Ben here is screwing my bastard of a husband for every damned penny he can get out of him,' said Nancy. The sultry purr in her voice was suddenly replaced with a vindictive sharpness.

A bitch of the first order, thought Hugh. But far from putting him off it added a spicy facet, making her more interesting by the minute. Nancy touched a latent core of savagery in him, something Diana had never been able to do. What a woman. She made other women, including Diana, seem insipid in comparison.

'On what grounds?' he asked.

'Cruelty. Unreasonable behaviour,' said Ben.

'I see,' said Hugh wryly.

Privately he thought the cruelty and unreasonable behaviour was much more likely to have emanated from Nancy. But that wasn't his problem, it was Ben's. He was being paid to untangle the details. As for the husband, it was his own fault for marrying her in the first place. Hugh was firmly of the opinion that no man should ever become involved with a woman he couldn't manipulate. He'd always prided himself on his ability to manoeuvre his female acquaintances to play the game he chose. Although he was careful to keep it hidden, it amused him letting Diana think she was the driving force in their marriage. Not that he underestimated her. He needed her. She was a pleasurable stable prop in his life. It was useful having a glamorous and famous wife, and even more useful being able to share in her wealth.

'My husband, Joseph, is loaded,' said Nancy with the same slow, calculating smile. 'But Joseph, poor misguided darling, made the mistake of thinking that I'd do as he wanted once we were married. He also had a weird idea that marriage is for ever.'

'Was he never married before?'

'Oh yes. But his first wife escaped by dying. However, I'm afraid I've no intention of being so accommodating. I'm divorcing him. I've given him five long years of free screwing, and now I'm bored.'

Ben shushed her, he wasn't used to such candid talk outside the office.

Hugh was filled with a surge of pure carnal lust which almost burst his fly buttons asunder. 'Lucky Joseph,' he said, 'to have had you for five years.'

Nancy drew on her cigarette. 'Yes, lucky Joseph. But now I'm claiming the back pay.'

'Five years of fidelity is a long time,' said Ben sanctimoniously in his best courtroom voice. 'And no consideration from her husband, not even an adequate personal allowance.'

79

'Are you going to use fidelity as the basis of your case?' Hugh didn't bother to hide his incredulity.

'Well,' Ben looked at Nancy who was still smiling at Hugh, 'I was thinking of playing that as our strongest card.' His voice wavered, and he began to sound doubtful.

Nancy turned to Ben. 'Fidelity? You'll have to think of something better than that. No-one said anything to me about fidelity.' She choked with sudden laughter. 'Good God, Ben,' she said, 'what is the matter with you? I was told you were a good lawyer, so think about it. Joseph is nearly seventy, and although he's as keen as the next man on fucking, he's not so hot on the performance. Now, surely you must understand that a normal young woman like me couldn't put up with that. I need vigorous satisfaction, often, with plenty of variety.'

'Do you mean to say that you have slept with . . .' Shocked to the core at this revelation, Ben spluttered into horrified silence, his glasses slipping down to the end of his nose.

Hugh nearly burst out loud with laughter at Ben's outraged expression. Poor Ben with his gold-framed spectacles, thinning hair and serious face. He had about as much sex appeal as a cold potato, and probably as much experience. Hugh suddenly realized that Ben was quite oblivious of Nancy's sexual aura, and up until that moment had obviously had no idea of her admitted promiscuity. He wondered if Ben was now regretting taking on her case. She wouldn't be an easy client for whom to act.

'Not everyone treads the straight and narrow like you, Ben,' he said with a grin.

Under the table Nancy's foot was slowly running up along the inside of Hugh's leg. She's slipped off her shoe, the bitch, thought Hugh, enjoying the sensation. Suppressing his quivering excitement, he felt her toes play a suggestive rhythm up and down his leg. He looked at her, but her face was impassive. The only thing giving her away was the unmistakeable lust shining from the depths of her black eyes. Hugh kept his gaze equally impassive, even though by now he was feeling sick with desire. But he couldn't prevent the knuckles on the hand holding his beer glass noticeably whitening.

Nancy turned towards Ben and smiled angelically. 'Do you mean have I slept with other men? Of course I have. Doesn't everybody? I need variety for God's sake! It's the only thing that keeps me sane. Haven't you heard the saying? An orgasm a day keeps the doctor away.'

'Don't you worry about AIDS?' asked Hugh curiously. He too liked frequent satisfaction, and plenty of variety and had forgotten his marriage vows the moment the words had left his lips, but he did worry about AIDS. Cursing the disease for cramping his style, he'd been much more careful of late.

'AIDS, darling? Good heavens you can still have plenty of fun without catching AIDS. Would you like me to show you how?' The smile was wicked now.

'For goodness sake, Nancy, keep your damned voice down,' muttered Ben. Puce with embarrassment, and sweating more than ever, he looked around nervously, praying that no-one had overheard. 'If I'm going to try and present you as the wronged but virtuous wife, you'd better start behaving like one.'

'Oh must I,' said Nancy, utterly unrepentant. 'Well, Ben, on second thoughts, perhaps you'd better think of something else. I really don't think being virtuous is quite me.' Then ignoring Ben, she leaned towards Hugh and whispered, 'surely you've heard this saying, *smart girls carry condoms*! It's practically the motto in women's magazines these days, especially the ones aimed at liberated ladies.'

'You're not supposed to be liberated,' grumbled Ben, 'you're supposed to be married.' He wondered why he was bothering to waste his breath.

'Is that where you get your ideas from, magazines?' asked Hugh. How ravishingly beautiful she looked when her black eyes sparkled so deliciously wickedly.

81

Nancy gave a soft laugh. 'Of course not. I'm a very inventive person in my own right. Which reminds me. What are you doing tonight, darling?' While speaking she slipped a small address card into Hugh's hand. 'Shut up, Ben,' she added as Ben opened his mouth to protest.

'I'm going to the National Theatre I'm afraid,' said Hugh, fervently wishing he wasn't. Shit! he'd much rather screw Nancy than sit through yet another version of Hamlet. 'It's to celebrate Diana's new directorship.'

'She might not get it,' said Nancy. 'You don't know for certain yet. And if she doesn't there'll be nothing to celebrate.'

'She'll get it.' Ben's voice was sharp with dislike. He'd finally recognized Nancy for the woman she was, and was thinking that he'd like to kill Tony Bodkin, his colleague at the Gray's Inn practice, for recommending him to Nancy. 'Diana is a very clever *lady*.' He emphasized the word lady.

'All right, Ben. Don't sound so bloody disapproving. We can't all be as pure as the driven snow.' Nancy turned to Hugh. 'Some other time then,' she said in a low voice, squeezing his hand still holding her address card. 'You know where to find me.'

'Time for us to get back to my office,' said Ben abruptly, draining the last dregs of his lager and standing up. 'We've got a lot of paper work to get through.' An awful lot, he thought gloomily. He was not looking forward to more intimate anecdotes from Nancy on the subject of her marriage. It was obviously going to be a very messy divorce, unless by some miracle Joseph Morris was a saint and didn't put up a fight.

Nancy made no secret of her reluctance to leave. She pulled a mocking face at Hugh. 'He's going to lecture me on being a good little wife, I just know it,' she grumbled, caressing Hugh's leg with her toes before withdrawing her foot. 'Give my love to Diana,' she said, smiling down into Hugh's mesmerized eyes. 'And don't forget, we must get in touch *soon*.'

The telephone in Hugh's office rang.

'Darling, I've got it.'

'Diana. Congratulations, when do you start?'

'Immediately, I'm just being dragged in for a celebratory luncheon, then I'll be home. Darling, do you realize that you are now talking to the Deputy Managing Director of Wycombe and Yatton?'

'I'm very impressed,' said Hugh, and meant it. Momentarily he forgot about Nancy, and thought of all the extra money Diana would be earning. 'I'll buy the best bottle of Dom Perignon they've got at the National tonight. This is really something to drink to.'

Diana laughed happily. 'Perhaps I'd better buy it, darling. Now that I'll be making so much money.'

'Certainly not. This is going to be my treat. I can afford it. See you later, darling. Take care.' And so I can, thought Hugh, a self-satisfied smile spreading across his face as he put the 'phone down. I can afford that *and* Nico.

He looked at his watch. Another hour and a half and everyone would be gone, they always left the offices early on a Friday. Then he could ring Nico. The thought of Nico reminded him of the previous night when Diana had unwittingly picked up the nasty reminder he'd received detailing how much money was owed. He prickled with perspiration even now at the thought. Christ! but that had been a close call, supposing Diana had unwrapped the note and read it. He hastily put the thought from his mind. There was no need to worry. The fact of the matter was she hadn't read it, and now he'd pay Nico off, and Diana would remain, as always, in blissful ignorance.

The time dragged slowly, but at last the flurry of goodnights, and goodbyes as the inhabitants of the offices left for the weekend stopped, and all was quiet. Hugh waited a little longer, listening carefully. All remained quiet in the adjoining offices. Good, that meant he could sort Nico out right now. The snow had been a bonus, it meant everyone had left a little earlier than usual this

Friday evening. There was no-one about to overhear. Picking up the 'phone it only took a moment to punch out the number he knew by heart.

'Pronto.'

Christ! Why can't that bloody woman speak English after thirty years in England? The fact never failed to exasperate Hugh, but hiding his irritation he said smoothly, 'can I speak to Nico, please.'

'Oo ees spiking?'

'A friend.' Hugh enunciated loudly and clearly as if to a child. In his opinion Nico's mother must be an idiot, and he spoke to her accordingly.

The phone crashed down, and at the other end of the line Hugh winced at the noise. He could hear a babble of voices in the background, then Nico himself answered. 'Hi, Nico here.'

'It's Hugh. Hugh Stratton. Can I meet you? Say in half an hour. The usual place.'

'Only if you've got what I want. Nice crisp little pieces of paper. You can't have all credit. I've got a living to make. I'm not running some fucking charity.'

'Yes, yes I've got it.' Hugh was impatient.

'How much?'

'Five hundred, just as you asked for. But for that I want some more packets and the usual credit.'

'OK.'

The high pitched whine told Hugh that Nico had put the 'phone down. He'd better move quickly. Pulling open the bottom drawer of his desk, Hugh had already inserted the key in the petty cash box when his office door suddenly opened. A grey bobble hat appeared first, followed by the bulky form of Miss Higgins, his secretary. She swayed, half in, half out of the office, her head at an angle around the edge of the door.

'Anything you need, Mr Stratton?'

'No, thank you. You go now before the rush hour,' said Hugh forcing a relaxed smile to his lips with an effort. What the hell was she still doing here? He'd thought she'd gone with everyone else. Silly old cow making him jump out of his skin. He pushed the drawer in softly with his foot, so that it was out of the line of her vision.

'Thank you, Mr Stratton. Have a good weekend.' The woollen bobble hat disappeared and the door closed.

'Same to you,' called Hugh cheerfully through gritted teeth.

Edging the drawer out carefully, Hugh bent down and turned the key in the lock of the cash box.

'Oh, Mr Stratton.'

Hugh nearly died of heart failure. It was Miss Higgins back again and this time she was leaning over the desk and could see quite clearly that he had the key in the cash box.

'That's what I came back for,' she said. 'There's all that money in the petty cash and silly me,' she giggled girlishly and Hugh wished he could strangle her on the spot, 'forgot to put it in the safe.'

'I was just about to do that myself, as you can see,' lied Hugh smoothly. 'Don't worry about forgetting it, you've had a busy day.'

'I'll do it now.'

'No you won't.' Hugh rose and put his arm gallantly around Miss Higgins. 'I'm not having you getting home late in this dreadful weather. I'll do it, and you are to go home immediately. That's an order.'

'Oh, Mr Stratton. You are good to me.' The face beneath the bobble hat was bright pink.

'Good secretaries are hard to come by. They need a little cherishing. Now off you go.' Hugh opened the door, and resisting the urge to push Miss Higgins flat on her face, gently escorted her through it. 'Goodnight again,' he said.

'Goodnight, Mr Stratton. And thank you ever so much.'

Hugh closed his office door and leaned against it sweating, his breath coming in short rapid gasps. Hell! he'd damn near died of fright. He decided to wait. Better make sure she bloody well had gone this time. He heard three doors slam, a sign that she was safely out of the front door and into the courtyard outside. But having no intention of leaving anything to chance again, he checked from his window, watching until the shapeless woolly form that was Miss Higgins finally disappeared from view. Only then did he quickly re-open the drawer to its full extent, open the box and take out five hundred pounds. He wasn't stealing, only borrowing. It would all be put back on Monday morning. He smiled, more relaxed now. No worries any more about raiding their joint bank account occasionally. Diana would never notice with all that extra money going in.

Carefully locking the cash box he pocketed the key, just in case Miss Higgins got in before him on Monday and wanted to open it. Then having stowed the box away in the wall safe, Hugh put on his overcoat and left his office.

The two elderly cleaning ladies who 'did' for the firm were coming up the steps to the building as Hugh pulled open the heavy front door to leave.

' 'Night, Mr Stratton. Anyone else left?'

'No, I'm the last. Goodnight.'

'Goodnight. Bit parky tonight, sir. You wrap up warm now, can't 'ave you catching cold.'

'I will, thanks.' Hugh pulled his overcoat collar up high against the bitter night air as he hurried out past them.

Secluded and peaceful, the ancient courtyards and passageways of the traffic-free Inns of Court always had a curious tranquillity, but tonight the snow added an eery quietness of its own. It lay clean and white, unsullied by milling crowds, and effectively deadening all sound. Unlike nearby Fleet Street, where the pristine white powder had already turned into ugly grey slush. But the timeless beauty of the Inner Temple was wasted on Hugh. He had no eyes for the allure of the warm pools of light shed by the Victorian street lamps, his mind was on one thing only. The meeting with Nico. Head down against the biting cold, he hurried through the cobbled alleys towards the Inner Temple Gateway. Good, Nico was already there, he could see a shadowy figure by the wall. Hardly pausing in his stride, Hugh handed over the five hundred pounds in cash, and took the envelope Nico handed to him.

'Hang on a minute. I'll count it.'

'Not here, you fool. Anyway, you don't need to. It's all there.' Hugh hurried on through the gate.

'It fucking well better *had* be.' There was no mistaking the evil menace in Nico's low voice floating after him.

Hugh stepped through the ancient wooden doorway which led through the gate, and was immediately caught up in the swirl and roar of the evening traffic surging along Fleet Street. Little shit, he thought venomously, wishing he could do without Nico, but knowing that he couldn't. Only the Nicos of this world had what he wanted. His fingers curled around the packet and he smiled. Sod Nico, he'd got it, that was all that mattered. Unmindful of others, Hugh pushed his way through the crowds towards his next destination. The quiet sanctuary of St Bride's, the parish church of Fleet Street. Once there, he settled himself out of sight at the back of the church in one of the tall wooden sided pews, and took out the envelope Nico had given him. The single envelope contained ten smaller packets. Hugh swore softly. A bad sign that. It was already split into grammes, and Nico knew he liked to split his own. But Nico was always looking to make a bigger profit, and knowing him he'd probably cut the stuff with cheap talcum powder. Carefully opening one packet Hugh touched it experimentally with his tongue. He smiled, his luck was in. Nico must have been feeling generous. The sharp bitter taste told him it was cut with paracetamol. Hugh liked that, he always got a bigger rush with that. Reckless now, it had been more than a week since he'd had a snort, Hugh put the cocaine on the back of his hand and sniffed it up through the rolled up five pound note he had at the ready. Two sniffs, half the powder through each nostril. Then he leaned back against the pew waiting for the rush.

A priest entered the church, silently moving up the aisle towards the altar, his flowing cassock almost brushing against Hugh hidden in the darkness of the pew. Through a mist Hugh watched him light the candles ready for evensong, and kneel, head bowed, before the cross. Then suddenly the candles flared, exploding brilliant and white in Hugh's head as the rush came. His whole body shook with an orgasm of frenzied intoxication and immediately he thought of Nancy. Fucking hell, if only she were here. He wanted her, *he wanted her now*. He felt his penis rise and harden and very nearly ejaculated there and then at the mere thought, but somehow managed to control himself. He waited, breathing deeply, savouring the moment. Then as soon as the first ecstatic rush died away he got up and hurried from the church, knocking over a chair near the font in his haste to get out.

'Who's that?' Disturbed from his devotions, the priest rose from his knees to face the direction of the noise.

'Sorry,' Hugh shouted to the startled priest, 'love to stay for the service, but can't.' He laughed. Still too high on the cocaine to control himself completely, it came out as a high pitched hysterical sound. 'I have a pressing engagement.' The main door to the church slammed, and he was gone.

'What a very strange young man.' Perplexed, the priest stared after Hugh.

'A junkie,' said the verger dismissively. He'd arrived in time to see Hugh's exit. 'Probably had a fix in one of the pews.'

'Nonsense, Charles. Don't be so cynical, it's a most unchristian attitude. Anyway, he couldn't possibly be a junkie, he was much too well spoken.'

The verger remained silent. He'd lived in London all his life, through the heyday of St Bride's before the Second World War, until now when it was a haven for winos and drug addicts if he forgot to lock the doors at night. He knew well enough the look of someone who'd just had a fix. Too well spoken indeed! They were the worst ones when it came to coke. He glowered at the priest, newly appointed; give him six months, then he wouldn't be so unworldly. Too well spoken indeed! Sighing mournfully at the state the world had come to, the verger shuffled among the pews putting out half a dozen hymn books. Three for the three old ladies who always came to evensong, and three in the vain hope that someone else might come too.

Hugh strode along Fleet Street. He had already forgotten the priest, St Bride's and everything else except Nancy. Still on a high, he caressed her naked body in his imagination. Firm white breasts, huge dark nipples, perfect for sucking. He almost drooled at the thought. On reaching Ludgate Circus, a cab coming down Faringdon Street with the yellow 'For Hire' sign illuminated caught his attention. The need to lay claim to it before anyone else temporarily drove thoughts of Nancy from his mind. Leaping out into the road, he ruthlessly beat off two umbrella waving elderly City gentlemen in bowler hats and a young woman, who also had their sights set on the same cab.

'If you were a gentleman, you'd let me have it. Especially on a night like this,' the girl wailed miserably, trying to hang on to the door handle of the taxi.

A sharp wrench of the taxi door prised the handle from her grasp. 'Fuck off,' Hugh snarled, pushing her aside violently. Losing her balance the girl slipped and fell into a deep pile of wet and dirty slush, but Hugh was totally unmoved. 'This is the era of emancipated women and equal opportunities,' he said with a disdainful sneer. 'You should have been quicker.' Slamming the cab door shut he leaned forward and gave his address. 'Cheyne Walk, Chelsea.'

Chapter Six

Diana was already in the shower when Hugh entered the apartment, but came out into the hall, holding a towel around her, to greet him. 'Darling, you're early. I thought you'd be late because of the snow.' She raised her wet face for a kiss.

'I got a cab straight away,' said Hugh slowly. His mind was still reeling from the cocaine-induced euphoria, and he stared curiously at Diana's reflection in the long mirror on the wall as he automatically kissed her. Captured in the golden oval-framed mirror with her damp hair curling in tendrils like a woman in a Pre-Raphaelite painting, her bare shoulders and thighs catching the light, she had an air of innocent sexuality. Hugh caught his breath. The erotic fantasies of Nancy bubbling just beneath the surface suddenly became unbearable, filling him with a raw uncontrollable lewdness. He was desperate for sex. So desperate that he threw all caution to the wind and forgot that Diana had never seen him so soon after snorting. All he could think of was that he had to have a fuck, now, now, NOW. He couldn't wait to get inside her. His head began to pound and his groin engorged and throbbing was hurting. He needed the release of a woman. Any woman.

'Hugh!' Diana's initial laugh of surprise turned into a gasp of horrified astonishment as Hugh flung aside his overcoat and jacket and unzipping his flies grabbed her from behind. Tearing the towel she held aside, he curved his body in behind hers and rammed his rigid shaft into her unprepared body. Briefly she tried to struggle free, but quickly realized that it was useless. There was an overpowering, primitive savagery about him that rendered fighting pointless. Like a man possessed by a demonic fever, his breath came in great gasping rasps. His hands burned cruelly into her flesh and his mouth on her shoulders wasn't kissing; he was almost eating her. Catching sight of their reflection in the mirror, Diana felt a choking sense of unreality. Who was this stranger with the widely dilated pupils and ghastly salacious appetite?

How could he do this? How could he? Her mind rebelled at the idea of registering that this man was Hugh. It wasn't Hugh. Not the husband she loved. No, it couldn't possibly be Hugh. It was as if the smooth pebble that was their life together had suddenly been flipped over to reveal dark vermin clinging to the underside.

Then it was over. As suddenly as he had grabbed her, Hugh let her go. Picking up his overcoat and jacket he walked past her into their bedroom. 'God! I needed that,' he said.

It was then that the chaos of her emotions suddenly fused into one overriding force, that of anger. An all-consuming, furious, blinding, anger. Hugh was now behaving as if what had happened was not important. Furiously she wanted to scream at him, how dare you, how dare you!

But she didn't, she remained silent. At all costs she mustn't lose her self control and more importantly she knew she must somehow regain control of their relationship. But how? Bending down she picked up the towel with trembling fingers and wrapping it around her, followed Hugh. In all the four years of their marriage he had never behaved in such a way before. Did he not realize that by this one violent act he had altered the whole substance of their marriage?

She came to the doorway. 'Why did you do that?'

'Do what?' Hugh asked vaguely, shrugging his broad shoulders into a towelling robe before walking into the second bathroom on the far side of the bedroom. He began to run a bath.

Diana followed him. She had no intention of letting it

91

drop, and behaving as if nothing had happened. 'Make
. . .' she stopped, tightening her mouth into a thin angry
line. No, damn it! She wasn't going to dignify the act by
saying *making love*, because Hugh's act had been nothing
to do with love. Nothing at all. 'Why did you jump on
me?' she said sharply. 'Like some sex-starved maniac.'

Hugh, catching a fleeting glimpse of his reflection in
the mirror before it steamed up, saw himself as Diana was
seeing him. Pale face, pupils dark, widely dilated; a
stranger's face. Suddenly ice cold needles of realism
abruptly punctured his euphoric mood. He recognized
with an unpalatable jolt of dismay that he'd betrayed his
true self to Diana.

But just as ruthlessness and logic were Diana's
strengths, so quick wittedness and the daring to take a
gamble were Hugh's. He knew what he'd do, he would
make light of it. She'd soon forget.

'Oh, darling, do be adult,' he said with a deprecating
laugh, mustering the most blasé voice he could. 'We don't
always have to make love the same way every time, do
we?'

Diana walked with slow deliberation across the bedroom and stopped at the bathroom door. 'Make love? It
was more like rape,' she said icily.

'Rape! Oh my God, now you *are* being ridiculous.'

'Am I?' Diana heard her own voice as if from afar, it
was ominously chilling, and that was exactly how she felt.
'I believe the dictionary definition of rape is the act of
taking something by force. And that is what you did. You
just took me, you didn't ask.'

Hugh turned towards her, carefully switching on the
charm which had served him so well over the years.
'Darling,' he said softly. 'I'm your husband. It never
occurred to me that I should ask. I wanted you. It's as
simple as that. I wanted you so badly, that I just had to
make love to you there and then. I couldn't wait, so I
made love to you in the hall. You've never objected when
we've made love outside the bedroom before.'

92

Diana stared at him, feeling strangely aloof. It was as if she were a spectator not a participant in this charade. Who were this elegantly unreal couple in their beautiful apartment, surrounded by expensive belongings? What did they have to do with her? But almost immediately the answer was there blazing back at her, and there was no avoiding it. This wasn't a charade, it was her life. This was the life she had schemed for, planned and chosen so carefully; and Hugh was part of that plan, part of the jigsaw of her life. The problem was that Hugh's piece of the jigsaw had moved out of position. How did she fit him back in? It was essential that she did. Diana couldn't bear to think of her carefully conceived plan going awry. But suddenly anger took over once more and she knew she didn't want to fit him back in, not yet. Not this Hugh. Not this stranger.

'No, Hugh,' she said coldly. 'You didn't want to make love to me. You just wanted sex. And it didn't have to be me, it could have been any woman. I was the unlucky one. I just happened to be there.'

'Oh, Diana,' Hugh protested, 'what a terrible thing to say. Of course it was you I wanted. There could never be anyone else. But you're right, I was selfish, thinking only of my own needs, and not yours. Forgive me, darling.'

Moving across to her, he put one finger under her chin and very gently tipped back her head a little. 'I had one hell of a day,' he lied. 'And when I saw you standing there wrapped in that towel, you looked so beautiful, so desirable, that I just couldn't help myself. I lost control. It's something that happens to all men at some time, and it's unforgiveable I know.' Burying his face against her damp hair, Hugh thought he sounded marvellously penitent. 'I know I don't deserve it,' he whispered. 'But I love you so much. Can you ever forgive me?'

'No Hugh,' she said. 'I don't think I can.'

He put his arms around her and glanced at his watch. There was time. 'Let's go to bed and start again,' he said softly, bending his head to kiss her.

But, Diana, feeling his arm move, instinctively knew he had looked at his watch. His calculated timing added to her icy determination not to be won over. They'd make it up later, when she felt it was right. Not now.

'No Hugh, there isn't time. And anyway I've got to wash.'

Hugh thought of Diana's new salary and swallowed the last remnants of his pride. 'All right, darling. But please, please, tell me I'm forgiven.' There was no reply and Hugh worried. 'Diana?' he repeated.

Diana turned and looked at him. 'I'll think about it,' she said, 'but right now I'm going to shower.'

There was nothing more Hugh could do but wait.

Diana showered, bathed and showered again, and only then did she begin to feel clean. She had to purge her body and soul of that brutal sexual act. All the while she was washing, she forced herself to think. Not of the humiliating episode in the hall, she didn't allow herself to think of that, but of the future. Her mind hummed with half-formed thoughts. So what do I do? Leave Hugh and divorce him? What good will that do? She thought of her new position at Wycombe and Yatton. I'm not yet secure enough to weather a domestic scandal. The hypocrisy of the establishment, sickening though it might be, is a fact of life, and something I have to live with if I want to go on succeeding. And I do, I do. If I'm to be known as Mrs Diana Stratton, the happily married, successful woman, I need Hugh. It is a good image to project, one of stability and respectability. The image, Diana decided firmly, she intended to keep.

She glanced at Hugh, now changing in the bedroom. Half an hour ago, she thought, I loved him without question. Now, it can never be quite the same again, but human relationships always change. I'm being unrealistic to expect otherwise. It might be difficult to pick up the threads again and weave them into something resembling our past rapport, but it can be done. It *has* to be done. She thought of the evening ahead at the theatre. It will be a strain, but that is no good reason for putting it off she told herself sternly. Somehow the fabric of our marriage has to be stitched back together as soon as possible.

'You look lovely, darling,' said Hugh casually, trying not to let the relief show in his voice. It was ten minutes before they were due to leave for the theatre, and as soon as she'd put on the beautiful green dress, he knew that their evening was going ahead as planned. She had forgiven him. 'New dress?' he asked.

'Yes,' said Diana briefly.

She looked at Hugh, handsome in his evening suit, flicking imaginary specks of dust from his shoulders. So, he had decided to pretend the incident in the hall had never happened. That much was obvious from his demeanour. Well, maybe, on measured reflection, that was for the best. There was no point in mulling over it, and the last thing she wanted to hear was a repeat of the feeble excuses he'd made earlier. No, much better to erase the whole grotesque incident, to deny its existence, deny that it had ever happened. That way, in time, it really would be as if it had never been.

Smoothing down the green velvet of the new Armani gown she said as casually as Hugh, 'It's a very expensive dress. But worth every penny.'

'Oh, talking of pennies reminds me,' said Hugh, immediately thinking of Nancy, and seeing a golden opportunity of further diverting Diana's mind away from the immediate past. 'Ben Rose introduced me to one of his clients today.'

'Oh?' Diana couldn't think of what interest that could be to her.

'It was your cousin, Nancy Morris, the one who put in such a brief appearance at our wedding. Now there's a woman who is hoping to get her hands on quite a few pennies. Those belonging to her husband if the divorce settlement goes as planned. She told me they are going to screw him for every last penny.'

'Huh!' Diana gave a distasteful snort. 'According to Susan she always was an avaricious little bitch. Used regularly to embezzle her school dinner money then plead she'd lost it.' Leaning forward she squinted into the mirror and carefully applied grey eyeliner. 'Age obviously has not changed her for the better.'

'That's a bit harsh. You don't know the facts of her divorce. Anyway, she sent you her love.'

Diana frowned. 'Her love! I hardly knew her, she's seven years older than me. I didn't invite her to our wedding, because I didn't even know where she lived.'

'You must know her. She lived with you didn't she?'

'For a while. But she left Mottisley when she was about fourteen.' Diana paused. 'It's a strange thing,' she said as much to herself as to Hugh, 'but I never did know why.'

'How come?' Hugh sensed a mystery.

'I was only six and a half years old. The age when nobody tells you anything. Anyway, even Susan didn't know and, as far as I know, still doesn't.'

Half-forgotten memories filtered back. Her mother's voice saying shrilly, 'That girl has got to go. I can't bear it. And if you won't agree then I'll . . .' A door had slammed then and the rest of the conversation was blurred. But whatever the reason, her mother's will had prevailed that time and Nancy had gone. Diana remembered being pleased, but at the same time very puzzled. Both her parents were tight-lipped about Nancy, and her name was never mentioned at Abbey House again.

'I think she'd like to renew her acquaintance with you again,' said Hugh cautiously, thinking it would do no harm to prepare the ground. Once Diana and Nancy had met, there would be nothing strange in his seeing his cousin-in-law occasionally.

'Really? Well I can't say the desire is mutual.' Diana picked up her shoes and slid her feet into them. 'Did you remember to book a table for dinner tonight?' The subject of Nancy was firmly dismissed, much to Hugh's disappointment.

'Yes, of course.' The reply was automatic, Hugh's mind still on the fascinating subject of Nancy; but it would be pushing his luck to show too much interest now.

Ready for the theatre, they were on the point of leaving the apartment and Diana had her hand on the door when the telephone rang. 'Leave it,' she snapped.

She was feeling restless and impatient. Blotting out the unpleasant happening of an hour ago wasn't proving to be as simple as she had persuaded herself it would be. But damn it, she would make herself do it. If she couldn't make herself forget, they might end up getting a divorce. To Diana a divorce meant failure. Her mouth set in the familiar straight determined line it always took when she made up her mind to do something. She was not prepared to accept failure in any part of her life, not in her marriage, not in anything. She could bear anything except that. Anything.

Ignoring her, Hugh picked up the 'phone.

Chapter Seven

'Hello.' The smile disappeared from Susan's face.

'What is it?' The wrinkled little woman standing beside Susan edged in closer, trying to hear the conversation.

Susan covered the mouthpiece of the 'phone. 'Hugh's answered,' she whispered.

'Well, don't let him fob you off with some cock and bull story about Diana not being there.'

'No, I won't.'

Susan smiled at the old woman's fierce expression. Dear Aunt May, always so concerned for her welfare. What would she do without her? It was an ever-increasing worry, Susan knew she really shouldn't rely on her so much. At seventy-nine Aunt May was hale and hearty, still able to do her share of work on the farm she owned; but no-one could live for ever. Not even Aunt May.

'Huh!' The diminutive woman beside Susan bobbed up and down with irritation, not entirely convinced. Circumnavigating Hugh to get at Diana was not easy, slippery customer that he was.

'Yes, Susan.'

'Hugh, what a nice surprise to hear your voice.' Susan hoped it sounded as if she meant it. 'Can I speak to Diana?'

'Yes, this is a surprise.' Susan noted that he didn't sound at all pleased. May obviously heard too, as she made a rude face and rolled her eyes heavenwards. Susan was forced into a reluctant grin and her spirits picked up a little. She had no reason to feel afraid, but why was it Hugh always made her feel nervous? 'You want Diana?'

'Yes,' said Susan injecting her voice with as positive an intonation as she could muster. 'It's important.'

'Important? Well, I'll tell her, but I'm sorry Susan, Diana isn't . . .' Hugh *is* going to fob me off, oh damn! Susan felt panic stricken. When will I see Diana again, it has to be soon. I've left it far too long already and Tony had been most emphatic. She could hear his voice now.

'You can never be sure,' he had said. 'You can never be sure.'

'Susan? What's wrong?'

The relief at hearing Diana's voice was great, Susan didn't know whether to burst into tears or laughter. She realized that Diana must have overheard Hugh's conversation and taken the 'phone. 'Oh, nothing is wrong,' she said happily.

Diana sounded worried. 'But I heard Hugh say important. What is important?'

'I want to see you, Diana. It's been such a long time. That's what I meant by important.'

May's head nodded in vigorous approval. 'Make her come down,' she hissed. They needed to get Diana down to Mottisley, Susan could tell her the reason later.

'But why?' Diana sounded even more worried. 'Are you very short of money, Susan? If you are you know I will . . .'

'Oh, Diana,' Susan tried not to show it, but couldn't prevent a sigh of exasperation escaping her lips. 'Why do you diminish everything by reducing it to monetary terms? No, I'm not short of money. Well, to be exact, no shorter than usual, and you know that never worries me. I might live on a shoe string, but, incomprehensible as that may be to you, I am happy.'

'Sorry.' It was Diana's turn to sound exasperated.

'It's been nearly a year since we last saw each other,' said Susan. 'But I ought to be honest. There is another reason. I want to ask you something, and I can't do it on the 'phone. So can you come down? How about next weekend?' There, she'd asked her. Now, what would Diana say? There was a long silence and Susan waited.

May, still glued to her side, raised a stubby hand with fingers crossed.

'I'm not sure about next weekend,' Diana said slowly.

'Then ask her about this one,' said May loudly, nudging Susan.

'Shut up!' Susan frowned fiercely. She didn't want Diana to know May was there. She might think they were ganging up on her.

Unrepentant, May cackled, her black eyes twinkling like jet buttons. 'Go on, ask her,' she commanded.

'I suppose it's too late even to think of this weekend,' Susan began tentatively.

'For God's sake, hurry up, Diana,' said Hugh. 'If there are two things I hate, it's women who rabbit on and on, and the other is being late for the theatre. Tell Susan to fucking well get lost.'

Susan gasped. She'd heard Hugh's sneering abusive voice, just as he'd so obviously meant her to hear. 'It doesn't matter, Diana,' she stammered unhappily. 'I'm sorry to bother you. I know you and Hugh are very busy, I shouldn't have . . .'

'This weekend is fine, Susan,' Diana said. 'I'll be with you in about an hour, traffic permitting.'

'But you can't go down to Mottisley now.' Hugh tried to keep his voice neutral, realizing that once more that evening he had overstepped the mark, and Diana's decision was his own fault.

His voice was neutral, but his face betrayed his dismay and Diana saw it. 'Of course I can,' she said, suddenly glad she'd acted on impulse. It was too soon yet to let Hugh think things were back to normal. If their marriage was to go on in the way she wanted, Diana knew she had to reassert her control over it. Leaving Hugh alone for the weekend would give him time for reflection.

'But those damned tickets cost a fortune. We can't afford to waste money.' He appealed to her prosaic sense of the materialistic.

'I *can* afford to. Susan wants to see me. I want to see

her. And I'm going.' The money was not important. The important thing was establishing the fact that she was her own woman, in her marriage as in everything else.

'You're being petty, just because of what happened.'

'You mean the tender loving rape scene?' enquired Diana, her voice strafed with sarcasm. That *was* the reason, of course. She didn't want to go to Mottisley any more now than she had ever done. Visiting Mottisley inevitably unsettled her, and now, already feeling uncertain and insecure because of Hugh's strange behaviour, she sensed that in some nebulous way she was putting herself at risk. But she should have visited Susan a long time ago, and Hugh's rudeness was the much-needed catalyst. Doubts were immaterial. She was going.

'I didn't say rape,' said Hugh.

'No, you didn't, did you.' Diana pushed past him and hurried back into the bedroom. Dragging out a suitcase she began to cram it with the few items she'd need for the weekend. 'However, think what you like. The fact is I have decided to go, and I'm in a hurry.'

'But what am I going to do all weekend?'

'I'm sure you will think of something,' said Diana briskly. His debonair mask had slipped, and he was staring at her as if he couldn't believe his eyes. Diana looked at him with icy detachment. He would have to believe. He would have all the weekend to deliberate over the fact that he couldn't do just as he pleased with her body or anything else. Marriage was a partnership. When she returned they would talk about it properly, and then perhaps they'd be able to pick up at some point near to where they had left off. She ignored the nasty persistent little voice telling her it could never be the same. Of course it would. She would make it so.

At last she was ready. Hugh escorted her to the door of the apartment. 'See you on Sunday night, then,' he said mildly.

Diana paused, her cool, competent brain ticking over, digesting this new, quiet Hugh. Only a moment ago he had been bewailing his lot. 'I'm glad you're not still angry,' she said at last.

'Of course not. As usual you're right. You *should* see Susan, and perhaps this weekend is the best time for both of us.' He bent and kissed her briefly as he opened the door. 'Do you want me to come down to the garage with you?'

'No, of course not. I'll be all right.' Diana smiled, but as she did so, she had a frightening vision of the carefully organized, perfectly sanitized life she'd built for herself crumbling into dust around her feet. It was only a fleeting vision, and then it was gone. By the time she'd gone down in the lift to the basement garage, only a faint echo of it remained, and she was cursing her over-active imagination.

Bryant was waiting for her. Diana had forgotten about him. 'It's not the theatre I'm afraid, Bryant. I'm driving myself down to Sussex, so you are free until Monday morning when you can pick me up for the office. I'm sorry it's such short notice and that I've kept you waiting,' she added, seeing the look of curiosity cross his face, 'but it's a family emergency.'

'Yes, ma'am.' Bryant touched his cap and left without further comment.

The moment the front door had closed behind Diana, Hugh sprinted into the bedroom and rifled through his suit pockets. His fingers closed around Nancy's card, thank God he hadn't lost it. Would she still be free? He prayed that she would. The whole weekend in bed, or wherever else the fancy might take them. The possibilities were endless. Diana forgotten, and almost slavering with excitement at the thought of taking Nancy to bed, Hugh punched the 'phone number in reverse order and got a Chinese Take-away.

'Special offer on flied lice with orders over £5,' intoned a sing-song voice.

'I don't want any fucking flied lice,' shouted Hugh,

slamming the 'phone down in frustrated rage. Then taking a deep breath, he started punching Nancy's number out again, concentrating hard this time.

'She's coming.' Susan put down the 'phone.

The stone flagged hall of Abbey House, with its high vaulted ceiling, had once been part of the original monastery on the site. Heating its cavernous depths had always proved an impossibility, and now, even after talking for only a few minutes, Susan was chilled to the marrow. Shoulders hunched and shivering violently she hastily retreated back into the warmth of the large untidy kitchen. I really must get that 'phone moved, she thought, but knew she wouldn't. It would cost money, and there was never enough of that to go around.

May followed Susan, she never felt the cold and her own farmhouse resembled one vast refrigerator. Susan remembered Diana always joking that May carried her own central heating system around with her. Now May plonked herself down on a chair at the table and snorted noisily. 'Huh! So she's coming, good. Wouldn't be though, not if that sod of a husband had anything to do with it.'

'Oh, May. Why must you always be so nasty about Hugh?' Susan said it as much to appease her own conscience as to remonstrate with May. She always felt that she ought to like her sister's husband, and that in some curious way it was a failing on her part because she didn't.

'Don't like him, the bugger,' came the growling reply. 'Never have and never will. A slimy bastard in my opinion.'

Susan laughed at May's fierce expression. 'All right, have your opinion. But please, for God's sake, don't call him a slimy bastard in front of the children. They are just as likely to repeat it to his face. And, May, we must both remember that Diana loves him in spite of what anyone else thinks.'

May sniffed loudly and looked cross, then seeing

103

Susan's anxious expression, relented and smiled. 'Anyway, lovey. Diana's coming, that's the main thing. And it'll do her good too, breathing in some decent fresh air. It's not natural living in a great big dirty city.' Standing up she plucked a po-shaped hat from a cup hook on the Welsh dresser and rammed it firmly on her head. 'I'd better be off. Bert will be waiting for his supper.'

Susan didn't want her to leave. Not yet, she still needed reassuring. 'Do you think I'm being silly, May? Worrying about the future, about the kids?' Knowing that she hadn't told Diana the real reason for wanting to see her was bothering Susan. It was against her gentle, honest nature. 'Perhaps I should have mentioned what I really wanted.'

May had no such scruples. She turned, regarding her great-niece affectionately, her brown walnut of a face crinkling into a benign smile. 'Time enough for reasons later,' she said. 'Anyway, you've got nothing to worry about now, ducky. Right as ninepence you are, thank God. I don't need any doctor to tell me that, I can see it for myself. But all the same you're doing the right thing. That sister of yours ought to be more involved with her own kith and kin. She doesn't come down to Sussex near enough.'

'Diana is a very busy woman,' Susan defended her sister.

'No-one should be too busy for family,' said May decisively. 'Takes after her mother in that respect,' she added, continuing with her preparations to leave. There was silence, save for the whistling sound of the air May sucked in through her teeth while she concentrated on winding a long knitted scarf around her neck, finally crossing it with a flourish across her bony bosom and tying it at the back. 'Now, Susan,' she said, 'help me into that coat, please.' She waved in the direction of a heavy leather jacket hanging on the back of the kitchen door.

Susan duly obliged. She was still thinking of Diana and wishing that she did see more of her sister. 'Perhaps if you were nicer to Hugh, they might both come down more often,' she suggested.

'I *am* nice to the bugger,' said May, bristling with outrage. '*Always!*'

Susan gave up the unequal argument, and changed the subject. 'How's Buggins?'

Buggins was a large and ancient horse, the apple of May's eye. Now retired from hunting, he spent almost as much time wandering through the vast kitchen of her farmhouse as in the stables. The general opinion of the populace of Mottisley was that he should have gone to the knacker's yard years ago, but May wasn't having that. She loved him, and treated him more like a dog than a horse.

Now, her wizened face noticeably softened at the mention of his name. 'He's a bit colicky today. Ate a box of apples Bert'd got down from the loft. Greedy old bugger.'

'Buggins is a bugger.' Timothy, coming into the kitchen in his pyjamas, trailing his dressing gown by its cord behind him, heard the end of the conversation. Affectionately known to everyone as Miffy, he was Susan's youngest son.

'Darling, don't swear,' said Susan automatically.

'Why not? Auntie May does.'

Susan wished she could think of a suitable answer, but there wasn't one. She couldn't deny the truth, neither could she denigrate May's choice of language which was part and parcel of her character. Miffy started to cough, his chest rattling as if it were filled with a bag of loose nails. 'Put your dressing gown on,' said Susan sharply. Small for his five years, and always prone to chest infections and asthma, Miffy had caused Susan many sleepless nights.

'Can't think where he gets that bad chest from,' said May, pausing in the act of buttoning up her coat. 'Not from his father, that's for sure.'

'Well, Tom was never strong, you know,' said Susan, busying herself tying Miffy's dressing gown cord.

'Ah yes, Tom,' said May. There was silence for a moment, broken only by Miffy's strident cough, then May reached into the depths of her coat pocket. 'That reminds me,' she said, 'I've brought some goose grease for his chest.' She handed Susan a small jar and a tattered piece of brown paper. 'Put this on his chest tonight and cover it with the brown paper. That'll ease that cough.'

'Mummy's called the doctor,' gasped Miffy between coughs, ignoring Susan who, behind May's back, was shaking her head urging him to keep quiet. May's opinion of the medical profession was not high. Miffy ignored her. 'I don't like the smell of goose grease,' he said in his high treble voice, 'it makes me go, ugh!' He gave an excellent imitation of someone vomiting.

'I thought I ought to be on the safe side,' said Susan apologetically, not wanting to hurt May's feelings. 'He might need a course of antibiotics. But thanks anyway for the goose grease. I'm sure it will come in useful.'

'Damned sight better than all those new fangled pills and potions young Tony Evans uses. He told me himself that the last pot I gave him worked wonders.'

'I don't like it,' croaked Miffy, 'I'd rather have . . .'

'Be quiet,' hissed Susan. Even in illness Miffy was always so extraordinarily determined. He regarded her now, his vivid blue eyes flashing a steely defiance. For a brief second they glowered at each other, then Susan picked him up and dumped him in the armchair by the side of the warm Aga. The solid fuel burning stove had been Susan's one concession to luxury. Kept burning night and day during the winter, it was the one thing that made life bearable at Abbey House, providing heating for the kitchen, and a means for cooking and heating the water for the icy bathrooms. 'I'll see you off, May,' she said, throwing a woollen cloak around her shoulders.

May bent down for Miffy to kiss her a dutiful goodnight, before accompanying Susan outside. It was intensely cold. The land stood frozen in solemn silence, and their breath flew before them in the bitter night air like pious incense from the censers of the long-departed monks. The snow clouds had cleared temporarily, and from their position on top of the West Sussex Downs it seemed possible to touch the myriad of stars glistening in the black velvet of the sky. Far away on the horizon, the floodlit spire of Chichester Cathedral pointed heavenward as it had done for the last nine hundred years. A magical sight, thought Susan.

May too was affected by the spellbinding enchantment of the winter night. 'Ah, the Downs,' she said, drawing in a deep breath and suddenly waxing poetic, 'the backbone of Sussex.'

But Susan's attention had already been diverted from the magic of the night. Her gaze was fixed in horror on a shiny motor cycle with a red crash helmet balanced on the top. It was standing amidst the snow in the gravelled yard which curved around the side of Abbey House. 'Good God, May,' she exploded. 'Surely you didn't come over on that tonight? And it's new isn't it?' she added accusingly.

'It's Japanese,' said May proudly, switching from the spiritual contemplation of the Downs to the practicalities of her awe-inspiring two-wheeled transport with ease. Popping the crash helmet on top of the po hat, she scrambled on to the machine with the agility of a monkey. Unable to avoid Susan's accusing glare, she had the grace to look slightly guilty. 'I needed a new one,' she muttered, 'my other one was dropping to bits.'

'Yes, but you promised me you'd use the car, and you told Tony that you'd sold your other one.'

'Well, so I did.'

'But you never said anything about buying another. How could you break your promise?' A ripple of vexation shook Susan. Why couldn't May be like other old ladies of seventy-nine? She'd break her neck one of these days.

'Never promised, only said I said I *might*.' Susan recognized the familiar stubborn growl, and knew May had absolutely no intention of switching to a safer mode

107

of transport. 'Anyway,' said May, now warming to the subject, 'this one will do two hundred miles an hour, it's much faster than my old one. Of course, I shall drive slowly,' she added hastily as Susan's mouth opened in horrified amazement, 'and this one is much, much safer because it's got broad wheels, you see.' Revving up the engine to an ear-splitting decibel level, she spun the wheels gleefully, showering Susan with a mixture of snow and gravel. 'Bye, dear,' she shrieked. Susan could hardly hear her above the powerful roar from the twin exhausts, as the machine, with May perched on top, disappeared.

The thunderous throb of the engine faded. Susan prayed that the snow wasn't too thick on the long drive that cut a swathe through the serried ranks of vines from Abbey House to the main road. She prayed too that May would make it safely back to Willow Farm. Why, oh why couldn't she be content with car? Especially *her* car. Most people would give their eye teeth to drive a vintage yellow Rolls-Royce.

Miffy who'd been watching from the window, jumped down as soon as Susan re-entered the kitchen. 'Why don't you get a bike like that?' he demanded, his voice thick with envy.

'Because I can't afford it. And even if I could I wouldn't. They're far too dangerous.'

'Auntie May doesn't think so. Auntie May is fun.' Miffy contemplated his mother crossly and scuffed his way back to the chair by the Aga. 'I suppose you're not going to let her take me for a ride on the back.'

'You suppose absolutely correctly.'

'But Auntie May said . . .'

Susan's patience snapped. 'One more word from you and I'll put this goose grease on your chest right here and now! Stay put in that chair while I go upstairs and make up another bed. Diana's coming to stay for the weekend.'

'Oh her. Mrs Snooty-pants.'

'Be *quiet*!'

Suddenly Susan felt exhausted. She was worried about

May's obstinacy in riding the motor bike, and was worrying too about Diana's impending visit. Some days everything seemed such a battle, and she wished, not for the first time, that her children liked Diana better. It wasn't Diana's fault, they didn't really know her. But Diana didn't help matters by not coming down so that they could get to know her. And when she did come, she was so coldly sophisticated that she put the children off.

Susan herself wasn't fooled by Diana's brittle poise. She could see through the chinks of her sister's sophisticated armour plating, and knew the Diana she'd known so many years ago, a warm and loving girl, still existed. And of course she had the positive proof in Diana's boundless generosity. Susan knew she only had to ask and Diana would have seen that she wanted for nothing. But she never did ask, and never did confess her fears and worries, and wondered now if that was part of the problem. Maybe *she* had shut Diana out and made her feel awkward. Maybe it was her fault that Diana and children were so uneasy together. But this weekend will be different, Susan promised herself. We'll get back on to our old footing, especially as Hugh isn't coming. Then she immediately felt even more guilty. I really ought to like Hugh, she told herself.

Hugh, however, did not make it easy for Susan to like him, and the main reason was Abbey House and the vineyard. Susan knew very well that she owed her home and livelihood to Diana and was grateful. She knew too that Diana had never given it another thought since the day the property and land was made over to her. Hugh was a different matter. He always managed to slip in a snide remark which left Susan in no doubt of his opinion. He didn't approve of Diana giving her the house and vineyard. May was right when she called him greedy, he didn't need Abbey House or even want it, but thought he should have a share of the money.

Wearily climbing the stairs, Susan sighed. It was hopeless trying to explain the complicated behaviour of adults to children, when most of the time the adults themselves were incapable of unravelling their emotions. As far as Diana was concerned, she could only hope and pray that as they got older the children would see her sister's true nature for themselves. If only Diana would unbend just a little and let them.

Downstairs, Miffy, knowing he'd pushed his mother too far, lapsed into sulky silence, broken only by his coughing; and Susan, making Diana's bed, worried about his cough and wished she hadn't shouted. The sound of a car being driven at a reasonable speed up the drive curtailed her bed making activities, and glad of the interruption she went downstairs to make her peace with Miffy and let in Tony Evans.

'Who was that maniac on a bloody great motor bike roaring away from here? Damned nearly killed me.' The gangling young man Susan let in walked straight over to the Aga and stood warming his back and rubbing his hands.

Miffy ran to greet him. 'That was Auntie May on her new bike.' The effort of running started off a renewed fit of coughing.

Lifting up the unresisting child Tony Evans put him back in the armchair by the side of the warm Aga. 'Oh no,' he groaned, 'I thought she'd given them up.'

'I'm afraid you thought wrong,' said Susan grimly.

'That woman ought to be certified,' said Tony, but he was beginning to grin. 'Well, she'll have to take her chances, I suppose, and the population of Mottisley will have to watch out!' Lifting his hand he waved it under Susan's nose. 'Look at that. Still shaking! And all because of a near head-on collision with the Amazon Queen of Mottisley.'

'Auntie May's not a queen,' spluttered Miffy, who was very pedantic about facts.

Tony turned his attention back to the small boy, the object of his visit. 'Bed, antibiotics and some nice soothing syrup for that cough,' he said firmly, noting that Susan

110

looked tired. 'I'll sort out this young man,' he said, picking up Miffy and tucking him under his arm, 'and if this damned thing goes off,' he placed his air-call bleep in the middle of the table, 'just take a message and tell whoever it is I'll be with them in about half an hour.'

'I'm not having goose grease on my chest,' warned Miffy.

Tony grinned. 'I'll have it. Marvellous for stopping the rust on our ancient lawn mower. I told May it worked wonders.'

'She thinks you put it on your chest,' said Susan. 'You misled her.'

'Not nearly as much as she misled me over that damned motor bike of hers,' said Tony, disappearing with Miffy through the doorway leading to the stairs.

Back in the kitchen twenty minutes later, he found Susan's other two children, twelve-year-old Clementina and nine-year-old Simon, sitting down to supper.

'Would you like some, Tony. Get *down* you wretch.'

The last remark was addressed to a fat tabby cat intent on helping himself to whatever he could reach on the table. Balancing on the edge of a chair with surprising agility for such a portly animal, the cat ignored the tea-towel Susan flapped around his ears.

'Mummy, don't be so nasty to Shakespeare,' Clementina lifted the cat tenderly on to her lap.

'I ought to go back and catch up on some paper work between house-calls,' Tony said half-heartedly, looking at the savoury minced beef spilling out from beneath a crispy mashed potato pie crust, 'but your food would certainly make a welcome change from pot noodles.'

'Sit down then. The bleep hasn't gone off.' Susan smothered a smile. Tony always contrived to call at supper time if it was an evening call-out.

'Damn the paper work. The Health Authority will have to wait for their statistics.' He sat down next to Clementina. 'Why is that cat called Shakespeare? It's something I've always meant to ask.'

'Daddy called him that. He found him before I was born. A stray in Stratford-upon-Avon.' Simon provided the answer.

'Stratford-upon-Avon, therefore, Shakespeare. That seems a good enough reason.'

'Of course it is.' Simon's eyes were almost black, as were Clementina's. They both took after their father. Only Miffy's were brilliant blue, quite unlike his father's or Susan's eyes which were grey. 'Do you really eat pot noodles?' Simon asked. 'Mummy says that's junk food.'

'Quite right too. But I'm too busy to do much proper cooking.'

'You wouldn't be if you got more time off,' said Susan. She thought it was disgraceful the way Edward Evans overworked his son. She knew, as did everyone else in Mottisley, that old Dr Evans, as he was called to distinguish him from Tony, was far more interested in digging up Roman remains and growing prize vegetables than he'd ever been in looking after his patients. 'You ought to persuade your father to retire,' she said. 'If you got another younger man in to work with you, then you'd get more time off.'

'I wouldn't dare mention the word retire,' said Tony. 'But talking of daring. Have you dared to do what I suggested?'

There was a long pause while Susan concentrated on dishing up Tony's supper. Trust him to turn the conversation neatly back on to her problems.

'Yes,' she said at last. 'In fact, Diana is coming down later this evening.'

'Good.' Tony sounded satisfied. 'I'm a great believer in insurance policies. Even when they're not needed.'

'What do you mean, insurance policies?' Clementina, still hugging Shakespeare and surreptitiously feeding him pieces of meat, was curious.

Her curiosity was destined to remain unsatisfied.

'You've got more homework to do, young lady,' said Susan sternly. 'So please hurry up and finish your supper.'

Chapter Eight

Diana huddled closer to the Aga and pulled Susan's thick old dressing gown tightly around her. 'Of course, none of the damned clothes I've brought are warm enough,' she complained to Tony. She stretched her benumbed feet towards the stove. 'Strange thing memory, isn't it,' she said. 'When I remember my time here in Abbey House, I can only remember the warm, sunny days.'

'Not even a single black day?' asked Tony curiously.

Diana's head jerked up. 'Black? I was talking about the weather, not moods.'

Tony watched her with renewed interest. He had obviously touched a raw spot. 'Oh, so was I,' he replied mildly. 'Perhaps I should have said wet or cold, not black. Expressing myself in anything other than medical terms was never one of my strongest points. It took me three attempts to pass O level English.'

Diana laughed but a niggling unease remained. Did Tony know about her abortion? But it wasn't possible, no-one except Dr Evans knew, not even Susan. Suddenly she knew she shouldn't have come, it was always a mistake coming back to Mottisley. Once there it was so much harder to keep unwelcome memories at bay. Unbidden they now came, tumbling over one another, spilling back into her mind.

Happy memories, which for some absurdly illogical reason always made her want to weep. Days full of sunshine. Running with Susan in the field beside the abbey, hair flying behind them, breathless with the exertion of forging their way through a sea of waist high buttercups. The smell of the warm moist earth, when, exhausted, they lay, noses pressed against the purple and

113

white heads of the nodding clover, the only sound the sleepy drone of bees. Warm, perfumed nights waiting with Susan for the moon to rise, and years later warm perfumed nights spent with Joe.

Joe! She put all the thoughts from her mind, refusing to succumb to maudlin sentimentality. All that was over and done with. She had a different, better life now, one of her own choosing. She'd always prided herself on being different from other women. She was not a woman to romanticize, and knew it was the height of stupidity to look back. It was like climbing on to an emotional carousel, spinning around in aimless circles. Yes, the height of stupidity.

'You know what they say, Tony. One only remembers the good days. Memory is notoriously unreliable, emotive and unscientific.'

Susan entered the kitchen carrying a large enamel bowl. 'Put your feet in this, Diana. It's hot water and mustard, and will stop you getting chilblains.'

Tony snorted. 'Now that's about as scientific as . . .'

'Memory?' Susan put the bowl down. 'Scoff as much as you like Tony Evans, but this does work.'

'So does dipping your toes in your own pee.'

'I haven't got any pee handy, and I think I prefer this,' said Diana gratefully, wriggling some life back into her numb toes. Typical of Susan to be so thoughtful. Diana began to feel happier.

'And eat this.' Susan plonked a plate of cottage pie on Diana's lap. 'You're much too thin.'

Diana opened her mouth about to point out that Susan was even more thin, but Tony interrupted. 'Yes, Diana, too thin. You're much taller than Susan, you could afford to put on some weight.'

'It's fashionable,' said Diana.

'Of course it is.' Susan agreed. 'And anyway Tony you will use the wrong words. You can say, slender, petite, but not thin, it sounds so unglamorous. Oh, hell!'

A noisy fracas echoed down the stairs claiming her

attention. Rushing out into the hall she shrieked abuse up to her scrimmaging offspring, before bounding up the stairs to sort them out.

Diana looked at Tony. Susan looked as if a puff of wind might blow her away, and as her doctor Tony must realize that. Susan had been ill, she knew that. But Susan had never been specific about the nature of her illness, and Diana had never pressed her for information. Now, she wondered and worried. Was it more serious than she had ever imagined? This was her opportunity to ask while she was out of the room.

'Is Susan well, or is she still ill?'

Tony hesitated for a moment.

Susan had forbidden him to discuss her recent illness with anyone. Although it went against his better judgement, he had to respect her wishes.

'Susan is well,' he said finally. 'At the moment she is very well indeed. She works too hard of course, but she has stamina and I'm certain she'll continue to be fit and healthy. Of course, there is always the . . .' his sentence remained unfinished as Susan came charging back into the kitchen with a sulky looking Simon in tow.

'Sit down there,' said Susan fiercely, pushing Simon on to a chair at the table, 'and finish your French homework. And you,' she glowered at Diana, 'finish your supper.'

Diana grinned at Susan's ferocious expression. 'Yes,' she said meekly. Relief overwhelmed her. Until that moment she hadn't dared to admit to herself how worried she'd been by Susan's fragile appearance, but now she could see that Tony was right. Susan *was* well. She might look frail, but she obviously had the stamina of a shire horse and at that moment the temper of a brood mare!

Relaxing a little for the first time since she'd set foot in Abbey House Diana began to enjoy her supper. 'I'd forgotten how good home-made food tastes,' she said.

'Do you live on pot noodles too, then?' Simon raised his head from his homework.

'Of course not, silly.' Tony answered for him. 'Probably on exotic fare from Harrods or Fortnum and Mason.'

'How did you guess?' Diana made light of Tony's remark, but it reminded her forcibly of how different her life was from those of the people at Mottisley. Guiltily Diana knew that most of them would die of shock if they saw the prices she paid for her food. But cooking doesn't come naturally to me, Diana excused herself. She'd always envied Susan her ability to conjure up a mouthwatering meal from the most mundane ingredients.

Simon flung down his pencil. 'French finished,' he announced.

'Mine too,' said Clementina, coming into the kitchen.

They both eyed Diana curiously. Their concerted gaze made Diana edgy. What was it about children that so unnerved her? Whatever anyone might say to the contrary, she always felt that they were much more perceptive than adults. Suddenly she imagined an interview with the boardroom table surrounded by solemn-eyed children, instead of elderly men. What a nightmarish scenario. They'd be impossible to flatter and manipulate. Give me old men any time, thought Diana.

'Time for bed, kids,' said Tony firmly.

Both children obeyed him. Rushing across to say goodnight, flinging their arms around him in a spontaneous demonstration of affection. The realization that he was obviously a very regular visitor at Abbey House made Diana wonder if Tony was sweet on Susan. It would be nice if she did marry again.

The children turned back to Susan and she put her arms around them. Once more Diana found herself plunged back into the past. It was always the insignificant moments that eroded the years.

She remembered now that hugs and kisses had been in short supply in her own and Susan's childhood. Mother had always been too busy and too aloof, besides which, her mode of dressing didn't encourage spontaneous hugs. It would have taken someone braver than her two daughters to disturb a knife-edged pleat, or a crisp lapel on one of her fiercely tailored business suits.

And now she thought about it, Diana remembered that even her beloved father hadn't really been a touching person. Loving and attentive, always willing to talk, but not physically demonstrative. Except with Nancy. But then Nancy was different. She was always clinging on to him like a leech. Diana felt a long submerged but familiar resentment welling up, and knew she was being ridiculous. It was all so long ago. But suddenly she wondered if that was the reason neither she nor Susan had liked Nancy. The cause was plain, old-fashioned, childish jealousy.

Watching Susan, Diana wondered if she consciously realized that she was giving her children what she herself missed. Or was it just instinctive maternal affection. For a few seconds Diana was aware of an empty void in herself, and wanted to be part of the noisy, laughing family before her. But the moment passed. She was an outsider looking in and could never be part of this family, because this was not part of her life.

She thought of Hugh and felt a bitter stab of regret. This was the first time they'd been apart since their marriage, except for the odd occasion when she'd been away on business. But this time it wasn't her work keeping them apart, it was her own decision to leave him alone for the weekend. Suddenly she felt confused. Perhaps I was wrong, and the situation wasn't as intolerable as I thought. Perhaps I should have stayed and then we could have talked and set things right between us.

What was Hugh doing now? Was he regretting their quarrel too? The more she thought about it, the more Diana's anger and anxiety concerning Hugh's violent behaviour towards her became sublimated by the cognizance that in spite of everything, she really needed him. Not just because of her new position at Wycombe and Yatton, not just because of her image, and not because she feared failure; but because she had no-one else she could be really close to.

Dragging her thoughts back to the present Diana became aware that a reluctant Clementina and Simon were being pushed towards her.

'Go on, kiss your Aunt Diana, Clemmy,' said Tony good naturedly.

'I wish you wouldn't call her Clemmy,' grumbled Susan, 'it doesn't sound at all ladylike.'

'Who wants to be a lady? Will you call me Clemmy, Aunt Diana?'

'Well, I . . .' Diana looked at Susan who shrugged her shoulders with a gesture of resignation. 'All right. But you call me Diana, not Aunt Diana.'

'I'll call you Diana as well,' announced Simon. 'I'm too old to call you auntie.'

'I think that's a back-handed compliment meaning you look too young to be an aunt,' said Tony.

'I'm flattered,' said Diana as they kissed her goodnight. Would she ever understand Susan's children. One moment standoffish and unfriendly, the next minute seemingly affectionate.

'Can we watch a film upstairs for half an hour?' asked Simon.

'Oh God, not that stupid Sci Fi thing you've got on video,' groaned Clemmy.

'It's not stupid, it's bloody good.'

'Don't swear,' snapped Susan.

'Aunt May does.'

'Aunt May does what?' The kitchen door opened, and a golden labrador roared in, goosing a peacefully sleeping Shakespeare. Enraged, Shakespeare puffed up like a sweep's brush, and hissing wildly lunged out with a right hook which missed, then made a hurried exit up the stairs towards the safety of the bedrooms.

'Swear,' said Clementina, flinging her arms around the dog's great golden girth and hugging it. 'Why does Sam always do that to Shakespeare?'

'Because he likes it I suppose.'

'Shakespeare doesn't.'

118

'He might. He just isn't letting on.'

The gorgeous redheaded woman who'd followed the dog into the kitchen looked familiar, and then Diana recognized her. Her name was April Harte, and her latest novel had caused well publicized controversy. It had been condemned as obscene by a Bishop in a celebrated TV question and answer session, in which April Harte had definitely come off best, her witty replies keeping the audience in fits of laughter. Diana had watched it, and remembered the Bishop finally stalking out of the TV studio in high dudgeon.

'Hi,' said April, smiling in Diana's direction.

'Hi,' replied Diana. April's open smile was infectious and she found herself smiling back.

A tall, broad shouldered man stepped forward from behind April, and whistled to the dog who immediately came and sat at his feet. Diana's smile faded. There was no mistaking Joe Kelly, although the years had turned his once black hair almost silver, and the lithe lean figure had matured into muscled bulk.

'It smells like a burger bar in here,' he said.

'Oh, that's Diana's hot mustard bath,' said Clemmy. Then remembering her manners she waved in Diana's direction. 'That's Diana.'

'We've met.' The abrupt words were uttered simultaneously, and Diana saw that his vivid blue eyes exactly mirrored her own emotions. A mixture of surprise, displeasure and hostility.

'Joe has finished renovating the manor house,' said Susan taking the two bottles of whisky Joe proffered.

'And I've moved in with him,' added April.

Diana felt annoyed. Why hadn't Susan told her Joe Kelly was coming. Common sense told her there was no reason why Susan should have done, but that didn't stop her feeling put out. Quickly removing her feet from the mustard bath, she slipped them into Susan's old slippers.

'The work cost a bomb,' said April. 'But it looks lovely now.'

'Of course. I'd forgotten. You're a millionaire now.'

Joe fixed Diana with a steely blue stare. 'Yes. I'm not the backwoods boy I used to be.'

Diana turned away to hide the flush she knew was staining her cheeks. I asked for that, she thought. But even so, she'd been shocked to see what she was sure was real hatred reflected in his eyes. Unlike Hugh, whose expression was always unreadable, Joe was like an open book. He made no effort to conceal his emotions.

'Excuse me, I promised to ring my husband.'

Bolting from the room into the hall she dialled the Chelsea number. Oh God, why did I come to Mottisley? I should have stayed and talked things through with Hugh. Rushing away like that was a mistake. Hasty decisions are always mistakes. Maybe I'll go back early, tomorrow perhaps; after I've spoken to Hugh. But there was no reply. The answer machine was on. Maybe he's gone to the theatre, but he hates being alone, and there was no-one else he could have asked at such short notice. Was there? Of course not, Diana told herself fiercely. Stop being melodramatic. He's probably feeling as miserable as me and gone out to eat somewhere. She started to make her way back into the kitchen, then changed her mind. April looked so glamorous, pride demanded that she couldn't stay wrapped in Susan's old dressing gown. Damn the cold, at least she'd look decent.

'That looks terrific.' Susan looked at her sister enviously as she came back into the kitchen. 'But will you be warm enough?'

'Judging by the length of the skirt, I should say not,' said Joe, pouring himself a generous measure of whisky. 'I'm not sure red and navy blue suits you.'

'I didn't buy it with you in mind,' snapped Diana acidly.

April laughed. 'Take no notice. It's gorgeous. I can recognize a designer suit when I see one, even if Joe can't.'

'Oh I can recognize clothes that cost serious money,' said Joe. 'That little number would probably feed the entire Third World for a week.'

'Joe!' April turned to Diana. 'Sorry, but the whisky loosens his tongue.'

Diana noticed that one bottle was almost empty, and knew that Tony hadn't drunk it. He was on duty. 'Takes after his father, I see,' she said, then immediately regretted her bitchy remark.

'Help me get out some bread and cheese will you, Diana.' Susan rushed to defuse the atmosphere. Diana followed her into the pantry and Susan turned on her fiercely. 'Joe Kelly and April are marvellous friends. Please try and be nice to them.'

Diana sighed. 'I'll try. But if Joe Kelly constantly needles me it's going to be bloody difficult.'

'Life is never easy,' said Susan tartly and marched out of the pantry carrying the cheeseboard. Diana followed with the bread. It was the first time in years that she had seen Susan cross.

The rest of the evening was a disaster. Tony stayed, as his bleeper didn't go off once, and together the foursome, Susan, Tony, April and Joe, laughed, joked, ate and drank their way through into the small hours. Diana tried 'phoning Hugh again, but still no reply. Where the hell was he? Miserable, she slipped back into the kitchen and poured herself another glass of wine. She felt an outsider, unable to join in the easy camaraderie of the others. April was kind, and tried to include her. But Joe's tongue was razor sharp, poking fun at her achievements and making her life with Hugh appear pretentious and empty.

'He doesn't mean it,' whispered Susan at one point.

'It's immaterial to me,' said Diana. But that didn't stop her sustaining her failing morale with one glass after another of wine.

Chapter Nine

Hugh screeched his black Porsche to a halt outside a house in Church Row, Hampstead. He always drove fast. It gave him a buzz of excitement to feel the powerful machine completely under his control. Soon after his marriage to Diana he'd changed his rather mundane car for the flashy Porsche. It had to be that particular car, nothing less would suit his social image. The fact that it gave him chronic backache on long journeys was immaterial. It was the image that mattered, and the image of himself, his virility and the car were inextricably bound together. The car, subconsciously a powerful phallic symbol, was worth any amount of backache.

The house in Church Row was Nancy's house, and Hugh was impressed. The elegant eighteenth century terrace was one of the most expensive streets in Hampstead, and the outside of the house gave a subtle hint of the splendour to be found inside. The wrought iron railings in front of the house sparkled blackly under the lamplight. Two perfectly pruned bay trees, decked now with neat little haloes of snow, stood sentinel either side of the wide stone steps leading to the front door where an enormous brass knocker gleamed invitingly.

The house itself was painted cream, and looking through a gap in the curtains of the lighted windows, Hugh caught a glimpse of vibrant colours, exquisite and ancient porcelain, rich fabrics and wonderful paintings. He took a deep breath of pleasure. This was his sort of world, this was the expensive ambience he needed in which to thrive. Nancy and he should get on well, their tastes were obviously very similar. He'd wanted to furnish their apartment in the same opulent manner, but although

Diana liked expensive things, she preferred a subdued, understated effect, and never bought anything flamboyant. As Hugh climbed the steps he idly reflected that Joseph, Nancy's husband, must be very well heeled indeed. No wonder she was determined to hang on to every last penny.

His hand never reached the brass knocker. The door opened the moment he reached the top step, and Hugh walked in.

The second he was inside his breath exploded in a gasp, and he hastily slammed the door behind him. Nancy was there waiting for him, stark naked. 'Jesus Christ!' he choked, 'the neighbours might see you.'

'Darling, don't be so provincial. Sod the neighbours. I don't want to waste any time. I've waited since lunch time today as it is, and I want a fuck now.' Laughing she pulled him down on the hall floor and spread her legs open wide. 'Kiss me,' she commanded, 'and for God's sake don't worry about AIDS. I'm all right, and as you live with the pure Diana I know you are too.' She pulled Hugh's head down on to her perfumed bush, which was just as black as he had imagined.

Later, in the early hours of the next morning, lying by the side of Nancy in a huge double bed, Hugh drifted between sleep and fantasy. He couldn't remember getting undressed, but supposed Nancy must have done it for him. She'd done practically everything else. Was there a single sexual permutation she didn't know? It seemed unlikely. Now asleep, her beautiful body relaxed for the first time in hours, Nancy somehow still contrived to look in command. Other people looked vulnerable in sleep, but not Nancy. Hugh looked at her sleeping form and smiled. Normally he always took the initiative, but Nancy hadn't allowed that. She'd led, and he had followed willingly. Eager to find out what erotic delights she would think of next.

He stretched luxuriously. Their orgy of sex had been carnal perfection itself. Hugh looked down at his now flaccid penis, marvelling that last night it had assumed a life of its own, surging upright like a great steeple time and time again. More times than he'd ever thought possible, and then always, the screaming bliss of that shuddering, pumping release whenever Nancy let him come. The night had been unbelievable. Nancy certainly put Diana, and every other woman he'd ever known, in the shade.

Suddenly he sat up. Shit! Diana, he'd completely forgotten about her. She was sure to have 'phoned last night, and must have wondered where he was. He turned towards Nancy and shook her shoulder. 'I've got to go,' he said. 'Diana's certain to ring again first thing in the morning, and I'd better be there.'

Nancy awoke immediately, and yawned, revealing small, white perfectly even teeth. 'Darling,' she said through her yawn, 'you are so conventional. So what? Let her ring. Let her wonder.'

'I've no intention of ever leaving Diana. You know that, don't you, Nancy.' Hugh wondered if he'd made that fact clear enough. Nancy had to understand that Diana was his bread and butter. He couldn't afford to leave her.

'Darling, of course I know that.' Pulling a face at him and laughing she turned away and fished a crumpled cigarette from a drawer of the cabinet at the side of the bed.

'So I don't want to give her any cause for getting a divorce.' It never occurred to him to consider the violent incident of the previous evening might be considered grounds for divorce. He'd almost forgotten it, and anyway he thought that even if Diana was still a little aloof, he was sure to be able to win her round easily once she returned from Mottisley. She'd be glad to get back to London, she always was after she'd been down to Sussex, and he'd make it up to her. I can afford to be generous, he thought feeling flushed with munificence. After all, it was Diana who'd given him the time off to be with Nancy.

All the same, he had to play his cards very carefully. Discretion was the name of the game.

Nancy lit the cigarette and inhaled slowly. Then reaching out she slipped a hand between Hugh's thighs and squeezed. 'Are you telling me, darling, that there won't be any more nights like last night?'

'Yes, of course there will. But I've got to be vigilant. Diana mustn't know.' Nancy's squeezing got more insistent. Hugh suddenly felt tired. His performance last night had been marvellous, but he wasn't sure that he was capable of repeating it so soon after waking; besides, he was worrying, he really ought to get back to the apartment. 'I don't think I can come again, Nancy.'

'Rubbish! I haven't shown you all the tricks yet.' She took another gulp from the cigarette and handed it to Hugh. 'Go on, take a puff.'

Hugh took the mangled cigarette and looked at it with distaste. 'A joint?' he asked. He liked everything neat and perfect, even his cigarettes.

'Yes, darling, pot. Haven't you ever tried it?'

'Of course. But not since university. I grew out of it.' For a second he wondered whether to confess that he'd progressed to something stronger, but decided the time was not yet right. He needed to know Nancy better, be able to predict her reaction.

Nancy laughed at his expression of distaste. 'Oh, go on. Take a drag.'

Hugh puffed unenthusiastically, reflecting that he'd rather have a snort. Nothing much happened. He took another puff, this time inhaling deeply. Not bad, not at all. He'd forgotten the hazy sensations it induced. He sucked fiercely at the limp cigarette and gradually felt an aura of well being enveloping him, and mixed with it were the stirrings of desire. Nancy was right. Why bother to go back to the apartment? It was too far, right on the other side of London. 'Maybe I'll tell Diana the 'phone was out of order,' he said.

'There, I knew you'd see reason,' purred Nancy,

bending over him and giving his left nipple a sharp nip with her teeth.

'Ouch!' said Hugh. 'That hurt.'

'Just wanted to make sure you were properly awake,' said Nancy, taking the joint away from Hugh and extinguishing it between her fingers. 'I don't want you to have too much,' she said putting it back in the drawer, 'it can affect the performance.'

'Whose performance?' muttered Hugh.

'Yours, of course, darling,' said Nancy climbing on top of him, firmly straddling his body with her long white legs. 'Cock a doodle doo,' she said in a guttural whisper, and bending over crammed the whole of his limp organ into her mouth, grazing it fiercely with her sharp little teeth.

Hugh felt the familiar fire begin to burn in his loins, but before he could start to enjoy the sensations pulsing through him Nancy stopped. 'Go on, for God's sake, go on,' he implored.

'Wait,' was all she said. Leaning across the bed and reaching into the drawer again she drew out a small packet.

Hugh felt ridiculous lying there on the bed with Nancy astride him. 'I can't keep it up like this for ever,' he said, slightly petulant.

'Oh yes you can.'

'What the hell!' Hugh stared at the rubber sheath she dangled in front of his nose. It glowed red and green, had little spikes and looked like a Christmas tree. Nancy flicked it playfully and the colours changed and shimmered.

'A late Christmas present from me for me,' Nancy said. 'And don't you dare come until I tell you,' she hissed.

Hugh began to think he could never last out while Nancy amused herself with varying gyrations, all the time her beautiful face was lit with a lewd wantonness which Hugh found almost frightening in its intensity. Just when he thought he would explode and come even though she had told him not to, she shouted, 'now, now, *NOW*.'

After that any thought of Diana was completely forgotten. Hugh was Nancy's willing captive, and the rest of the weekend was spent in an erotic haze of lovemaking. They made love in the bath, under the shower, in the kitchen, in the hall. Nancy knew how to make any place exciting. Hugh even relaxed enough to let her see him take a snort of coke, and Nancy approved.

'God, Hugh,' she said when he came almost immediately after snorting. 'I like you like this. You're so much harder, and rougher.' She rubbed herself against him. 'It's almost as good as being raped. Come on, do it again. Any way you like.'

And he did. Taking her from behind because it gave him an enhanced sense of power. Nancy pretended to struggle, but he knew she was loving every minute of it. Briefly he thought of Diana. She was so bloody puritanical when it came to sex. Why couldn't she be more like Nancy?

On Saturday morning Diana awoke after a restless night. She had a splitting headache. I drank too much, she thought. Then remembered why. The whole damned evening had been one long unmitigated disaster, only serving to reinforce her view that she had made a mistake and should never have come down to Mottisley. It was as if Abbey House, Susan, Joe Kelly, all of them, were her nemesis. But immediately that thought struck her, Diana rejected it, cross with herself for even allowing such a thought to creep in. She had nothing to be afraid of, and no-one to be afraid of either. And she'd been willing to be civil, even though she had felt angry with Susan for not mentioning that Joe would be coming for the evening. Common sense told her there was no reason why Susan should have thought to, but that didn't stop her feeling disgruntled. And what an evening it had been. Joe had brought two bottles of whisky, most of which he'd drunk himself. And Diana had lost count of the number of wine bottles Susan had opened.

With a determined effort she swung her feet over the edge of the bed and stood up. Her head spun. Serves you bloody well right, she told herself, for behaving like a timid teenager, instead of the mature woman you are. I'm thirty-one, she reminded herself, a long way off from being a teenager.

The freezing cold forced her introverted musing to come to an abrupt halt. Although bright sunlight shimmered in her room, it was bitterly cold, and now Diana looked about her properly she could see that the inside of the glass of her window was covered in a thick frost. The sunlight sparkled on the mixture of swirling patterns, some symmetrical and some like exotic leaves and ferns. Heavens, this is like living in an ice house Diana thought, shivering violently.

There was a knock on the door and Clemmy came in. 'I just want to see what pictures you've got,' she said, crossing to the window. After inspecting them carefully, she turned to Diana who'd wrapped herself in the duvet and was sitting on the end of the bed. 'Mummy says that people with central heating don't have ice pictures,' she said in a pitying tone.

'No they don't,' said Diana, thinking she'd give anything to swap the ice pictures for central heating. 'Is the bathroom free?'

'Yes. Miffy and Simon never wash in the mornings, dirty little devils. But I have.' Clemmy sounded self righteous.

'Is the bathroom heated?' It was a vain hope that Susan might have put an electric radiator in there.

'No, of course not. But the water's hot.'

'Thank God for that.'

Her hasty wash reminded Diana of Mrs Loveday, their awful housekeeper when she'd been a child. 'A cat's lick and a promise is all you need,' she used to say when they'd complained about the freezing conditions in the bathroom. And that's certainly all I'm bothering with until I get back to London, thought Diana, hastily struggling into

128

the warmest clothes she'd brought, a pair of cords and a cashmere sweater.

At the top of the stairs, she paused and sniffed and immediately felt better. Freshly brewed coffee and hot bread, Susan had been busy.

Miffy joined her at the top of the stairs. He was carrying a bottle of cough syrup and wrapped in a thick dressing gown. He regarded Diana suspiciously, and took a swig of the cough syrup from the bottle. 'I don't like you,' he said.

There was something about the piercing dislike in his blue eyes, and the way he swigged from the bottle that made Diana think again of Joe. That was how he'd looked at her last night.

'And I don't like rude little boys,' she snapped. 'Hasn't anyone ever told you that it's bad manners to drink from the bottle?'

'Yes,' said Miffy. 'But I don't care.'

They stood glowering at each other. Then suddenly Diana burst out laughing. 'This is ridiculous,' she said. 'Why are we being so nasty to each other? We ought to try to be nice, for mummy's sake.'

Miffy regarded her silently, his blue eyes still suspicious and wary. 'Were you really a little girl with my mummy?'

'Yes.'

'And do you love her?'

Diana dropped to her knees so that her eyes were level with Miffy's. 'I love her very, very much,' she said gently. 'Just because I don't see her often doesn't mean that I've stopped loving her.'

Miffy digested this piece of information, then said graciously. 'All right, if you love mummy, then I'll try to like you.'

'Thank you,' Diana heard herself saying humbly.

Susan called up the stairs. 'Come on you lot. Breakfast is ready and it's late. Good heavens, it's gone eight o'clock already.'

'That's the crack of dawn,' called back Diana, following

Miffy who clattered down the stairs in front of her.

'Not to me,' replied Susan, 'I've been up for hours.'

Once in the kitchen Diana could see that she must have been. When they'd finally gone to bed the previous night there'd been bottles, glasses and the remains of supper scattered across the kitchen table. Now it was all cleared away. A cheerful yellow checked table cloth gave an added glow to the sunlit room, and on the table was a pot of coffee, a freshly baked loaf, butter, jars of honey and home-made jam and a mountain of individual small cereal packets.

'Bags I the one with the Ninja Turtle in,' said Simon, who although last into the kitchen somehow succeeded in sitting first at the breakfast table. He dived among the cereal packets and extracted a box.

'That's not fair. You had one yesterday.' Miffy hurled himself across the table in fury and tried to snatch the packet from Simon.

'Quite right, you did.' Susan deftly retrieved the box from a disgruntled Simon and tossed it over to Miffy. 'Now you two, sit up, eat up and shut up.'

'Boys are pests,' said Clemmy smugly.

Diana secretly agreed, and marvelled at Susan's tolerance. 'It's just as well I'm not a mother,' she said to Susan, 'I would never have your patience.'

'It's something you acquire when you need it,' said Susan matter of factly, concentrating on pouring Diana a coffee. 'But you do like children don't you?'

The unexpected question caught Diana unawares. 'Well, I . . .' she hesitated, an uneasy presentiment was telling her that her answer was important. Which was absurd. What difference could it possibly make to Susan whether she liked children or not? But then she thought she understood. It was important to Susan that she should like *her* children. All mothers thought their children were the best in the world, even if they were little monsters! 'Oh yes, I like them well enough,' she lied hastily. 'But I'd never be as well organized as you, Susan.'

'Nonsense. You'd be better. For instance, you'd never fritter your money away on silly things like those.' Susan waved at the cereal packets. 'You'd be businesslike and buy in bulk.'

'But then we wouldn't get the Ninja Turtles,' said Simon.

'True,' agreed Susan. 'But neither would you be spoiled as you are now.'

'I'm glad *you're* not businesslike,' said Simon.

'A put-down for me,' said Diana with a wry grin at Susan.

The warmth of the kitchen and the steaming cup of coffee gave her a sense of well being, enabling her to view things with a more benign eye. Susan's kids weren't bad on the whole. They were reasonably well behaved, and perhaps most importantly they adored their mother and she them. She was even able to regard Miffy, who was still watching her with his very unnerving blue eyes as he munched his way through a large slice of bread and honey, with an amused tolerance. Funny little thing, so self-possessed and determined for his age.

Susan was busy filling an enormous earthenware dish with steak and kidney, Guinness and bay leaves. 'For our supper tonight,' she said seeing Diana watching her. She popped it into the oven of the Aga. 'By tonight it should melt in our mouths and, later, I'll make some dumplings to go with it.'

'Are you trying to make me fat?'

'I just want to be happy while you're here,' said Susan seriously.

'Food and happiness are synonymous with mummy,' said Clemmy. 'That's what Joe always says.'

Joe! Damn Joe. She didn't want to think of him again. Diana poured herself another coffee, sipped it too soon and scalded her lips. Damn Joe!

A loud thud under the kitchen window, as a bicycle was dumped, signalled the arrival of the postman. He let himself in, accompanied by Sam, Joe's golden labrador.

'Mr Joe sent him over to see if you're all right,' he said.

'Good God, you make him sound as if he's the Lord of the Manor,' said Diana, glad to see that it was only the dog who'd arrived, not Joe himself.

The postman laughed and accepted the offer of a cup of coffee, and while Susan was gossiping Diana took the opportunity to 'phone Hugh again. She prayed that there'd be an answer this time. The pretence had been so hard last night, letting everyone assume that he'd been there, that they'd had a conversation, and then that she'd forgotten something vital and had needed to speak to him again. Pride had prevented her from admitting there'd been no answer either time.

The kitchen door thudded to a close as the postman left and Susan poked her head into the hall. 'Give my love to Hugh,' she said.

Diana put the 'phone down. 'He isn't there,' she said bleakly.

Susan studied her sister carefully. Diana had cultivated the habit of not showing her emotions over the years very well, but now her distress was quite unmistakeable. Susan had a flash of insight. 'And there was no answer last night either?' Diana shook her head. 'Then there must be something wrong with the 'phone. We'll report it. Why on earth didn't you mention it last night?'

'Because I didn't want *them* to know. I mean Joe and April. And because,' Diana hesitated, she hated admitting, even to herself, that anything in her life was less than perfect, but she *had* to tell someone. 'And because we had a quarrel before I came down, and I wanted to try and sort it out. But if I can't speak to him, how can we even begin to put things right?'

'Oh, Diana.' Susan put her arms around her sister. 'You didn't quarrel about me did you? I know Hugh's not keen on Mottisley. You shouldn't have come if it meant quarrelling with him.'

'We didn't quarrel about you. It was something else.'

132

And please don't ask me, Diana prayed. I can't tell anyone about *that* she thought.

But to her relief Susan didn't ask her. Instead she said, 'Diana, you know there is some perfectly logical explanation why he's not answering, and the most likely one is that the 'phone is out of order.' Without further ado she picked up the 'phone and reported a fault on Diana's London number. 'There, that's done,' she said turning back to Diana. 'They said it might not be until Monday before they can check. You know what telephone engineers are like. One pace only, dead slow!' She led the way back into the kitchen. 'For goodness sake stop worrying about the 'phone and your quarrel. I loved Tom dearly, but believe me we didn't see eye-to-eye on everything. We had some blazing rows, I even considered divorce at one point.'

Diana followed her. Sam lumbered across from the Aga and nudging Diana's hand demanded a stroke. Absent-mindedly she pulled at his silky ears. 'I can't imagine you and Tom ever rowing,' she said. Although now she thought about it, it was unrealistic to suppose that any marriage could exist without the occasional disagreement. It was all a matter of perspective. 'Did you?' she wondered whether she should ask then decided she might as well. After all, she didn't have to say exactly what. She could keep it on a general level. 'Did you ever quarrel about sex?'

Susan stopped dead in her tracks and stared at Diana. 'Why do you ask?' she said. Her voice was quite different. Sharp, defensive, hard almost.

'Oh God, I've offended you. I should never have asked such a personal thing,' said Diana in a panic, the last person she wanted to upset was Susan. 'But I only asked because that's what Hugh and I quarrelled about and I was very angry at the time, but now I'm beginning to wonder if I over-reacted. Forget that I ever asked.'

Susan gave a sudden wry smile. 'Diana,' she said, 'of course we quarrelled about sex. Too much or not enough of it, one or the other. All couples do. Why should you and Hugh be an exception? Don't tell me anything else, whatever the problem is you've got to sort it out between you.' She came over and hugged Diana. 'I know you will. You'll be all right.'

The warm familiarity of the kitchen, the fat cat lolling with complete abandonment on the sunny windowsill, the smell of food and coffee, all had a pacifying effect. Of course Susan was right. What was the matter with her? The 'phone was out of order, and as soon as she and Hugh were together again she'd sort things out. The saying that you couldn't put the clock back was wrong, of course you could, if you were determined enough.

'You're right,' Diana said firmly, 'we *will* be all right. Hugh's a good man.'

*   *   *

'Now cut back to this bud, and then the same on the other side.' Susan's breath smoked in the frosty air, and she waved at the rows of vines planted with military precision. They stretched down the hillside away from Abbey House. 'I've planted and trained the vines using the Double Guyot method,' she said. 'With the limited acreage I have, I need to aim for a good average yield in order to make it pay.'

'And does it?'

Diana shivered, her teeth ached from the sharpness of the cold, and she wished she was doing the usual thing she did most Saturday mornings, having beauty therapy at the Aphrodite Club. The Sussex Downs, early on a January morning, were beautiful but the bitter cold chilled her to the marrow of her bones. Diana marvelled at Susan's stamina, knowing that she pruned, come snow, rain or shine, every morning from December to February. But as Susan had pointed out, it was a question of having to, there was no-one else to do it.

'Most of the time,' said Susan, in answer to Diana's

question. 'Now come on, or we'll never get two rows finished by lunch time, and that's my target for today.'

Diana followed Susan. They each pruned every other vine; Susan's suggestion so that they would be near enough to chat while pruning. Sam kept them company, nose glued to the ground as he wove up and down and in between the rows following exciting scents in the frozen snow. 'Does that dog stay with you all the time?' asked Diana.

'No, Joe and April will collect him soon,' said Susan. She cast a wary eye in her sister's direction.

Diana caught the glance. 'I suppose you're thinking that Joe and I didn't hit it off very well last night.'

'Yes,' said Susan bluntly, glad that Diana had brought up the subject. 'I must admit I was surprised to find you both so,' she searched for the right word, 'hostile,' she said eventually.

'I wasn't hostile.' Diana was incensed. 'It was Joe. Poking sarcastic fun at Hugh and me and our life style. It's no business of his.'

'No it isn't,' Susan agreed, 'and I was disappointed with him, and you.' She stopped pruning. 'Diana, you ought to know that Joe is very, very special to me. He's been a good friend for many years, long before Mum and Dad were killed, although I always kept quite about it then because for some reason they both disliked him, and Joe wasn't overkeen on them either. During this last year since April's been with him, I've grown very fond of her too. She's good for him, he's more stable now than he's ever been, and they're super with my kids. To tell you the truth I don't know how I'd have managed without them. They, Tony Evans and, of course, Aunt May and Bert, have all been absolute towers of strength.'

Diana blew on the tips of her fingers poking out of the borrowed mittens, they were colourless and frozen. She felt guilty, and at the same time irrationally put out that Joe should be held in such high esteem by Susan.

'I should have been your tower of strength,' she said,

'and I would have been if I'd known you needed help, but you didn't tell me anything.'

'Don't stop pruning,' said Susan, snipping quickly while she talked, 'we'll get out of sequence. And, Diana, I don't expect you to help me every time I have a problem. It wouldn't be fair to be on the 'phone every five minutes. I know how busy you are. Also you're too far away.'

She smiled, and Diana was suddenly struck by the delicate beauty of Susan's face. It must have been her imagination last night, Tony Evans couldn't possibly prefer April Harte to Susan. In comparison to Susan, April Harte, although striking, was blowzy. Diana decided it was probably Tony's way of covering up the fact that he was in love with Susan.

'Well, so long as you remember that I'm always there. Promise me that you'll come to me for anything really important.'

Susan looked serious. 'I'm so glad you said that,' she said, 'and I promise you I will. I'll save you for the important things in life.' Their conversation was interrupted by a yodel at the far end of the vineyard. Sam, recognizing Joe's voice, hurtled down the hill towards the two figures making their way towards them. 'Now try and be nice to Joe,' said Susan.

'I'll try. The point is, will he?'

Diana did not feel hopeful, and viewed the approaching figures with apprehension. The weekend was turning out to be very different from the peaceful one she'd envisaged.

It was that damned newspaper article which had started it off, and then meeting up with him so soon afterwards and finding him so bloody minded had been the last straw. But I'll be pleasant to him she resolved, if it kills me. And once this weekend is over I'll make damn sure our paths never cross again.

Joe kissed Susan then turned to Diana and held out his hand. 'Hi,' he said.

Warily Diana extended her own hand towards him. 'Go

136

on,' said April, 'he won't bite. He's on his best behaviour. He knows he was bloody rude last night, I told him so.'

'She's a great one for telling me things I don't want to know,' said Joe. 'I'm glad to see Susan's got you working, it must be a change from telling other people what to do.'

'In my world that *is* called work,' said Diana.

'Come on, you two. No sniping,' said April severely.

'Hear, hear,' echoed Susan.

'Susan tells me that you've both been a great help to her,' said Diana. I'm not going to let that man rattle me, she thought fiercely, no matter how hard he tries. I'm going to be nice as pie, just as I promised Susan.

'Joe has known Susan for much longer than me,' said April. 'I've only known her since we moved into the manor house.'

Susan fished out two more pairs of secateurs and gave one each to Joe and April. 'You can work over there,' she said jerking her head to the opposite row. 'That is, if you're staying.'

'We'll come with you down to the end of the row, then we'll have to go. April's meeting her agent for dinner in town tonight, and I said I'd drive her up.'

'Yes,' said April gloomily, 'I don't know what he'll say when he hears I'm way behind with my schedule. It's all Joe's fault, he keeps distracting me by persuading me to choose new colour schemes for the redecorations.'

Diana remembered that in her youth the manor house had been practically derelict. Old General Humphries and his wife had plenty of airs and graces, but not a bean with which to bless themselves. Even in those days, the house and the extensive land which went with it had gradually been reverting back to nature. As children they'd often trespassed on to the land when riding their ponies. Winterbourne Thicket was part of the manor estate, and Diana wondered if Joe remembered its significance, but then decided that it was extremely unlikely. After two wives, who'd remember a brief affair conducted mostly on wet grass?

They worked their way slowly down the rows, snipping, then putting the clippings in the baskets Susan had brought. In the summer the clippings would be sold as aromatic barbecue fuel.

'Why did you come back to Mottisley, Joe?' Her voice sounded awkward in her ears, but Diana was bent on keeping her promise to Susan. His answer was unimportant, but at least she was appearing to be friendly. Whether or not he answered was up to him.

'Unlike you, Diana. I never really left. I've proved that you don't *have* to live in London to make money. I bought the lodge house first from General Humphries when he was strapped for cash. He was a widower by then, poor old thing, living from hand to mouth. Then later, when he died and the whole estate was put up for sale I bought the lot.'

'Well, tell her *all* of it,' said Susan, her busy secateurs pausing for a moment in their snipping, as she gave a wicked grin.

'You tell her,' said Joe.

'He also bought the Lordship of the Manor at auction. It gives him droit de seigneur and the right to drive his sheep from Mottisley to Chichester on the main highway.'

April shuddered. 'Thank God we haven't got any sheep. Joe threatened to use his rights, and I had awful visions of poor little sheep being mown down by bloody great lorries.'

'And what about the droit de seigneur?' asked Diana drily, thinking that in view of Joe's history that seemed a particularly superfluous right.

'Village virgins are non-existent these days,' said Joe, his blue eyes suddenly twinkling impudently.

'And if there are any, I'm not letting you near them,' said April. 'Come on, darling. We really ought to be going.'

They'd reached the end of the row and were at the bottom of the hill. 'What about Joe's parents?' asked Diana as she and Susan trudged back up the hill together, carrying the two baskets laden with prunings. 'If I remember correctly they weren't too popular in Mottisley.'

'Oh Joe sorted them out,' said Susan. 'He moved them. Romany caravan, assorted buses, horses, dogs, cats, the lot; all moved to a remote field on the edge of his estate. They are quite happy there, and can make as much mess as they like without bothering anyone.

'They obviously haven't changed then,' said Diana. 'How embarrassing for Joe to have such delinquent parents.'

'Embarrassed? Joe? Not a bit of it,' said Susan. 'Joe's not ashamed of his roots, and he's very fond of his parents, although not of their life style.' At the top of the slope on one side of Abbey House, stood an ancient tithe barn. Here, Susan and Diana stowed away the prunings. 'Now,' said Susan, 'I think we've done enough work. Let's visit Aunt May and Bert this afternoon.'

The rest of the weekend disappeared like a puff of smoke, and it was only when she was almost on the point of departure, that Diana remembered she hadn't tried to ring Hugh again. By now completely relaxed, it no longer seemed so important. Hugh and I can sort ourselves out when I get back to London, thought Diana.

'One last cup of tea,' said Susan, 'before you go.'

It was peaceful in the kitchen. The children were outside frantically trying to make a snowman before the snow disappeared. The usual perversity of the English weather had prevailed, and a thaw had set in as rapidly as the snow had arrived.

Inside the soporific, womb-like warmth of the kitchen, Diana sipped her tea. 'You know, I'd forgotten how eccentric May and Bert are,' she mused. 'Fancy living together for more than fifty years but never marrying because neither wants to give up their freedom.'

'Not eccentric,' said Susan, 'just ahead of their time. Everybody does it nowadays.' She watched Diana. I ought to ask her outright, she thought, not just leave it as a vague promise in mid air. 'Diana,' she said.

'Yes?' Diana was still thinking about May and Bert.

'I've been worrying a lot recently, about the children.'

'Worrying?' Diana was surprised. 'They seem fine to me.'

'Oh, yes, they are. No, I worry about who would care for them if anything happened to me.'

'What on earth could happen?'

'Well, I could die, get run over by a bus, fall downstairs and break my neck.' Susan's eyes suddenly filled with tears. 'People do die you know.'

'For heaven's sake,' said Diana firmly, thinking Susan was remembering the early death of Tom, her husband, 'stop being so melodramatic. I've never heard such nonsense in my life.'

'But if anything should happen,' Susan persisted. 'Would you make sure that they are looked after properly?'

Diana reached across the table and clasping Susan's hands in hers drew them up against her cheek. It was true, people did die. But not Susan. To Diana, Susan seemed as much a part of Abbey House as the lichen growing on the walls. Although their meetings were few and irregular, Diana couldn't imagine life without knowing that Susan was there, living in Abbey House, her old home. Suddenly she understood that in spite of her reluctance to go back to Mottisley, part of her held it sacred, regarding it as a haven should things go wrong, and part of that haven was her sister, Susan. Diana kissed her sister's thin fingers.

'Look, I know I'm a rotten sister, and I'm never here when you need me. But nothing has really changed since we were children. I still love you, and because of that I love your children too. Blood is thicker than water, isn't that the saying? You said that you'd save me for anything important, and I'd be hurt and disappointed if you didn't. I promise you now, that if anything should ever happen to you, I will look after the children. It would be the very least I could do. What sort of woman do you take me for, that you can even doubt it?'

'Oh, Diana, what can I say?'

'You can say something happy. I want to go back to London on a cheerful note, not one of gloom and doom.'

Chapter Ten

'Why, Hugh,' Diana said in surprise as he leaped up and rushed to take her bags as soon as she set foot through the door of the apartment on Sunday evening. 'You've prepared dinner. It looks wonderful. And,' she picked up the chilled bottle of of Sancerre from the ice bucket, 'my favourite white wine.'

'A romantic dinner à deux,' said Hugh, gently brushing her cheek with his lips. 'All out of the deepfreeze, but the best I could do. Diana, darling, I missed you terribly. I know I don't deserve it, but am I forgiven for my behaviour on Friday?' That was the first hurdle to clear and Hugh was determined to get over it as soon as possible.

'Oh, Hugh.' The relief of making up was so great that Diana almost burst into tears. Flinging her arms around his neck she hugged him, revelling in the deluge of relief washing over her. He would never behave like that again, she knew it, just knew it. 'I missed you too,' she said.

'Thank God,' said Hugh, carefully injecting just the right amount of reverence into his voice. 'I couldn't bear to go on living if you left me.'

It was only much later in bed that Diana remembered about the 'phone. 'I tried to ring you twice but there was no answer. We reported it as a fault.'

Truly fate was a marvellous thing. Diana had just handed Hugh the perfect alibi on a plate. 'Oh yes,' he answered, yawning, feigning sleepiness, 'the engineer rang just before you arrived to say the fault had been fixed. I told him that I didn't even know there'd been one.'

Hugh put his arm around Diana and pulled her close.

142

He yawned again loudly, and prayed that Diana wouldn't want to make love.

'Are you very tired?' Diana snuggled closer.

'Exhausted. I worked the whole weekend on a case for Archie Herbert. You know what an old slave driver he is, every 'i' has got to be dotted and every 't' crossed, and in addition to that I was worrying that you'd leave me.'

Diana sighed and yawned too. It was infectious. 'I'll never leave you again,' she murmured sleepily. 'Not even for a weekend.'

'I shall insist on it,' said Hugh firmly. 'I've been far too selfish. You must go down to Sussex and see your sister and her family more often.'

Diana relaxed and prepared to enjoy her therapy session at the Aphrodite Club. A massage, body wrap, face-pack, manicure and pedicure – that was her Saturday morning therapy whenever she had time.

She felt the manicurist begin to work on her nails. 'We missed you last week, Mrs Stratton. Working hard again I suppose?'

'No, I went down to the country for the weekend.'

Diana stifled a yawn. Heavens she felt tired, last night had been particularly late, although Hugh had thoughtfully waited up for her and warmed a pizza. But at least the copy for the advert concerning the new secretarial posts was finished ready for the newspapers. The wording was vital if the right type of people were to be attracted to Wycombe and Yatton, and Diana hadn't trusted anyone else. A trace of a smile flitted across her features. Alan Sinclair didn't know yet that his secretaries would be departing *en masse*. She'd tell him that on Monday.

'Lovely hotel was it?' Tracy, the manicurist, dragged Diana's mind away from business matters.

'I stayed with my sister. She runs a vineyard in Sussex.'

Tracy stopped filing. 'A vineyard,' she squeaked. 'How exciting. I suppose your sister is just like you. A real career woman.'

'Yes,' said Diana, in a tone of voice that precluded further conversation.

Tracy took the hint and lapsed into silence, and Diana lay back waiting for the pleasant soporific state between waking and sleeping which usually descended upon her during her beauty treatment. But it didn't come. Only disturbing thoughts of Mottisley and its inhabitants buzzed aimlessly around inside her head.

'*I suppose your sister is just like you.*' She'd said 'yes,' to shut the girl up, but it couldn't be further from the truth. Although sisters they were completely different. In outlook, life style, everything. And Susan is so happy. The thought touched a sensitive spot somewhere deep in her subconscious, almost as if there was something telling her that she, Diana, was not happy. Ridiculous! Of course I'm happy. Look at me now. I'm in pampered luxury, while Susan is out pruning the vines. For a brief moment Diana saw the special beauty of the rolling Sussex Downs. She could see them softly rounded, shimmering with light as they sloped away from Abbey House down to the sea. The bare branches of the winter trees standing out with startling clarity in the clear, crisp air, the only colour the hips and haws shining in the pale sunshine like drops of blood. The ground glittering with hoar frost. But it would be cold, she reminded herself, the opulent luxury of the Aphrodite Club was much more to her liking.

The images of Mottisley faded but Diana left the club feeling unaccountably unsettled and restless, and at the same time, angry with herself. The anger helped control the wayward emotions. Nothing was wrong, certainly nothing that a good lunch at the Savoy Grill with Hugh couldn't put right.

The girls in the Aphrodite Club leaned on the counter watching Diana. 'I wish I was like Mrs Stratton.' Tracy, sighed enviously, as the tall slender figure of Diana hurried through the crowd thronging Covent Garden. 'She's so self-assured, so beautiful.'

'And so rich,' added the receptionist.

144

'With a handsome husband who adores her, and not a worry in the world. It just isn't fair. Some people have everything.' Tracy sighed again at the injustice of life.

'Have you really got to go?'

Nancy stood, naked, staring out of the window of her bedroom. Her beautiful predatory face had a sulky expression.

'You know I have to. It's Saturday morning. I told you. Diana only spends the morning at the Aphrodite Club. She'll be expecting me to meet her for lunch at the Savoy Grill.' Hugh rolled off the bed and went into the bathroom.

'Oh, come on, Hugh. Once more.' Nancy followed him, rubbing her sleek body against his.

'Nancy, I can't. There isn't time.'

'There is. I can make you. Wait.' Nymph-like she sped back to the bedroom and then returned. 'Here, let's both take a snort. It'll make us come quicker.' Without waiting for Hugh's reply she emptied the white powder on to the back of her hand and handed Hugh a piece of rolled up paper. Hugh hesitated. He was snorting too much. Three times already this week. 'It'll only be half a dose because I'll have the other half,' Nancy whispered persuasively. 'We've never fucked after we've both snorted. Come on, it'll be fun.'

Hugh laughed, he'd noticed Nancy never said make love, and knew it was because love had nothing to do with it. All she wanted was pleasure. The temptation was too great. Hugh gave in and snorted some of the cocaine. 'You're an unprincipled bitch, you know that don't you.'

'Yes,' shrieked Nancy, switching on the shower, and turning away. 'Now, come and get me,' she teased. 'I'm not going to make it easy for you.' Hugh grabbed Nancy and plunged into her from behind. The rush came and he ejaculated in rough, jerking thrusts while Nancy screamed in pleasure. 'More, more, more,' she shrieked, bucking her hips backwards and forwards.

Half an hour later Hugh was dressed and ready to leave. 'Jeez! I feel exhausted,' he said.

Nancy lay on the bed smoking a joint. 'When are we going to get together again?'

'I'll ring you.'

'Don't leave it too long. Otherwise I'll have to find some other diversion.'

Hugh straightened his tie and checked his appearance in the mirror. 'Don't worry. I don't want to do without you for too long either. I'll find a way to get to Hampstead. With any luck Diana will work late again every night this week as well, and as long as I get back to the apartment before she does, everything will be OK.'

Nancy laughed, a guttural purr at the back of her throat. 'And you're sure she doesn't suspect?'

'Of course not. I get something out of the freezer and put it in the microwave, and she thinks I'm the bees' knees for waiting up and getting supper.'

'Good.' Nancy watched him through narrowed black eyes. She didn't want Diana to spoil their fun. Hugh was perfect. Carnal enough to satisfy her most depraved needs, and weak enough to be completely under her control. 'And don't forget you're nearly out of coke. You'd better get some more.'

Hugh felt a brief flicker of unease, but then it was gone. He knew how to control his coke habit. He'd cut it down next week.

'I'll get it,' he said, and left the house without a backward glance.

Smiling, Nancy stretched luxuriously, and idly curled the black hairs of her bush into little corkscrews.

Three months later, Diana had almost forgotten her trip to Mottisley. Wayward thoughts no longer bothered her. She'd spoken to Susan once on the telephone, and since then had been busy on an enormous project; an ambitious jungle theme park which would involve covering vast tracts of Norfolk under a gigantic plastic bubble.

'We'll drain the waterways first, then erect a plastic bubble over the whole area and keep it in place by air pressure which will ensure that the humidity and temperature is right for the flora and fauna. Once that is done we can start planting trees, making artificial lakes and swamps, and finally bring in the animals and insects.'

She could see Alan Sinclair almost rubbing his hands in glee at the thought of the enormous profit potential. Greedy little man, she thought, then squashed her own irritating conscience which reminded her that she stood to gain considerably as well.

'That seems fine, Diana,' said Alan. 'But there'll be the inevitable outcry from the conservationists.'

Diana had already thought that point through. 'Don't worry about them. I'll organize the planning application and speak at the public meetings. By the time I've finished, even the conservationists will end up thinking what a good idea it is.'

Alan Sinclair grinned. 'God, you're frightening, Diana. When you get a bee in your bonnet there's no stopping you. I thought it would take at least six months to get this off the ground, and you've prepared the whole thing in less than three.'

'I've worked damned hard,' Diana reminded him.

'But not been neglecting that husband of yours, I hope.' Alan's only concern was that Diana's concentration should not be distracted by marital problems.

Diana laughed at the idea. 'Hugh never complains.' And it was true, he didn't. Their life was back to normal now. That fateful Friday evening, forgotten – almost.

'I'm having a dinner party next week,' Alan continued. 'I'd like you and Hugh to come.' He forestalled her refusal by adding, 'as far as you are concerned I'm afraid, it will be a working dinner. I want you to sell the jungle theme park idea to the Secretary of State for the Environment, and I'm relying on Hugh to use his enormous charm on the battleship of a woman who passes as his wife.'

'I see. Priming our guns *and* keeping the gunpowder dry,' said Diana wryly.

Alan laughed. 'Into which category do you slot Sir Timothy Drisdale?'

'Oh, he's the gun. He needs priming *and* loading! That man has never had an original idea in his life.'

'I look forward to seeing if you can win him over.'

'It's as good as done,' said Diana.

'Glad to hear it, my dear.' Alan placed a pudgy hand on her knee and gave it a squeeze. 'We make a perfect couple don't we?'

Diana smiled, adroitly removing his hand. 'The perfect couple,' she agreed smoothly.

Alan Sinclair lived in a neo-Georgian house in Dulwich. The electrically operated gates opened for Hugh and Diana to drive up the gracious sweep of the gravelled drive.

'Alan must be damn well heeled to be able to afford a place like this,' observed Hugh enviously.

'We could afford something like this,' said Diana, 'if that's what you really want. But we'd need a gardener and handyman. I can't imagine your cleaning out the drains and planting the bedding plants.'

Hugh grinned. 'And a housekeeper. I can't imagine your rushing round with a cleaner or slaving over a hot stove.'

'Well, keep your fingers crossed. If I get this theme park off the ground and built, my bonus will pay for the lot, house as well.'

Hugh whistled slowly. 'I didn't realize that you stood to gain that much.'

'Why else do you think I agreed that we'd have dinner with Alan Sinclair? It's only the thought of all that money that keeps me being civil to the man.'

Hugh took her arm. 'I'm a lucky man,' he said, and meant it.

Diana looked stunning in a new Armani creation. A

shimmering affair of gold and silver threads which some-how contrived to look casual and dressy at the same time. She was the epitome of a fragile, cool English beauty. But she couldn't stir Hugh the way Nancy did. Nancy always dressed in black or red, the colours of the devil. She was the dark side of his life, Diana the light. Diana provided the means and Nancy the method to satisfy his sybaritic longings. He needed them both.

'Let's go and be nice to everyone,' said Diana smiling up at her handsome husband. 'I know you'll charm the pants off Lady Drisdale.'

'Do I really have to go that far?' said Hugh.

Besides Sir Timothy Drisdale and his enormous prune-faced wife, Lord Bing, Secretary of State for the Depart-ment of Trade and Industry, and his equally unattractive wife were also present at dinner. Diana approved of that move, it meant she'd be able to kill two birds with one stone by convincing both men of the soundness and, more importantly, the financial attractiveness of the jungle theme park. The blessing of both Departments was essential to the plan.

Diana played her part well, being in turn, businesslike, then feminine and slightly seductive as the need arose. She noted with amusement that Hugh's charm eventually coaxed ill-fitting girlish smiles from both Lady Drisdale and Lady Bing.

'Oh, Hugh!' They were soon tittering like sixth-form schoolgirls at his jokes.

We make a good pair, thought Diana. On an evening such as this we are the perfect foil for each other, and she was glad that their lives had settled down into the old routine. How foolish she would have been to let one little incident mar what was otherwise a perfect relationship.

As the last of the plates were cleared away by the Sinclairs' Filipino housemaid, Sir Timothy leaned back and poured himself another generous measure of port. 'Well, dear girl,' he boomed. 'I understand that you are the architect of this ambitious scheme.'

Diana gritted her teeth at the 'dear girl', and smiled ingenuously.

'You flatter me, Sir Timothy,' she said, 'but a lot of the credit must go to Alan as well.' It would never do to let them know it was all her idea, a token man was always necessary to keep the male egos ticking over happily. Before they had time to ask too many questions she proceeded to blind them with science, periodically slipping in disarming little asides. 'Of course, I know I don't have to explain the nuts and bolts of this to you, but I always feel happier when all the cards are on the table.'

Judging by their glazed expressions, Diana knew that most of the information was going straight over their heads. What little intelligence they had was now totally befuddled by alcohol.

'Well, it all seems quite straightforward to me,' said Lord Bing, who was heavily into the brandy. He motioned his empty glass towards Alan who hastily refilled it. 'Should make plenty of money, and everyone likes that. Might even invest in it myself.' Diana and Alan exchanged glances, this was going even better than they had hoped. 'Of course,' Lord Bing belched loudly, 'I'd get my son to do it for me. Never do to let the newspapers get wind that I was involved. Next thing you know, they'd be printing a load of rubbish about me having a vested interest. No, best use one of his off-shore companies.'

'And of course you *would* be helping the public.' Diana stepped up her sales pitch. 'Joe public will have some- where different to go for his holiday without the need for expensive foreign travel. That should please the Treasury, as in turn this will prevent the outflow of sterling as well as attracting tourists from abroad.'

Lord Bing nodded ponderously. 'Good point, m'dear.' He turned towards Sir Timothy. 'Of course the actual park will be in your constituency Tim. What do you think the electorate will think?'

'Think? Think? Don't think they ever do, dear chap. Never shown any signs of thinking before. Hardly likely to start now.' He snickered disdainfully.

'There is one snag.' Diana had saved this until she was sure they were enthusiastic about the idea. 'A small village is in the way. A hamlet really, five houses and a farm. They will need to be demolished. I suggest that they be offered good compensation and the promise of employment in the theme park.'

'They can't grumble at that. No problem.' Sir Timothy waved his hand nonchalantly, mentally brushing the village and its inhabitants aside.

But Diana wanted to be sure. 'Supposing they are awkward, and don't want to move? A long-drawn-out enquiry would ruin my costing.'

Sir Timothy laughed. 'Don't you worry your pretty little head about that. Bing and I will back it. The Whitehall mandarins set the wheels of bureaucratic machinery turning, and then it'll take more than a few Norfolk yokels to stop it. Before they know where they are the decision will have been made, and it will be too late for protests.'

A toast was drunk to the future of the Jungle Theme Park and Sir Timothy and Lord Bing departed with their spouses; wafting out of the house on a fog of alcohol.

'One law for them and another for us,' said Alan sourly, watching them drive off. He'd lost his licence nine months earlier on a drink driving offence.

Diana laughed. 'Never mind, Alan. We'll make them pay dearly for their privilege. With a little judicious arm twisting, I have a feeling that they and their companies will finance the majority of the theme park. Wycombe and Yatton need only put up the front money.'

'You ought to be in politics. You'd run rings around them.'

'Not enough money in it,' said Diana simply. She turned to Hugh and slipped her arm through his. 'Let's go home,' she said.

That night they made love, and it was just as it had

been at the beginning of their marriage. Hugh was tender and considerate, and Diana responded, giving her whole self. I love him, she thought, and this is where I belong, here with Hugh. She looked into his dark face, intent now only on her pleasure, and tried to imagine life without him. It was unthinkable. But he has his failings; she didn't want the dark voice to remind her, but the galling fact was it would never completely go away. She answered it back. So what? Everyone has failings. But Hugh is my husband, the man I've chosen to be with for the rest of my life. Nothing will ever separate us. All we need is each other.

'The 'phone at this hour. Who the hell can it be?'

Hugh was irritable. He'd hardly slept at all last night. He knew why. It was the strain of playing the gentle, thoughtful husband when what he longed for was the lewd abandonment he always had with Nancy. And more than that he needed a snort. The fact that his supply of coke had run out made the need more urgent. Damn Nico. Why the hell did he have to go on an extended holiday to Sicily? He'd ring again today and see if he was back.

The 'phone kept ringing. 'Damn,' he said again, and slamming down his coffee picked up the 'phone. 'Yes?'

A man's voice. 'Can I speak to Mrs Diana Stratton, please?'

'She's busy. I'll take a message.'

'It is important that I speak to her.'

'Look, I told you . . .'

'This is Dr Evans. I'm speaking from Mottisley.'

'Who is it, darling?' Diana called out, her voice raised against the gushing water of the shower.'

'Some Dr Evans from Mottisley. Wants to speak to you.'

'Tell him I'm coming.'

'She's coming.' Hugh put the 'phone down and went back to his coffee wondering if there'd be time for him to slip out and see Nancy during the day, and when Nico would be back. He was only vaguely aware of Diana, wrapped in a robe, talking on the 'phone.

It was the ominous chill of the silence which finally caught his attention. Diana was sitting at the breakfast bar, elbows on the table top, hands in her chin, her face drained of colour, white and expressionless.

'What is it?' asked Hugh.

'He apologized . . . should have rung sooner. But no-one realized. They thought . . . but she didn't. The virus was deadly. Deadly, silent and swift. So swift.'

'What virus?' The stilted half sentences made no sense to Hugh.

'The pneumonia virus. The one that killed Susan.'

Diana turned and looked at Hugh, but all she saw was the laughing face of Susan. Somewhere, far away in the distance, she could hear a voice. It was her own. How calm it sounded, how remote. It was saying:

'Susan is dead.'

PART TWO

DOUBTS

Chapter Eleven

Diana arrived at Mottisley and found a household stunned. The children crept about, small, grey, desolate ghosts. May and Bert drifted in and out of Abbey House, their eyes red rimmed from weeping. And Diana couldn't bear it; not any of it. To her the children's grief, although mostly silent, seemed like a raw ugly wound, and the anguish from that wound seeped into every nook and cranny of the old house. She longed to be able to staunch the flow of pain, to make it better, to promise them that everything would be all right. But she couldn't. She didn't know how to begin to comfort them, knowing that nothing she could say or do would ever make it all right. So she left them to themselves, and instead buried herself in the day-to-day practicalities which had to be dealt with.

She summoned Griselda to Abbey House. Griselda was the village piano teacher who had once taught Diana. Lately she had helped Susan in the house as well as giving the children piano lessons. The meeting took place formally in the library. Diana sitting behind the large old writing desk, Griselda, on the other side, perched nervously on the edge of a chair. 'I have a proposition to put to you,' Diana said.

Griselda, looking more worried than usual, peered short-sightedly at Diana. Even when Diana had been a small girl she'd found her unnerving. Now as a fully grown woman she found her terrifying. 'A proposition?' she quavered.

'One that I hope you will find agreeable,' said Diana briskly.

How was it possible for a female to grow into such a pale grey imitation of a woman? Apart from teach the piano, what had she ever done with her life? For a second Diana remembered how easy she'd found it to bully Griselda when she'd been a child. I was a little brat, she thought, and felt sorry for the older woman.

'Oh yes?' Griselda sounded slightly more confident.

'Yes. I know you helped Susan with the children and sometimes did a bit in the house, and I was wondering if you would be interested in the position of full-time housekeeper? At least for the time being.'

'Well, I . . .'

'At the moment I'm afraid I cannot say exactly how long a housekeeper will be needed. Long-term decisions will need to be made once the value of Susan's estate is known, and also, of course, once we know what provisions she has made for the children.'

'Hasn't Mr Grimble told you?'

Diana sighed with irritation. 'Mr Grimble is being very stubborn, and won't tell me a thing. Apparently Susan left instructions for the will to be read after the funeral, and he is sticking to the letter of those instructions. In the meantime, and probably for some weeks to come, the children need someone they know and trust to look after them.'

'They have you,' said Griselda timidly.

'They don't know or trust me,' said Diana sharply. 'Playing the part of a mother is not something life has equipped me for.'

'And you think it has me?' For once in her life Griselda answered back without stopping to think. 'I'm a spinster.'

'Of this parish.' A wan smile flitted across Diana's face. 'That's the important part, don't you see. They know you. I could hire a housekeeper from an agency in London, but the last thing they need is a stranger, they need you.'

'Well, if you think I can do it.'

'Of course I do. I wouldn't ask you if I didn't.' Not quite the truth, but it would have to do. Diana didn't allow herself to doubt Griselda's ability to keep order. Assertiveness may not be one of her characteristics, but with

Aunt May in the background, Diana thought, she'll manage. Anyway, she'll have to. It was the best thing to do in the circumstances. She wrote an amount on a piece of paper and pushed it towards Griselda. 'This arrangement is between you and me. Would this amount per week be suitable?'

Griselda gasped her appreciation. 'That's a very generous salary.'

'I shall expect you to earn it,' said Diana abruptly, and rose to show the interview was at an end. 'You can move your things into Abbey House today.'

In the week preceding Susan's funeral, Diana organized everything that needed to be done with her usual cool, calm, ruthless efficiency, inwardly hardly aware of what she was doing. For the first time in years Diana felt afraid. Really afraid. And the fear stemmed from the fact that she could feel nothing. No sorrow, no sense of loss at Susan's death. Just a cold, bone freezing nothingness. A great empty void where she knew some kind of emotion ought to be. God in heaven, Susan was my sister! I loved her. I should be weeping as I did for my father. I even wept for mother, and I felt little enough for her.

But there were no tears. Her eyes ached with dryness, not tears; and worse than that was the guilt of being unable, and if she was truthful, unwilling, to comfort the children. The truth was that the sight of their tear-stained faces repelled her, and their pathetic tendency to cling on to anyone who came near terrified her. She didn't want them clinging on to her, dragging her down into the mire of *their* agony. She wanted her *own* grief. If only it could surface. Once it did, then she'd be able to deal with it. Conquer it. It was always easier to deal with an enemy one knew, because knowing made it a reality. Shadowy, insubstantial emotions amounted to nothing.

So Diana shut herself off, and engaged Griselda to feed the children, clothe them and see to their material needs. The children had no need of her, and Diana was a realist, knowing that the task was beyond her capabilities. Besides, there were plenty of other people making an effort to alleviate their heartbreak. May and Bert, Tony Evans, who was always popping in, and of course Joe Kelly and April Harte.

'No-one can tell me it's right, because I won't believe it.' May's voice quavered with worry. 'It's just not natural, showing no feeling at all.'

'It's Diana's way of coping,' said Tony.

'I hope you're right.' May leaned on Bert. Her usual pugnacious spirit dissipated. 'It should have been us,' she said looking up at Bert. 'We're both too old to be of much use to anyone. Why didn't we die?'

'It wasn't our time. The Lord decides that.' In spite of rarely attending church, Bert held deep-rooted religious convictions which had survived the years of May's perpetual debunking.

'Bugger your Lord,' said May, a little of her old spirit surfacing. 'If ever I get face to face with Him, I'll tell Him a few home truths.'

Joe was still thinking of Diana's strange behaviour. 'If grieving is natural as you told me,' he said to Tony, 'then Diana is behaving in an unnatural way. But I suppose that's because she *is* unnatural. She's a bitch.'

His voice was harshly condemning. Being so open himself, he couldn't understand Diana's tight, self-constrained aloofness. Susan was so different, like him she'd been open with all those who knew her, and over the years he had grown to love her like a sister. Once he'd thought himself in love with her, and liked to think that Susan was a little in love with him. That was when Tom, her husband, had first started to be so ill. Susan, despairing of the future and lonely because Tom had shut himself in with his illness, had turned to Joe for comfort. Not her parents, because they didn't care, and not her sister, because she was so busy making money that she was isolated from real life. 'Susan was the sister I never had,' he added slowly. 'I should have done more.'

'You were a good brother, Joe,' Tony said gently. 'Susan couldn't have asked for better.'

'But she would never let me help her financially. Never,' said Joe in anguish. 'If only she hadn't worked so hard, then maybe she . . .'

'She would have died anyway,' said Tony. 'Sooner or later, it was inevitable. I always prayed that it would be later, but I knew, and so did Susan, that she was never destined to be an old lady.'

'And she wanted to be independent,' April reminded Joe. 'You know she did. You mustn't blame yourself.'

Tony tried another tack. 'If it's any consolation I know Diana tried to help her too. But Susan would never accept a penny from her either.'

'Diana! That cow!' was Joe's angry reaction.

'I think you're too hard on Diana,' Tony was quietly authoritative. 'Whatever you think, now is not the time to quarrel with her. She is trying to do her best. Leave her alone.'

'Oi agrees,' said Bert, his slow country drawl interrupting the conversation unexpectedly. He was a man of few words, but those he did utter were usually sensible. 'Now, Joe, yous best be gettin' along 'ome and 'aving a shave. May and me'll 'ave the kids over at Willow Farm until the funeral.'

'A good idea,' said Tony briskly. In the three days since Susan's unexpected death Joe had been at Abbey House the whole time, and not once shaved by the look of him. April, coming in every day to do the cooking, had tried to persuade him to leave once Diana had arrived, but he'd snapped her head off, and had insisted on staying. Diana had made no objection, in fact she hardly seemed to notice.

'I seem to be outvoted,' said Joe slowly, looking at the anxious row of faces before him.

'You are,' said Tony. 'And for your own good. Take him home April, I'll explain to Diana.'

* * *

161

No explanations were necessary, for Diana didn't notice their going. Neither Joe and April, nor the children. She was too busy in her makeshift office.

As it was unseasonally warm that year for mid-April, it was warm enough to turn her bedroom into an office, so using a portable telephone and a desk she'd had brought up from the library, Diana did all her organizing from there. She could have used the library, but the windows, shrouded by overgrown rhododendron bushes, let in little light, and the gloomy atmosphere depressed her. The bedroom caught the sun most of the day, and she felt more at ease there. She was busy on the 'phone all the afternoon and only realized the house was empty when Griselda called her down to supper.

Supper consisted of omelette, chips and salad, and Griselda's apologies. 'I'm not such a good cook as April,' she said looking earnestly worried. It was her permanent expression, partly due to the large, immensely powerful glasses she was obliged to wear, and partly due to the fact that she usually *was* worried about something. 'But I think you'll find it all right.'

'I'm sure I will,' said Diana with a polite smile. She felt impatient, and wanted to start planning the children's future. A move to a smaller house with a permanent housekeeper or foster parents, or a boarding school; those were two possibilities. But she could do nothing until she had the facts and figures and heard the terms of Susan's will. Until then, Griselda Morgan would have to do.

'Shall I open a bottle of wine?'

'Good idea.' It was then that Diana noticed that the table was only set for two. 'Where is everybody?'

'May and Bert have taken the children to Willow Farm, and Joe and April have gone back to the manor house. Tony thinks it might be a good idea for the children to stay at the farm until the morning of the funeral.'

'Yes it is,' said Diana feeling relieved and yet guilty at the same time. 'It's a pity it's the Easter school holidays.

School would have helped them forget their mother's death.'

'I doubt that anything could do that.'

Griselda sounded disapproving, and Diana felt a flash of resentment. She was just the same as all the others, judging her, and finding her wanting. Oh, I know, thought Diana, I know what you all think. But you're wrong. I shall do the best I can for Susan's children, just as I promised, and to hell with the lot of you! She glowered at Griselda, who glowered back through her pebble lensed glasses.

'It's a fact of life they will have to get used to, Griselda,' said Diana. 'Their mother is dead, and nothing will bring her back.'

'They'll get used to it,' said Griselda sombrely, 'but they won't forget.'

Partly because of the empty desolation inside herself, Diana clung to her life in London with an obsessive determination. Although physically in Mottisley, she made certain that Wycombe and Yatton still occupied much of her time. Combining all her duties at Mottisley and keeping up with her workload in London made life doubly hard. All the dealings had to be done over the 'phone, and the fax she'd had installed, but nevertheless she did it with a gritty determination, finding a kind of solace in concentrating her mind on the things she understood. Plans and projects, concepts and facts. They were things she could manipulate and control, unlike the people around her at Abbey House. The constant ebb and flow of their heartache and sorrow was something over which she had no control whatsoever, and made her feel isolated and alone. The dealings of Wycombe and Yatton were familiar and comforting, and in that world nothing was beyond her capabilities. In that world she felt strong.

The day before Susan's funeral found her working harder than ever. Because the portable 'phone had a fault she had been forced to use the 'phone in the hall. Apart from the 'phone, her briefcase and a stack of papers was all she needed, and she was soon submerged in business, and with it came blessed normality. Griselda made a point of cleaning the rest of the house, steering well clear of the hall. She had made it quite clear to Diana that she thought she ought to spend the day with the children, and been sharply put in her place.

'Goddamn it, Diana,' said Alan as they were on the point of winding up for the day, 'I hate doing business like this.'

'Oh, do stop complaining. Nothing has gone wrong yet has it?' When dealing with Alan Sinclair, Diana was always practical to the point of brutality.

'No, but I want to know when you're coming back up to town.' Alan sounded plaintive. 'Lord Bing has been asking to see you. He wants to take you to lunch.'

'I'll be back in London just as soon as I've made proper arrangements for the children.'

'And when the hell will that be?'

'It won't be long, Alan. I promise you that. Get that secretary of mine to book me a luncheon date with Lord Bing for the end of next week. I'll be there.'

Diana put the 'phone down. She could understand Alan Sinclair's frustration at her absence, and sympathized with him. It would be good to get back to London.

'My God! If I hadn't heard it with my own ears I would never have believed it. But, no, on second thoughts, perhaps I would. You're a cold fish, Diana Stratton. Not a thought for anyone in the world. All you care about is your own bloody career. You make money like other women do knitting.'

Diana turned. 'I've always thought knitting a singularly useless occupation,' she snapped icily.

Joe stood in the doorway from the kitchen to the hall, his blue eyes glittering with a dislike he took no trouble to conceal.

'I like women who knit,' he said illogically.

'What an absurd statement.' Diana turned to leave.

'I've more important things to do than listen to your ravings. If you want Griselda, I think she's upstairs.'

Joe grabbed her by the arm, the force spinning her round to face him. 'I don't want Griselda. I want you, because I want to know what is going to happen to Clemmy, Simon and Miffy.' His face was very close to hers and the expression in his eyes made Diana falter.

But it was only a moment before she regained her composure and with it anger. 'I don't think that is your business. I'm their next of kin, and I shall do what is best for them.'

'There's a lot of bloody nonsense talked about biological ties. Blood isn't thicker than water. You don't feel anything for those kids. Let me adopt them.'

Logic told her that Joe's suggestion would be the perfect solution, because he loved the children and they loved him, and he could more than adequately provide for them. But Joe Kelly was the very last person from whom she wanted help. The ties, broken by herself so many years before, needed to remain severed. Diana dismissed the idea out of hand.

'Adoption by you is a non-starter. And if you had eavesdropped a little more carefully, you would have heard that I said I'd go when I've made proper arrangements for the children, not before. And I'm doing just that. Already I've persuaded Griselda Morgan to take up permanent residence at Abbey House as housekeeper for the time being. I can't replace their mother, but I can make sure their material needs are met, and plan for their long-term future.'

'Material needs! Long-term future!' Joe sneered. 'That's boardroom speak, all you're capable of. Children have emotional needs too. But, of course, I forgot, you don't have emotional needs do you? So it's hardly surprising you can't understand theirs.'

'Of course I understand.'

'When have you wept with them?'

'I haven't cried for years,' said Diana. What was the

matter with the man? Subjecting her to this tirade. 'Weeping with them won't change things, neither will it help in the slightest way. Strength, to cope with things the way they are now, and are going to be in the future, is what they need. And they won't get that if I start snivelling too.'

'Haven't cried for years,' Joe pounced on her words. 'That I can believe! You didn't come down when Susan was ill, and I don't suppose you've even asked why she died. Irrelevant. You deal with facts, nothing else. Facts and figures. Susan is dead, and that is that. Just another statistic to be stored away in the enormous computer you have instead of a heart.'

White with rage at the injustice of his words Diana wrenched her arm from his grasp and stepped away. 'Of course I asked, and Tony told me. Susan had a severe form of pneumonia. A lethal virus, there was nothing anyone could do.'

'Did you read the death certificate?'

'No. I didn't need to read a certificate to know my sister was dead.' The truth was Diana couldn't bring herself to read it, but she couldn't admit that to Joe or anyone else. She remembered holding the official scrap of paper in her hand, thinking it seemed such an ignominious way to record the ending of a life. Just a sheet of paper, and that was that. She'd felt then as if Susan had never existed, so she'd passed it straight over to the undertaker, still folded and unread.

'You should have done, then you would know why she had pneumonia. You would have known something that you should have known more than a year ago.'

'What should I have known?' A sudden dryness afflicted her throat.

'That Susan had leukaemia,' shouted Joe, at that moment hating Diana, hating the smart, slick, creature he saw before him. The hatred made him brutal. 'But you didn't know that did you? You knew she'd been ill these past eighteen months, but not once, *not once*, did you ask what it was, and Susan was too proud to tell you. She underwent all that bloody painful treatment, and all the worry, alone. You never came down to see how she was, because you didn't damn well care.'

Too late Diana realized the significance of Susan's frailty, of Tony's hesitant explanations. Too late she wished she had taken the time and trouble to visit Susan more often. Too late, too late. She stumbled backwards away from Joe, away from his hateful accusations of not caring, away from the abomination that was the truth. Leaning against the wall of the hall for support, her fingers spread desperately on to the uneven rough stone of the house, and she clung to it. The house, the only reality there was. Everything else, Joe's words, Susan's death, that wasn't real, it was a nightmare. But Diana knew that she wasn't going to wake up, because it was the truth. It had been there all the time, but she had never seen it. The shadow of ambition had blocked the light of truth.

At last Diana spoke. 'Leukaemia,' the word was a ragged whisper. 'Oh my God. Leukaemia.'

'Yes,' said Joe.

'But she was so well that weekend I came down. So full of energy, so happy.' Diana shook her head, still not willing to accept Joe's words. 'I don't believe it,' she said shakily. 'It can't be true. She was so well, so well.'

'She was in remission, and had been for some months. A really good one, so good in fact that we were all hoping, praying that . . .' Joe's voice roughened and broke.

The tears came now. Spilling down Diana's cheeks, scalding and bitter. What a waste. How cruel the hand of fate. Why Susan of all people? Susan who had never harmed anyone and had always been a truly good person. Not like me, thought Diana, suddenly humbled, an arrogant superwoman always grasping after something new. For the first time since she'd arrived in Mottisley she acknowledged what a gap Susan's death was going to leave in her life. Susan had always been there. Solid as a rock and totally undemanding. Oh, Susan, she wept silently, I took you for granted, always thinking you were part of the past I despised, never realizing until now, too late, that I need you.

'Why didn't she say?' she wailed. 'Why didn't someone else tell me?'

Christ! I shouldn't have been so bloody brutal. Joe panicked, wishing that he'd been more gentle in the telling. What now? Joe hated weeping women, they unnerved him. Deliverance from his dilemma arrived in the reassuring form of Tony Evans. Tony took charge, and soon calm was restored with the aid of a pot of coffee and a glass of brandy.

Tony took Griselda aside. 'Just make sure that no-one comes into the kitchen for the next half hour.'

Griselda, eyes as big as organ stops, scuttled off to do his bidding.

Tony sat down beside Diana and motioned for Joe to leave. But Joe was reluctant. 'I told her. I ought to stay,' he said, still riven with guilt for breaking the truth so pitilessly.

'Get out,' snapped Tony, then seeing Joe's stricken face he softened his tone and added, 'look, tact and patience are just not your forte, Joe. You know that. At the moment Diana and I need to talk quietly.'

Joe nodded. Tony was right. He was always opening his great big Irish mouth and putting his foot in it, and he'd done it again. He hovered by the doorway, trying to catch Diana's eye, but she only stared into her coffee. 'I'm sorry,' he said at last. 'Sorry that it had to be me to tell you, and sorry for the way I did it.'

'It doesn't matter. Somebody had to tell me.' Diana didn't look up.

'Go,' said Tony sternly.

Joe went, striding off down the slope between the vines towards Mottisley Manor, and with each step his rage grew at the unjustness of life in general. By the time he reached the manor house he'd decided there was nothing for it but to get blind, stinking drunk.

*　　*　　*

'Talk to them,' Tony told Diana, when she'd confessed to him how she felt towards the children. 'Then everything will fall into place.'

Diana put it off. 'I will after the funeral,' she said. 'When I know what I've got to do. Everything hinges on Susan's will.'

'The longer you leave it, the harder it will be,' he warned.

Long after Tony had left Diana stayed sitting in the kitchen. She poured herself another brandy, splashing a generous measure of the golden liquid into the glass. The window was still open. Outside in the lavender twilight of a spring dusk she could hear a tractor growling along the uneven flinty lane between the vineyard and the abbey. It reminded Diana of the tractor standing in the tithe barn, and the fact that the vines were sprouting dark green buds. There must be work that ought to be done in the vineyard. Susan had said every month there was something. But what? She had no idea. Another matter needing to be dealt with later when the children were sorted out. *When the children*. Everything came back to the children.

She sipped the brandy. At least she felt better now, not quite so guilty. Tony had been marvellous, not like that sod Joe Kelly. Susan hadn't wanted her to know, he'd said, if she had, she would have told her. And then he'd apologized for not having told her himself the moment she'd arrived, it was wrong of him to keep the knowledge from her. Not that it would have made any difference. Knowledge hadn't been able to save Susan, and knowledge certainly couldn't raise the dead. She didn't like brandy, it burnt the back of her throat, but she went on drinking it and poured herself another glass. From the rookery at the back of the house she could hear the rooks squabbling noisily as they settled down for the night. Like a lot of children, she thought, through a haze of brandy.

Children, always back to the children, and the big question mark. Why didn't Susan tell me? Ever since Joe had rubbed her nose into the painful truth she'd been asking herself the same question, over and over again. Was that really the reason? The one Tony had put forward, that Susan didn't want Diana to worry unnecessarily. Or was it that Susan didn't trust her? Did Susan think that I might have refused to be responsible for the children if I had known there was a very real possibility that she would die soon? Diana tried to answer herself honestly. Would my answer have been the same unqualified yes? Or would I have wriggled out of it? Made another suggestion, a more practical solution to the children's future which did not include me. Everything was blurred and confused, even her professed love for Susan became uncertain. What would my answer have been if I had known?

Chapter Twelve

'Jesus! How long does this affair have to take?' Hugh fiddled irritably with his tie.

The funeral was over, and the whole family were crammed into the dingy gloom of the library, to hear Mr Grimble read the will. Diana had thought she couldn't feel more depressed, but found she was wrong. The library lowered her spirits even more, and she wished she'd taken May and Griselda's advice and used the kitchen. Too late now. Everything was too late now.

'This will take as long as it has to,' hissed May to Hugh. 'You don't have to stay if you don't want to. You're not *proper* family.'

'I'm Diana's husband.'

'Never could understand why Diana married him,' May said loudly to Bert who turned his weatherbeaten face in Hugh's direction and glowered.

Hugh glowered back.

'Why did he bring that Nancy with him?' asked Bert.

'Yes, why did you?' repeated May. She leaned over and peered at Hugh fiercely, her beady little black eyes sparkling suspiciously.

'Nancy rang and asked me for a lift down from London,' lied Hugh glibly.

May wasn't so easily satisfied. She fired the next question before Hugh had a chance to draw breath. 'How come you know her?'

'Nancy's a client of Ben Rose, a lawyer friend of mine. He knows Diana. I told him Diana's sister had died, and knowing Nancy was her cousin he told her. Once she knew, it was only natural that she should wish to come and pay her last respects. As she doesn't drive,

171

she rang and asked for a lift. I could hardly refuse, could I?'

May seemed convinced, for she relaxed her probing stare and sat back in her chair. 'No, I suppose you couldn't. Strange though that she should want to come. She hasn't been back since . . .'

'Since when?' asked Hugh.

'Since she left,' snapped May, suddenly irritable again.

From across the other side of the room Hugh saw Nancy raise her dark eyebrows expressively, and knew what she was thinking. She was as bored as he was. However, that didn't stop her putting on a convincing show of cousinly sorrow. But Aunt May was the object of Nancy's real devotion. As she'd told him before they'd left London. 'Great aunt May must be worth quite a bit, and it can't be long before she's pushing up the daisies. If I play my cards right, she's bound to leave something to me. Diana and I are her nearest relatives.'

Diana, sitting next to Hugh, hadn't heard any of the conversation. Her thoughts were still in the abbey churchyard. Had she done the right thing in allowing the children to go? Tony had said yes, grief was natural and had to be expended. But she had her doubts. They were calm, too calm. In the abbey and at the graveside, the three children stood silently, hand in hand. They were so young, and yet to Diana's eyes they looked like old people. The shroud of grief and bewilderment had drained away their youth, and they'd become colourless, indistinct and old. Diana watched them with a helplessness tinged with anger at her own impotence. Even now, when she really wanted to help, she couldn't. They didn't want her. They hadn't said so; in fact they had been scrupulously polite, and everyone else had told her how much she was needed, but Diana knew differently. Susan's children had bonded themselves together in mourning, pulling their sorrow around them like a cloak, effectively excluding her.

Everyone from Mottisley and the surrounding villages attended Susan's funeral. It had never occurred to Diana before how well known and well liked Susan had been. The abbey overflowed with people, and the masses of spring flowers, sent as tributes, filled the air with a heady mixture of fresh and delicate fragrance. The abbey churchyard looked beautiful in the brilliant April sunshine, the spring grass sprinkled with daisies, the lichen blooming yellow and orange on the tombstones of ancient, long forgotten graves. It was a perfect spring day. People Diana didn't know came and offered their condolences and spoke in praise of Susan. Joe's parents, the Kellys, were there, his father sober for once, and with them April and Joe. Dr Evans and, of course, Tony Evans. The Reverend Pincher took the service, and Tony gave a short, but very moving, account of Susan's life, and why she had meant so much to everyone who knew her.

But now all that was over. Susan was lying beside Tom, her husband, in the silent, sunlit churchyard, and the family were awaiting the arrival of her solicitor.

Hugh caught Bert looking at him again. There was something alarming about the old man's gaze, as if he pierced straight through Hugh's hypocrisy and could see him for what he really was. Which of course was ridiculous. But the old man had him rattled, and to salve his conscience he reached out and took Diana's hand in an ostentatious show of solicitude.

Diana responded gratefully, turning towards him and smiling. Soon, she thought, this will be over and I'll know what I have to do. Maybe there will be nothing I need do. Maybe Susan, knowing she could die at any time, has already made watertight provisions for the children. The thought cheered her. Almost certainly Susan would have done that, and that was why she'd never told her about her illness. She suddenly felt an enormous sense of relief. Once Mr Grimble had read the will, she'd be able to go back to London with a clear conscience, and forget about all of the disturbing interlude at Mottisley. She could get on with the life she had chosen, her life with Hugh, and Wycombe and Yatton.

The faint hum of conversation died away as Mr Grimble entered. Putting on his half-moon spectacles he began to read.

His voice droned on. Like the hum of an elderly bumble bee, thought Diana. Heavens, I feel tired. What a week this has been. Still, nearly over now. 'I, Susan Jane Wentworth, being of sound mind . . .' all the usual formal words that preceded the nub of a will. Her thoughts drifted away. The buds of the rhododendron bush outside the window were hugely fat, some almost open. Vivid slashes of pink showing, where in a day or two there would be an exotic bloom. They were early this year, maybe that meant a good summer.

Her attention was drawn back into the room at the mention of her name. 'To my sister, Diana Stratton, I leave all my worldly goods and chattels, Abbey House, and the business known as Abbey Vineyard and all the assets that go with it.'

A faint hiss echoed around the room. The intake of a dozen breaths as the import of the words sank into everyone's consciousness.

'All to you,' whispered Hugh. He sounded pleased. 'Should amount to a tidy sum.'

Diana turned and stared at him. Surely he realized she couldn't possibly take it? 'But I don't want it. Why did she leave it to me? What about the children?'

Mr Grimble cleared his throat noisily and frowned in their direction. 'I have not finished,' he said sternly. 'There is a codicil written in Susan's own hand.' He cleared his throat again, then continued. 'I have willed everything to you, Diana, because I love you and would have trusted you with my life. Even though as you hear these words, my life will be ended, there are other lives more important to me than my own. Those of my children; Clementina, Simon and Timothy. I appoint you, Diana, their legal guardian and entrust their health, welfare and happiness to you. I know that you will use the inheritance for their benefit, and will ensure that they grow up in a happy and secure environment so that one day they will take their place in the world as responsible, well-balanced adults. I realize that this will be a heavy burden, but I know you have the strength and determination to do it, Diana. But more than that, I know that you will keep the promise you made to me to care for the children should anything ever happen to me. If things should ever get difficult, which I pray they will not, I ask you to remember the words of the poet John Donne.

> All other things, to their destruction draw,
> Only our love hath no decay;
> This, no to-morrow hath, nor yesterday,
> Running it never runs from us away,
> But truly keeps his first, last, everlasting day.

There was a hush as Mr Grimble folded the will and slowly removed his spectacles.

'Are you sure your sister wasn't mad?' said Hugh. 'Fancy putting a poem into a will.'

Diana didn't answer. Susan's codicil made her feel very humble, it also made her feel very close to Susan. Mr Grimble came across and handed her the will. 'Quite a responsibility you've been handed, young lady,' he said.

'And one she could do without,' Hugh was already foreseeing difficulties. 'We have our own lives to lead. We don't need the encumbrance of children.'

'They won't be an encumbrance, Hugh.' Diana turned towards him. 'And I did promise Susan to care for them, just as she said. And I shall keep that promise.'

'Let's hope it doesn't take up too much of your time.'

Diana smiled, Susan's words rang in her ears. Suddenly she felt confident, sure that she could manage everything with her hands tied behind her back. 'It won't. All it means is that our family has increased rather suddenly.'

'Your family,' said Hugh, 'not mine.' He went across to the sideboard and poured himself a large whisky.

'Some inheritance,' whispered Nancy. 'If Susan had left

175

everything to me, I'd put the kids in an orphanage, sell up and keep the money.'

'Just as well she didn't then,' said April, overhearing Nancy's remark. 'Poor little sods wouldn't stand much of a chance with you as a foster mother.'

'I'm not sure Diana will be all that good at it,' said Hugh. 'Personally I think Susan must have been a bit strange. Surely she could have thought of a better solution.'

'Well, I think it's marvellous,' said May, joining the party at the sideboard. 'Hugh, pour me out a whisky, will you? A large one. None of your half measures.'

'Terribly sad about Susan, Aunt May,' said Nancy piously.

May's black eyes swivelled round and looked Nancy up and down. 'Sad, yes,' she said, taking the whisky from Hugh, 'but suddenly I feel much happier. I know now that everything is going to be all right.'

April made her way over to Diana who was still standing in the same place, her thoughts with Susan. 'Susan must have loved you an awful lot,' she said. 'If I had kids, I'd be very wary about who I'd entrust them to.'

'Yes, I suppose she did. I only hope I won't disappoint her.'

'You won't,' said April. She put an arm around Diana's shoulders. 'If you need any help, never be afraid to ask me. I love those kids too, you know. I'd like to think that I could do something. Now, would you like a drink.'

Diana suddenly shivered. The euphoria of hearing Susan's words written especially for her, suddenly began to wear off. In the place of the euphoria was a nagging worry. What the hell should she do? Would she really cope as easily as she had so blithely told Hugh she would?

'I'd like a large brandy,' she said.

Chapter Thirteen

'I'm walking over to Abbey House to give Diana a hand,' said Nancy.

May's bright little eyes skimmed over the glamorous creature before her. Both she and Bert had been suspicious of Nancy's arrival with Hugh for Susan's funeral. The explanations they'd both given had been a little too pat to ring entirely true. Always relying on her instinctive gut reaction, May concluded that Nancy was either having, or wanted to have, an affair with Hugh.

'Stay with us, my dear,' she'd said as soon as the reading of the will was complete. 'It will be company for us, and for Diana too now that she has to stay on at Mottisley for a while.'

May didn't like Hugh, but he was Diana's husband. Therefore, she had no intention of allowing Nancy unlimited access to Hugh while Diana was detained in Mottisley.

Nancy, surprised and flattered at the invitation to stay had accepted. 'It's a marvellous opportunity to show May what a wonderful niece I am,' she'd whispered to Hugh when he'd complained that he didn't mind leaving Diana, but he did mind leaving her. 'And I can find out what she's worth at the same time.'

Now, after three weeks, Nancy was beginning to feel very restless. She'd had her fill of cows, horses and outside lavatories, and the strain of playing the permanently sweet-natured niece was beginning to tell.

'I dare say Diana could do with a hand,' said May. 'She's got Ronald Pugh and old Isaac Skelton going over to spray the vines for her today.'

'Rumour has it she's going to sell, so why is she

177

bothering to do that?' In spite of her ostentatious show of concern, and frequent visits to Abbey House, Nancy hadn't bothered to enquire too deeply into Diana's problems.

'If she neglects the vineyard now, she'll not get a good price if she does sell.' May sniffed disparagingly at Nancy's ignorance.

'Let's hope, for her sake, that she sells it soon,' said Nancy, hoping nothing of the sort. Once back in London, she would much prefer to have Diana safely tucked away down in Mottisley. Hugh would then be available whenever she wanted him, and after three weeks of celibacy Nancy was impatient.

'Yes,' snapped May, who also didn't want Diana to sell, although for entirely different reasons.

She wished she was young enough to run the vineyard and look after the children herself. Old age, what a curse it was. Knowing your time is measured; not being able to plan long term. It was no use making a fuss. Diana would see the children through to adulthood, and by that time she would be long dead and buried. And if I'm not, she thought, ever the realist, I'll be no damned use to man nor beast!

If only Diana could find it in her heart really to care. Then she would finance the running of the vineyard herself; Susan had been naive to imagine that Diana would stay permanently in Mottisley. But May fervently believed that if only Diana could be persuaded to put her own money into it, then she would remain part of Abbey House, part of the children's lives, even though the links would be financial not love. But May was also an optimist, and believed that love could grow in the most unexpected circumstances, provided there was a bond, however tenuous.

May's bright eyes, half hidden when she dropped her wrinkled eyelids, watched Nancy. She well remembered the precocious dark haired child and all the trouble she'd caused. The child had grown into a beautiful woman, no doubt about that. But after observing her for three weeks May decided that Nancy was vain and shallow, and completely self-centred. She worried, ought she to tell Diana about Nancy? Warn her in some way?

Blissfully unaware of May's doubts about her, Nancy gave her the benefit of her sweetest smile. 'See you later then. Any messages for Diana?'

'No.' May turned abruptly and went inside Willow Farm. What was Nancy up to now? 'Don't trust that Nancy as far as I could throw her,' she said to Bert, who'd come in for his second breakfast after milking the cows, and moving the bullocks from the top field.

Bert snorted through a mouthful of egg and bacon. 'Sly as a fox, that one,' he pronounced.

Once certain that May was safely inside the house, Nancy set off down the lane away from Willow Farm. It was much quicker to walk across the fields to Abbey House, but the one and only public telephone was in the square at Mottisley, and she wanted to ring Hugh without being overheard.

The telephone in Hugh's office rang. It was Nancy.

'For God's sake come down this weekend and take me back to London,' she said, getting straight to the point. 'Please, before I go stark raving mad.'

'You're not the only one going raving mad, but I can't just come down and get you. What the hell will Diana think?'

'Get Ben Rose to ring Willow Farm and leave a message for me. Tell him to say it's imperative I return on Saturday. Something to do with evidence for my divorce, anything will do. You can think of a reason. And then later, you ring Diana and tell her you're coming down for the weekend.'

'Great idea. Yes, yes, don't worry I'll think of something.' And he would, the thought of Nancy had incredible power to fire his imagination. 'I'll come down on Friday night, and we can leave on Saturday.'

179

'What are you going to tell Diana?'

'Don't you worry about that. I'll keep Diana happy Friday night, then you must come and beg me to take you back to London on Saturday. Between us we should be able to convince her.'

'I can't wait until Saturday,' Nancy's laugh echoed down the 'phone, wicked and maliciously provoking.

'You must,' said Hugh, afraid that she'd turn up at Abbey House as soon as he arrived. 'I've got to have some time with Diana alone.'

And I must make Diana happy thought Hugh. But more than that, he knew he had to get her back to London soon. The bonus for the jungle theme park, which had at one point seemed so tantalizingly near, had now receded into the distance. Alan Sinclair had put the scheme temporarily on ice until Diana returned. In the meantime Hugh, who'd rather rashly paid Nico all his dues from their joint back account, was now worried that Diana might notice the depletion in the balance. In future he'd have to raid the petty cash once a month and ask Nico for credit again, until she got another bonus. At the moment the cash box was empty, and would remain that way until the Firm's accountant sent down a cheque to be cashed at the end of the month. Bloody Miss Higgins with her scrupulous attention to detail, he'd almost had to physically prise her away, from the damned box. But now, as he talked to Nancy, he could feel the key to the locked bottom drawer of his desk sticking into his leg from within his trouser pocket. It was a comforting feeling. At least Miss Higgins couldn't get her hands on it while it remained there.

'Hell! if only you knew how much I long to get back to civilization,' grumbled Nancy. Opposite the 'phone box she could see Griselda Morgan, clad in a plastic mackintosh, ankle socks and open toed sandals in spite of the fact that the sun was shining and it was quite hot. She dismounted her bicycle and entered the Newsagents and General Store. 'This place is full of weirdos,' Nancy said. 'And I'd better go before one of them wonders why I'm in the 'phone box.'

Hugh laughed. 'Don't worry about them, you'll soon be back with me. And I'm very normal.'

'Well not *too* normal I hope,' came the sharp reply. 'I couldn't stand the boredom.'

After supper one evening Diana went over to Willow Farm to tell May what she had finally decided. She knew the news would not be well received, but in her opinion there was no viable alternative. She sat down in May's cluttered kitchen, in front of the open grated kitchen range where the hot coals glowed bright orange. May kept it burning day and night, winter and summer.

'Where are the children?' May asked.

'With Nancy. I asked her to stay while I came over as it's Griselda's night off for choir practice in the abbey.'

'Huh! She *has* got some uses then,' said May bad-temperedly. She knew very well why Diana had come, Griselda had dropped in on her way to choir practice and told her.

'Yes she has. I don't know why you're so against her. Especially as you asked her to stay.' Diana had found Nancy's company a welcome relief from Griselda's permanently disgruntled demeanour. She also served as a reminder of the more sophisticated world outside of Mottisley. The world to which Diana hoped she would be returning soon.

May put a large black kettle on top of the hot coals. 'Cup of tea?'

'Yes please.' Diana fended off Buggins who'd clopped into the kitchen, and was now trying to get his huge velvety nose into her pockets. 'May, for God's sake, tell him I haven't got any sweets, and get rid of him. We've got some serious talking to do.'

Smacking the horse soundly on the rump May bellowed 'Bert! Settle Buggins down for the night will you? Give him some oats and shut the stable door once he's in.'

181

Bert's voice echoed in answer across the stable yard and Buggins clattered off in happy anticipation of his evening feed.

May sat down in her favourite chair by the side of the range, and gave Diana her full attention. 'Well?' she said.

Diana took a deep breath. Ever since the bombshell of Susan's will she had known that sooner or later she would have to make a final decision. Having made it, she'd chosen to tell May first.

'Susan's will gave me sole guardianship of the children, and also left to me the entire estate and Abbey House,' she began.

'I know that,' interrupted May impatiently.

'Now that I have had time to assess Susan's legacy, I realize that she did the only thing possible,' said Diana cautiously. I must approach this carefully, she thought. Prepare May gently for the changes that are about to occur. 'Susan left very little money, only a few hundred pounds in the bank. The rest of her estate is Abbey House and the vineyard, the winery, the machinery which is pretty dilapidated, and the tithe barn full of assorted agricultural machinery, half of which probably doesn't work.' Diana paused. 'How she survived I'll never know.'

'With a lot of help from her friends,' said May. 'Although she always managed her money very well.'

Diana ignored May's interruption. 'I've thought long and hard about this and believe me, May, my decision has not been made lightly. I've decided to sell Abbey House, the vineyard and winery as a going concern. With luck some fool keen to get back to nature and lead the so-called good life will buy it for a reasonable price. The tithe barn will be sold separately, I've already applied for planning permission for a change of use. When granted, as I'm assured it will be, it can be sold as a barn for conversion into a house. Someone from the City will pay a mint for an eleventh-century tithe barn.'

'Where will the children live?'

'I shall invest the money from the sale of the estate,

and it will be used for their keep. In term time the children will go to boarding school, and in the holidays they can stay with you if you want, or I shall make other arrangements.'

'What other arrangements?' asked May suspiciously.

'I'm not sure,' said Diana truthfully, who'd been thinking in terms of short-term fostering for the holidays, maybe even with Griselda who had a small house in the village. 'It all depends on how much money I can realize from the sale of Susan's assets.'

'Do you have to sell? Couldn't you stay here and commute to London? Griselda could stay on as housekeeper and then the children needn't be uprooted.'

Diana shuddered. It was difficult to imagine a more ghastly scenario. Living in the country, children under her feet every day of the year and Griselda as housekeeper. Hugh would go mad, and so would I, she thought. But reminding herself that May was only trying to be helpful, she merely said, 'it would be too exhausting to commute every day.'

'Mr Black does,' May growled stubbornly. 'And *he* lives in Mottisley, in the white-pantiled cottage opposite the abbey.'

'Neither Hugh nor I have any intention of commuting,' said Diana firmly. There was no point in May hoping for miracles, she couldn't, wouldn't stay, and May must understand that.

May tried another approach. 'All right, pay for Griselda to look after the house and children on a permanent basis, and get someone in to run the vineyard. You can't just sell it.'

Diana bit back the temptation to be irritable at the old lady's stubbornness, and tried to speak calmly. 'There is no alternative, May, believe me. There isn't even enough money in the bank to pay the outstanding bills as it is. I'll have to settle those, but I cannot afford to pay for a housekeeper and a viticulturist as well. A vineyard isn't just any old farm, it needs specialist knowledge.'

'Susan taught herself.'

'I won't be here, and anyway, I'm not Susan.'

'I know that,' said May, her tone of voice leaving Diana in no doubt that she came a very poor second to Susan. 'But you could afford to pay someone to run Abbey House and the vineyard. Everyone knows how much money you earn. Joe showed me a report in one of those fancy London papers. You're a rich woman.'

'Bloody Joe, trust him to interfere.' Diana's temper began to rise, but taking a deep breath she resolved to keep calm, no matter what. 'May, please understand this. I am not so rich that I can afford to waste money on what I consider a useless venture. At best the vineyard will only ever break even, and that's not good enough. I'd be permanently out of pocket on that, plus I'd have the expense of running Abbey House and supporting the children.'

'You could afford it,' said May, doggedly sticking to her side of the argument. 'You're being selfish.'

Bert clumped into the kitchen, his big farm boots leaving a trail of mud from the back door to the chair where he sat himself down. He regarded Diana passively from beneath his flat cap, as he reached up for his tobacco jar. *You're being selfish*, the words echoed in Diana's head making her dizzy with sudden anger. Bert's chair and tobacco jar were the straws that broke Diana's resolve not to lose her temper.

'How can you sit there and tell me what *I* can afford, when this whole house is stuffed full of priceless antiques.' She pointed at Bert's chair. 'Do you know that is a Charles II giltwood carved armchair and worth at least three and a half thousand pounds.' Bert looked down at the chair with an alarmed expression. 'And that tobacco jar he uses every day, is a Louis XV ormolu-mounted tortoiseshell casket, which would fetch another three thousand at auction.' Bert clutched the tobacco jar possessively to his chest as if Diana were about to snatch it away and sell it at that very moment. 'If you sold just half your possessions, most of which you don't need, you'd be able to run Abbey House and support the children for some considerable time to come.'

It was tantamount to waving a red rag at a bull. May, like the rest of her family before her, had always hoarded as if her life depended on it. It was almost a form of religion, and not something to be tampered with.

'I'll not sell a stick of furniture from this house,' said May, her eyes glittering jet black with anger. 'Everything has been here since the day it was bought and there have been Marshams at Willow Farm since 1741.' She drew herself up to her full minuscule height, and thumped her chest dramatically. 'And while there is breath in my body no-one is going to touch any of it.'

'All right, don't sell the furniture,' said Diana in exasperation. 'But since you are so keen for me to dip into my bank account, how about dipping into yours. Everyone knows that your grandfather made a fortune in South African gold at the turn of the century, and what is more, everyone knows that it has never been touched. It just sits in the bank, growing bigger every day.'

'That is my private affair,' shrieked May outraged.

'And so is *my* money,' shouted Diana.

'But Susan left *you* in charge of the children, not me. And Susan never asked me for money.'

Diana stood up and made for the kitchen door. Where is my self control? she thought in panic. What am I doing fighting with May about money? The sooner I can cut myself loose from all this the better. She felt suffocated, everything was closing in on her, the village, the family, children; everything she had striven to escape from. The bloody children!

'I intend to do what I think is best for the children in the long term, and you will have to accept it. Just as you must accept that I have another life, away from here. I'm sorry, May, but that's my last word on the subject.'

Once back at Abbey House Diana got the whisky from the cupboard and poured herself and Nancy an enormous

185

glassful each. For once in her life she felt a real kind of kinship with Nancy. They both hated the country.

'I only stayed because May asked me and I didn't have an adequate excuse to say no,' said Nancy. 'Besides I didn't want to hurt the old girl's feelings. But as soon as things start moving in my divorce case I'll be leaving.'

'And I'll be leaving as soon as I get this financial mess sorted out,' said Diana grimly.

Griselda, coming in from choir practice, oozed disapproval from every pore as soon as she saw the whisky bottle. 'No thank you,' she said primly, refusing Diana's offer of whisky. 'I'm going to bed.'

'I don't think she likes you,' observed Nancy.

'*Nobody* likes me,' said Diana. She emptied the rest of the whisky bottle into her glass. 'But to hell with the whole bloody lot of them.'

The next day Diana followed Isaac Skelton and Ronald Pugh into the tithe barn. They'd come in answer to her request for help and had stood in the kitchen politely doffing their caps, but managing at the same time to make her very aware of the fact that they disapproved of her. Because I'm selling up, I suppose, thought Diana, and felt annoyed. It was none of their business. She'd forgotten during her years in London, that the inhabitants of Mottisley thought everything *was* their business.

Well, they're not dealing with a country girl now, thought Diana, as she followed them. Even their damned backs managed to look surly! If Susan could run this place, then I certainly can. And until I've sold it, this place is going to be transformed into a model of efficiency.

She cleared her throat. Sounding confident and knowledgeable should put them in their place. After all, she was *paying* them, they weren't doing her a favour. Hastily consulting Susan's wine diary which, after searching through the whole house, she'd eventually found under a pile of socks waiting to be darned, she said, 'I understand that in mid April, during bud burst, the vines should be sprayed with mancozeb. And that is what I'd like you to do this morning.'

Her tone of voice would have made anyone in the office of Wycombe and Yatton jump to attention, but the effect it had on the two men was so minimal, Diana began to wonder if they were both stone deaf.

Eventually Isaac Skelton answered. ' 'Tis beginning of May,' he said morosely.

Both men stood and stared at her blankly. Diana stared back. She could hear May saying, 'you'll not find a better pair than those two. Could never do enough for Susan.'

'Well, you know what they say. Better late than never,' said Diana, determined to remain cheerful in the face of their taciturn approach to aiding her. If this was being helpful, what the hell were they like when they were unhelpful? But she held her tongue. This was not the time to lose her temper, not when she needed their assistance.

Ronald Pugh ambled over to the back of the barn. 'Do you know why you're doing it?' he asked filling up a large tank from a container he'd unearthed.

'Unfortunately I'm not an expert on viticulture. I only know what it says here.' Diana consulted the book again. 'It's apparently to prevent dead arm disease.'

'Huh! Should have been done two weeks ago.' He signalled to Isaac and the two men hitched the now full tank on to the back of the tractor.

'Are you telling me it's too late then?' Diana hid her impatience with difficulty.

Isaac Skelton started up the tractor. 'Happen it is.' He looked gloomier than ever.

Ronald Pugh put on a protective hat, mask and thick gloves, before climbing up on to the rear of the tractor above the tank, and picking up the spray. 'And happen it isn't,' he said.

Diana watched them drive out of the barn. Bloody men! It's not my fault I'm not Susan, and it's not my fault I know nothing about viticulture. Why the hell couldn't they have come and reminded me? She struggled to close the big double doors of the barn, ending up with splinters in the palm of her hand and a grazed thumb. This place needs an army of helpers she thought bad-temperedly, not two reluctant old men putting in a few hours work and the services of a half blind ex-piano teacher. If Griselda had darned the socks, she would have found the wine book earlier and got the spraying done on time.

She turned and looked at the vineyard. The hazel hedge which bounded one side of it was awash with sunshine. Catkins hung in yellow profusion, dancing every now and then with the passing breeze blowing up from the far distant sea. There was no chill to the air this morning, the southerly breeze was warm and balmy, a perfect spring morning. Diana walked down to sit on the ancient rustic bench, set against the hedge, halfway down the slope. She had to think. It was all very well May and Bert telling her she ought not sell Abbey House and the vineyard, but it wasn't their problem, neither were the children.

Oh Susan, I am doing my best, but I wish you were here to help me. The silent cry went unanswered, and a kaleidoscope of thoughts swept through Diana's mind. Shifting, moving thoughts, never settling into a clearly defined pattern. She wondered if Susan had had any idea of the difficulties the legacy would cause. Probably not, Susan had always seemed to manage her life incredibly well. But that was the main problem, it *was* the remnants of Susan's life she was trying to sort out, and she wasn't Susan. She was Diana Stratton and she was in danger of being wrenched in two. Her life with Hugh tugging her in one direction, and the relentless pull of the ties of Mottisley tugging her in the other.

The beauty of the bellying sails of white clouds scudding across a cerulean morning sky, and the delicate perfume from the late primroses and violets, still nestling in sheltered hollows of the hedge, passed unnoticed by Diana.

Although she tried to keep it at bay, the acrimonious

conversation she'd had with May the night before intruded, blotting out everything else.

Griselda's thin reedy voice jerked her back into the present. She was calling from the kitchen door. ' 'Phone call for you, Diana.'

Hurrying up the slope towards the house, Diana told herself there was no point in re-running the unpleasant scenes of the previous night. That would achieve precisely nothing. Of course she and May would patch up their quarrel. They had to. For the children's sake it was important not to be bad friends. For the children's sake! She still felt resentful. All the trouble she'd taken not to have a family herself, and now she was lumbered with someone else's. Susan's, her conscience reminded her. Your own flesh and blood. Not just *anyone's*.

Reaching the top of the slope, she cheered up. The Planning Officer had promised to ring her about the tithe barn this morning. Perhaps it was good news. Hurrying into the hall she picked up the 'phone. But it wasn't the Planning Officer. It was Hugh.

'Darling, do you think you could put up with me this weekend?'

'Put up with you?' Suddenly she noticed the sunshine flooding the countryside outside, and spilling over into the house. 'If only you knew how much I miss you.'

'I'll be down early on Friday night,' said Hugh.

Diana laughed with sheer happiness. 'I'll put a hot water bottle your side of the bed.'

'Don't bother. We'll generate quite enough heat on our own. Any chance of getting rid of the kids for a few hours?'

'I'll think of something,' Diana promised. 'I want you all to myself.'

'Just us here? I can't believe my good luck.'

Diana slid her arms around Hugh's neck. 'Just us,' she whispered. 'I've packed Griselda and the kids off to the cinema in Chichester.'

189

Dumping his bags in the middle of the kitchen Hugh carried her upstairs. 'I can't tell you how much I've longed for this moment.' His mouth kissed each part of her body as he gently undressed her.

'I feel just like I did the first time we made love,' exclaimed Diana in delight as his hands began to work magic on her body. Her arms across his broad back held him close. They were together, she loved him, that was all that mattered. Everything would be all right, no need to worry about Mottisley.

Then Mottisley was forgotten as Hugh's fingers became more urgent. Reaching down she drew the pulsing shaft of him into her, and let her body take control, all conscious thought held at bay by the surging tide of explosive pleasure.

'That was wonderful.' Hugh kissed her and reached for his cigarettes. The lighter flared, illuminating his face.

'Perfect,' said Diana. They'd made love just the way she liked it, slow and gentle, and now she lay contented in the crook of his arm. From Hugh's point of view it was a physical release, the mere prelude of better things to come with Nancy. But for Diana it was utter bliss. For the first time since the day of Susan's funeral she felt relaxed. With Hugh she knew who she was, he was part of *her* world, the world she belonged to; not the unfriendly world of Mottisley where she could never put a foot right, and where everyone continually compared her with Susan.

'You know it's strange,' she told Hugh, glad to be able to talk to someone, 'I'd always thought Susan mismanaged her life. But here, in Mottisley, she's held up as a paragon of virtue. And she certainly ran this place better than I'm doing at the moment.'

'No comparison,' said Hugh. 'You are completely different.'

'You're right. I'm just not a family person.'

Her sister's laughing face flashed before her inward eye. I promised I'd do my best and I am, Diana thought. I mustn't think about Susan.

'What time are the monsters due back?'

'Late. I gave Griselda the money to take them to McDonald's after the film. And they're not really monsters. They're frightened, upset children, whose parents are dead, and whose world is being turned upside down by me. I've told them that everything is to be sold, and that they are to go to boarding schools.' She paused remembering the moment. 'The awful thing was they didn't say a single word.'

'Thank God you've finally made up your mind,' said Hugh. 'I was beginning to think you'd never come home.'

'With any luck I'll be back in London permanently within a week. I've advertised for a viticulturist to take over the vineyard temporarily, until the place is sold, and Griselda has agreed to stay on as long as she's needed. And I've made appointments to view two boarding schools next Monday.'

'This sounds more like the old Diana,' said Hugh giving her a squeeze. 'Getting everything organized, telling people what they're going to do, not asking them.'

Hugh took another draw on his cigarette, and said casually, 'Anything else happened? Have you seen much of Nancy?'

'Quite a bit. It's strange, but I don't mind her so much now. I suppose it's because we've both grown up. She comes over most days for a bath. Willow Farm has only one modern amenity, the telephone. I think Nancy is fed up with the outside loo and cold washing water.'

'Why on earth doesn't she leave then?'

'She's going to. As soon as she hears from Ben Rose.'

Hugh smiled at the ceiling. He hadn't wasted time asking Ben Rose to do him a favour, instead he'd told Miss Higgins to call Willow Farm and relay a fictional message from Ben. 'Let's hope for Nancy's sake that he makes that call soon,' he said. Stubbing out his cigarette, he turned and drew Diana closer. 'Is there time before the kids come back?' he whispered.

Diana slid her arms around his neck. 'We've got hours

191

and hours tonight,' she said, 'and then there's tomorrow and the day after.'

'Darling, you don't mind me snaffling Hugh do you? It's absolutely imperative that I get up to Ben's office by twelve noon today. And you know what the train services are like on a Saturday. Absolutely hopeless.'

Behind Nancy's back, Hugh shrugged his shoulders apologetically. Nancy had put him in an impossible position, to have said no would have been downright churlish. Diana could see that, but it didn't stop her feeling annoyed. Their first weekend together for three weeks. Why couldn't Nancy have got a taxi? Angrily Diana watched her blithely throwing her handbag behind the passenger seat. Nancy hadn't changed much really, only superficially. She was just as selfish as ever, and Diana found herself feeling just as resentful as she had done as a child, when Nancy always managed to monopolize her father.

'You'll come back down once you've dropped off Nancy?'

'Well, darling, if I'm going back up to town, I might as well get on with the casework I ought to have been doing anyway. It's a terrible waste of time driving backwards and forwards. You know what the traffic is like.'

Diana heard an echo of herself from years gone by. How many times had she used that excuse. The traffic, a waste of time. A waste of time to make the effort to be with someone you loved.

'Yes, of course.'

Reaching out Hugh pulled her against him. 'Hey,' he whispered, making his voice pulse with tenderness. 'You told me last night that you'd be back in London within a week. I'm holding you to that. Promise me.' Kissing her gently he caressed her face with his fingers. 'Promise me,' he repeated.

Diana clung to him for a moment. How stupid, being jealous of Nancy. She was not a child now. It's this damned place. Once I get back to London and Hugh, all my troubles will be over. 'I promise,' she said, straightening her mouth in a determined line and letting Hugh go. 'Now get going, or Nancy will be late for her appointment.'

Griselda joined Diana in the doorway and watched Hugh's Porsche pull away down the drive towards the main road. Stretching out shyly, she touched Diana's sleeve. 'Shall I make a cup of coffee?'

Diana turned and looked at her. What a sight the woman looked. Her iron grey hair stuck out at all angles, looking as if it had been cut with a pair of blunt garden shears. Her shapeless skirt and jumper might have come from some jumble sale stall, and knowing Griselda, probably did; and on her feet were the perennial white ankle socks and sandals. All in all, she contrived to give the appearance of a scarecrow assembled in a hurry. But looking close, Diana saw concern in the pale, myopic eyes behind the thick glasses, and kindness in the nervous mouth. Why had she never seen it before? Because you never looked her conscience told her, you have only ever seen what you wanted.

'A coffee would be lovely. We'll make it together,' said Diana.

Following Griselda back into the house Diana put all doubts about Hugh from her mind. There was nothing to worry about. Why should there be? Nancy might be very attractive, but Hugh was her husband and he loved her. Trust was an essential element of marriage. Irrational jealousy could lead down treacherous paths.

Chapter Fourteen

'Mornin' Joe.' Albert Carter paused from cutting back the hazel in Winterbourne Thicket. 'Got some good shoots here, considerin' it's not been looked after right. Once I gets it in good order, the Manor will have plenty of hurdles for market every year. Make a tidy profit I shouldn't wonder.'

'Yes,' said Joe. 'Well done, Albert.'

Joe's opinion was that the sale of hurdles would probably never make enough money to cover what he paid Albert Carter. But it kept the man employed, retained his self respect, and enabled him to feed his family. Joe, once short of money, claimed government benefit, and the indignity of the system stuck in his gullet. Now, when he saw an opportunity of preventing someone else having to endure the same humiliation, he took it. The copse was badly overgrown, it needed thinning, Albert was doing a good job. A miracle could always happen, maybe in time it would pay for itself.

He looked around, remembering that this had been their secret place, his and Diana's. Which tree had been the meeting point? That oak over there? No, it was too large, too mature. But thirteen years ago it would have been younger, more slender. Just like me, thought Joe wryly. He wondered if Diana remembered the spot. Doubtful he decided, she would have ruthlessly erased it from her memory along with everything else she disliked about Mottisley.

Diana, the object of his visit to Abbey House. He thought of his first reaction when May told him the news that Diana was putting everything up for sale, it was one of fury. But both Tony and April had made him see that she had no choice. The children had to be cared for and educated, and that took money. Diana had a husband and job in London, and it was unrealistic of May to expect Diana to keep things as they were and subsidize it from her own purse. She was doing the only thing possible in the circumstances. It was Tony who'd suggested that if Joe really wanted to help, he could buy the estate from Diana and make sure he paid enough to maintain the children and leave a bit over to be invested for their future.

His accountant thought it crazy. 'From what you've told me, Mr Kelly, it seems that sentiment for this family is ruling your head rather than business acumen. The amount you intend to offer is far too high, and what on earth are you going to do with another house and a vineyard?'

'You've always told me that land is a good investment,' Joe had said stubbornly.

'Only if it can be developed, Mr Kelly.' The accountant's voice droned on, dry and dusty. 'I've looked into it carefully, as carefully as I can in the short time you've given me. A time limit of two hours is really not the best way, but,' Mr West, Joe's accountant sighed, and continued, 'Abbey House and the land cannot be developed, it is in a clearly designated green belt area. Now if you were proposing to buy the land around Willow Farm, that would be a different matter altogether, as far as I can find out there is no bar to developing that as it's just outside the green belt zone.'

'Willow Farm is not for sale. Abbey House and the vineyard is.'

'And your proposed offer is too high, it won't be easy to sell it on.'

'Thank you for your advice,' said Joe, and Mr West knew he had no intention of taking it.

Now, Joe rehearsed what he would say to Diana. Businesslike and straight to the point, that's how he'd tackle her. She'd not refuse his offer. Only a fool would do that, and when it came to money Diana was no fool. She'd take the money, send the children away to boarding school, and leave Mottisley for good. Send the children away, that was a pity. He'd miss them. But he'd see them during the holidays when they came to visit May, and at least Diana would be gone.

Joe stopped walking and looked up the rise of the land towards Abbey House. From this point he could only see the ancient tiles of the roof glowing russet brown in the morning sun. Diana, what was it about her that disturbed him so? He was not attracted to her, far from it. The emotion he felt was confusing, a mixture of fascination and abhorrence, and somewhere beneath that he knew he felt pity. Why pity? Pity for himself or for her? Pity for what she'd become? He caught his breath with annoyance, this was being ridiculous. Such sentiments were unwarranted. Diana had got what she wanted out of life, and so had he.

He started walking again. Buy the bloody place and done with it, he told himself. Then Diana would leave, and this confusion would leave with her. He refused to let himself think how empty Mottisley would seem without Clemmy, Simon and Miffy. Reaching the bottom of the field, he slipped through a gap in the hedge and into the vineyard.

'What the hell are you kids doing?'

Three forlorn faces with dull, opaque eyes turned towards him. Joe was struck by the contrast before him. The children's cold, set expressions, contrasted sharply with the vibrant brilliance of the May sunshine, streaming like liquid gold up the rows of vines, lighting each gnarled branch with life. But there the life stopped. None of it spilled over on to the children. They stood before him, small, sad wraiths from another world.

'We're rubbing off the bottom buds, so that the grapes will be bigger.' Clemmy turned her back on Joe.

'We always used to help Mummy do it. But she's not here any more,' Miffy said breathlessly. The words fell out in a tumbling rush, and Joe knew he was desperately trying not to cry. It broke his heart.

'We're being sent away.'

'I know,' said Joe. Would it help if he told them he was as upset as they were, but could do nothing about it.

'I shall hate, *hate*, whoever buys all this,' Simon waved his arms encompassing the land and the house. 'It's our home,' he said fiercely. 'It belongs to us. Why did mummy leave it to that cow, Diana?'

'Because she thought it was the right thing to do I suppose,' said Joe, feeling very inadequate.

'Diana doesn't like us,' said Clemmy. 'We shall have to leave everyone. Aunt May, Bert, you; we won't even be here to put flowers on mummy and daddy's graves.' She was still facing away from him, but Joe could tell she was crying.

A sudden onslaught of black, ungovernable rage washed over him. The bloody unfairness of it all. They had suffered enough, why should they be uprooted from everything they loved as well? Diana had to be made to see that selling was the one option she *didn't* have. There had to be another way.

'Don't worry,' he heard himself saying. 'It will be all right. I promise.' One thing was certain, he couldn't possibly buy it. It would be a betrayal to Susan and the children. He couldn't add to their already heavy burden of grief, and more than that, he couldn't bear to think of them hating him. 'I promise,' he said again, and turning, started the climb towards Abbey House.

Be careful, be tactful, he told himself. This isn't going to be easy. I've got to persuade her that between us we can come up with some other solution, and whatever happens I mustn't lose my temper.

'You can't sell it. You just can't,' Joe roared. Griselda half expected to see the plates come crashing down from the Welsh dresser, such was the power of his voice.

'May has put you up to this, I know it.' Trembling with

197

anger at the unannounced interruption, Diana put down her coffee cup and stood up. She should have known her brief moment of peace and new-found companionship with Griselda couldn't last, that it would be shattered by someone.

Joe glowered. 'She did not. She doesn't even know I'm here.'

'In that case, get out then. Because it's none of your business.'

'But I promised the children you wouldn't sell. *I promised them*,' Joe shouted even louder.

Sam scuttled out of the kitchen into the peace outside, and Griselda jumped nervously, upsetting her coffee over the kitchen table. 'Oh dear, I'm terribly sorry, so clumsy of me.' She dabbed ineffectually at the puddle of coffee with a tea towel. 'Diana, shall I . . .' she stopped, realizing that neither of them had heard a word she'd said.

'You'd better follow me.' Diana led the way into the library. From the look on Joe's face it promised to be a stormy session. At least the library was relatively private. Slamming the door shut, she turned on him.

'I promised them,' he repeated before she had the chance to open her mouth.

Diana's voice was softly glacial. Joe could bellow and shout if he wanted, but she was *not* going to lose her temper as she had last night with May. No, this time she would remain calm, and in command, even though the fact that everyone seemed to think they could tell her what to do was driving her mad.

'Joe, may I point out to you that you are in no position to promise anything. I am the legal owner of the property, and the legal guardian of the children. The decision is for me to make, and I've made it.'

'Sod it. I know that,' growled Joe, trying to lower his voice a little. He knew shouting at Diana wasn't going to work. Why on earth couldn't he keep his temper when it mattered? Why had he let her cool dismissal when he'd first stepped into the kitchen goad him into a rage? They'd not even discussed the matter properly. 'I don't know why Susan didn't make *me* their guardian, then things would be different.'

'What, a man who's had two wives and God knows how many mistresses?' Outrage spurred Diana on cruelly to drive home the point. 'Susan knew what she was doing. You're probably HIV positive, you won't live long enough to be able to make a difference.'

Joe immediately forgot about keeping his voice down. 'I'm bloody well not. I've had a test to prove it.'

'The fact that you even needed a test speaks volumes,' said Diana acidly.

'What have those poor kids done to deserve a bitch like you?' Joe was beside himself with rage, how dare she slander him, or was it libel? he couldn't remember. 'You're a cold-blooded cow,' he said, eyeing her nastily. 'You don't give a bloody tinker's cuss for anyone. Never have and never will.' Seeing Joe's expression, Diana moved behind the desk and sat down, feeling it prudent to put something solid between herself and the man towering opposite her. 'What I want to know,' said Joe, leaning across the desk, 'is what difference does my past make? I love those kids, dammit, that's what counts.' He thumped the desk with a clenched fist. 'I love them,' he bellowed.

'I heard you the first time. I'm not deaf. You love them.'

'Yes, I do, and you don't.' Diana opened her mouth to protest but Joe didn't give her the chance to speak. 'And you didn't love Susan either. I thought you did, but I was wrong, because if you had any feelings at all you couldn't possibly sell up so soon after Susan's death. Can't you see that the children need at least a year in their own surroundings so that they can come to terms with their mother's death. And this year's harvest would be a fitting memorial for Susan. Keep the vineyard, it was so important to her and she worked so hard. It's the very least you can do.'

His words touched a raw strand of memory. Her own

voice saying '*I'd be hurt and disappointed if you didn't save me for the important things in life.*' *Her* promise, *her* vow to do her best. And I am, and I will, if only people will let me get on with it and stop interfering. Diana stared at Joe. She didn't mean to say it, but some evil gremlin drove her on, and the words were out before she could stop them. 'In view of all this love and admiration you profess, I'm surprised you didn't marry Susan. Then Clemmy, Simon and Miffy would have been your step-children, and you could have done just as you liked.'

Joe turned away and looked out of the window. 'I did ask her,' he said, his voice suddenly quiet, 'but she wouldn't have me.'

His answer was a bombshell, stunning Diana into momentary silence. She looked at him, partially turned away so that she had profile view of him. He'd grown into a great big bear of a man, still athletic looking, but bigger and stronger than when she'd imagined herself in love with him. More battered too. His profile made her realize just how badly his nose must have been broken at some time. But, against her will, Diana had to admit that he was still attractive. Attractive and a millionaire and he'd asked her sister to marry him. Suddenly, without warning, Diana was swamped with irrational jealousy. She'd always regarded Joe as part of *her* past, it was unsettling to discover that he was part of Susan's past as well. Shock sharpened an icy edge to her tongue.

'My sister had more sense than I thought. I'm not surprised she turned you down. You're not good enough for her.'

Joe swung round to face Diana. 'Still on the same tack,' he snapped angrily. 'Measuring everything and everybody and finding them wanting by your standards. Well, let me tell you something Diana Stratton, you don't come out very well when the measure is applied to you.'

'What's that supposed to mean?'

'I'll explain. It means that you are a superficial, empty shell, with not a thought in your head except how to add two and two together and preferably make it come to five. Acquisition and position mean more to you than people. And why? because you have no real feelings. A money-making robot, not a normal human being, that's what you are.'

The words hurt more than Joe knew. Was that how he really saw her? Did everyone see her like that? Unfeeling, uncaring, concerned only with her own needs. May had hinted at much the same thing, but it wasn't true, and worse, it was so damned unfair. Diana decided she'd had enough. There was no point in this conversation. Why should she let him stand there and insult her? Why couldn't he leave her alone to get on with what she had to do? Why couldn't they all leave her alone?

'Get out,' she said.

'Not until you tell me you'll not sell. Look, I'll even give you the bloody money to run the place if you're so damned mean you won't use your own.'

'I wouldn't take a penny from you, not even if I were starving.'

'Don't flatter yourself, I'm not offering the money for your benefit. I don't care a shit what happens to you. I only want to . . .'

Diana picked up the heavy glass paper weight from the desk and threw it. It missed Joe and smashed the mirror behind him. 'Get out,' she screamed, the last vestige of self control whizzing across the room with the paper weight. 'Get out, and mind your own bloody business.' Leaping up she wrenched open the library door. 'Go away, and stay away. Don't you dare come to Abbey House again.'

It was only when Sam came rushing in, tail wagging furiously, and leaped up at Joe, that Diana and Joe realized they had an audience. Squeezed into the narrow space by the coat rack in the hall were the three children and Griselda.

Without a word Joe rushed past them and out through the kitchen.

Left alone in the library Diana looked at the stony faces of Griselda and the children. How much had they overheard? Enough, obviously. By this afternoon everyone in Mottisley would be repeating an embellished, garbled version. But it would make no difference, she would not change her mind.

'Griselda,' she said imperiously.

'Yes,' eyes as big as organ stops, Griselda took a nervous step forward. Good God, thought Diana irritably, I'm not going to throw anything at you!

'Kindly get a dustpan and brush and clear up this mess.'

Griselda tiptoed over and looked at the pieces of the broken mirror scattered over the library floor. 'Oh dear,' she said gloomily. 'You know this means seven years bad luck.'

Chapter Fifteen

Nancy turned away from the bookshelf. 'Nothing exciting here. Not a single dirty book. All Diana's I suppose. She always was too clever by half.'

Hugh watched her. The long black hair was wet and shining, plastered to her body where she was still wet from the shower. A trail of water marked her progress around the apartment. 'Don't make too much mess, Diana will wonder what's been going on.'

'Jesus! now I have to worry about what Diana thinks. This is turning out to be a dull evening. No porno videos, no dirty books, and now you don't want me to drip on the floor. We should have stayed at my house as I wanted.'

'You know we couldn't. Diana is going to ring. I've got to be here.'

'Oh, Diana, Diana,' Nancy pouted, 'it makes me think you're not interested in me at all.' She flopped down beside Hugh on the huge leather settee. 'Oops! sorry.' Hugh dragged her up and threw a dry bath towel beneath her. 'I know, don't tell me, Diana might notice.'

'Exactly,' said Hugh. He felt exhausted. Perhaps having Nancy round to the apartment was not such a good idea. She was being bloody minded because he had insisted she come, and because he wouldn't take a snort until after Diana had 'phoned. He had to switch her mind on to something. Keep her occupied until after the 'phone call. 'Tell me what you found out at May's. Has she got pots of money?'

It worked. With a reminiscent giggle she sat up and clasped her naked knees to her lovely breasts. Hugh watched her in admiration as she told him of her three weeks at Willow Farm. 'Not pots of money, darling,' she said, 'but bloody great trunkfuls. Of real money I mean. May doesn't believe in banks, not for the farm money anyway. But gossip has it that she has a fortune invested in the bank anyway, which she never touches. So I snaffled a few hundred quid while I was there, seemed such a pity to leave it lying around. And then there's the house. No electricity, only oil lamps, no hot water, no inside loo, but crammed full of priceless antiques. All collected by May's ancestors. I must say they had exquisite taste.'

Hugh sighed enviously, thinking of all the money he owed Nico. 'Good God, next time I'll come with you. I could do with a few extra thousand.'

'She's my aunt,' said Nancy quickly, 'you can't steal from her.'

'But you can?'

'Of course.' She laughed. 'But tell you what. I'm going down again soon to catalogue and photograph some of those antiques for a valuation, and when I do, I might bring you back a little token. But only if you're nice to me.'

'I'm always nice.'

'I want you to be nice now.' Nancy undid his silk dressing gown, and slid her hand down in between his legs. 'Lovely balls,' she whispered, massaging them gently, 'nice and firm and just the right size.' She started kissing his stomach. 'I want us to be depraved,' she groaned.

'We already have,' said Hugh, extricating himself and doing up his dressing gown. 'It's no use, Nancy. I can't concentrate until after that damned 'phone rings.'

Nancy giggled. 'Is that why you've got your dressing gown on? Afraid that Diana might see you naked?' She started burrowing again, determined to arouse him.

The 'phone rang. 'Oh God. Stop it,' gasped Hugh. He kissed her roughly. 'Now, just let me get this 'phone call over and done with, then we'll be as depraved as you like. I promise.'

'Oh, goody, goody.' Nancy skipped across the room

like a naughty child. 'I'll get the coke now. Don't let her talk for too long.'

'Hello,' said Hugh, 'it *is* Diana,' he whispered, holding his hand over the mouthpiece.

'I shall be back at the end of the week,' said Diana.

'What, found a buyer already? Well done, that's good going.'

'No, I've made alternative arrangements. It might mean we have to pull in our horns a little, but at least it means I can come home to you, and get on with my real work again.'

Hugh gasped. Nancy was back and pulling aside his dressing gown, slid on top of him. The gyratory movement of her hips was making him lose concentration. He could feel an erection beginning, if he wasn't careful she'd make him come there and then. 'Oh, oh,' he gasped.

'There's no need to sound so shocked, darling,' said Diana. 'I only said pull in our horns a little.'

Hugh tried to concentrate, and clamped his free arm around Nancy to stop her moving. 'What do you mean? Pull in our horns?'

'What horns?' whispered Nancy, collapsing in a fit of giggles on his chest.

'What's that noise?' said Diana.

'The television,' lied Hugh, his brain working overtime. 'Some stupid comedy programme. When did you say you'll be back?'

'Friday night. I'll fill you in on the details when I arrive. 'Bye, darling.'

' 'Bye. Don't forget I love you,' said Hugh, putting down the 'phone with relief.

'What a hypocrite you are,' said Nancy.

'I'm not.' Hugh was indignant. 'I love Diana as much as I ever loved any woman, probably more. And I intend to stick with her, so don't you dare fuck it up for me.'

'Love!' Nancy laughed, 'you love her money. She keeps you in a style to which you've become accustomed. But don't worry, I won't fuck it up for you as long as you keep fucking me.' She grasped his penis and gave it a vicious twist.

Hugh choked. 'Bloody hell! Be careful, you nearly had it off.'

'Just what I intend to do, darling,' said Nancy, flicking him a small white packet. 'There you are, one for you, and today one for me as well. I want to feel white hot with lust.' She carefully poured the white powder on to the back of her hand. Dark eyes blazing, she looked at Hugh. 'I want to come, and come, and come,' she said, 'until I drop from exhaustion.'

Hugh had been about to say that they couldn't afford to keep snorting coke together. It was getting too expensive. But the reckless profligacy in Nancy's expression drove all coherent thoughts from his mind. He couldn't wait to snort and feel the ecstatic rush explode in his head and loins. Sex with Nancy after snorting was a uniquely debauched experience.

'I'll make you beg me to stop,' he said, sniffing two long hard sniffs through the funnel of rolled paper Nancy handed him.

She sniffed too. 'Never,' she whispered, eyes shining with a fierce unnatural light. 'Never.' Then hurling herself at him she ground her body against his, groaning and shuddering with orgasmic pleasure. Nancy had started without him.

The roar of a motor bike racing up Abbey House drive, cut like a swathe through the bird song, temporarily silencing their symphony to the coming of summer.

'It's May,' said Griselda unnecessarily. She wondered whether she ought to confess to Diana that she'd told May about the change of plans.

'It's Tuesday,' said Diana, looking up in surprise from her paper work at the kitchen table. 'I thought May and Bert always went to the cattle market on a Tuesday.'

'Not today,' said May, already in the kitchen by this time. 'I've come over to see if this rumour I've heard is true.' Taking off her crash helmet she put it down on the pile of papers Diana was working on.

Diana smiled mischievously, 'What rumour?' she asked, knowing very well what May meant. It was difficult to keep a secret in Mottisley.

'That you're not selling. That Griselda is staying on here as housekeeper to look after the children. And they are not going to boarding school.'

'Correct. But haven't you missed something?'

'You've appointed some man to look after the vineyard.'

'Yes,' said Diana. 'I interviewed him yesterday, his name is Sheridan Porter, and he's very suitable. He's young, straight from college, a little lacking on practical experience but the excellent course he did on oenology in California more than makes up for that. He'll live in Abbey House. We're converting the attic floor into a flat for him. If anyone can get decent wine to sell from this vineyard, I'm sure he can.'

'They say in the village he's black,' said May.

'More coffee coloured actually.'

'But there's never been a black man in Mottisley.'

'First time for everything,' said Diana briskly. 'Now, May, please move that helmet, I'm in the middle of some very complicated calculations.'

May obediently moved the helmet. 'And are you staying as well?'

Diana sighed. Please don't let May be difficult, she prayed silently. 'You know I can't,' she said.

'Oh,' there was no comment other than that. Then May asked. 'Who is paying for all this?'

'Me, of course. It's what you wanted isn't it?'

May drew up a chair and sat down beside Diana. Her wrinkled brown, bird-like hand closed on Diana's, strong and firm. 'Oh, yes, my dear,' she said. 'It's what I wanted.'

Diana finally looked at her aunt, and was shaken to see the bright beady little eyes awash with unshed tears. 'It matters to you much more than I thought,' she said slowly.

'Of course it matters,' said May fiercely. 'Anything that is *family* matters. The fact that you care enough to take the time and trouble to organize everything, *and* to take on the financial burden, that matters. The children are staying in Mottisley and that matters. This is where they belong, where their ancestors have lived for centuries. Oh, they'll grow up and go away, perhaps never come back. But if they stay here during childhood they'll have proper roots, and they'll always know who they are. If you know that, you can thrive anywhere.'

Diana smiled wryly. She didn't totally agree with May's philosophy, and refrained from reminding her that she hadn't been willing to take on the financial burden herself. No point in telling her either that many happy and immensely successful people had been shunted around from pillar to post during childhood, often suffering terrible physical and emotional deprivation. But it was the sort of philosophy that Susan had subscribed to. Suddenly Diana wondered if Susan had purposely put her to the ultimate test when she'd made her will. She'd always known how much Diana had tried to shake the dust of family and Mottisley from her feet, and had always thought it wrong and tried to draw her back. Diana knew why. Susan had wanted her to share the happiness she'd found herself, and was sure that it could work for Diana too. She was wrong of course. Diana knew only too well that what worked for one person did not work for another. Ties of blood were one thing, but difference in personality was a far stronger motivation for people's actions. All the same, she had to admit that deep inside her there was a nice comfortable feeling, knowing that her final decision had pleased so many people.

'I haven't told the children yet. They've got an idea, but don't know for certain. I had to wait until Sheridan had signed his contract. But, May, you must understand, and I'll make it clear to the children too, that it is only for a year in the first instance. Then I'll do a feasibility study and review it.'

'Yes, of course, dear,' said May comfortably. In a year's time hopefully Diana would have forgotten all about feasibility studies and stupid things like that. She'd see that everyone was happy, and leave it at that. 'What made you change your mind?'

'I realized that I couldn't justifiably muck up the children's lives for no good reason, other than money. Which wasn't a good reason.'

'Oh? And who started you off thinking like that?'

'No-one,' said Diana quickly, reflecting grimly that she was damned if she was going to give Joe any credit. Although his words had struck hard and deep and were responsible for her sitting down, and giving serious thought to funding the whole project, the more she thought, the more arbitrary and unfair her decision had seemed. She missed the knowing look which passed between Griselda and May.

'Hum,' said May, and changed the subject. 'Well, where is this black man then? I'd like to see him.'

Her wish was granted almost immediately. After a discreet tap on the kitchen door it opened, and May found herself staring up at an enormously tall, good looking, man.

'Come in, Sheridan.' Diana leaped up, and dug her elbow in May's side. 'Please do not mention the word black,' she hissed fiercely in her ear. She pushed May forward, 'this is my great-aunt May. She farms near here. I expect you'll be seeing quite a lot of her.'

'Delighted to meet you, ma'am,' said Sheridan in his slow American drawl, and taking May's knobbly old hand in his, he bent over, with all the elegance and grace of a courtier, and kissed it.

'Oh!' May withdrew her hand and looked at it suspiciously. 'No-one has ever kissed my hand before.'

'And I don't suppose you've been kissed by a black man either,' said Sheridan.

'No.' May looked him up and down. 'You're the first one I've met,' she said. 'Diana said I wasn't to mention the word black.' Diana rolled her eyes heavenwards wondering what was coming next. 'But as you have, I don't see why I shouldn't. Tell me something, do you mind being black?'

'Ma'am, the good Lord didn't give me any say in the matter. He put me on this earth just the way I am.'

May snorted with laughter. 'Come to think of it, I suppose that goes for the rest of us too. You know, when I was young, I always wanted to be tall and beautiful. But I was destined to be short and ugly.'

'You have character, ma'am. I can see it in your face, and that's a form of beauty which never ages.'

May puffed up, pleased with the unexpected compliment. 'I think we'll get on very well,' she said, her face crinkling into a wide smile. 'As soon as you've got time, you must visit Willow Farm, and don't hesitate to borrow any of my machinery if you need it. I want Abbey vineyard to be successful.'

'Ah yes, talking of the vineyard.' Sheridan turned back to the kitchen door, opened it and beckoned. Isaac Skelton and Ronald Pugh ambled into the kitchen. 'Now, Mrs Stratton,' he said, turning back to Diana, 'I want your permission to engage these two guys on a regular basis. There's a lot of work to be done in that vineyard, and I can't do it all myself. I need a couple of reliable hands, and Isaac and Ron have volunteered for the jobs.'

'Are you thinking then that we could actually make money?' Diana hoped so, and started doing rapid calculations in her head. She hadn't made provision for paying two extra wages. Could she afford it?

'In the long term definitely,' said Sheridan confidently. 'In the short term we should break even. But only if we take good care of it. By the way there's a lot of good wine ready for bottling in the winery. I'd like to get on and do that.'

'There you are,' said May, 'he's practically paid for himself already. Once you sell the wine you'll be making a fortune.'

'I know where Susan kept all the labels,' said Griselda eagerly. 'I always used to help her do the labelling and corking.'

'Right,' said Diana. 'Let's make it our target to break even this year. And that means covering the costs of all the salaries, including the two extra helpers.' She nodded at the two men lurking behind Sheridan. 'I'll talk to you in the library in a moment about your rates of pay. Griselda if you want to help of course you can. But only after you've finished your duties in the house.' A fortune was unlikely, but breaking even would be acceptable.

'Thank you, ma'am,' said Sheridan. He turned to the two men behind him, and held out his hand. Both men shook it, grinning from ear to ear, they obviously liked him too.

He must be at least six foot four, thought Diana, he makes them look like pygmies. She also felt the familiar stab of irritation at the way they reacted to Sheridan. With her they'd been surly to the point of insolence. The same old story, men hating being told what to do by a woman. If I were running that vineyard I'd have to prove my-self before they showed me respect, but a bloody man doesn't have to prove anything. They don't know whether Sheridan Porter is any good at his job or not, just the fact that he is a man is enough. Why always this presumed assumption that a man is bound to know what he's doing? It infuriated her.

A loud thump outside the house announced the imminent arrival of someone. 'It can't be the postman,' said Griselda, 'not at this time of day.'

It was the Reverend Pincher. He was hot, flustered and out of breath. 'I dropped by to tell Griselda that choir practice has been changed. It's tonight this week instead of Thursday.' Collapsing on to the nearest chair, he gasped, 'do you think I could have a glass of water?'

'I was just going to make coffee,' said Griselda.

'Why didn't you 'phone?' asked Diana. She didn't like the Reverend Pincher. He was round and pink, with ginger hair, flapping hands, and a permanently sweating face. She knew why he hadn't used the 'phone, he was as nosy as everyone else and had used the choir practice as an excuse to come up and find out what was going on in Abbey House.

'Can't afford to. Country vicars aren't like you city people. We have to watch every penny.'

'Well, you've got the right name for doing that,' said May, who didn't like him because he was always trying to persuade her and Bert to get married.

'Oh, May, you're so funny.' He burst into a ripple of laughter, a surprisingly feminine sound, thought Diana.

'Funny ha ha, or funny peculiar?' snapped May.

'Oh, ha, ha, of course.' Swivelling round in his chair, he looked up at Sheridan. 'So this is the young man I've heard so much about?'

'What exactly have you heard?' asked Diana, an ominous note to her voice.

'Well, I . . . er,' the Reverend Pincher mumbled, desperately trying to think of something tactful to say.

He couldn't very well say that Mrs Graystock, leader of the Mothers' Union and Women's Institute had practically had hysterics at the thought of a black man living in Mottisley, and was convinced that within weeks Mottisley would be the centre of a thriving drugs racket. Or that Freddie Martin, chairman of the Conservative Club and a Parish Councillor, had called a special meeting to discuss the influx of foreigners to Mottisley. Rumours were rife, one of them was that the black man Diana Stratton had employed was married with ten children. Miss Prudence, head mistress of the local Church of England School, had left a note at the vicarage saying that in her opinion the addition of black children to the school would cause a racial imbalance, and lead to strife.

'That you've engaged someone specially trained in viticulture to run the vineyard.' He crossed his fingers, said a little prayer, and hoped that Diana would believe him.

'I have. Although for the life of me I can't see what that has got to do with anyone in Mottisley.'

'Everyone is interested in what happens in Abbey House.' The Reverend Pincher smiled expansively at Sheridan as he spoke, hoping that he too believed him. Never do to let him think there might be racism in Mottisley.

'So it seems,' said Diana dryly, well able to guess at some of the rumours flying around.

'What I mean is, everyone knows how difficult it must be for you, filling your sister's shoes.' Reverend Pincher floundered under Diana's direct gaze. She was a very unnerving young woman, not at all like her sister.

'Well, Reverend Pincher, you can tell everyone that I am not, nor have any intention of, filling my sister's shoes, as you put it. I intend to do things my way, with or without the approval of the population of Mottisley. So I suggest that you cycle back and tell the lot of them to go to hell.'

Reverend Pincher blushed an unbecoming shade of magenta which clashed violently with his ginger hair. 'I can't possibly say that.'

'Have a coffee,' said Griselda quickly, filling the awkward silence that followed. She passed a tray round, and paused at Sheridan. 'Do you sing? We're very short of men in the choir.'

'Bass,' said Sheridan. 'I love choral singing, I was in the choir at University. Ah, ah ah ah!' The power of his voice reverberated around the room as he sang a scale.

Reverend Pincher leaped up and clapped his hands. 'Wonderful,' he cried. Mrs Graystock, Freddie Martin and Miss Prudence could take a running jump – he couldn't quite bring himself to even think the word hell – he wasn't going to turn down a talent like that. 'Can you hold a harmony line?' he asked excitedly.

'Sure. I read music, man. Play the organ too.'

'Sheridan, may I call you that?' Reverend Pincher didn't wait for Sheridan's reply but rushed on excitedly.

213

'We'd be very honoured if you'd join the choir. We're doing a concert version of "Show Boat" in the autumn to raise funds for an extension to the church hall, and you'd be perfect to sing the part of Joe.'

'But you said Mr Fairburn could sing it,' said Griselda.

'Yes, because he was the only bass in the choir. Now we've got two, I'll hold an audition.'

'Sheridan hasn't said "yes" yet,' said Diana, amused at the Reverend Pincher's sudden enthusiasm.

'Ma'am, I'd like to, if you'd permit.' Sheridan turned to Diana.

'Permit? Good heavens, you're not going to work twenty-four hours a day, seven days a week, and you don't need my permission for what you choose to do in your spare time. Go ahead if you want to. I think it's a good idea. A good way to get to know the people of Mottisley. You might as well start tonight. There's nothing else you need do.' She beckoned to Isaac Skelton and Ronald Pugh still lurking by the kitchen door, 'come into the library with me, and we'll sort out how much I'm to pay you.'

'So it's true then?' Clemmy sat on the edge of her chair in the shapeless navy pinafore tunic and grey shirt of her Chichester Girls' school, swinging her skinny legs clad in wrinkled navy blue tights.

'It depends on what you've heard,' said Diana cautiously, wondering why on earth it wasn't possible for schools to come up with more attractive uniforms for adolescent girls.

'I want to know officially.' Simon was very serious.

'Me too,' said Miffy, then he frowned. 'What does officially mean?'

'Any information that comes from me,' said Diana, 'is official. That means you can believe it.'

'Would you please tell us then?'

Diana could see that Simon was suspicious. Unlike Clemmy he didn't believe the rumours he'd heard. The

214

boy had an anxious look at the back of his eyes. She was glad that her words could be reassuring.

'I've decided that I was wrong to think of selling everything and sending you away to school. Instead, you are to stay here, and stay at the schools you go to now. Griselda will be your housekeeper, and a sort of foster mother. I expect you to be good, or as well behaved as children can be, and not play her up too much.'

'I'm always good,' said Miffy serenely.

Diana decided to let that pass. Griselda would be dealing with them on a day-to-day basis, not her. She continued. 'The vineyard will be run by Sheridan Porter, whom you've already met. He is going to live upstairs in the attic rooms. Those rooms will be his, and are private. You are not to enter them unless he says you may do so. Do you understand?' Three heads nodded vigorously. 'Sheridan will be helped in the vineyard by Isaac Skelton and Ronald Pugh, and anything to do with the vineyard and winery is under Sheridan's control. I'm sure he will be pleased if you want to help, but you must remember to do as he asks, not what you think should be done.' Diana paused for breath, then said. 'Well, that's about it, I think.'

'Does Sheridan come from Africa?' Miffy wanted to know.

'Of course not, stupid. He's American,' Simon said with all the superiority of a nine-year-old.

'But he's black.'

'There are lots of black Americans. Aren't there, Diana?'

'Oh, yes,' said Diana, praying she wouldn't have to embark on a history lesson.

'I see,' said Miffy, who clearly didn't. Then he perked up. 'I remember now, I've seen them on the television.' To Diana's relief he lapsed into silence.

'Are you staying here?' Clemmy asked Diana.

'No. I am leaving Mottisley on Friday. I must go back to my job and earn some money. Which reminds me. This arrangement is for a year to start with. It all depends on how the money works out. I'm afraid there won't be lots of spare cash, but if you need anything special for school Griselda will let me know.'

'We're used to not having any money,' said Simon. 'We never need anything special. As children go we're very cheap to run. Mummy always said that. But we can eat less if you want us to.'

Diana felt an unfamiliar emotion close around her heart, she couldn't name it, but the feeling nearly choked her. 'That won't be necessary,' she said gently. 'Whatever you need you shall have. I promised your mother that I would see that you were cared for, and I will. So for her sake you must take care, eat properly and keep well.'

Miffy climbed down from his chair and edging round the kitchen table came to where Diana was sitting. He put his small hand on her knee. 'Are you going away because I said I didn't like you?'

Diana shook her head. 'No, it's because I must earn some money. For all of us.'

Miffy heaved a sigh of relief. 'That's all right then. I've changed my mind anyway, now that you're letting us stay. I've decided to like you.'

Clemmy held the cat up. 'Look, even Shakespeare is smiling now that he knows he's not going into a cats' home.'

'He wouldn't have gone into a home, he'd have been put down, silly,' said Simon realistically. 'But he needn't worry. Everything is going to be plain sailing from now on. Isn't it Diana?'

Oh my God, thought Diana guiltily, I hadn't even thought about the cat. 'Yes,' she said with an over-whelming sense of relief. 'From now on everything will be plain sailing.'

Chapter Sixteen

'What exactly did you mean on the 'phone by *pulling in our horns*?' asked Hugh over dinner. To celebrate Diana's return to London they were dining out.

'Oh, it's nothing much,' said Diana, surprised at Hugh's worried expression, then concluded that he had every right to look worried. He must be wondering what on earth she had let them in for, with all her talk of being careful. It sounded much worse than it really was. 'It's no big deal, Hugh. I'm thinking of little things. For example instead of eating out here at Langans once a week, we'll come once a fortnight, and we won't change our cars this year. But these economies won't be for long. The vineyard will soon start bringing in money when the wine is bottled and sold. And now I'm back in London, the Norfolk theme park project can go full steam ahead. The bonus from that alone will be very substantial.'

'I still don't see why we should suffer for the sake of your sister.'

Diana frowned. 'I didn't have much choice. Surely you can see that?'

Suffer? Did Hugh really think that giving up a few luxuries was suffering? Surely not, Hugh wasn't as small minded as that, or as selfish. Although perhaps because we have never needed to think of anyone but ourselves, we've both become selfish; the thought had never occurred to her before, and she wondered why. '*We're used to not having any money . . . we can eat less if you want us to.*' It was Simon's voice, as clear as a bell. Suddenly Diana remembered the tense anxiety in his dark eyes, and the pathetic bravado of Clemmy and Miffy, and an unexpected rush of emotion caught at her throat. The

217

children knew what it was to suffer. The very least she and Hugh could do was to go without a few luxuries. The very least.

Hugh watched the expressions flicker across Diana's face. What was she thinking? 'Of course you didn't have a choice. I know that,' he said carefully. But the prospect depressed him. Nico wouldn't wait for ever for his money.

'We'll hardly notice the difference.'

You might not, thought Hugh bitterly. *But I damn well will*. 'You know you have my full support for whatever you decide,' he said softly. 'I think you're being an absolute angel to that family. I only hope they appreciate it.'

Diana smiled, thinking of the children's faces when she had told them they were staying in Mottisley. And May too. Dear, funny old May. Yes, they did appreciate it, and in a strange way she'd gained something from them. A new, and unexpected, warm glow inside. She tried to explain to Hugh. 'Giving is a two-way thing,' she said. 'I wish you could have been there when I told them what I was going to do. If only you could have seen their faces. I know you would have felt the same as me then, and known it was the right thing to do.'

Hugh doubted it, but forced himself to smile. Reaching across the table he took her hand and kissed it. 'I think you're wonderful,' he said.

The day after Diana returned to London, Ben Rose's secretary summoned Nancy to his office.

She arrived at the offices of his firm in Gray's Inn, half an hour late, looking absolutely stunning in a pillar box red outfit, floating in on a cloud of exotic perfume. Men appeared, as if by magic, from all directions, from every nook and cranny of the old building.

'Bloody hell,' whispered Valerie, the office receptionist, 'why can't I attract men like that?'

'You could if you were permanently on heat,' said Ben's secretary sourly. 'Believe me, she's a bitch. But my boss

218

has got her sized up all right. She doesn't make him go weak at the knees.'

Ben ushered Nancy into his office and held out a chair for her. His secretary's statement was not quite true. Nancy did, in fact, make him go weak at the knees, but from terror, not admiration. He lived in fear of her next indiscretion. As soon as she was seated he came straight to the point.

'Your husband has engaged a private detective.'

'What? To spy on me? How exciting.' Nancy looked with distaste at Ben's cluttered office. Why was it solicitors' offices always looked as if they never filed anything? She wondered if Hugh's office looked the same.

'It's not exciting, Mrs Morris. It's very serious.'

'Really?' Nancy looked at the large NO SMOKING sign on the wall, and ostentatiously lit up a cigarette.

Ben ignored the cigarette. He had other things on his mind. 'If you don't modify your behaviour, I'm afraid you are going to have a nasty shock and find that your divorce settlement could be very little indeed.'

That got Nancy's attention. 'What the hell do you mean? Modify my behaviour?'

'I mean,' said Ben slowly. 'That you've got to stop this affair with Hugh Stratton. Everyone in The Temple and at Gray's Inn knows about it. I refuse to answer for the consequences if you carry on seeing him.'

Nancy frowned, and inhaled deeply. 'You mean the private detective will find out?'

'Of course he will.'

'And that will affect my settlement?'

'Too damn right it will. You could come out of this with virtually nothing. After you've paid my fees, of course.'

Nancy fixed him with a stony stare from her black eyes. 'I might not pay you at all if you muck up my case.'

Ben fiddled with some papers on his desk, then said casually. 'Fortunately for me that problem won't arise. All fees are deducted at source. There is no question of your husband dealing with you direct.' He looked up and

219

smiled. He was not a vicious man, but it gave him venal pleasure to put Nancy down.

There was a long silence while Nancy concentrated on blowing two perfect smoke rings towards the ceiling. Then she stood up and stubbed out her cigarette in Ben's empty coffee cup. 'Right,' she said, 'that settles it, doesn't it. I can't afford to take the risk. Hugh will have to be put on ice for the time being. Pity, but there it is.'

'You'll stop seeing him?' Ben could hardly believe that she was being reasonable for once.

'Better than that, darling,' said Nancy, patting him on the top of his head as she made for the door. 'I'll leave town. I'll go and stay with my aunt at Mottisley. There are one or two things I have in mind to do down there.' She laughed, 'I guarantee you, the private detective will find life very dull in the country.'

'I wish I knew what Nancy Morris was up to.' Tony had dropped in to the Manor House after his mid-morning house calls. 'Why is she staying with May and Bert?'

'Probably casing the joint,' said Joe idly.

'Yes, that's what I'm worried about. That house of theirs is a gold mine. May and Bert are incredible for their years, but they're no match for someone like Nancy.'

'I think you are underestimating that old couple, not many people could pull the wool over their eyes. And, anyway, what have you got against Diana's cousin? She's not so bad.'

'I wouldn't be so sure about that. Thanks,' Tony accepted a cup of coffee April passed him. 'I get vibrations from that young woman, and they're not good.'

April laughed, 'Oh, Tony, you sound like Joe's mother. And talking of Joe's mother, you've changed your tune since the last time we talked. If I remember correctly, you pooh poohed her forecasts for the future.'

'Oh, God! You haven't been listening to my damned mother have you?' Joe was exasperated. 'What did she say?'

'That there would be changes in Mottisley, and that Diana is lightness and Nancy darkness,' said April lightly.

'Is that all?'

'What else did you expect? Her prophesies never make sense.'

Joe was annoyed. 'You shouldn't encourage her fortune telling.'

'You can't stop her, Joe,' said Tony. 'And although I hate to admit it, she performs a useful function. People often go to see her for reassurance instead of pestering me. They'll accept her advice, but all they want from me is a packet of pills. But to get back to Nancy Morris, it's not that rubbish about lightness and darkness that makes me worry. It's the fact that she's making an inventory of the contents of the farm.'

'Is that all?' Joe laughed. 'Well, why not. I expect she's hoping to get her hands on some of it when May kicks the bucket, but knowing May she's probably left the lot to a home for old horses.'

'Hum.' Tony changed the subject. 'Have you been up to Abbey House since Diana left?'

Joe shook his head. 'She expressly forbade me to go there,' he said.

'And me?' said April.

'I don't think that order applies now,' said Tony. 'After all, she changed her mind about everything else, so I think it's safe to assume that she changed it about you too.'

'One should never assume anything where Diana is concerned,' said Joe. Too late, he realized that he'd let the bitterness show in his voice.

April looked up at Joe quickly. 'It sounds as if she hurt you.'

'Diana didn't hurt me,' said Joe abruptly. 'But she certainly did hurt those kids, even if she has made reparation of sorts now.'

Tony drained his coffee cup, and looked at his watch. 'Hell, I've got a surgery in half an hour. I'm off.' He paused at the door. 'Do me a favour. Pop over and see

May and Bert, but be surprised at Nancy's presence. I don't want her to think we've been talking about her, she's insufferably conceited as it is.'

'I've got a feeling you don't like the lady,' said Joe.

'You're very perceptive.'

April laughed. 'I'll go. I'm going into the Post Office now anyway. I'll drive past Willow Farm on the way back.'

They left Joe staring absent mindedly out of the window.

'I wonder if Joe is harbouring something for Diana,' mused Tony out loud.

'Of course not,' snapped April. 'Don't be so bloody stupid.'

Her car roared off down the drive, gears crashing, and at the wide main gates she turned right so violently that huge skid marks were left in the road.

Chapter Seventeen

Summer arrived in London, taking everyone by surprise as usual. Every bush and tree burst into luscious leaf. Bright green and buoyant the supple leaves fluttered and waved in every passing breeze, too young to be dulled yet by the polluting grime of the city. The formal flower beds in the Royal parks blazed with colour; geraniums, fuchsias, bégonias, all set out with geometric precision by the gardeners, and along the river the hanging baskets reflected bright splashes of colour on to the ironwork of the lampposts.

Diana took to walking to work, letting Hugh have the services of her chauffeur. Bryant dropped him off at his office in The Temple. Hugh thought Diana was mad to walk.

'You'll be exhausted before you even start work.'

'On the contrary. The walk wakes me up, besides it seems such a pity to miss all this wonderful weather. Once I get to the office I'm stuck in a high rise, air conditioned, building, and I feel out of touch with the real world. It's claustrophobic at Wycombe and Yatton.'

'All that fresh air you got in Mottisley has addled your brain,' Hugh laughed.

His remark was made on a teasing note, but Diana suspected he was irritated because she was departing from their routine. Hugh always liked everything planned. And so do I, thought Diana – usually. But it was fun to do something different occasionally, and it was true what she'd said about the office being claustrophobic. Perhaps Hugh was right, and it was something to do with the weeks spent in Mottisley, because the feeling of being shut in was not something she'd ever noticed before.

She *had* been affected by the vast spaciousness of the West Sussex Downs. If she was absolutely honest, Diana knew she had felt the same sense of freedom she used to feel as a child, in spite of all the problems and the constant nosiness of interfering villagers. And now she was back in London, fleeting visions often slid into her mind when she was least expecting them, and she saw the Downs. Sometimes they were sunlit and benign, the sun sweeping over the gently swelling hills and hollows, a perfect pastoral symphony; at other times they were bleak, as they were when a southwesterly gale was blowing, and the salt from the sea left a bitter taste on the lips of all. Diana began to accept the fact that her country roots were deeper than she'd ever suspected.

And in spite of Hugh's scoffing she enjoyed the walk. On a still June morning, the River Thames shone with a pearly lustre, and in the distance it was just possible to see the dome of St Paul's, dwarfed by the high rise developments of the City. As she walked, she planned her day. The first week back at Wycombe and Yatton had flown past in a series of board meetings. Defining strategies for new projects, picking up the threads of old ones. Without her dynamic push it seemed that many things had been allowed to lapse. She had been annoyed, and had very nearly come to blows with Alan Sinclair over, what she thought, slack management.

'Are you accusing me of being lazy?' Alan demanded furiously.

Sorely tempted to say yes, Diana had managed to keep her temper. 'You're too lenient with everyone, Alan. Why did we lose our options on that golf village complex in Florida? I'll tell you why. The architect you engaged was too slow. Wycombe and Yatton didn't get the proposals in by the deadline, because his damned specifications were late.'

'Russell Stuart-Johnson is a good friend of mine. He's very highly thought of.'

'By you, perhaps,' said Diana tartly. 'I only think highly

of people who deliver the goods on time.'

'In that case,' snapped Alan, turning nasty. 'Perhaps you'd get your finger out and go and have lunch with Lord Bing and Sir Timothy Drisdale. *That* project is noticeably behind schedule.'

'It'll be pushed through on time,' said Diana, determined that it would be. She needed that bonus for Abbey House.

'The board will certainly be disappointed if it isn't. The loss of that particular project could adversely affect our half yearly figures. Questions would be asked at the shareholders' meeting.'

As she walked Diana remembered Alan's words, and fumed yet again at the veiled threat. She worked harder than anyone else at Wycombe and Yatton, and just because she'd been away for a month shouldn't have meant everything grinding to a halt. But it had, and now she was having to work twice as hard to make up for it. Today she was lunching with Sir Timothy Drisdale at some discreet venue organized by Sir Timothy's private secretary.

The car arrived at Wycombe and Yatton's City office at twelve o'clock on the dot. Its only occupant, a sandy haired, slightly chubby, bespectacled, earnest looking young man. 'We are proceeding to the venue separately, for security reasons,' he told Diana. 'My name is Thomas Younghusband, Sir Timothy's Parliamentary Private Secretary.'

'Security reasons! Are the IRA on the war-path again? If so, I hope you've had the restaurant searched by sniffer dogs.'

'Oh nothing like that. Sir Timothy doesn't worry about the IRA.' Thomas Younghusband looked smug. 'Neither do I.'

'Maybe you should,' said Diana. His self-righteous expression gave her a malicious urge to disturb his composure. 'They do seem to blow up politicians with monotonous regularity.'

225

'The security is against the Press,' said the young man, his composure intact, ignoring Diana's remark. 'This Jungle Theme Park in Norfolk is a potential hot potato if the Greens get to hear about it.'

'But not too hot for the Secretary of State to be interested in it.' Diana smiled. 'That's good.' She noted that Mr Younghusband was now looking rather put out.

'Personally, I am of the opinion that it would be better if he had nothing to do with it,' he said.

'Lucky for me then, that he obviously doesn't take your advice.' Diana leaned back in the car stretched out her legs and crossed her ankles. She was beginning to enjoy herself. Nothing better than a battle for stimulating the mind. For the first time since she had returned from Mottisley she felt a surge of adrenalin streaming through her. This was going to be a successful encounter with Sir Timothy. She knew it; in spite of pompous Mr Young-husband.

'I've asked Thomas to join us for lunch. I hope you don't mind, Diana. May I call you that?' Sir Timothy brushed back his thinning grey hair self-consciously, and extended his hand in greeting.

He's conceited, thought Diana, an asset to be exploited when the occasion arose. She also noted the empty bottle of claret on the table. Good! nothing like a bottle of wine at lunch time for slowing down the cognitive powers.

'Please do,' she smiled. 'And of course I don't mind your private secretary joining us.'

'Thomas is very fussy about notes,' Sir Timothy said on a grumbling note. 'He's a stickler for accuracy. Personally I'm quite happy to keep it all up here.' He tapped his forehead.

Oh, so Thomas, like Diana, thought Sir Timothy's faculties were not likely to be reliable after a good lunch. But she hadn't counted on him wanting to be in on the act. Bloody annoying, but nothing she could do about it. Diana hid her annoyance behind a charming smile. 'Good, that's the way it should be. It saves so much trouble when you know that all the facts are one hundred per cent accurate.' Thomas wasn't going to have the satisfaction of knowing that she would have preferred Sir Timothy to herself. 'I've got duplicate sets of all the facts and figures. I'll let you have a copy, Thomas.'

'Later, later. We'll eat and talk. Then look at the figures.' Sir Timothy picked up the menu. 'I'm starving, *and* thirsty.' Snapping his fingers at the waiter, he ordered another bottle of claret. 'To tide us over,' he said.

Thomas demurred when the waiter tried to pour him a glass. 'I'll wait until the meal.'

'No, you won't,' thundered Sir Timothy. 'I know you're new at the job, but you'd better learn right here and now that I'm not having some wet-behind-the-ears young puppy who can't hold his drink as my private secretary.' He fixed the waiter with an imperious stare. 'Pour the young man a glass of wine.'

'Yes, sir,' the waiter did as he was told, and Diana hid a wry smile.

'Now drink it, Thomas.'

'Yes, sir.' Obediently Thomas took a small sip, then seeing that Sir Timothy was watching, took another. With only a tenuous footing on the political ladder, he couldn't afford to alienate his new boss.

Diana watched with amusement. With any luck Thomas would end up as befuddled as Sir Timothy. A fact which made it all the more important that *she* should keep a clear head. 'I wonder if I could have some white wine, Sir Timothy. Red never seems to agree with me.'

'Of course not, m'dear. My wife's the same. Hasn't got the stomach for a strong red. A man's drink, eh Thomas?' He refilled Thomas's glass.

'Thank you,' said Thomas, faintly. He was trying to lose weight and had not eaten breakfast, with the result that the wine had gone straight to his head. He began to wish he was a PPP to a teetotal minister.

'Choose what you like from the wine list, Diana.'

227

Snapping his fingers again, Sir Timothy commandeered the services of the wine waiter.

Diana chose a low alcohol white wine. She was pleased to see that the bottle arrived in an ice bucket, firmly wrapped in a white napkin, so that neither Thomas, nor Sir Timothy knew that what she was drinking was practically neat sugar water. She matched them glass for glass during the meal, and enjoyed herself. Perhaps it was due to her month's absence from the fray, but she knew without a doubt that her conversation was sparkling, informative, although not too informative, and very definitely inspirational.

Even Thomas became enthusiastic, and Diana noted thankfully that he had abandoned note-taking very early on. 'This could be enormously important for the balance of payments problem,' he said solemnly, enunciating with the care of someone who has drunk rather too much.

He's pissed thought Diana with delight. 'Oh yes,' she said, marvelling at the sincerity she managed to inject into her voice. She put her hand over Thomas's and gazed into his watery blue eyes. What a wimp he is, she thought, and what a bitch I am. But it has to be done. Business is business. 'I think it is the duty of every one of us to make an effort to do something about that. It's up to us to put the great back into Britain, and we all know that can only be done with money. This scheme will syphon money in, especially from the continent.'

'Yes, I'd like to do those European bastards down,' growled Sir Timothy. 'The French are too bloody cocky, and the Germans are too bloody rich. The rest don't count.'

'Then you agree it is absolutely essential that we don't miss this opportunity?'

'Absolutely,' said Sir Timothy and Thomas in unison.

The protracted luncheon over, they went their separate ways. With a quick flick of her hand Diana had deftly muddled up the papers as she went to hand them over. She apologized profusely to Thomas.

228

'So silly of me. It will take me ages to sort them out now. I'll have a set collated and sent over by special courier to your office this afternoon. Will that be all right?'

'Quite all right.' Thomas was looking a bit green around the gills, and in no fit state to read anything. All he wanted to do was to go and lie down.

'Thanks.'

Diana wanted to go through the papers again carefully. Her intention was that anything that could possibly be construed as potentially prejudicial would be deleted at this stage of the game.

It was only on the way back to the office that she suffered a twinge of conscience. Susan would have hated what I'm doing she thought, and remembered her saying, '*you specialize in pulling down things, and erecting huge concrete buildings.*' Well it wasn't concrete, no-one could accuse her of that. But the Jungle Theme Park was going to change that part of Norfolk irrevocably, destroy the ancient heritage of that part of England. At this point Diana put a firm brake on her wayward thoughts. Thinking like this does no good at all. This is my work, I have a job to do, and I'm good at it. More than that, I need the money to support the Abbey House venture.

Two carefully edited versions of the project were sent over to Thomas Younghusband's office that afternoon, and the following week Diana had an equally successful luncheon with Lord Bing. The Planning Application was filed with the Norfolk District Council and the County Council, and a date set at the end of June for a confidential meeting with the two Secretaries of State, the financial backers, Alan Sinclair and herself.

Everything was going as planned. Normally Diana got a physical high from her work. But this time her pleasure was marred by a vague disquiet. An uneasiness she couldn't put a name to. Everything was as it should be. Her life with Hugh followed the usual pattern, although their lovemaking was less frequent. On the night she'd fixed the final meeting for the theme park, she lay in bed listening to Hugh splashing around in the bathroom. Suddenly she wondered what other couples' lives were like. What did they talk about? Did they discuss politics, the theatre, the meaning of life? Anything deep? She and Hugh never did, but then there was no need. They agreed on everything – at least she thought they did. The thought was disquieting. She didn't really know. We say I love you, she thought, but what exactly does that mean? In her present frame of mind it seemed an empty, meaningless, phrase. But then she chastised herself for being stupid. What was she worrying about? They were the three most important words in the world.

Hugh slipped into bed beside her and Diana turned, wrapping her arms around him. She wanted to share her day with him. And she wanted reassurance that the theme park wasn't such a bad idea after all. She wanted to still the conscience which had been getting a little out of hand lately.

'We fixed the final meeting for the Jungle Theme Park today. The financial backers are lined up, and it's all systems go.'

Hugh kissed her briefly on the forehead. 'Great,' he said.

'You don't sound very excited.' Diana raised herself on one elbow and looked down at him. He looked strained, there were lines around his mouth she'd not noticed before. 'In fact you don't look too well.'

Hugh smiled, and pulled her head down on to his chest so that she couldn't look at him. 'I feel a bit low,' he said. 'The result of struggling with a difficult case, with not much prospect of a good outcome. But the theme park news is good.'

'Do you really think so? You don't think it'll be too much of an environmental blot on the landscape?'

'Of course not. It's going to make money. That's all that matters. When will you get the bonus?'

It was not the reply Diana had wanted, but she knew she couldn't really blame Hugh for that. 'Not until everything is signed and sealed,' she said.

'How long does that take?'

'Several months. It has to go through the planning stages, but I've been assured by Lord Bing that they are merely a formality. I gather they've got the District and County Councillors, the ones that matter anyway, in their pocket.'

'How long is several months? two? three?'

'Oh, at least five, maybe six. But it doesn't matter, I'll get there in the end.'

Hugh felt a gnawing fear in the pit of his stomach. How was he going to keep Nico at bay for six whole months? He'd been counting on Diana's bonus coming sooner than that. His fear spilled over into irritability. 'Of course it matters. You've been playing around with this project for months. It's about time you had something to show for it. And to think I've taken the trouble to look at houses in Dulwich.' That was untrue, but he knew how much Diana had admired Alan Sinclair's house, and hoped it might spur her on to hurry things up.

But Diana was hurt. The vague uneasiness she'd been feeling suddenly crystallized into a more identifiable form. She saw their relationship, hers and Hugh's, spread out like a map before her. It looked like a game of Monopoly. That was the sum total of their lives, making money and buying things. The hurt gave way to sudden anger. He'd been looking at houses in Dulwich to buy with her money without even consulting her. *Our* money, her conscience reminded her. You are married and you have promised to share. But anger was the stronger emotion and overcame her conscience. Diana put her anger into words. 'Do you think that I've been put on this earth to provide solely for you?'

'Diana, I didn't mean . . .'

'But you did mean it, Hugh. I'm beginning to think that money is all you want from me.'

231

'Diana, that's not true. I love you because you're you,' he said fiercely, holding her tight.

'Yes, but would you feel the same if I didn't have a penny to call my own?'

As she spoke Diana thought of Susan and her friends in Mottisley. That was something *she* didn't have, a multitude of friends to call on in times of need. Not for money, but for support, encouragement, and comfort. Suddenly Diana knew why Susan had been so happy living on next to nothing. She'd always had her friends around her, like a great heart-warming life belt. Because of them Susan had known that nothing really bad could happen to her or her children. Even in death she'd been surrounded by love. But I only have Hugh, thought Diana. Could we manage on next to nothing and be happy? The answer, she knew, was an unequivocal no.

'Of course I would.' Hugh caught Diana's face between his hands and pulled her round to look at him. He had to convince her, *had* to. 'If you really feel that way,' he said slowly, 'why don't you hand in your notice? Become an ordinary housewife, and wait here every day for me to come home. I'd provide for both of us. We wouldn't be as well off, but at least then you'd see whether or not I still loved you.' Positive it was a challenge she wouldn't take up, Hugh felt quite safe in voicing the idea.

'I'd be bored to tears,' said Diana with a shaky smile.

A smothering blanket of panic caught at her breath, caused by the uncomfortable knowledge that if she didn't work, they really would have nothing at all to talk about. But almost immediately the determination and common sense with which she'd disciplined herself over the years, came into play. Stop it, she told herself. Stop behaving like a typically irrational, emotional woman, the kind of woman I despise. My marriage is a good one, a successful one, it will last for years. To doubt, was to play with fire; and fire very often consumed everything in its path.

Hugh kissed her. 'If you were bored, I'd be afraid to

come home,' he teased. 'A bored Diana would frighten me to death.'

Diana agreed. 'I'd most likely be unbearably grouchy.'

'Most definitely,' said Hugh, rolling her on her back and cupping her breasts in his hands. His mouth closed over a nipple.

'Hugh, I do love you,' whispered Diana, clenching his thick dark hair in her fingers. 'I love you so much, and I need you.' It was true she did need him. Without him she'd be terribly alone. Their years together had been good. Why was she doubting? What was the matter with her?

'Me too,' murmured Hugh, stroking her slender limbs. She wanted him to make love to her, and he must if he was to convince her that all was well. But it wouldn't be easy. One of the distressing withdrawal symptoms, since he'd stopped snorting, was his lack of sexual desire. Increasingly, he was finding it difficult to become aroused. Guiding Diana's hand down to stroke him, Hugh prayed that it would be all right.

Chapter Eighteen

'I think I'll make a start on the front parlour today.'

Nancy had told May she thought it would be a good idea to make an inventory. The decision to tell May had been forced on her for two reasons. First, the difficulty in doing it clandestinely, and second, the fact that April Harte and the local doctor, Tony Evans, had both developed the unnerving habit of dropping into Willow Farm unexpectedly.

To her surprise May had been quite amenable to the idea. 'Yes, it's about time it was done,' she'd said. 'I don't know what I've got, or how much it's worth. When you've done it I'll get it valued.'

'I think that would be wise. You should be insured. My husband always maintained that one should be adequately insured.'

May pricked up her ears. Nancy very rarely mentioned her husband. 'How is that husband of yours?' she asked. 'And when are you getting this divorce? or have you changed your mind?'

'I haven't changed my mind.' Nancy decided to let May know a little of what was going on, reasoning that it couldn't do any harm, and might even encourage May to regard her in a sympathetic light. 'As a matter of fact, he's been quite nasty, and had me followed by a private detective. Although what he hoped to find out I don't know,' she added virtuously. 'Anyway, that's the real reason I asked if I could come down and stay. I needed some peace.'

'Why didn't you say so before, my dear.' May had a shrewd idea why a detective should be following Nancy, and hoped he hadn't latched on to the liaison between

Nancy and Hugh Stratton. For Diana's sake Nancy must be kept away from London as long as possible. 'You can stay as long as you like, and do the inventory for me while you're here.'

Now, Nancy paused, sucking the end of her pencil while she regarded the grand piano in front of her. It hadn't been polished for years, and was covered in a dull sticky film. She lifted the lid, the once white ivory keys grimaced at her like old yellow dentures. She noted the name carefully, Erard of Paris. It meant nothing to her, but to an expert it might. Flicking back the pages of the notebook in which she was making the inventory, she did a rough calculation. By no means an expert on antiques, she knew enough to feel certain that what she had listed so far represented a sizeable fortune, a part of which would be hers, if she had anything to do with it.

'Nancy,' May shrieked from the other end of the house. 'There's a telephone call for you. A Ben Rose.'

Ben! Nancy dropped the pencil in her haste. About time. Good news she hoped. She wondered how much her settlement would be. 'Ben, darling, how are you? What news?'

In his Gray's Inn office Ben winced at her cheerful voice, and wished she wouldn't call him darling. He took a deep breath. Better get it over and done with. 'Nancy, I'm afraid the news is not good.'

'Oh?'

'I was too late with my warning about the detective. He'd already been at work months before we knew anything about it. As a result your husband knows about many of your previous indiscretions. The ones you assured me he knew nothing of. But worse than that, he also knows about your affair with Hugh Stratton. He has issued an ultimatum through his lawyers that unless you accept his terms, he will parade the whole sorry mess through the courts.'

'If I go to court, what are my chances of winning a decent settlement?'

'About zero, I should think,' said Ben, who had no intention of putting his own neck on the line for her. He knew he should be fighting for his client, but couldn't help thinking the stupid bitch was getting what she deserved.

'What is he offering, do you know yet?'

'The house in Hampstead, and the contents.'

'And?'

'That's it. Just the house, nothing else.'

'No money?' Nancy was aghast.

'Only what is already in your own bank account. Otherwise nothing.'

'But I couldn't *exist* on that, let alone *live*!'

'My advice is to take it. If you start quibbling now, he can withdraw the offer, which personally I think is very generous in the circumstances. The value of the house and contents has been estimated at about a million pounds. Not something to be sniffed at.'

'But it's not money. I still need cash for day-to-day living.'

'You could sell up. Move somewhere cheaper, and invest the remaining capital,' said Ben with some relish. 'Alternatively, you can go on a secretarial course and learn to type.'

'Never!' said Nancy emphatically. There was a silence, then she said, 'All right, accept the offer, and bring the case to a close.'

Ben put the 'phone down and turned to his secretary. 'She's agreed, thank God. Now I can wind up the proceedings, and get that damned woman off my back.'

'Greedy bitch,' said his secretary echoing Ben's sentiments exactly.

At Mottisley, Nancy put the 'phone down slowly and walking back to the parlour looked around at her surroundings. Willow Farm, stuffed to the attics with antiques, and the odd bundles of money May left in teapots, boxes and other out the way corners. So far, on this visit, Nancy had left the money alone, now she emptied the carved sandalwood box on the mantelpiece of the one hundred pounds it contained and stuffed the notes in her pocket. There was plenty more in the house, she'd take it all before she left. When she'd started her inventory, it had been for malicious fun as much as anything, and the desire to make sure that she got her share. Now, things were different. A share wasn't good enough. She needed it all. How good was May's health? She couldn't afford to wait too long.

The 'phone rang in Diana's office, causing her to click her tongue in annoyance. She'd asked not to be disturbed. Flicking the intercom switch she called to her secretary. 'Take it for me, please, Shirley. I must finish what I'm doing before I talk to anyone.'

Diana bent her head back over the mountain of paperwork. She'd just finished chairing an exhausting meeting concerning a regeneration development project in Liverpool. For once she could honestly hold her head up high and say it was a perfect scheme. Environmentally sound, with the potential of providing work in an area of high unemployment, and when finished it would provide low cost homes for several hundred families. But in spite of all these plus points, she'd met nothing but opposition from government planners at both national and local level. Pettifogging objections raised all along the line, and Diana knew why. There was just not enough money in it to satisfy the fat cats of big business. Their philosophy was why drink milk when they could have the cream.

A year ago she would have ditched the project without a moment's hesitation, and switched to something more profitable. But now, she was surprised to find herself thinking – why? Why ditch it? It would make money. Not a lot, but enough. Why couldn't she persuade someone to take a smaller cut but at the same time actually do some good? Exasperated, she was determined to do her damndest to get the Liverpool scheme off the ground. At the back of her mind was the thought that if she could, it would compensate in some way for the monstrosity that was the Jungle Theme Park. She hated admitting it, but more and more often she found herself acknowledging what a hideous obscenity the Norfolk project actually was.

'This is a fine time in my life to start getting a conscience,' she muttered, angry that her mind was cluttered with contentious thoughts.

Shirley buzzed on the intercom. 'Mrs Stratton,' she sounded anxious. 'It's a Miss Marsham on the line, and she won't take no for an answer, and she won't leave a message either. She wants to speak to you.'

Diana astounded her secretary by exclaiming in obvious delight. 'Oh, it's May! Of course I'll speak to her.'

Suddenly the all-enclosing pale cream walls of the office melted away, and Mottisley seemed to be all around her. The fresh, earthy smell of early summer, the quietness of the lane by Abbey House, and the neat rows of vines blazing a fiery green in the sunlight. It seemed more real than the world of red buses and black squat London taxis hurrying past outside her window.

'Diana? Is that you?' May's familiar voice bristled down the line.

Diana smiled. She recognized the tone of voice. May wanted something and was determined to have it. In the background she heard shrieks, must be the children arriving back from school. They sounded happy, and she was glad, although at the same time obliquely put out, which was silly. I can't expect them to miss me, she thought, I may be their nearest relative but they hardly know me. There was more noise, and surely that was the sound of a dog barking.

At Abbey House, May turned round and shushed the children, all of whom had come swooping into the hall, followed by a dog, jumping about excitedly like a kangaroo.

'Can we have him? Oh say we can?' Simon flung himself at May.

'I haven't asked her yet.' She tried to cover the mouthpiece with her hand, but Diana heard.

'Asked me what?'

'After Galahad died it was always the intention to get another dog.' May decided to approach the subject with caution. 'But somehow . . .'

Miffy couldn't bear it a moment longer and snatched the 'phone. 'His name is Seamus and he's Irish, and he's been given to us.'

Clemmy and Simon crowded round Miffy. 'He's terribly handsome, and aristocratic looking.'

'And absolutely enormous.'

'Fool,' hissed Clemmy, 'don't tell her that.'

'But eats hardly anything,' added Simon hastily. 'And is black and white.'

'He needs a home, and if we don't have him he's going to be shot at dawn.' Clemmy's voice quavered with emotion as she imagined a firing squad.

'That girl is probably going to be an actress,' remarked Joe from his position in the doorway. 'She always goes over the top.'

'At dawn,' said Diana, sounding suitably horrified. She had suddenly realized that they were talking about a dog. 'Will he be blindfolded and stood against a wall?'

'Don't be so bloody daft.' Snatching the 'phone back May heard Diana's last remark. 'Well. Can they have this dog? It seems to have taken to them.'

'And from what they've said they seem to have taken to him,' said Diana. 'So how can I say no? Just one proviso, Griselda has got to agree.'

'Griselda thinks he's wonderful. She loves greyhounds. Don't you, Griselda?'

Griselda nodded doubtfully. 'He seems good natured,' she said.

Diana knew she'd been steamrollered into a decision, but there was no harm in their having a dog. He would be an added security for the house, and cheaper than a burglar alarm. 'All right,' she said. She knew May must have relayed the information because of the deafening screeches of wild excitement echoing down the 'phone.

'When are you coming down?' May decided now was a good time to try and persuade her. 'You ought to see the new addition to your family.'

'As soon as I can, May.' My family, she'd never thought of the children like that before. My family, what a strange feeling. She wasn't sure whether she liked it or not. The word 'family' reeked of responsibility, ties, an intricate web of emotions that bound a person tight, and could be suffocating. Suddenly the rosy glow of Mottisley faded, and she was back in familiar territory, her office in London's square mile. 'As soon as I can, May,' she repeated. 'But I am very busy at the moment.'

'She won't come unless she has to,' said May sadly, putting the 'phone down.

'Did you really expect her to?'

Joe turned and walked back into the kitchen. Why should he feel disappointed? He had wanted Diana to leave. Perverse, that's what his mother always called him, and perhaps I am, thought Joe. It was uncomfortable being perverse. Why can't I be content with things the way they are? But thinking of his mother made him even more uncomfortable. Why did she keep telling him to let April go so that she could find her own true happiness? True happiness? What true happiness? April wanted to marry him, Joe knew that. They weren't in love, even though April thought she was. But Joe knew better, it wasn't love, but they were fond of each other, and she was in love with the thought of settling down. Joe also knew that he probably would marry April eventually, and then what would his mother say? It would throw her claims to have second sight into a turmoil.

'Can we take Seamus for a run?' The children swung on his arms.

'Why not. We'll race him up and down the hill, between the vines. He'll love that.' Joe led the way outside. He refused to think about his mother and her prophesies for the future. She was as nutty as a fruit cake, damn her!

* * *

240

A week later, Shirley caught Diana the moment she stepped through the door. 'Hartmanns of Belgravia on the line for you.'

Diana paused. 'Take a message, please, Shirley.'

'But they've rung three times today already, and they won't leave a message.'

'Damn!' Diana looked at her watch. She was on her way to chair yet another meeting on the Liverpool regeneration scheme. Paul Scott-Johnson, her new personal assistant, had been dredging through potential backers and had come up with some new ones. The last thing she wanted was to be late for the meeting. She made a decision, she could spare five minutes. 'OK, Shirley, I'll take it in my office.'

It was Malcolm Hartmann himself, the owner. He seemed embarrassed. 'Sorry to bother you, Mrs Stratton,' he said. 'But recently you wrote a cheque payable to Hartmanns for nine hundred and fifty pounds.'

'Yes.' Diana was impatient. 'What about it.' She remembered the cheque, it was for a service and four new tyres for Hugh's Porsche.

'I regret to inform you that we've presented it to the bank twice and they refuse to honour it.'

'You mean they've bounced it?' Diana was astonished.

'Er . . . yes.' He sounded even more embarrassed. 'I'm sorry to have to . . .'

'Nonsense,' said Diana briskly. 'You should have told me the first time it was refused. I've been away and since I've been back I've been so busy that minor details, such as topping up my current account, have slipped my mind. I'll transfer some money immediately. Please present it again and I assure you it will be honoured. My apologies for your inconvenience.'

Diana put the 'phone down. She felt uneasy. She'd written so many cheques for Abbey House she'd lost count. I need an accountant, she decided. Abbey House and my own personal money will have to be separated. She made arrangements with the bank to transfer money from her investment account to the current account, reprimanded them for not informing her that the current account was low, and engaged an accountant she knew by reputation to be sound. His name was Norman Leadbetter, and she arranged to see him at the end of the week. On her way to the scheduled meeting, Shirley handed her a large envelope. It was from Sheridan Porter, the promised report. Diana stuffed it into her briefcase. No time to read it now.

Diana read Sheridan Porter's report that night when she got home. 'He writes a very businesslike report,' she told Hugh.

'Good.' Hugh didn't bother to disguise the fact that he wasn't interested.

'He's started selling wine from the barn. He and Griselda have made a little shop.'

'Maybe you'll get some of your money back,' said Hugh. That interested him.

Diana carried on reading out loud, although she'd hardly heard Hugh's comments. She'd become immersed in the doings of Abbey Vineyard, and found herself wishing she was there to help. 'They're spraying once a fortnight, using four different fungicides. And now it's turned hot they're using a foliage feed spray as well. Oh dear, he says the rabbits and deer are problems. He's had to buy masses of netting to protect individual vines from the rabbits, and has erected a perimeter fence against the deer.' She sighed, there staring up at her was an invoice for the fencing. An expensive invoice. 'I'll have to give him some more money,' she told Hugh.

'The sooner you get rid of that place, the better,' said Hugh, feeling bad tempered. 'It will always be a drain on your resources.' Nico had been particularly persistent lately. But he'd drained both his sources of money for the time being; Diana's account and the firm's petty cash. He wished Nancy would come back. Maybe she would cough up some cash if he asked her, after all she'd had her fair share of both the coke and pot.

'But I promised I'd give it a year, Hugh. I can't break that promise.' Diana looked at Hugh, unhappy that he didn't understand.

Hugh caught the glance, and cursed. He should have been more careful. Diana must never know how worried he was about money. God forbid that she should think of checking her bank balance.

'I know, darling,' he said softly. 'I know you think I don't understand, but I do, and I admire you for sticking to your promise. I just hope it doesn't turn out to be too expensive. Perhaps you should ask Sheridan to be more careful. Set him a budget, so that you don't have un-expected bills turning up out of the blue.'

'Yes, I will,' said Diana, thinking of the bounced cheque. When she met Norman Leadbetter on Friday, she'd ask him to go through her accounts with a fine toothcomb.

'Have you gone mad? What the bloody hell do you want to hire a sodding accountant for? We've never needed one before, and we don't need one now.' The agitated mixture of fear, fury and resentment churning inside Hugh boiled over, and he flung down his knife and fork. Needing to take out his temper on someone besides Diana, he snapped his fingers at a nearby waiter. 'I said I wanted this steak rare, not bloody raw. Take it away.'

'Yes, sir.' An expressionless waiter bore the offending steak away.

Diana stared across the table at her husband. Astonished at this ashen faced, black eyed, furious stranger. Hugh's savagely rancorous reaction to the news of her engagement of Norman Leadbetter, the accountant hired to sort out the vineyard's financial affairs, astounded and shocked her. Why on earth was he so angry? What was happening to him? To them? Using foul language, to her, his wife. Something he'd never done before. Diana

243

felt that slowly the whole tenor of her life was changing, and not for the better. What was wrong? But even as she thought, the word *wrong* clanged with such a dolorous portent that she veered away from trying to analyse the problem. Not wanting to admit that there was anything wrong.

'*We* don't need one, Hugh. But *I* do. And I've told you why,' she replied quietly. 'I've probably been spending too much money on Abbey House and the vineyard, and I just don't have the time to sort out all the different accounts myself.'

'Why didn't you tell me?'

Diana shrugged, uncertain of what to say to this strange, bellicose, Hugh. 'I didn't think it that important. It just seemed sensible to hire an accountant to do it for me.'

'I could do it, *and* save you money.' Hugh made an effort at pulling himself together. 'You should have asked me first.'

'I didn't want to bother you with what is essentially my family problem,' said Diana coolly. 'And anyway you don't have much time either. It wouldn't have been fair of me to ask you.'

That wasn't the whole reason. But as with everything else between herself and Hugh, Diana refused to let herself even begin to think, let alone admit, that there could be an underlying, more serious, reason.

'I can make time,' said Hugh, forcing himself to sound genial.

It was on the tip of Diana's tongue to point out that he'd never felt that way before, in fact quite the reverse; always making it perfectly clear that her sister's family, and indeed anything to do with Mottisley, was not only boring, but outside his terms of reference as a husband. But she bit the words back. No need to go out of her way to make a quarrel, they seemed to manage to quarrel quite enough lately without any effort on her part. All the same, Hugh's remark stuck in her gullet, making her even more stubbornly determined to hang on to the accountant she'd appointed.

'The business of running the vineyard at Abbey House is my problem, Hugh, and it is turning out to be more complex than I thought. Not only do I have salaries and insurance and so on to pay, but there are also things like bonding the wine, then Customs and Excise duty to pay when the wine is out of bond, plus tax when there is a profit. So the money for Abbey House and the vineyard must be quite separate from my own, and Norman Leadbetter is well qualified to sort it out for me. And that is what he's going to do. Concentrate on Abbey House, not our personal financial affairs.'

'Well, you know best, darling,' Hugh said, forcing a reluctant smile. At least their joint personal accounts were not included in the accountant's remit. He raised his wine glass in a gesture of tribute. 'You usually do.'

'Your steak, sir.' The waiter returned, the head waiter following in close attendance.

'And we hope this one is to your satisfaction,' the head waiter said obsequiously, knowing perfectly well that there had been nothing wrong with the first one.

'I'll let you know if it isn't,' said Hugh abruptly. He turned back to Diana. 'I think this restaurant is going off, don't you? They're trading on their reputation and getting slack.'

'Perhaps,' said Diana non-committally, not wanting to disagree with him yet again. It was their favourite French restaurant, below Tower Bridge, overlooking the Thames. Personally she thought the food as delicious as ever, and suspected Hugh had sent the steak back because he was in a temper. Suddenly she felt depressed. It was Friday night, and normally she looked forward to the weekend, but now it stretched ahead bleak and boring. Even the wonderful sunset, shooting ribbons of orange and pink across the purple dusk of the Thames, failed to lighten her heart. They had to do something to fill in the time until Monday. You could always go down to Mottisley –

the thought popped up in her mind. No, not there. It'll unsettle me, and God knows I feel unsettled enough already. 'Let's go and see that new play at The Globe tomorrow night,' she said on impulse.

'What about conserving money for the vineyard?' Hugh raised his eyebrows.

'Damn the vineyard.'

Hugh laughed. 'That sounds more like the Diana I know and love,' he said. 'Determined to have her own way.'

Is it? thought Diana. Is that the way I appear to everyone else? Determined to have my own way? Of course it was. It was the image she'd cultivated. But how true was that image? And how well does Hugh know me? How well do I know myself? More to the point, how well do you *really* know the man who is your husband? The unwanted thought struck suddenly, searing into her consciousness like a red hot needle. All the instances of his unpredictable behaviour over the recent weeks flashed before her mind, and then, against her will, she found herself reliving the incident in their apartment all those months ago, when he'd come in and virtually raped her. Yes, raped me! The anger surged again. I hate him for that, and always will. The thought was frightening.

Later that night in bed, Hugh pulled her into his arms, and started to peel off her nightdress. But Diana wriggled away. 'I'm tired,' she lied.

Ridiculous though she tried to tell herself that it was, she still felt angry, not wanting him to touch her. But there was another reason; although as usual, with anything unpleasant, Diana tried to ignore it. The reason was that there was a difference lately in their lovemaking. Unknown to Hugh, Diana had noticed when he'd failed to climax, aware of him withdrawing still hard and unfulfilled. But she'd said nothing, hoping that it was something temporary, and that if she kept silent he'd get over whatever the problem was that was causing it. In the meantime, the act of love had become a mechanical duty,

246

not a pleasure. She worried about the cause. Something was missing in their relationship. And lately, even more worryingly, she had found herself wondering if the missing ingredient was affection.

'Tired?' Hugh said. 'Poor darling, you've been working much too hard. You definitely deserve that trip to the theatre tomorrow.' He kissed her chastely on the forehead. 'Sleep tight, my darling.'

But far from sleeping tight, Diana lay awake for hours, trying to pinpoint the unsettling unease which assailed her senses. Was it Hugh's fault? Had it started when he'd taken her forcibly in sex that Friday night? Or were the roots deeper than that? She couldn't decide. Finally she fell asleep. But peace still evaded her. She dreamed of Mottisley, Joe Kelly, and the child denied of taking a breath. Of Susan, and her children, now Diana's children. Only they're not, they're not mine. I don't want children.

'I don't want children.' She awoke to find herself muttering the words out loud.

Raising herself on her elbow she looked at Hugh in the dim light of the bedroom. He was sound asleep, and looked calm now. His face handsome in repose. Outside, the hum of the never-ending traffic, rumbling along the Chelsea embankment, started to rise in pitch as a prelude to the first traffic jams of the day. And the slate grey light of a London dawn spilled over into the room. Diana looked at Hugh more closely. Why is it, she wondered, that I've never noticed before that his mouth is weak?

Chapter Nineteen

Nancy punched out Hugh's office number with the end of one long red finger nail.

Miss Higgins answered. 'Mr Stratton's office.'

'Put me through to Mr Stratton.' Nancy never said please.

'Who shall I say is calling?'

'You don't. Just put me through.'

'I'm afraid Mr Stratton always likes to know which of his clients is calling him. He insists I give him the name first.'

Nancy laughed. 'So that you can then say he's out I suppose. Well, he'll not be out for me I can assure you. Just put me through.'

'I'm very sorry. But really it's more than my job's worth to do that. I must insist on a name.'

Debbie came in with the post. 'Difficult customer?' she whispered.

'Very,' Miss Higgins whispered back, her hand over the mouthpiece, 'won't give her name.'

'Put the 'phone down on her,' was Debbie's practical advice.

At the other end of the line Nancy seethed. She was damned if she was going to give Hugh's nosy old secretary her name. Then she smiled, her sloe black eyes glinting wickedly. 'You can't have my name, but you can give him a message. It's this – an orgasm a day keeps the doctor away. Got that?'

'Er . . . yes, I think so.' Miss Higgins scribbled down the message, and switched the 'phone on to hold.

Debbie, peering over her shoulder started to giggle. 'I've heard through the office grapevine that he's got a bit on the side,' she said. 'This must be her. What a bleedin' cheek she's got. Fancy getting you to pass on sexy messages.'

'Oh dear, I don't think I can say this to him.' Miss Higgins's double chin quivered at the thought.

'I'll say it.'

'Say what?' Hugh came into the outer office.

Miss Higgins looked imploringly at Debbie who gleefully siezed the piece of paper. 'There's a female on the telephone who wants to speak to you,' she began.

'Don't you mean *lady*,' snapped Hugh. He didn't like Debbie. Not only was she immune to his charm, something he was unused to, she was also much too cheeky.

'Oh no, she's no lady, sir. Ladies don't give messages like this.' Holding the paper aloft she read out loud in her clear young voice. 'An orgasm a day keeps the doctor away.' Lowering the paper she stared challengingly at Hugh who had gone bright pink. 'Will you take the call, *sir*?'

Bloody girl, but try as he might Hugh couldn't outstare her. 'Yes,' he spluttered, retreating back to his office. He had to say something, something credible. 'It's, it's . . . er my cousin. She's a great practical joker.' Slamming the door shut he collapsed at his desk and picked up the 'phone.

'At last,' said Nancy. 'The Pope is more accessible than you.'

'Why did you give a message like that?' said Hugh irritably. 'Do you have to embarrass me?'

'Sorry, darling. But I had no intention of giving that old hag of a secretary my name. Anyway the message is very apt. I haven't had one for ages, an orgasm I mean. Can you get over to Hampstead at lunch time, and bring some coke with you? I have a yearning to have you at your fucking best.'

Hugh felt a rush of adrenalin at the thought of Nancy's body. He could picture it in every detail. She was back in London. Thank God, now he'd be able to get back to normal. But then he remembered, he didn't have any coke, and couldn't afford any either. 'I haven't got any, and it's impossible for me to get any before lunch. I'm due over the road at the High Court in ten minutes. Anyway, what are you doing here? I thought you were in hiding in deepest Mottisley.'

'I was, but there's no need any more. But don't let's waste time talking about that. Give me your Italian friend's number. I'll fix the coke.'

Hugh hesitated. Somehow the thought of Nancy meeting Nico filled him with a shadowy disquiet. But the need for cocaine, and lust for Nancy, overcame his angst. 'You'll have to pay for it. I'm broke.'

'Broke?' Nancy was disbelieving.

'Absolutely, stony. I've used up Diana's money *and* the spare money from the cash box here. So if you want me on a high you're going to have to pay for it this time.'

'I do,' said Nancy. 'So give me the number, and come over as soon as you can.'

When Hugh arrived at Nancy's Hampstead house just after one o'clock, his usual parking place was taken by a silver Jaguar. It took ten minutes of shunting up and down Church Row for him to find a space, and by then he was very bad tempered and impatient.

Nancy let him in, clad in a diaphanous robe beneath which she was clearly naked. Hugh felt a heat stir in his groin at the sight of her. 'Darling, I've missed you,' he said, reaching out to slide his hands beneath the robe.

But Nancy neatly side-stepped his grasping hands and led him into one of the opulent sitting rooms. 'I have a visitor,' she said.

It was Nico. He was lounging on a chaise longue, his tie awry and his shoes off. His normally sallow face was slightly flushed, and he wore what could only be described as a satisfied expression. Hugh nearly exploded with jealousy. The bugger! He'd just had sex with Nancy, he was sure of it. Nancy too, looked relaxed, and her nipples were sticking like a couple of corks through the thin material of her robe. A sure sign she'd just been aroused.

'What the hell is he doing here?' Hugh grated.

Nico stretched, lit a cigarette slowly, then started to put on his shoes. 'Don't be like that, old son. Haven't I just done you a favour and delivered the packets your little lady wanted?'

Infuriated, Hugh wanted to strangle him. 'Looks like you've done a damned sight more than deliver a package. Get the hell out of here.'

A nasty smile flickered across Nico's sallow face, and his black eyes narrowed. Hugh Stratton, what was he? nothing more than upper class shit. They were all the same, thought they could treat anyone who wasn't one hundred per cent English as scum. But he'd show him. It was about time Hugh Stratton knew who held the whip hand.

'Look mate, you're in no position to tell me what, *or who*, to do. Just thank your lucky stars that your lovely lady friend has paid up what you owe.' Shoes on, he got up and leaning forward, ran a finger down Hugh's cheek in a menacing manner. 'Remember,' he whispered, 'She's paid. Pity really, I was just beginning to think that a little plastic surgery was called for.' The evil menace in his voice sent a shiver down Hugh's spine.

Nancy laughed. The threat excited her. 'Why, Nico. I believe you mean it.'

'Believe it,' said Nico.

Nancy ushered him from the room. Hugh heard her say. 'I'll ring you when we need some more.'

'Remember, I'll want hard cash next time.'

'And how did you pay him this time?' asked Hugh as Nancy stepped back into the room.

Nancy laughed. 'Darling, don't worry. He didn't ask for much.' She slipped down on to her knees and unzipped Hugh's trousers. 'Um, delicious,' she whispered, sucking hard.

'How much?' Hugh was torn between the excruciating

251

sensations Nancy was inducing and his jealousy of Nico.

'Let's just say it was the easiest four thousand pound bill I've ever paid.' She tugged his trousers down. 'Shall we snort now, or later?'

'Now,' said Hugh, forgetting Nico. 'Now, damn you, *now*.'

Alan Sinclair regarded Diana from the leather depths of his office chair. 'Glad to see that the preliminary planning applications for the Theme Park have been passed by the Norfolk Local Authority.'

'Lord Bing assured me that there'd be no problem.' Diana felt weary. Unusual for her. And it was only Monday. Alan's office was stuffy, his cigar smoke hung in a great smudge of blue haze in the centre of the room.

'All the same, I think it would be politic to take him out to dinner. The old boy is very smitten with you.'

'Can't say it's mutual. But if needs be, I suppose I must.'

'You must,' said Alan. 'And I'll come with you. I've booked a table for tomorrow at the Waldorf.'

The 'phone on his desk buzzed. Alan switched on the intercom. It was Shirley, Diana's secretary. 'There's a call for Mrs Stratton. A Mr Joe Kelly.'

'I'll take it in my office.' Diana made her way to the door.

'By the way,' Alan called after her, 'you'd better bring an overnight bag in with you tomorrow. The dinner is at the New York Waldorf Astoria. We're popping over on Concorde. Lord Bing is tickled pink.'

'Pink!' said Diana acidly. 'Does the Prime Minister know? I thought she liked all her ministers true blue.'

Bribery and corruption, that is what this business is really about, she thought moodily as she walked back to her own office. But it had always been like that. It was not something that had ever bothered her before, so why should it now? She wished she knew the answer.

Back in her own office she picked up the 'phone. 'Yes, Joe. What can I do for you?'

'I'm afraid there are problems.'

Diana looked at a file on the desk, her mind still on office problems. 'Problems?' she said vaguely.

'Griselda's fallen off her bicycle and broken her leg. She's in hospital.'

'But how . . . ?'

Joe was smiling, she could hear it in his voice. 'How? The silly, short-sighted woman was waving at Mr Merryweather as he stood outside his chemist's shop, and careered straight into the back of a parked car. It could have been worse, but as it is she's likely to be hospitalized for several weeks.'

So aware of the unexpected warmth that the smile in his voice generated, it was several seconds before the full impact of his words struck Diana. The children. There was no-one to look after them. 'Oh God, the children.' she said.

'Look,' said Joe. 'I'm really sorry to dump this problem on you. Believe me if there was something I could do here I would. But April's away in London for a week and I'm flying out to New York tonight on business. It's not something I can cancel at this late stage.'

'I don't expect you to cancel anything. It's my problem,' said Diana.

'I know. But I worry.'

'There's no need to worry. The children will be OK.'

'I know that. I know you won't let them down. But I, I mean *we*, all worry about you too. How are you going to manage? It's no good for anyone trying to tear themselves in two.'

'I've done it before. I can do it again,' said Diana. 'I'll ring May now and see if she can be at Abbey House for the children after school. And then I'll have to try and fix up a temporary housekeeper as quickly as I can.'

'I'm sorry,' said Joe again.

Again that warm glow. He really *was* sorry he couldn't help. Suddenly Diana realized that the only other people who had ever given her that feeling lived at Mottisley too.

Aunt May, Susan when she'd been alive, the children sometimes, and funny old Griselda, now in hospital with a broken leg. Why was it she didn't get even a faint echo of such warmth when she was with Hugh? He cared for her. He loved her. He was her husband for God's sake. Oh, hell! what was she thinking of? With a great effort Diana gave herself a mental shake and concentrated on the predicament now facing her.

'There's no need to be sorry, Joe. As I said before, it's my problem. But thanks anyway.'

By the time Diana rang her, May had already heard about Griselda's accident and was more than willing to be at Abbey House when the children arrived home from school. 'Damn silly woman,' she grumbled. 'It's all Mr Merryweather's fault.'

Diana smiled at May's indignation. 'How can you possibly blame him? It's not the poor man's fault.'

'It is. He shouldn't have put ideas into Griselda's head.'

'Ideas! What ideas? When?'

'About thirty years ago,' said May. 'But that's a long story, far too long for now. You'd better be getting on your way. What time shall I expect you down?'

Mottisley, London, New York. Her separate worlds were on collision course, and Diana knew she had to choose. But not yet. There might be a way round it without having to tear herself in two as Joe had said. It was worth a try. 'I'll ring you back, May,' she said. 'And let you know. There are one or two things I must sort out here.'

It was as she'd thought of Mottisley that the idea had come. Clearly, as if she were there, Diana could see the village main street, the Parish Council offices in the old Corn Exchange, and opposite, the General Stores where Mrs Lomax ruled the roost, and charged the inhabitants of Mottisley a pound a week to put advertising postcards in her window. The window was always full, advertising everything from old lawnmowers to *cordon bleu* cooking.

Someone might be looking for the job of housekeeper. It was worth a telephone call.

Mrs Lomax herself answered the call. 'Yes, yes, Mrs Stratton. I've heard about Miss Morgan's accident. Yes, I can see that it is a problem. A housekeeper you say. Wait a minute I'll have a look.' Diana hung on to the 'phone impatiently, awaiting Mrs Lomax's return. 'You're in luck, Mrs Stratton. There is just one, and it was only put in yesterday. I didn't take it myself, so I didn't meet the lady. Gladys my assistant took the card. *Gladys!*' she nearly deafened Diana as she shrieked down the shop from her partitioned office at the end of the store. 'What was this woman like, this Mrs Wright who put the ad in for a housekeeping job?'

'Never mind, Mrs Lomax,' Diana interrupted. 'I'll find that out for myself. Just tell me what she says on the card and give me the telephone number so that I can contact her.'

Rather disgruntled that Gladys's opinion wasn't wanted, Mrs Lomax imparted the information. 'Mrs Millicent Wright, Mottisley 823493. Position of housekeeper wanted. Anything reasonable considered. Unattached.' She sniffed, 'that means divorced I expect. You want to be careful, Mrs Stratton.' In Mrs Lomax's opinion divorced women were very suspect.

'I will be. Thank you, Mrs Lomax.'

Diana dialled the number given, and a woman with a strong Yorkshire accent answered. 'Millicent Wright speaking.'

She sounded nice, had a warm, comfortable sort of voice. Diana explained her predicament, ending with, 'so you see I do need someone rather quickly. Someone who is experienced with children.'

'Then you've rung the right person,' said Millicent Wright. 'I'm divorced.' Diana thought of Mrs Lomax's warning, and ignored it. 'And I've come down south to make a new start in life. I've had five children of my own, and if that's not experience I'd like to know what is. Of

255

course they're all grown up now, but I haven't forgotten what they were like when they were little, and I could start tonight if you wanted me to. I'm in bed and breakfast accommodation. I can walk out the minute I want to.'

I ought to get references, I ought to see what she looks like, I ought to ask May's advice – oh damn, there isn't time to do any of those things. Diana firmly squashed the stirrings of unease before they had time to get a hold on her. Unconventional crises needed unconventional remedies. She would ring May and tell her, then speak to the children later in the evening.

'In that case, Mrs Wright, I should like you to start at Abbey House this very afternoon. My aunt, Miss Marsham of Willow Farm, will be there and I'll tell her to expect you. I can't tell you at the moment how long this position will last, but you do understand, don't you, that it's only temporary.'

'Oh yes, dear. Don't you worry. I'll stay as long as you like, and go the minute you don't want me. And I'm so glad of the chance to work. You won't regret the day you hired Millicent Wright.'

Diana put the 'phone down congratulating herself on having solved a difficult problem so easily.

'All I can say, Diana, is that I hope you won't regret being so hasty. Fancy engaging someone over the telephone.'

'Needs must, Aunt May.'

'I do wish you'd at least come down and see this woman.' Far from thinking it the ideal solution to the crisis, May was being stubbornly awkward.

'I've already told you I can't. I just can't.'

'Why not?'

'Because I'm flying to New York tomorrow for an important meeting.' Could dinner with Lord Bing really be classified as an important meeting? Knowing May would definitely think it wasn't, Diana kept that detail to herself.

'Joe's going to New York today. You're not meeting him there are you?'

'Of course not. I'm going with Alan Sinclair on business for Wycombe and Yatton. It has nothing to do with Joe.'

'Oh,' said May, and sounded disappointed.

For a moment Diana was annoyed, then the emotion changed to resignation smattered with a sense of the farcical. If she was not very much mistaken May was hoping that there was something between herself and Joe. 'Aunt May,' she said sternly, determined to scotch any such notion before it had time to take hold, 'I am married to Hugh, and Joe is as good as married to April Harte, and we are not having a secret liaison in New York.'

'Oh,' said May again, still sounding disappointed.

'Now promise me you'll be nice to Mrs Wright and show her where everything is. I'll ring later tonight when the children have had a chance to meet her.' Diana crossed her fingers, praying that their reactions would be favourable. 'And I'll write to Griselda now telling her not to worry about a thing.'

'What about her pay?' May asked. 'She was worried about that.'

Again Diana felt annoyed. Yet another salary she was now having to pay from her own dwindling resources. 'I'll pay her, of course,' she said abruptly. 'I told you she has nothing to worry about.' Once again she wondered why May was so obstinate where money was concerned. Why wouldn't she dip her hand into her own pocket? She had plenty of money which she never spent.

'Good, she'll be pleased about that,' said May.

She knew very well why Diana was abrupt. But she was damned if she was going to help financially, at least, not yet. Let Diana get in really deep, then she was bound to become more involved in the children's lives. Because she wanted that so badly, May stubbornly believed that she could drive Diana into doing what she wanted; failing to recognize that in her great-niece she was up against a stubbornness as great as her own.

Good as her word Diana hastily scribbled a letter to Griselda as soon as she'd finished speaking to May; reassuring her that her position and salary were safe, and telling her not to worry. She also ordered an expensive bouquet to be delivered to the orthopaedic ward of St Richard's Hospital, Chichester, which was where Griselda was incarcerated. She wondered, as she wrote, what Norman Leadbetter her new accountant would have to say about the additional expenses when he knew. He'd already clicked his tongue censoriously when given the list of her undertakings as far as Abbey House was concerned. This surely would be another click of consternation. But she couldn't help it. Accidents were beyond her control. For a moment Diana felt overwhelmed by events. Everything that happened at Mottisley seemed to be beyond her control. But quick as a flash she extinguished the flicker of uneasiness. Nonsense, of course it wasn't. *Nothing* was beyond her control, never had been, never would be.

Hugh was late home that night. Diana, used to finding him already in the apartment, usually with the evening meal prepared, was surprised. He hadn't rung saying he'd be late.

She busied herself setting the table and deciding what they'd eat that night. Gazpacho soup to start with, fillet of salmon with fennel compote and thyme sauce, new potatoes and salad for main course, finished off with fromage frais and coffee. It was only as she started opening all the packets that Diana began to add up how much the prepared, pre-packed meal was costing. Then she felt guilty. It was as much as she had been paying Griselda to buy food for two or three days at Abbey House. She and Hugh were terribly extravagant. Perhaps Norman Leadbetter had a point, suggesting that she separate all her financial matters from Hugh's, and that he look at everything including her personal finances.

Opening a packet of croutons, and putting on an egg

to hard-boil as the garnish for the gazpacho, Diana thought of that afternoon's conversation with her newly hired accountant. He'd taken the unusual step of ringing her at the office, and as a result of their conversation Diana had given him permission to have access to all her accounts. She'd also, reluctantly, agreed to close all her joint accounts with Hugh.

'This afternoon,' Norman Leadbetter had said. 'It will enable me to straighten out your affairs so much more quickly. The last thing you want is to have the Inland Revenue breathing down your neck concerning irregularities connected with Abbey Vineyard.'

The thought of additional problems at Mottisley forced Diana to agree, and she had duly closed all the accounts that afternoon. I must remember to tell Hugh, she thought, looking at her watch again.

It was nearly nine o'clock, and she forgot about Norman Leadbetter. Hugh was unusually late, surely he couldn't still be at the office? She decided to ring Abbey House while she waited, might as well take the opportunity of seeing how the new housekeeper was getting on.

At Abbey House Millicent Wright was going down a treat with the children. May had also thought that she seemed all right, and concluded that Diana had struck lucky when she engaged her. Tony Evans, who had come round to inspect Griselda's replacement, and give an up-date on Griselda's condition, was less certain. Although once she had asked him to stay to supper and he'd tasted her cooking he began to revise his opinion.

The children, Sheridan, Tony and Millicent Wright were seated around the kitchen table eating supper. Seamus, the greyhound, now an established member of the household, stood, nose resting hopefully near the casserole on the table. Something Griselda would never have permitted. And Shakespeare was doing his usual balancing act and being fed by Clemmy.

'Do you mean to say you are not going to make me do

my homework?' Clemmy leaned her elbows on the table, another thing Griselda would never have allowed, and spooned up the gravy from the casserole.

'It isn't Millicent's job to make you. You are old enough, and sensible enough to know you've got to do it,' said Tony sternly. 'And that goes for you too, Simon.'

'I don't know why,' muttered Simon rebelliously.

'So that you don't end up as a dustman,' said Miffy.

'It's all right for you. You don't *have* any homework. Anyway, I'd *like* to be a dustman. There's nothing wrong with dustmen.'

'Of course there's nothing wrong with them, but you might change your mind,' said Tony. 'And if you haven't done your homework, there won't be any choice.'

'Crumbs, this is really delicious Millicent,' said Clemmy as she finished her supper, neatly switching the subject off homework. 'Where did you learn to cook so divinely? And what did you put in it?'

'Two bottles of red wine, and loads of steak,' said Simon, helping himself to a glass of red wine from the bottle on the table. 'I say, do you really think this is OK? Griselda never lets us drink wine.'

Millicent sniffed. 'Griselda sounds a bit of a kill-joy. Fancy not drinking wine.'

'No,' said Simon, always anxious to be fair. 'She's just serious.'

'It is only for this evening, isn't it,' said Tony, fixing Millicent with a stern eye. 'Just to celebrate your arrival.'

Slightly daunted by his fierce expression, Millicent patted her rigidly permed grey hair. 'Of course,' she said, smiling sweetly.

'And you'd better not drink *all* the wine,' said Sheridan getting up from the table and whipping away an unopened bottle. 'We are supposed to be selling it.'

'You're a kill-joy too,' grumbled Millicent, watching the departing wine bottle with longing eyes.

'Perhaps, but Mrs Stratton has got to pay us all with something, and the wine brings in money.' He put on a jacket. 'Coming Tony? I'm off to the "Show Boat" rehearsal now.' He turned back to Millicent. 'Make sure those kids are in bed before I return.'

'I'm in charge of the house and children, not you,' said Millicent. 'Mrs Stratton's orders.'

'And I'm in charge of the wine. So don't you be taking any without my permission.'

'As if I would.' Millicent looked outraged at the suggestion.

'You took this.'

Sheridan waved the bottle, and wished there was a more secure way of locking the vineyard shop. He must try and persuade Diana to purchase new doors that could be securely padlocked. Lucky for them Mottisley wasn't peopled with alcoholics. If it had, they could have got all they wanted, free and gratis, from Abbey Vineyard with no trouble at all.

'You'll have to keep an eye on Millicent,' Tony said to Sheridan once they were outside. 'I have a feeling she likes her tipple.'

'I suppose you know about these things.' Sheridan was more concerned with getting to rehearsal on time.

'Yes,' Tony felt gloomy. Why the hell hadn't Diana come down and vetted this woman?

'But at least her cooking is bloody good.'

'Yes.' Tony cheered up. 'She must be on the ball if she can cook that well.'

'For God's sake, man, don't start thinking she's an alcoholic. I only mentioned it because I don't want her drinking my profits. Or rather, Mrs Stratton's profits.'

All the same Tony would have felt a lot happier if Diana had actually done the hiring herself. Telephones were all very well, but not for important matters.

Millicent sniffed again once the door had closed behind them. 'I used the wine for cooking, and he ate it,' she said in an aggrieved tone. She turned to the children. 'What a cheek that Sheridan has. Still, at least you appreciated my cooking, didn't you.'

261

'Yes,' chorused Simon and Clemmy in unison.

'Very nice, thank you,' said Miffy in a muffled voice, through a mouthful of beef casserole.

The 'phone in the hall rang and Millicent answered it. 'Hello, Mrs Stratton. Yes, I've settled in very well. The children are absolute angels, and Seamus and Shakespeare are adorable.'

Rather an exaggeration, thought Diana, but remembered that Mrs Wright had been very eager to get the job. She was hardly likely to complain about anything, not even the animals, on the first night.

'Can I speak to the children?'

The children came on to the line. They sounded surprisingly happy and excited, and were laughing and giggling a lot. Diana was taken aback, thinking that they would have been upset at their routine being disturbed yet again.

'We're going to visit Griselda tomorrow in hospital,' shouted Miffy. With his mouth full by the sound of it, thought Diana. 'And we're going to take a bag of grapes. Our own, from the greenhouse. Sheridan says they're ready now.'

'Good, she'll like that.' As she spoke Diana immediately thought of money and felt happier than she had all day. Sheridan had got an order from an up-market restaurant in Chichester to supply them with English grapes as soon as they were ready. She wondered how many pounds of grapes there were and hoped the children wouldn't eat too many. The money from the sale of the fruit would help swell the coffers. Heavens, I'm beginning to think like Susan! Diana was uncertain whether to be pleased or worried, but she had to admit it was certainly a change for her. Fancy being pleased at the thought of swelling the bank balance by a few pounds, when she normally dealt in half a million at a time.

'Mrs Wright, I mean Millicent, is very nice.' Simon's voice. Why was he giggling? Unlike him.

'And a *marvellous* cook,' said Clemmy. 'Seamus is just finishing up the casserole, listen.' There was silence, broken only by the sound of a dish scraping noisily along the kitchen tiles. 'Hear him?' asked Clemmy.

'Yes. Not very hygienic, letting him lick the plate.'

'A peck of dirt never did anyone any harm,' pronounced Clemmy.

'Oh! Who told you that?'

'Millicent. She said we didn't need to wash before dinner tonight. And, anyway,' Clemmy rushed on, suddenly sensing Diana's long distance disapproval at her statement, 'we've got to go now. We're taking Seamus rabbiting over the Downs. Bert's coming with his shotgun. Byeee!'

Diana stood holding the dead 'phone. The children out on the Downs with Bert. Bert with a loaded shot-gun at this time of night. She hoped he'd be careful. Was his eyesight all right? She only just stopped herself from ringing back to Abbey House and forbidding them to go. Common sense stopped her. Why was she fussing about like some anxious mother? It was June, the evenings were long and light, and nowhere longer and lighter than over the glowing contours of the South Downs.

She looked out of the window. The Thames glowed with reflected light, and the sky was smudged with a pinkish purple haze. The products of pollution hanging over London, although it looked pretty. But on the Downs the light would shimmer with the clarity of crystal; a perfect night for catching rabbits. Diana remembered trailing behind a much more youthful Bert in her own childhood, gathering the furry creatures he'd shot, when they were still warm to the touch. It hadn't seemed repellent, it had been natural. Rabbits were pests, and good for the pot too. Later she and Susan would watch, in May's kitchen, as they were cleaned; then they would hang each one up by the back legs, the heads in brown paper bags, the stomachs propped open with rough wooden stakes. Hanging game made all the difference.

Diana remembered the delicious rabbit pies and stews May used to make.

She looked around the kitchen at the meal she'd prepared. How different were the meals of her childhood from those she ate today. Everything she bought now was ultra hygienic, sanitized into virtual tastelessness. All coming in plastic bags or boxes. It was hard to imagine any of the meat or fish actually running about, or swimming in seas or rivers. But it was progress. A strange phenomenon.

Diana looked at her watch again. Where *was* Hugh?

Chapter Twenty

Diana was late arriving at Terminal 4, Heathrow, and only made the 7.00 p.m. Concorde flight by the skin of her teeth. The rest of the passengers had already boarded.

'You're late,' grumbled Alan bad-temperedly when she slid into the seat on the other side of the aisle from his.

Yes, because I had to sort out a balls-up you'd made, Diana was tempted to reply, but she said instead, 'problems at the office, I'm afraid.' And last minute 'phone calls to Mottisley to make certain all was well, and to Hugh because she'd wanted to reassure herself that all was well between them too. He'd been curiously preoccupied when he'd eventually got in the previous evening. But even now, after speaking to him for twenty minutes on the 'phone, Diana still felt a tingle of disquiet. Something was happening to them, she wasn't sure what, but these matters were private, not something to be mentioned to Alan Sinclair.

'I had hoped Diana was sitting with me.' Lord Bing's shining bald pate popped out beside Alan.

Diana and Alan changed seats. Lord Bing patted Diana's knee and smiled flirtatiously. And that's all you are going to pat thought Diana, feeling cross. Some men never progressed to maturity as far as the opposite sex was concerned. Did he seriously think a bald head and a portly stomach was a turn on?

'You look disapproving. Patting a knee doesn't come under the heading "sexual harassment", does it?' joked Lord Bing.

'I'm tired,' said Diana, 'not disapproving.' She smiled, reminding herself that she only had to be sweet for a short time. Tomorrow morning they'd be winging their way back to London.

'I've already ordered the champagne, the best, of course,' said Alan importantly. 'Once we're airborne, we should be the first to be served.'

'That's what I like. Being well looked after.' Lord Bing settled back in his seat, looking smug.

Surrounded as he inevitably was by sycophants like Alan and herself, Diana thought the likelihood of his being anything other than well looked after, was remote. She too settled back, watching the orange runway lights flash past, and bracing herself against the steep upward tilt as Concorde took off and sped away from London towards the sun.

Three hours later she watched the coast of Long Island, New York come into view, and soon they were flying low over the awe-inspiring towers of Manhattan Island.

'5.30 p.m. New York time,' said Lord Bing, altering his watch. 'What time do you think we'll reach the Waldorf Astoria, Alan?'

'About 7.00 p.m. with luck.'

Diana thought that an overly optimistic estimate, but kept her thoughts to herself.

'We'll sail through immigration, thanks to Lord Bing,' Alan said.

And they did. A Minister of the Crown got the VIP treatment, and Diana, used to the hassle of Kennedy airport immigration, began to think that Lord Bing did have something in his favour after all. They were whisked through immigration and customs, everyone all smiles and politeness.

The fourteen miles to the centre of New York, however, was another matter. The traffic was solid, and much to Alan's obvious exasperation, it took more than two hours to get to Manhattan. His constant apologizing got on Diana's nerves.

'Alan, I think Lord Bing realizes that you are not

266

personally responsible for the New York traffic,' she said sharply.

Alan lapsed into sulky silence and Diana wondered if he was regretting not taking Lord Bing out to dinner in London. It would have been a damned sight simpler. But Alan always wanted to impress.

At last the taxi pulled to a halt, and the liveried doorman opened the door with a flourish. All Diana could think of when walking through the canopied entrance into the Waldorf Astoria Hotel, was how much she'd like to have a hot bath and go to bed. It might only be 8.45 p.m. New York time, but for her it was gone midnight. Alan and Lord Bing seemed unaffected, and buzzed happily along behind her like two excited schoolboys. They were looking forward to their dinner. Diana found herself wondering how the new housekeeper was getting on at Mottisley. They'd all be in bed there now. And how long would Griselda be off work? It was a worry having to pay an extra salary, one that she hadn't budgeted for, and Norman Leadbetter, true to her expectation, had not been enthusiastic.

'I really do think you must be very careful, Mrs Stratton,' he had said. 'You could easily run into problems.' Potential financial problems were a new and worrying experience for Diana, and not, she thought, something to be recommended.

'Diana, are you dreaming? I said, see you in half an hour.' Alan's voice interrupted her worries.

'Yes, of course.' Diana switched her mind back to the present, reminding herself that this was work, this would earn her money. This would help pay for Millicent Wright and everything else at Abbey House. She wondered again how the children and Millicent had got along on their second day. Had she done the right thing? Yes, of course she had. There was no alternative. Now she had to get on with the business in hand. She smiled at Alan. 'It won't take me long to change.'

Later, soothed by alcohol and food, Diana found that

dinner was not as tiresome as she had anticipated, and parried Lord Bing's flirtatious advances with amused dispassion.

'Tell me, my dear. Doesn't your husband get jealous? Doesn't he want you to stay at home with him, rather than flying off around the world?'

'My husband supports me in everything I do,' said Diana, wishing it was true. Lately Hugh hadn't been supportive at all, especially not where anything to do with Abbey House was concerned. 'He's not one of these men who has the archaic view that a woman's place is in the home.'

'I can see that you manage your home life as efficiently as your business life. You're a remarkable woman.'

'Not remarkable. A twentieth-century woman,' said Diana, wishing she had actually *seen* Millicent Wright rather than merely speaking to her. One read so many awful things in the papers these days. Supposing the woman was a compulsive child murderer! It was no use telling herself that there were plenty of other people at Mottisley to keep an eye on things. She had made the decision to hire Mrs Wright, and therefore she was responsible. Twentieth-century woman or not, it didn't stop her worrying.

The weariness afflicting Diana the day of Griselda's accident stayed with her in New York and throughout the following week. The only bright spot was the fact that all her fears had proved unfounded; Millicent Wright and the children seemed to be getting on very well. All the reports from Mottisley were good. Only Tony seemed to have some reservations, but then as he'd told Diana himself, he was always cautious.

She looked at the calendar. The end of June, only two and a half months since Susan's death. It seemed like years, and it was a different woman who had picked up the 'phone that morning in April to be told the news by Tony Evans. Diana knew she had changed since then. She didn't *want* to, had never planned it. But it had happened none the less, was still happening, slowly, gradually, but very, very surely. Was it because she was now responsible for lives other than her own? Was it that which made her approach things from a different angle? Diana wasn't sure. But whatever the reason, the certainty was that she *had* changed. Perhaps that was why she found herself so often disagreeing with Hugh lately. No, disagreeing was the wrong word. Quarrelling was the word to use. The smooth calmness of their previous well-ordered existence had disappeared, to be replaced by a life lived out on an emotional see-saw.

Diana put her head in her hands. She felt like weeping. Oh, damn you Susan for handing the children to me on a plate, and leaving their stewardship to my conscience. Damn, damn, *damn*, you! And damn too my own stupidity for being faint-hearted. Now my marriage is at risk and there is no-one to blame but myself.

Knowing that Hugh would hate Norman Leadbetter's idea of closing all their joint accounts, she had put off telling him that although the accounts were still there, she'd transferred all the funds to her own accounts. A cowardly act for which she had paid dearly last night. Last night! God, what a row. The mother and father of all rows. She tried not to think of it, but the angry, then increasingly vindictive, words rumbled round and round inside her head.

It had started when Hugh had roared, yes, that was the word, *roared* into the apartment. His face was unhealthily pale, the paleness thrown into greater relief by the bulging veins on his neck and forehead. He was waving their, once valid now defunct, joint cheque book.

'You bitch,' he howled, throwing the cheque book at her feet. 'You underhanded, nasty, deceitful bitch. How dare you humiliate me like this.'

Diana was alarmed. Of recent months she'd seen Hugh lose his temper, but never, never had he looked like this.

269

He's mad, thought part of her brain, and then immediately rejected it. Of course he wasn't. He couldn't possibly be. 'What do you mean, humiliate?' she asked.

'I mean closing the fucking joint accounts without telling me. I suppose it gives your power mad mind a kick to know that I tried to use the account, and got hauled in front of the bank manager? I looked a fool. Not knowing what my own wife had done.'

Diana gasped. It hadn't occurred to her that Hugh would try to use one of the old accounts. There was no need, all their bills were paid by direct debit, and that hadn't changed, she was still paying them. 'But I only changed them a week ago, and of course I was going to tell you, but I've been busy and . . .'

'Oh yes, you've been busy all right. Busy making sure that your husband would look a fool. Making sure that I'd not have access to your money.'

'Hugh, that's not the reason. I'm not shutting you out, or trying to humiliate you. I had to do it. For tax reasons. The vineyard and the Abbey House estate have made things very complicated. Norman Leadbetter insisted.'

'Fuck, Norman Leadbetter,' Hugh snarled, and coming up to Diana he gripped her arm so tightly that she felt the trapped blood tingling in her fingers. His eyes were black pools of seething fury. 'Think you're so clever, don't you,' he whispered. 'Well, two can play at that game. If you're going to keep your money separate, then perhaps we should live separately as well. Divorce means splitting everything down the middle. Let's do that. Then you'd *have* to give me half.'

'Divorce?' whispered Diana. She could hardly believe her ears. 'Is that what you want? Just because I did as the accountant suggested?' As she spoke she began to feel angry. Hugh was being unreasonable, quite absurd. She should have told him, of course she should. But how was she to know he'd use the account? He had no need to. Not now, not at this time of the month. He had no bills to pay. She put her thoughts into words. 'I didn't know you'd use one of those accounts yet. You don't need to. Really, Hugh, if all I am to you is an easy access bank account, then perhaps you are right. Maybe we *should* get a divorce.'

Am I really saying this, she thought. Hardly able to believe the words issuing from her own lips. I don't want a divorce. I don't want to join the other millions who haven't made a success of their marriages. Suddenly she was frightened again. As frightened as she had been as a child when she feared her parents would divorce. Why was it she was so afraid to admit failure? Equally, why did she equate divorce with failure? Many women were much happier after separation. But I won't be, she cried silently, I know I won't. She knew what it was she wanted, it was stability, security and to be with Hugh who'd always symbolized those things to her. She wanted nothing to change. Why couldn't they go back to how things were when they were first married? Recapture their early happiness. Not go on as they were now, bickering continually, usually over money and the Abbey Vineyard. But even as the thoughts flared up they immediately guttered down to extinction. It was futile. There was no going back, not for her, not for anyone. One could only go on. Through no fault of her own she had picked up responsibilities which she didn't want, but nevertheless had to shoulder. Hugh could support her, not obstruct her. But he was turning life into one long obstacle race.

Hugh looked at Diana standing before him. Pale, slender, beautiful but nondescript, he thought viciously. Not like Nancy. She couldn't turn him on like Nancy. She'd never sniff coke or agree to sexual experiments. She was dull. He didn't need her. He needed Nancy. Walking into the bedroom he pulled down a suitcase. 'Yes,' he said coldly. 'Yes, I think a divorce would be a good idea. I'll go now.'

'Where?' asked Diana.

'None of your bloody business,' he said.

Diana stared at him. I ought to be trying to persuade

271

him not to go. I ought to be telling him I love him. But the words stuck in her throat. She had apologized once, and was damned if she was going to apologize any more. Anyway, did she want him to stay? That thought stopped her dead. Did she want him to stay, or was their marriage over? Really over? No, she couldn't bear that. Something had to be said to stop him leaving.

'Hugh,' Diana reached out and touched his arm. 'Look, I'm really sorry you had to find out about the accounts in such a way. I didn't intend that it should be like that. It's my fault for not telling you sooner. But you're wrong about me wanting power. I don't want to lord it over you, I never have. I want us to be partners, and more than that I want us to be happy. Don't let's act rashly. Please stay, darling.'

Hugh paused in his packing and looked at her. His black eyes held not a hint of warmth. 'Tell Norman Leadbetter to go to hell, and re-open our joint accounts. Then I'll stay.'

A hard, cold feeling suddenly lodged in Diana's chest. It almost choked her. He wanted to bargain with her. Negotiate the price of their remaining together. And a strange bargain it was he was trying to strike. Love didn't feature at all, only money.

'I can't do that, Hugh,' she heard herself saying.

'Drop dead, then,' snarled Hugh, and left.

That's when I should have taken the sleeping pills, thought Diana, pressing the buzzer for Shirley to come into the office, not hours later. If I'd taken the Mogadon then, I'd be able to concentrate now.

'Yes, Mrs Stratton.' Shirley arrived in answer to the buzzer.

'Strong black coffee, please, Shirley, with plenty of sugar.'

'Yes.' Shirley turned to go, then looked back, anxious. 'Are you sure you're all right, Mrs Stratton? You look awful. Shall I ask Mr Sinclair to cancel the meeting with Sir Timothy Drisdale and Lord Bing?'

'Certainly not. I'm all right. A bit of a headache, that's all.'

'Here you are, Mrs Stratton.' Shirley returned to Diana's office and put the coffee on her desk. 'Would you like some biscuits?'

'No thanks, the coffee will be fine. Thank you, Shirley.'

Oh God, only half an hour before *THE* meeting on the Norfolk Theme Park. Diana took a scalding mouthful of coffee, two aspirins, and prayed that her head would clear. Half an hour later she sat down in the boardroom and surveyed the array of masculine faces staring at her through a blue haze of smoke. She wished they didn't all have to smoke so early in the morning, it was like working in a chimney; and why did they talk so loudly? She noticed Lord Bing at the far end of the room, he studiously ignored her. For someone who'd been so expensively wined and dined the week before, he looked strangely aloof. Sir Timothy had a new aide fluttering around him, whispering in his ear. Whatever the aide said must have been funny, for Sir Timothy suddenly brayed with laughter. Diana wondered if he knew his laugh sounded like an over-excited donkey? Regarding him from beneath lowered eyelids, she decided he didn't. If he did, he'd surely be quiet.

Alan opened the meeting. The contingent from the Norfolk District Planning Committee had come up to London especially for the meeting. They sat together, looking red-necked and uncomfortable in old fashioned shiny suits. Out of place countrymen surrounded by suave city gentlemen. Diana suddenly felt a pang of sorrow for them. They'd been outmanoeuvred, bought and betrayed by the city gentlemen sitting around them. Not that any of them were real gentlemen. In reality they were well disguised cut-throat gangsters.

Alan turned to Diana. 'I leave the ball in your court,' he said, smiling at her. 'I know you've got all the latest facts and figures.'

Diana looked at the open file in front of her, the writing

on the page blurred, then swam about crazily. It didn't matter. She knew it by heart anyway. She launched into the now familiar spiel of the minimum environmental damage, and the maximum benefit for the UK as a whole.

She finished by saying, 'and so you see, Norfolk itself will benefit by the additional tourism, and so will the rest of Britain as money is siphoned in from abroad.'

'You make it sound as if it is some huge monster, intent on swallowing everything in its path.' That was, Diana peered at his name plate, CHARLES MONTGOMERY, Junior Minister for the Environment.

'Did I?' she said. Sir Timothy gave a high pitched snigger. 'I didn't mean to.'

'I'm passing all the points to be disputed over to Charles,' said Sir Timothy, 'he's really on the ball where anything green with a capital G is concerned.'

'Points to be disputed?' Alan flashed Diana a worried look. 'I thought we'd gone beyond that stage.'

'Not quite,' Charles Montgomery fixed Diana with a searching stare. 'I've read all your reports very carefully. Would you agree that you've given pre-eminence to the financial side of the scheme?'

'Certainly,' said Diana. She felt sick. What would they say if she threw up on to the beautifully polished mahogany table? 'Ultimately the financial viability of any scheme is the only thing that matters.'

'You mean a nation needs to count all its wealth in cash?' Charles Montgomery smiled at Sir Timothy, who smiled back.

Diana began to feel uneasy as well as queasy. There was something going on she didn't understand. 'Ultimately, yes,' she said. Then doubt struck at her. No, that wasn't true. That wasn't what she meant. Yes, damn it, it was. Hell, that was what the Norfolk Theme Park was about, wasn't it? Money. Nothing else, just money.

'I take it, you think non-pecuniary schemes don't have any quantifiable value?' Again that strange smile from Charles Montgomery.

'Such schemes are difficult to quantify,' replied Diana cautiously. Where was he going with this line of argument?

'I disagree. I think the village you propose to eradicate if the scheme goes ahead would have no difficulty in quantifying their value. Although the measure would be in sociological and ecological terms rather than remunerative.'

Diana became aware of the contingent from Norfolk all nodding their heads. They recognized that statement. Suddenly she realized they had been primed. Such long-winded jargon wasn't likely to be their natural métier. There was a sudden buzz of disjointed comments.

'A small dairy farm, but a good little Friesian herd. Just big enough to manage.'

'That's right, and two nurseries.

'Aye, Mr and Mrs Beckett grow marvellous roses. Sold the length and breadth of England.'

'And don't forget Henry Burstow, best reed thatcher in Norfolk.'

'So you see, Lady, and Gentlemen,' said the Junior Minister for the Environment looking at Diana, 'this little village is, in fact, what we would term nowadays, a centre for thriving cottage industries. And it is this, that it is proposed to eradicate.'

'Diana, *say* something,' hissed Alan.

Casting her mind frantically around for inspiration, Diana remembered a speech she'd heard at a CBI meeting only the previous week. The disdainful sentiments expressed then fitted the present discussion perfectly. 'By cottage industry, I suppose you mean a sort of subsistence farming,' she said. 'And surely you must admit, that this type of industry is not cost effective. At most the workers make just enough to live on, at best they get some form of personal satisfaction.'

'Exactly.' Charles Montgomery looked triumphant. 'Personal satisfaction,' he said in ringing tones as if he'd just invented it. 'You see, work is not only work when the worker is paid by somebody else to do it. Even if it's good pay, such a distinction is meaningless. Work means a way of life. These country people are the glory of the British nation. They are the mainstay of family life in this land. Something the Conservatives cherish dearly. Their lives provide the primary spring for personal contentment, and this is something we ought to encourage. We must stand by these people, for they are our heritage *and* our future.'

'Well said, Charles,' said Sir Timothy, leaning back in his chair. 'We must not let them down.' Contrary to his original belief, his constituents had left him in no doubt that he could not count on their votes if he backed the scheme. So a *volte-face* had not only been desirable, it had been crucial.

'And they all bloody well vote Tory,' muttered Alan angrily. 'Go on, Diana. Decimate him.'

Diana looked at the junior minister sitting opposite her. It was all very well Alan ordering her in for the kill, as if she was his own personal Rottweiler, but for the life of her she couldn't think of one decent argument to put against Charles Montgomery's statement. 'I suppose you're right,' she said slowly. 'There *is* something special about country people.'

'Holy shit, Diana. What was the matter with you?' Alan Sinclair was beside himself. Pacing the length of the now empty boardroom, he swung round to face Diana. '*Something special about country people,*' he ground the words out from between his teeth. 'What a load of bloody claptrap.'

Diana stared at him. Apart from the fact that Hugh was tall and slim, and Alan was short and rather overweight, there was a ghastly similarity between the two of them when they were angry. Both behaved like spoilt children. Both wanted their own way. Both wanted money more than anything else. And she was tied to both of them. To one by marriage, and the other by occupation. She supposed she could still call herself married. She hadn't heard from Hugh since he'd walked out the previous night. Where had he gone? Not that it seemed to matter at the moment. Her headache was worse, screaming like a jet engine behind her eyes.

'They are,' she said, answering Alan's remark and thinking of May and Bert and everyone else in Mottisley. 'Country people *are* special. And we were wrong to think of turfing them out of their homes.'

'Don't tell me you buggered up this meeting because you suddenly changed your mind. You're nothing but an incompetent bitch. That's the long and short of it. You were bloody incompetent.'

'In all conscience, Alan, there was no fair argument I could level against the junior minister's comments.' That was true enough. She hadn't purposely lost the argument, but at the back of her mind she knew her heart hadn't been in the fight.

'I wanted the money that project would bring in,' bleated Alan, suddenly petulant. Then his face screwed up in fury once more. 'And since when have you had a bloody conscience?' he sneered.

'Since this morning, Alan.' Suddenly the pain in her head became unbearable and Diana's already frayed nerves snapped. All she longed for was to leave. Leave the boardroom, leave the Wycombe and Yatton building and go to Mottisley. She felt as though she was groping her way along a slippery, long dark tunnel, and there at the end, peeping tantalizingly through the darkness, could be seen the peaceful green tranquillity of the countryside. The tranquillity of Mottisley, unscarred by the passage of time. A place where people still had the time to care for each other. Where money and its acquisition were not important.

'*Since this morning!*' Alan strode down the length of the boardroom and came to a full stop before Diana. Leaning forward he thumped the table. 'A bloody fine time you've picked to have a conscience. Do you realize how much money you've lost us? Not to mention what it's already cost in expenses. That little junket across the Atlantic last week cost me a pretty penny, plus all the other sweeteners I've had to pay for.'

'If it had been a good scheme, it wouldn't have needed sweeteners,' said Diana slowly.

'Not need sweeteners?' Alan practically screamed. 'Have you gone stark, raving mad? That's the way we always work.'

'Yes, and it's the wrong way.' Diana stood up. She knew now what she had to do. 'I've not gone mad, Alan. I've suddenly become sane. Sane enough not to want to work with a slimy little shit like you.' Alan gasped, but Diana continued before he had time to speak. 'My mistake was in ever persuading myself I could work with a manipulative cheat at all. I had my doubts, right from the beginning, but I squashed them. I know now that I was wrong. I should have listened to my conscience then. I always knew what you were really like. A greedy, grasping, oversexed, undersized, unintelligent little runt. Unable to keep your sticky little hands off other men's women or their money. I'm not going to spend another moment breathing the same air as you. Like everything else around you, it's polluted.'

Diana picked up her files and swept from the boardroom.

Alan followed her, practically jumping up and down with fury. 'I want your notice in writing,' he howled.

'If it will help, I'll write it in my own blood.'

'And clear out your office before you go, and don't think you'll get driven home by a chauffeur. From this moment on you haven't got a car or a chauffeur.'

Shirley handed Diana the typewritten letter for her to sign. 'Oh, Mrs Stratton. I wish you weren't leaving. We all do.'

'I have to go, Shirley.'

'I know. I heard the row with Mr Sinclair.'

'Oh dear. I hope not too many people heard.'

'We all listened,' whispered Shirley. Then she looked up, her eyes shining with tears. 'But we're glad someone told him what a horrible man he is. Perhaps,' she added hopefully, 'he'll be a bit different now.'

Diana smiled wearily. 'I wouldn't count on that, Shirley. He's too old a leopard to be changing his spots.' She signed the letter and passed it across the desk.

Shirley took it reluctantly. 'Mrs Stratton, can I ask you something? When you get your next job, if you need a secretary, will you please think of me.'

'If I do need another secretary, of course I'd offer the job to you, Shirley. You're very good. But I don't think I'll be staying in London. I'm thinking of working in the country.'

Bryant drove her back to the apartment contrary to Alan Sinclair's instructions. He had caught up with Diana as she walked down The Strand.

'Mr Sinclair has told me to take the Bentley and just go for a drive,' said Bryant. 'He said I could go anywhere I fancied. So I'm going to Chelsea. Do you want a lift?'

Diana hopped in gratefully. Every taxi had whizzed past, all already occupied. There was always the tube, but the long walk from Pimlico station to the apartment in Chelsea was daunting, especially when she was burdened with two briefcases filled to bursting and a mountain of extra paper files.

'Thanks, Bryant. I take it you've heard that I've given in my notice.' The thought suddenly struck her. 'Oh dear, I hope I haven't made you redundant.'

'Plenty of chauffeuring jobs about,' said Bryant philosophically. 'More, I dare say, than deputy managing directorships.'

Diana smiled ruefully. 'On that, you are one hundred per cent right, Bryant.'

On reaching Cheyne Walk, Bryant carried her cases and bags up to the apartment for her. Diana wondered if

Hugh had come back in her absence. She could see no sign of his presence. Which hotel had he slept in last night? Had he been comfortable? Was he regretting their quarrel? Was she? The answer to that was yes, she did regret it. They'd both been far too hot tempered, and now she was longing to confide in Hugh, tell him about the row with Alan Sinclair. Tell him how she really felt.

'I'll be off now, Mrs Stratton.' Bryant's voice interrupted her straggling thoughts. 'And don't forget. If you ever need another chauffeur, remember me.'

Diana watched the lift doors close on Bryant's tall figure, then turned and entered the apartment. Nice of Bryant saying he wanted to work for her again. Unlikely though that he would. The germ of an idea which had been conceived in the boardroom during her row with Alan Sinclair, was slowly beginning to formulate into a more concrete plan. The more she thought about it, the more attractive it seemed. She wondered what Hugh's opinion would be. Then abruptly stopped wondering.

Picking up the 'phone Diana dialled Hugh's number at the Lincoln's Inn firm. She could never stand uncertainty. She had to know. Was he coming back, or was he not?

'Mr Stratton's office.' That was Miss Higgins's quavery voice.

'This is Mrs Stratton. Is it possible to speak to my husband?'

Miss Higgins who had only just taken a call from Nancy nearly dropped the 'phone in panic. This was too much. His mistress 'phoning him one minute, his wife the next. 'I'll see if he's available, Mrs Stratton.'

Diana looked at the 'phone in puzzlement. Was it her imagination, or did old Miss Higgins sound scared out of her wits? Next moment, without further ado, she found she was abruptly switched through to Hugh.

'Diana?' he said cautiously. Nancy had told him last night in no uncertain terms that her finances wouldn't stretch to the two of them sharing her home, or sharing the cost of their expensive habits. She'd told him that if he wanted to continue their affair, then he *had* to go back to his wife. Diana was, after all, as Nancy had so pithily pointed out, the one with all the money.

'You're a fool to have lost your temper,' she'd told him. 'There's more than one way of skinning a cat. Go back, make it up, and go on milking her for every penny she's got. This accountant is only a temporary hiccup. It's up to you to find a way round him. You want her money, don't you?' Hugh did, and now Diana had telephoned him, it seemed there was a chink of daylight in the blackness of their quarrel the previous night.

Diana hesitated, and Wycombe and Yatton were temporarily forgotten. What should she say to Hugh? Then from a practice born of years of experience, she knew the answer. The best way was always the simplest. She came straight to the point. 'I rang, Hugh,' she said. 'Because I wanted to know if you were coming home.'

Hugh breathed a silent sigh of relief. She wanted him to come back. She was making it easy for him. 'Of course,' he said. 'Did you think I wasn't?'

'That would hardly be surprising after last night.'

'Water under the bridge,' said Hugh breezily. 'Hot words, spoken in haste.'

'Oh,' said Diana, thinking I ought to be glad. Overjoyed, in fact. Instead I feel indifferent. A moment ago I wanted him back. I wanted to talk to him, confide in him. Now, I'm no longer so certain. She wished Hugh didn't have the irritating habit of sweeping away their quarrels as if they had never happened. They never *really* talked. Hugh was averse to delving. He was speaking again. Diana tuned in to his words.

'Look, darling.' Heavens, we're back to darling already. Diana couldn't help feeling that was a little precipitate. 'I can't talk on this 'phone. That old hag, Miss Higgins, listens in I'm sure.' Diana thought she heard a faint click. Perhaps Hugh was right. Could that be Miss Higgins putting down the extension? She smiled. Poor Hugh, fancy having his conversations monitored. Not, though, that they were likely to be very interesting. 'I'll try and get off a little early tonight,' he was saying. 'And we can have a relaxing evening. How did the meeting go today?'

So he had remembered. Diana realized that Hugh thought she was 'phoning from the office. 'It's all over and done with now, thank God,' she said ambiguously.

'That's my girl. I knew you'd get it right in the end.'

'Yes, I got it right in the end.' Would Hugh's definition of 'right' coincide with hers?

Chapter Twenty-one

Sheridan cycled along the lane from Mottisley village to Abbey House. The incline, deceptive to the eye, was steeper than he'd thought when he cycled down, and he struggled for breath as he rounded the last curve in the lane. The next moment he was lying, flat on his back, in the ditch.

'You all right, me lad?' May Marsham, the cause of his demise, screeched above the revving of the motorcycle engine.

'Yes, but no damned thanks to you!' Sheridan struggled to right himself. 'Why must you drive so fast? And aren't you supposed to toot your horn before you come round a bend in these parts?'

May watched him get up, and switched off the engine. He really was the most gorgeous chocolate-coloured young man, no wonder half the girls in the village were besotted with him, and apparently even the Reverend Pincher had mentioned him in his sermon last Sunday. The talented stranger in our midst, he'd said, according to Bert. Even Mrs Pincher was not so anti Sheridan now. 'I'm in a hurry,' she said.

'Don't let me detain you then.' Sheridan was annoyed. Sometimes he liked May very much, although she perplexed him, and other times she drove him to distraction. The problem was, she didn't behave like an old lady; more like an ancient Hell's Angel, and this threw Sheridan.

'No need to be bad-tempered,' said May, peering at him from beneath her crash helmet. 'You're not hurt as far as I can see.' Having ascertained that fact, the matter was closed as far as she was concerned.

It wasn't for Sheridan. 'I might have been,' he said

crossly, unbending the buckled mudguard on the front wheel.

'But you weren't. And anyway, what are you doing skedaddling around country lanes on a bicycle? Why aren't you using the estate car?'

'Because somebody at Abbey House has to make some economies. Millicent certainly isn't. She's overspent the housekeeping yet again this week, and this is only her second week. I've given her some money from the wine sales, we can't keep asking Mrs Stratton to top us up.'

'Diana can afford it,' said May.

Sheridan who had a much more realistic perception of what could and could not be afforded, felt even more exasperated. 'She needs to invest in the vineyard, not subsidize Millicent Wright's extravagances. I've just posted a report to her suggesting that we plough and plant the remaining six acres of land here. That will cost a minimum of £4,000 an acre.'

'Then why plant it?' asked May.

'So that eventually she gets a good return on the land.' Sheridan forgot his annoyance with May as he warmed to his pet subject, viticulture. 'If we planted some more Black Hamburg and Seibal grapes, we could make an additional quantity of good quality rosé wine. The one Abbey Vineyard already makes is very popular, it would be sensible to extend in that area.'

'So you think you're still going to be here in four years' time? That's good. That means Diana and the children will be here too.'

Sheridan who had already been told by everyone in Mottisley of Diana's original plans to sell the vineyard, guessed at May's worries. They were his also. 'I'll only be here if I can make this place pay. That's why we've got to be careful with what we spend. Mrs Stratton is a good businesswoman, but she's not going to be willing to go on financing a lame duck enterprise *ad infinitum*.'

'I see what you mean.' May tapped her teeth thoughtfully, then came to a conclusion. 'All right, you lean on

Millicent; persuade her to do a little less of the *cordon bleu*, and stick to plain cooking. Although how we'll wean the children off this fancy stuff now I don't know. Meanwhile, I'll have a word with Diana and get her to wield a big stick too. We can't have the temporary housekeeper plunging Abbey Vineyard into financial ruin.'

She climbed back on to the motorcycle and revved it up. Then roared off in a flurry of dust, leaving the once peaceful country lane throbbing with the sound of her exhaust.

'Bloody woman.' Sheridan climbed back on to the bicycle. She meant well, but he suspected she had no idea of how much money Diana was, in reality, having to spend.

It was early evening and Diana had just put down the 'phone when Hugh arrived home. She had felt a little disturbed when May had told her the new housekeeper, Millicent, was not keeping to her budget. But only a little disturbed, not unduly. If she followed through the plan she had in her mind, that little problem would soon be sorted out. She hadn't told May that she'd left her job. Time enough for that when her plans were finalized.

Hugh arrived with an enormous bouquet of flowers. 'With my abject apologies,' he said, handing them to Diana. 'And of course, congratulations.'

'Congratulations?' Diana felt a slight quiver of surprise, followed by delight. He must know that she'd given in her notice, and he approved. 'So you've heard then?'

'Of course. You told me yourself. It's all over and done with, you said.'

Diana felt deflated. It was stupid to think that Hugh would have known. How could he? Nothing for it but to tell him now. 'It's true I did say that. But it didn't mean what you think.'

'What did it mean, then?' Hugh felt a chill of unease.

'I've left Wycombe and Yatton. Given in my notice.'

Diana remembered the row with Alan, and suddenly smiled. 'You are looking at an unemployed woman.' For the first time since she had woken up that morning she realized that her headache was gone, and that she felt wonderful. More free, more alive. Truly mistress of her own destiny.

'What!' For a moment Diana thought Hugh was going to snatch back the bouquet from her. But then he sat down, rather quickly, as if his legs would no longer support him. 'Why, for God's sake, *WHY?*' he asked plaintively.

'Because I'd had it up to here with Alan Sinclair.' Diana drew her hand across her throat. 'And I told him so. After that I had no choice but to leave. But don't worry, I know what I'm going to do.'

'What are you going to do?' asked Hugh faintly. His mind was reeling with shock. No bonus, no salary coming in, no money. Jesus Christ! *no money!* 'Will you get a golden handshake?' he asked hopefully.

'You must be joking. After what I said, Alan is probably planning to bring a libel suit against me. No, there'll be no golden handshake. Anyway, what I've been thinking is this. We sell this apartment and both move down to Mottisley. You can commute to London, it's not so far. You could go by train, I'd drop you off at the railway station in Chichester, then stay behind at Mottisley and run the vineyard with Sheridan. That way I'm sure I could soon make the whole enterprise a paying operation, *and* I'd be able to keep a proper eye on the children.'

'If that is what you really want to do,' Hugh said very slowly, choosing his words with care.

Diana looked at him in surprise. She'd been expecting vociferous objections. 'You wouldn't mind?'

'Look,' said Hugh, mentally crossing his fingers and praying that he was handling the unexpected situation the right way. 'Forget all the harsh words we exchanged in the heat of the moment last night, and remember other times. Remember the time I told you to leave your job if that was what you wanted. You said then, you'd be bored. But perhaps if you were busy running the vineyard you wouldn't have time to be bored. So I think, let's give it a go.' He linked his arms loosely around Diana, and looked down at her.

Diana looked up at him, and slowly slid her arms around his waist. She felt very happy. Their quarrel had cleared the air. Hugh had come back and now he seemed to be more understanding of her needs, much more considerate. 'You really mean it?'

'Darling, of course I do.' Hugh bent his head and kissed her slowly. 'Let's go to bed,' he whispered, 'and then later I'll take you out to dinner.'

Diana smiled and let her head rest in the hollow of Hugh's shoulder. Who would have believed that a day starting out in such a disastrous fashion could end on such a sublime note. 'I was foolish to think I could do without you, Hugh,' she said. 'I do need you.'

'I never for one moment thought that I could do without you,' lied Hugh. 'If only you knew how hard it was for me not to turn right round last night, and walk back. I don't know what forced me to leave. Stubborn pride, I suppose.'

Diana took one of his hands and laid it against her cheek. 'It was pride which made me tell you to go,' she admitted. 'I'm sorry.'

'So am I.' His lips sought and found hers. His last thought, before drawing her purposefully towards the bedroom, was how to persuade Diana to change her mind. He had no intention of letting her rusticate in Mottisley, she would have to get another post, and somehow he had to persuade her into thinking this was what she wanted.

Diana responding to the pressure of his mouth, followed him into the bedroom.

* * *

287

Diana rang Norman Leadbetter the following morning and told him the news of her resignation.

'You'd better come and see me,' he said. 'This morning, in my office.'

Diana walked to his office in Sloane Square. The spell of fine weather had lasted, and now at the end of June the plane trees were in heavy summer leaf. It was wonderful not to be rushed. To have time to stroll up past the handsome iron gates of the Chelsea Physic Garden, through which could be glimpsed some of the rare and curious plants which grew there. Her mind on Mottisley, Diana wondered if vines were cultivated at Chelsea. She knew there was an olive tree, supposedly the northern-most tree in Europe to bear olives, but vines? She wondered. Still revelling in her new found leisure, she passed the Military Museum and came to the Royal Chelsea Hospital. The gardeners had been working over-time. Massed banks of colour filled the flower beds. Not a square inch of earth could be seen, the plants were packed in so tightly. Very beautiful, thought Diana, but somehow a little tame when compared to the haphazard colours of the wildly overgrown garden of Abbey House. That had a more natural beauty, in harmony with the deep, shadowy lanes, and sunbleached humps of the Downs. There, the sound would be the constant murmur of bees and other insects, not the constant hum of traffic. She felt impatient, suddenly aching to get there. The sooner they packed up and left London, the better.

'You can't possibly live in Mottisley and run the vineyard without taking out an enormous loan.'

Norman Leadbetter was in a dilemma. How much should he tell Diana? It was always tricky when dealing with a husband and wife situation. Did she know that her husband had taken vast sums of money from their joint accounts? Instinct told him that Hugh Stratton had taken most of it without Diana's knowledge.

'But I'm not destitute,' protested Diana. She was

disappointed, Norman Leadbetter was the last person she had expected to put a dampener on her plans. 'I've been earning plenty of money, and we are going to sell the apartment. That will raise extra capital.'

'As well as earning a lot, Mrs Stratton, I must point out to you that you've also spent a lot. You and your husband, like most young people today, have lived to the limit of your income.' He breathed a little easier, that had been a tactful way of letting her know the coffers were more or less empty. 'And as for selling your apartment, it's not something that will raise capital immediately. And is your husband agreeable to this? The property is, after all, jointly owned.'

'Oh yes.' Diana smiled remembering Hugh's passionate lovemaking the previous night. 'He thinks it will do us both good to move away from London.' Hugh hadn't actually said that, but she was sure that was what he'd meant.

'Yes, Mrs Stratton, I'm sure it would,' Norman Leadbetter, sensing Diana's affection for her husband felt his way carefully. The last thing he wanted was to be responsible for rocking an apparently secure marriage. 'However, I must advise strongly against such a move in the immediate future.'

'Why?'

'Let me show you the projected vineyard accounts. These include the suggestions Sheridan Porter has made concerning expansion. He's given me some tentative figures for planting another six acres with,' adjusting his glasses, he peered at the papers, 'Oh yes, with Black Hamburg and Seibal grapes so that the production of your rosé wine can be increased.'

Diana leaned forward to see. 'I haven't had those figures,' she said.

'Mr Porter is sending you the finalized figures as soon as he's costed it properly. But as you can see from this, even a small expansion is extremely costly.'

'But the vineyard has revenue.'

'Not much. The initial investment borrowing your sister made is still being paid. A good harvest this year could see that paid off if you are lucky, and then you can begin to think about breaking even, perhaps making a small profit. But only, and I must emphasize this, only if the overheads are kept to the absolute minimum.'

'Heavens, you make it all sound very depressing,' said Diana staring at the figures. It looked horribly expensive. The new machinery urgently needed in the winery for pressing the grapes was costed at upwards of £80,000, and that was just one of many items.

'I'm afraid it is. Viticulture is not plain sailing as I've found out since I've been investigating the possible returns and profit margins for you. So much depends on luck with the weather. Good management alone is not enough.'

Diana suddenly remembered her own disparaging words to Susan years before, when the vineyard was first established. Always will be subject to the vagaries of the weather, she'd said. But Susan had persevered and survived, so why couldn't she? 'My sister and her family lived off the proceeds,' she said.

'God knows how.' Norman Leadbetter looked at Diana kindly. Did she have any idea at all of how hard up her sister had been? 'Your sister must have been a very remarkable woman,' he said gently. 'She kept meticulous records of everything she spent, even down to the children's new shoes. I can tell you there was precious little left over for her own needs.'

Once again Diana had the *dèja vu* feeling of being measured against Susan and found wanting. 'I could do it.' She wanted to prove herself, prove that she could cope with hardship as well as success.

Norman Leadbetter guessed what was in her mind. 'I didn't say you couldn't. But if you really want to put that vineyard on its feet, then you'll find another well paid job and underwrite the enterprise until it *is* viable.' He passed a piece of paper across to Diana. 'Scott and James, an excellent headhunting firm, I can personally recommend them. Go and see them. There are plenty of other openings for a talented person like yourself.'

Diana took the sheet of paper. Suddenly she was back in the dark tunnel again, the longed for tranquillity of life at Mottisley, that yesterday had seemed so overwhelming, so near, receded into the distance. Now it was just a faint spot of light, hopelessly out of reach. 'I suppose you're right,' she said slowly. 'I owe it to Susan to underwrite the vineyard, because, in truth, I only hold it in trust for the children.'

'And it's sensible to do what you can do best.' Norman Leadbetter encouraged her. 'You're a corporate woman by experience, and, I suspect, instinct. I'm not sure that you're cut out to run a small business with all its attendant day-to-day hassles. I have a feeling that you'd get irritated with the milieu.'

'And I thought I could escape,' said Diana so sadly that the accountant began to have doubts.

Perhaps he should have let her follow her dream. But no, without her money the vineyard and the little family she'd inherited would all go under. But with her money, now that was different. And now he had charge of her accounting, that husband of hers wouldn't be able to help himself so liberally to extra cash whenever he felt like it, and she'd soon accrue a healthy bank balance.

Diana looked at the paper again. Scott and James, they had an office in Westminster. In spite of what he'd said, she knew that Hugh would be pleased if she decided to stay in London. Perhaps yesterday's longing to escape had been the culmination of stress caused by working with Alan Sinclair, and she was wrong in thinking she'd be happy in Mottisley. Perhaps this was the right place for her. After all, what had she been longing to escape from? If she was absolutely honest she wasn't really sure. Running down to Mottisley wouldn't solve any problems between herself and Hugh, only aggravate them, and anyway, maybe she'd been exaggerating that too. Last night Hugh had been so understanding, just like he'd been in the early days of their life together. He wanted their marriage to work just as much as she did, and all marriages had their sticky patches. He had to be considered as well as the children.

In fact, when viewed from a sensible angle, instead of from an illogically emotional one, she could see that it would be much easier dealing with Mottisley and the children from a distance, rather than in person all the time. The telephone was more impersonal. I can love the children more, provide for them better, when I'm away from them. A ridiculous thought, perhaps, but strangely true. Long-distance affection was more agreeable, not so intense, not so all-enveloping.

Norman Leadbetter was right. She *would* stay in London, and she would not let herself dwell on that irrational little part of her that was still stubbornly rooting for Mottisley. That idea would dwindle down to nothing and eventually die away completely, once she got going on something else. There was nothing like the challenge of a new job to stimulate the intellect and get the adrenalin surging. Once she was doing something she enjoyed once more, then the tranquillity of Mottisley would seem dull again.

'Well, what are you going to do?'

Diana stood up and smiled at Norman Leadbetter. A determined smile. Wycombe and Yatton was the past. Who knew what the future held, it was mysterious and exciting. 'No time like the present,' she said, brandishing the Scott and James paper before putting it in her briefcase. 'I shall go and see them today.'

Mike Menzies Scott and Charles James were two hyperactive, super-efficient young men and soon presented Diana with mountains of documents appertaining to firms they considered suitable potential employers. Norman Leadbetter had been right, they were good at their job, and nice too.

'No hurry,' said Mike. 'Take these papers home with

you and study them at your leisure. In the meantime we'll prime the companies and tell them they might be lucky enough to get the services of the talented Diana Stratton.'

'And the fact that you walked out of Wycombe and Yatton is a bonus point,' added Charles. 'Everyone in the City hates Alan Sinclair.'

'I'll read them all day and tonight,' said Diana and staggered back to the apartment at Chelsea, from where she 'phoned Hugh and told him of the latest developments.

Overjoyed that everything had fallen into place so neatly, without any effort being needed on his part, Hugh was his most tender, solicitous self. 'Don't you dare even think about cooking tonight,' he said. 'I'll prepare dinner. You just give those papers your undivided attention.'

Joe arrived at Willow Farm at the same moment as Tony, to be greeted by an irate Bert.

'I'm perfectly all right. I don't need any doctor. Or anyone else.' The last remark was directed at Joe.

'I'm not *any* doctor, Bert. I'm yours, and I'm going to check you over.' Tony Evans gently but firmly escorted a reluctant Bert Slocombe back into his armchair by the side of the kitchen range. Then he paused and wiped the sweat from his forehead. 'God, it's hot in here, May. Why don't you let that fire out now it's almost July? And for God's sake move that sugar from that shelf up there.' He pointed to the shelving above the range where two hundredweight bags of sugar were stored. May always believed in buying in bulk. 'It's a fire risk. And what's in those old cartridge boxes above the sugar?'

'It certainly is a fire risk,' said Joe. He had a horrible suspicion that the cartridge boxes actually contained cartridges, and was about to ask, but May cut him short.

'I didn't ask you round to poke your nose in Joe Kelly, and I asked you, young Dr Evans, round to look at my Bert, not tell me what to do. And for your information that fire's not been out since my mother's day and you

293

know it, and what's in those boxes is my business, not yours.'

Tony and Joe looked at each other, shrugged their shoulders, and gave up.

'And I'm all right,' growled Bert, doing up the buttons on his shirt almost as fast as Tony was undoing them.

'People who are all right don't fall off tractors,' said May fiercely to Bert. 'Now, just you sit still, undo your shirt front, and let Dr Evans have a listen.'

'My heart is as sound as a bell,' grumbled Bert mutinously as Tony placed his stethoscope on his chest.

Tony listened, and then proceeded to give Bert a thorough going over. As thorough as was possible, in view of the fact that he had to burrow his way through layers of underclothes, all buttoned and zipped in the most inaccessible places. About half an hour later, after much grumbling and grunting from Bert, Tony put his instruments back in his black medical bag and snapped it shut.

'You're right,' he told Bert. 'Your heart is as sound as a bell, but your blood pressure is high.' He wrote out a prescription. 'I'll give you some tablets for that.'

'What about driving the tractor?' asked May. 'Can he do that?'

'Course I can, woman.' Bert looked outraged.

Thinking that Bert's blood pressure would probably shoot sky high if he suggested otherwise, Tony said, 'I don't see why not. Although I think you ought to remember that you *are* eighty-two, Bert. Maybe you should get someone in to give you a hand now and then.'

'I've run this farm single-handed, except for casual labour, for the last sixty odd years. I've never needed help, and I don't need it now.' Putting his battered flat cap back on his head, he stood up. 'I'm going down to the bottom meadow to finish cutting the hay.'

Tony gave up. He knew that neither May nor Bert would heed his advice, they'd always done exactly as they pleased. He might as well save his breath.

'Have something to eat first,' May said to Bert. She

294

looked at Tony, and then at Joe. 'Fancy a glass of cider, and some bread and cheese?'

May's food, all farm produce, was not something to be refused lightly, and they both nodded assent.

Clearing the clutter from the table into an old laundry basket with one deft sweep of her arm, May piled the kitchen table with fresh bread, butter from the dairy, strong cheddar cheese, also from the dairy, and three different sorts of home-made chutney and pickles. Joe brought up two earthenware jugs of ice cold cider from the cellar, and they all sat down to eat.

'Try not to think about the cholesterol,' said Tony, who knew Joe was watching his diet.

Joe grinned, and spread a piece of bread with butter. 'I'm not,' he said.

'Eat up.' May piled Tony's plate high. 'By the way, talking about eating. Did Diana get on to Millicent about cutting down on her food bills?'

'Yes,' said Tony. 'but she hasn't had much time to follow it through. Since she's left Wycombe and Yatton she's been busy being interviewed and studying the management strategies, and long-term prospects of various firms. At least, that's what she told me when I spoke to her on the 'phone. Personally, I don't understand all this executive jargon. To a simple-minded country doctor like me, a job is a job. I wouldn't know a management strategy if I saw one.'

'What?' May put down the bread knife with a bang. 'Are you telling me that Diana is out of work?'

'Only temporarily,' said Tony.

'But why hasn't she told me? Why doesn't she come down here and work at Abbey House?'

'Presumably she doesn't want to,' said Joe.

He tried to imagine Diana settling permanently at Abbey House; taking over where Susan had left off. But the picture didn't gel, somehow didn't seem feasible. Diana had made it plain enough in the past that she didn't want to settle back in Mottisley. But then she had another job, other commitments, and now she was free. Now she could come, but she hadn't. A wave of ineffable sadness washed over Joe, surprising him with its bitter intensity. Diana had rejected the place, and everything in it, including himself. She would never come back, and because of that, he thought that for May, Mottisley would always be lacking something.

'We'll see about that. I *want* her back,' said May, almost as if she was reading Joe's mind. Her wrinkled jaw jutted forward at an ominous angle. 'I'm going to find out where she is, and talk to her. I'll ring that bastard husband of hers.'

'Poor old Hugh,' said Tony. 'You've always got it in for him.'

'With good reason,' said May grimly. 'But that's none of your business.' She looked through her telephone book, then dialled Hugh's office number. 'I want to speak to Mr Hugh Stratton, May Marsham here,' she said.

'One moment please.' Miss Higgins switched the 'phone through to Hugh. 'There is a May Marsham wanting to speak to you.'

'Oh, Jesus,' groaned Hugh.

'Shall I tell her you're out?'

'No, better not. It's my wife's great-aunt. I'll have a word with her.'

As soon as May was switched through she came straight to the point. 'I want to know where Diana is, and why she didn't tell me she had left Wycombe and Yatton.'

'Because she thought it had nothing to do with you,' snapped Hugh. He held the 'phone an inch away from his ear. May's voice was deafening.

'It has everything to do with me. I'm her aunt. She could come and work down here.'

'Of course she can't. Diana has too many brains to waste her time in Mottisley. She has bigger fish to fry.'

'Huh!' May snorted. No point in talking to Hugh, Diana was the one she needed to talk to. 'When can I speak to Diana?'

'Tomorrow at the earliest,' said Hugh, unable to keep the malicious satisfaction at thwarting May out of his voice. 'This afternoon at 3.30 p.m. she has an appointment at Scott and James, a headhunting firm. Headhunters are people who match the right person to the right job, specializing in the financial and contractual aspects of top jobs. Top jobs only,' he emphasized. 'It's an important meeting, so I'm afraid Diana won't be available to talk to you today.'

'Oh,' said May, and put the 'phone down. 'I can't speak to her,' she said to Joe and Tony.

'Didn't think you would.' Tony got up from the table. 'Thanks for the lunch, May. I've got to go and start my afternoon surgery now.' He turned to Bert. 'Now take it easy, and don't go mad cutting that bottom meadow. The hay can wait. The weather forecast is dry for tomorrow as well.'

'I'm all right,' said Bert stubbornly. 'Never needed to see you in the first place, and don't need any pills either.'

Joe rose too, and picked up the prescription. 'Don't be so bloody ungrateful, you bad-tempered old man. I'll get the pills and you'll take them even if I have to ram them down your throat myself.'

'You'd have made the perfect doctor,' said Tony. 'Such a wonderful bedside manner.'

'Awkward old bugger.' Joe walked outside with Tony. 'What is wrong with him? Why do you think he fell off that tractor?'

'Might have been a very slight stroke, his blood pressure is on the high side. But basically, it's old age, and there's no cure for that.'

'I never think of May and Bert as old,' said Joe slowly. 'I can't imagine Willow Farm without them.'

'Nor me. But they can't live for ever.'

'Sure, nothing stays the same.' Joe was suddenly swamped with irrational, maudlin self-pity. Clasping his hand to his chest he recited in ringing tones and with a heavy Irish accent. ' "O who could have foretold, that the heart grows old?" Yeats,' he told the astonished Tony.

'I didn't know you were well versed in poetry.'

Joe grinned, his mood switching back down to his normal plane. 'The only two damned lines I can ever remember.' He changed the subject. 'May really wants Diana back, doesn't she.'

'Well, we can't all have what we want in this life.' Tony thought of April. He wanted her but he couldn't have her. 'And that includes May.'

'I don't know *what* I want,' said Joe. He too was thinking of April, but her face kept being pushed out of focus by Diana's.

'Considering you change your women almost as often as you change your socks, I'm well aware of that,' snapped Tony, suddenly feeling bad-tempered. He jumped into his car and roared off without saying goodbye.

Joe watched him drive away. What had got at him? Or who? Tony Evans was usually the mildest mannered man he'd ever known. Never bad-tempered. Joe began to wonder if Tony had been hoping Diana might uproot herself and come and live in Mottisley. Perhaps he was in love with her. The idea was unsettling.

Chapter Twenty-two

Diana was finding it difficult to concentrate on the papers before her. Outside the Chelsea apartment the sun was still blazing fiercely over London. A couple of skiffs sculled upriver, the incoming tide carrying them along so fast the rowers appeared to be jet propelled. On the opposite bank, in Battersea Park, Diana could make out small shapes, the figures of people taking an evening stroll along the river footpath.

'Well, darling.' Hugh passed by on his way to the kitchen, and, stooping, planted a kiss on the back of her neck. 'How goes it? Have you decided yet?'

'No. I'm reading through them again.' That was a lie, she hadn't read through them once yet. At least, not properly.

The 'phone rang. 'The answerphone's on,' said Hugh. 'Just leave it.'

'It could be important.'

'Nothing is as important as you making up your mind about a job.' Hugh glanced at Diana, she was on the verge of answering the damned 'phone. He didn't want her concentration disturbed. He came back and slid his arms around her shoulders. 'It's probably someone trying to sell us double glazing. They always ring at this time of the evening.'

'Yes, I suppose so.' Reluctantly Diana stayed where she was and the 'phone clicked into silence.

'Dinner in half an hour,' said Hugh. 'We'll talk about your decision then.'

Ten minutes later the 'phone rang again. This time Diana picked it up. 'God Almighty, where have you been?' It was Joe.

Diana held the telephone away from her ear. He was in one of his roaring moods, something must be wrong. 'What's happened?'

'What hasn't happened, more bloody likely. That bloody woman you engaged, Millicent, Millicent . . .' he fumbled over the name.

'Wright,' said Diana crisply.

'Wright! Well, I can tell you one thing, she's not right, she's all bloody wrong. In bed, the woman is. Drunk as a lord.'

'Are the children OK?' Diana wasn't too worried about Millicent being drunk, Joe was probably exaggerating in order to make her feel guilty.

'Yes, I suppose you *could* say that, although no thanks to you. Miffy has been playing with matches and set fire to the kitchen curtains. Don't concern yourself about that though, the Fire Brigade and Police are here. Simon has locked himself in the toilet and is threatening to drown himself in the lavatory pan, and Clemmy is having hysterics in her bedroom. Finally, two bloody social workers have turned up and are talking about taking the children into care as there is no responsible adult here in charge of them.'

'Oh God,' said Diana.

'It isn't God that's needed, it's you. And don't think of asking May, because she's not well. Tony has packed her off to bed with Bert. They're both unwell, and even if they weren't they're far too old to cope with this lot.'

'I'll be down.'

'About bloody time,' said Joe. 'I take it you mean now, tonight. Not next week, or the week after, when you've finished something more important.'

'I mean now,' said Diana grimly and put down the 'phone. Bloody man. To listen to Joe one would think she had personally poured the booze down Millicent's throat.

'But you can't go now,' was Hugh's immediate reaction when Diana had told him what was happening.

'I must.' She wondered, was it possible to drown oneself in a lavatory pan?

'But you were going to make a decision tonight. It's important.'

'Don't rush me. I've got at least a week to make up my mind.' Diana was irritated. Why couldn't Hugh get the priorities right. 'At the moment things at Abbey House are more important.'

By the time Diana arrived it was dusk, the Fire Brigade and Police had departed, and only the social workers remained. A brooding presence, they perched on stools in the corner of the kitchen making copious notes. From time to time peering at the other incumbents of the room, before writing more notes.

'You'd think we were some sort of strange species of animal,' Diana said to April in an undertone. It annoyed her that she should find their presence intimidating.

'Huh! *they're* the strange species.' April quite obviously didn't like them. 'But we'd better be careful.' She pulled a face. 'In sociology speak, they're probably evaluating our role allocation as a group and our social interaction with regard to behavioural patterns of the children.' Seeing Diana staring at her, she laughed. 'I did an article recently. *Is Sociology a Science?*'

'No it isn't. It's a load of bloody rubbish,' said Joe loudly, glowering at the two women. 'I'm going upstairs again to see if I can winkle Simon out of the lavatory.' He stopped by the women. 'You're supposed to be the experts on children. Why can't you get him to come out?'

'The child is disturbed. It's a job for a psychiatrist,' said one.

Joe exploded. 'Rubbish.'

Diana decided it would be more tactful to get Joe out of the way. 'Perhaps you could tell Simon that I'm here,' she said, 'and that I'll be up in a moment.' There was no point in antagonizing them unnecessarily. They were only trying to do a job. She walked across to the two women, and smiled. 'Thank you for coming. I am the children's

301

official guardian, their aunt, Diana Stratton.' She tried to sound friendly, although their combined unblinking gaze was unnerving. She held out her hand. Neither woman moved, so after a moment Diana withdrew her hand, unshaken. 'There's no need for you to stay.' She made no effort to sound friendly now.

'I'm afraid there is.'

The older woman spoke. She had short dark hair, and in her plain button through dress, and sensible lace-up shoes, she looked like a particularly severe headmistress.

'We need to complete our notes for the case conference tomorrow,' the second social worker said sternly.

'Case Conference! On *my* children.'

As she said the words it was as if the mirror that reflected her life suddenly cracked; split wide open, to allow another Diana to emerge like a butterfly struggling to escape the ugly casing of a chrysalis. For a moment they stood side by side. The sophisticated, materialistic, self-assured, corporate woman, and the other Diana, a woman she didn't yet know. For a moment she felt vulnerable. What category did her new self fit into? But the moment passed, swept aside by the new possessive, protective rush of emotion she was feeling towards the children. They were *hers*. They belonged to no-one else. Most of all not to the two uninvited women sitting in the kitchen of Abbey House. She glared at the second social worker, a fatter version of the older one. 'A case conference won't be necessary.'

'On the contrary.' The fat woman was patronizingly smug. 'There's obviously been a major breakdown in the caring structure of the children. They've been emotionally traumatized. The case conference may decide that they should be placed in foster homes.'

A white hot rage swept over Diana at the mere idea. How dare they even consider making decisions about *her* children without consulting her.

'Emotionally traumatized!' Diana managed to keep her voice controlled with difficulty. 'And do you really think

302

placing them in foster homes will be less traumatic? Their mother died in April of this year. That was traumatic enough. They're not over that yet.'

The women remained coldly impersonal. 'We'll see you tomorrow, Mrs Stratton. Will you be available if we need to speak to you?'

'Yes. I shall be here. I'm not going anywhere.'

They packed their clipboards into woven linen bags and stood up. 'If you need any advice from either one of us, we can be contacted at the Social Services Department, Chichester on this number.' The older woman got out a card. 'My name is Tara Cotton, and my colleague is Dorothy Stoodley. Just ask for us by name.'

'Thank you, but I won't be needing you.' Diana didn't want to take the card, but had no choice as it was thrust into her hand.

'You'll be glad of us when you return to London,' said the fat one, Dorothy Stoodley, with what April described later as a treacle like smirk. 'I think you'll find foster parenting will be the only answer then.'

'I'm not going back to London,' Diana heard herself saying. 'I'm staying here and looking after the children myself.'

'Are you?' asked April.

'Yes.' Diana knew that as she said that single word, her new unknown self was plunging into uncharted waters. Nothing she had ever done or learned had prepared her for surrogate motherhood. It was not the path of her choosing, and she had fought against it ever since Susan's death. But quite suddenly she realized the fight was pointless. For better or for worse, this was her fate, her destiny. The two social workers, with their disinterested, matter of fact impersonal plans for the children, had proved to be the catalyst which jolted her into action. 'I promised Susan I'd look after them, and I bloody well will,' she told a dumbfounded April. 'And what is more I'm going to put Abbey Vineyard on the map. We're not going to scrape by on a hand-to-mouth existence. It's not going to be some run-down, poky little operation. Abbey Vineyard is going to be successful. Something everyone in Mottisley will be proud to be associated with.'

A slow handclap came from the doorway of the kitchen, the door that led upstairs. 'Well said.' Tony leaned against the door jamb grinning delightedly.

Joe at his side looked less enthusiastic. 'I'll believe it if you're still here in six months' time,' he said dourly.

'I'll still be here.'

'What about Hugh?' asked Tony. 'How will he like living here? I presume you are including him in your plans.'

'Of course I am, and I know he'll support me,' said Diana. The first prickle of apprehension began to dent the bubble of her new found elation. 'He'll understand.'

And so he would. Hadn't he said once that if she thought she wouldn't be bored running a vineyard to give it a go? Well, maybe not exactly those words. But more or less. Of course it was true that since then things had changed, and he was now expecting her to take on a well paid post in the City. One of the three possibilities put before her by Scott and James. But he'd get used to the idea of her staying in Mottisley. Of course he would. She straightened her back resolutely. He'd *have* to.

Suddenly there was a commotion in the doorway, and Joe and Tony parted as Simon squeezed past them before slowly edging his way into the kitchen. 'Are you really staying?' he asked.

'Yes, really,' said Diana. To her surprise Simon was not looking wild eyed and distraught as she'd been expecting. True his dark eyes looked enormous, but by no stretch of the imagination could they be called distraught. In fact, he was grinning sheepishly. She felt an immense sense of relief. 'You were conning us, weren't you?' she said. 'You didn't really mean it about committing suicide.'

'I tried,' said Simon with an attempt at bravado. 'But

my head was too big for the bottom of the pan, and it smelled horribly of bleach.' He paused, then added. 'But would you have cared?'

'Of course I would have cared.' Diana flung her arms around him and tried to kiss his cheek, but unused to such demonstrations of affection from Diana, Simon shuffled sideways in embarrassment. Pleased embarrassment though, Diana noticed with relief, judging by the wide smile he gave her.

'He only did it to frighten them.' Clemmy, having decided that being hysterical upstairs without an audience was no fun, came into the kitchen. She scowled in the direction of the social workers, now departing in a smart looking Renault down the drive. '*Silly cows!*' she screamed after them at the top of her voice.

'Shut up,' shouted Simon, annoyed at Clemmy belittling his suicide threat. 'Anyway *you* can't talk. All you did was have a fit of the screaming abdabs!'

Clemmy burst into noisy tears. 'I didn't know what to do,' she sobbed. 'The curtains were on fire, and Sheridan was down in the bottom vineyard and couldn't hear us calling, and Millicent was asleep. Well,' she sniffed loudly, 'drunk actually.' Diana handed her a handkerchief, and Clemmy blew her nose and wiped her eyes. 'But I did dial 999.'

'Well, let's thank God for that,' said Diana. 'You did the right thing. If you hadn't done that, Abbey House might not still be here. It could have all been burnt to a cinder.'

There was a shocked silence as they all thought about that fact.

'A cinder?' said a small voice. Miffy emerged nervously from beneath the kitchen table, where he'd taken refuge. Seamus, looking equally nervous, emerged with him. Miffy clung on to the dog's neck.

'Yes,' said Diana, trying to sound as stern as possible. 'A cinder.'

April took Diana's arm. 'Don't be too hard on him,'

she whispered. 'All small boys play with matches given the chance.'

Diana was finding it was difficult to be hard on Miffy anyway. Sensing her weakness, his blue eyes twinkled in a seraphic smile as, still clutching the dog, he sidled across to Joe. 'I knew you'd come if there was a fire.' he said.

'Is that why you did it?' Joe looked down at Miffy, now swinging happily on his arm.

'Yes,' he said simply.

'A bit drastic, old son.' Suddenly Joe looked across at Diana and grinned. 'With initiative like that he should go far,' he said. 'Ten out of ten for enterprise, wouldn't you say?'

But Diana didn't reply. For a moment she could have sworn that her heart actually stopped beating. Joe and Miffy stared at her and she stared back at them. Why had she never noticed it before? They were so alike. Miffy could easily have been Joe's son.

'What are you going to do about Millicent?' April's voice cut across her thoughts. 'Sack her?'

'Oh, please don't do that.' Clemmy rushed at Diana, flinging her arms around her with such force that she was nearly knocked off her feet. 'She didn't mean to get drunk.'

'And we do like her. She's fun,' said Simon.

'And she makes lovely puddings,' added Miffy, whose main concern in life was his stomach. 'Much better than Griselda. She can only do rhubarb crumble. Ugh!'

'Anyway Griselda isn't going to be able to run a household for some months yet,' announced Tony. 'She's coming out of hospital tomorrow, but she'll need some help herself. So she'll not be of much use here.'

'And everyone should be allowed a few mistakes,' said Joe.

Diana reeled under the unexpected barrage of support for Millicent. 'I ought to sack her,' she said slowly, thinking how daunting it would be trying to run Abbey House on her own. Not only was the house huge, there was the children's washing, and the cooking; something she'd never excelled at. Besides she wanted to get to grips with the vineyard, not be bogged down by domestic chores. 'But I won't. I shall speak sternly to her on the matter of her alcohol consumption, and after that we'll consider the matter closed.'

The children cheered wildly. A little too wildly thought Diana. They didn't cheer like that when I said I was staying.

'When Griselda comes out of hospital tomorrow, why don't you have her back here?' suggested Tony. 'She'll be a stabilizing influence on Millicent.'

'And even on crutches, she can still do something useful, like peeling the potatoes,' pointed out April.

And so it was settled. Millicent would stay, and Griselda would come to Abbey House to convalesce. Diana put off thinking about what she would do when Griselda was fully recovered. One thing at a time was quite enough.

Diana went to bed mentally and physically exhausted that night. Sheridan took her aside once the children were in bed and wanted to talk about his ideas for the vineyard, but Diana put him off until the next day.

She rang Hugh telling him of her decision to stay at Abbey House for good, but he refused to believe her.

'We'll talk about it tomorrow, darling,' he'd said. 'When you've had time to think things through.'

'But tomorrow won't change anything.'

Hugh thought hard and fast. A long distance row was *not* the way to make Diana see sense. 'I'm sure you're right,' he said soothingly, wondering if it was too late to see Nancy that night. 'But I still think it wise to talk in the morning. You must be tired.'

'I am,' agreed Diana. 'Absolutely shattered.'

'Go to bed then, darling.'

Diana took his advice. But before going to bed she moved her belongings into Susan's old room at the back of the house; a symbolic sign of her permanence. The room overlooked the southward facing slopes of the vineyard, and Diana hung out of the window breathing in the air, letting the stillness of the approaching night soak into every membrane of her mind.

A star hovered, silent and solitary, in the darkening blush of the sky. The serried ranks of vines, now in full leaf, looked dark and mysterious, the faintest tinge of mist creeping up over them from the lower slopes. Tomorrow was going to be hot. Leaning out she put her hands against the stones of the house. They were warm to her touch. How many years ago was it she and Susan had done just that together, feeling the old house breathe beneath their touch? Too many years. So much had happened, and yet at the same time it seemed that nothing had changed, and that the years had disappeared in the space of time it took to draw a breath.

She waited, as she'd done so many years before, until the moon rose above the dark shadow of the yew tree. A full moon, a great, glowing orb, standing out white against the navy blue of the night sky. She thought of her father and wondered if he would have approved of her decision to stay. She hoped so, just as she hoped Hugh would. But at the same time, she knew deep within her, that Hugh's approval or disapproval would make no difference whatsoever. She had made a decision, and she knew it was right. Explaining it logically in the cold harsh light of day might prove difficult, but she was prepared for that. Gut instinct was telling her she was right, and the same instinct would help her deflect any disapproval or difficulties. Nothing, and no-one was going to persuade her to change her mind now.

Once lying in the big double bed in Susan's old room, her mind wandered idly. Incredible how relaxed I feel, she thought sleepily. It must be the country air. She'd left the curtains pulled back wide, and the full moon flooded the room with silvery light. Somewhere at the bottom of the vineyard a vixen barked, a shrill yap, yap, warning her cubs perhaps of some hidden danger. The scent of the evening primroses, which still grew in untidy yellow clumps around the walls of the house, drifted up and into the bedroom.

A hazy vision of Miffy and Joe as they had stood side by side, floated through Diana's mind. How strange nature was, making two completely unrelated people bear such an uncanny resemblance to one another. But she was too tired to think about that or anything else.

Turning over and burying her head in the softness of the pillow, Diana fell asleep.

PART THREE

Resolution

Chapter Twenty-three

Hugh was furious. 'The middle of July. It's three bloody weeks now and still no sign of her changing her mind.' He was beginning to feel despairing. Never for one moment had he dreamed that Diana would resist his pleas to come back to London. Or, come to that, the pleas of Norman Leadbetter. For once they had been in complete agreement. But Diana was absolutely adamant. She was staying in Mottisley and wanted Hugh to join her. 'I'm getting desperate,' he told Nancy morosely. 'All my bloody salary is going on the mortgage for the Chelsea apartment.'

'You could sell it.'

Nancy was preoccupied with her own thoughts. They were lunching together at the Cheshire Cheese, Wine Inn Court. She was waiting for Ben Rose. He had promised to pop in during the High Court lunch recess. Apparently he'd persuaded her husband to part with some more money. A final financial settlement. Nancy was wondering how much.

'I thought you didn't want me to live openly with you.' Hugh said petulantly. Nancy was being very difficult in the circumstances, not a bit helpful. Nico was pressing *him* for money, not her. The little sod had started tightening the screws as soon as he knew Diana was no longer employed in the City. 'If I sold the apartment, I'd *have* to live with you.'

'Certainly not,' said Nancy sharply. 'We must be discreet.' There was more than one reason why she didn't want Hugh living in her house. Any permanent man was an inhibiting millstone around her neck as far as Nancy was concerned.

'Perhaps I should ask Diana for a divorce.'

Nancy switched her full attention to Hugh. At all costs he must be prevented from doing anything rash. Not yet, anyway. Switching on her most beguiling smile, she leaned forward and stroked his cheek with her long white fingers.

'No, no, darling, don't do that. We must play this game very, very carefully. Remember it isn't just your marriage which is at stake, it's my future too. If you move in with me, or divorce Diana, that will antagonize May, and we don't want to upset her do we? It could cause me to forfeit my share of her fortune.'

'*You* don't want to upset May,' grumbled Hugh, 'but why should I care? Your inheritance isn't going to do *me* much good. Anyway, what you seem to forget is that she isn't dead yet, and not likely to be for some considerable time. All that bloody country air seems to make them live for ever.'

'Wrong,' said Nancy, a slow gleeful smile stretching her lips back across her small white teeth. 'When I rang your beloved wife to commiserate at her fate and offer my help . . .'

'You don't intend going down there as well do you?' Hugh interrupted, horrified. Being short of money was one thing, but being cut off from Nancy's skilled sexual ministrations was quite another. At least when he lost himself in Nancy's voracious body he forgot all his troubles. Even Nico receded into oblivion then.

'Of course not.' Nancy was impatient. Sometimes Hugh was incredibly dense. 'I only offered my help because I knew she'd refuse. But during the course of conversation, she did tell me something interesting. Both May and Bert are unwell, and Tony Evans says it's old age.' She laughed. 'Poor Diana, she's very worried because nothing much can be done. Me, I have no such worries.'

'Oh,' Hugh perked up at the news. 'When May kicks the bucket Diana stands to inherit quite a bit too.'

'Exactly.' Nancy's blood red nails drummed on the table top in a rhythmic pattern. 'And we do want to make

314

sure we can get our hands on both halves of the money, don't we, darling. So now you see why you must humour Diana, and not divorce her. And you must keep going down every weekend to reassure her. Just keep stalling about the final move. I'll come down with you this weekend and play the solicitous niece. I'll take May and Bert some hot broth, or whatever it is invalids have these days.'

'Humouring Diana is one thing. There's still the problem of Nico. It's me he's threatening, not you.'

'I've spoken to him, and fixed it.'

'You have? How?'

'I've told him you've agreed to make a few drops.'

'Drops? Do you mean be a pusher?'

'For God's sake, darling, do keep your voice down. And don't look so bloody horrified.'

'I won't do it.' Taking drugs was one thing. Selling, quite another. The thought terrified Hugh.

'Of course you will. I'll be with you, it's only a little risk. In fact, it'll be fun. All we've got to do is go to three nightclubs next week. Have a meal, enjoy ourselves, and pass on a little package while we're there. After that our debts to Nico are cleared, and we'll be in credit.'

'If that's all there is to it, why can't Nico do it?'

'Because the Drug Squad know him, darling. They'll be looking for him. But no-one will be looking out for us.'

'I don't like it.'

Nancy laughed, supremely confident and thrilled at the element of danger the operation involved. 'Don't worry, we won't have to do it too often. May will soon snuff it, and then we'll be in clover. Ah look, there's Ben. In a rush, and hot and sweaty as usual. I wonder if he's like that in bed!'

Hugh seeing Ben, laughed. 'Probably,' he said. Nancy was right. It was only a small risk, and one worth taking if it got Nico off his back for a while.

'Hello.' Ben slid into the seat they'd kept for him. 'Do

you think it's wise you two being seen together like this?' he said nervously.

'Why not, darling?' Nancy was amused. 'Joseph knows all about us, or so you tell me. And Hugh is my relation by marriage. So what could be more natural than a brief luncheon together to catch up on family gossip. Which, believe it or not, was just what we were doing.'

Ben fumbled in his briefcase. 'I hear Diana has left Wycombe and Yatton, *and* you,' he said to Hugh, a small note of satisfaction in his voice. Serve him right, the upstart. About time he got what was coming to him.

'Wycombe and Yatton, yes.' said Hugh coldly. 'Me no. She's had to go down to be with those wretched children at Mottisley. But it's only a temporary measure.'

'Never mind about that.' Nancy was impatient. 'Where are the papers you promised? How much is Joseph going to give me?'

Ben found the papers, and pushing their salad plates and lager glasses out of the way, spread them on the table. 'Not much,' he said. 'Apart from the previous settlement which you agreed upon, he's also agreed to add the sum of forty-thousand dollars a year for the next three years. After that the payments will cease.'

'But that's less than twenty-thousand pounds sterling.'

'Take it or leave it. If you want it, sign here.'

'Sign,' advised Hugh. 'You won't get any more.'

Nancy did so with an ill grace. 'That old couple down in Mottisley better not last too long,' she said crossly. 'I need their money more than they do.'

'What is she talking about?' Ben looked at Hugh, mystified.

Hugh pretended he hadn't heard. 'I'll get you a drink, Ben,' he said, and made his escape to the bar. The last thing Ben needed to know was that Nancy stood to inherit a sizeable fortune from her great-aunt. If it reached the ears of Joseph Morris it could cause him to withdraw his offer, and unlike Nancy, Hugh was much less optimistic about when she was likely to inherit. He had a premonition that May would live until she was a hundred.

Seamus rocketed down the sloping ground between the vines. Spinning round in bouncing circles, turning somersaults in sheer exuberance at being out and free so early in the morning. Too happy and excited to even bother with the rabbits who scuttled back into the hedgerows at the sight of the large dog.

Diana laughed as she watched him. It was such a wonderful morning she knew just how he felt. 'If anyone had told me a month ago that I'd be out checking vines at 5.30 in the morning, I would never have believed them. Yet here I am, and I'm actually enjoying it.' She bent down and pricked out a straying side shoot from one of the vines. In July the grapes flowered, all spraying of fungicides stopped for a couple of weeks and everyone prayed for fine weather so that the flowers would pollinate well. Sheridan had taught her that once the flowers had set, which by now they had, the vines needed all their strength so that the grapes could grow fat and juicy. Side shoots were not needed or wanted. They were to be pinched off.

Sheridan grinned at her enthusiasm. Before, she'd been a distant employer, someone in London to whom he'd conscientiously reported. But now he was beginning to get to know and like her. Once she'd made up her mind to get involved in the vineyard she'd plunged in with all guns blazing. She wanted to know everything, and was proving a brilliant pupil. Her thirst for knowledge was insatiable, and her ability to store the information formidable. Sheridan's attitude had changed too. From being hopeful of success, he was now certain they'd achieve it.

'And if anyone had told me a month ago that you'd be here I would never have believed it,' he said. 'Damn and blast it.' He bent down and looked at the base of a vine. 'Bloody rabbits,' he muttered.

'What is it?' Diana too bent down to look.

Sheridan showed her where the rabbits had gnawed. 'Luckily this vine is well established,' he said. 'No permanent damage done. I'll get Ronald Pugh to come down and mend this wire. But we really do need to buy some new wire netting, for rabbits and the deer.'

'Damn! and I haven't got any money. Well, not enough for new netting and the new wine presses we need.'

'We also need plenty of paint and wood for the shelving in the craft shop, if you intend to open it by the end of this month.'

'I most certainly do.' Diana shrugged her shoulders. 'God! but it's bloody being poor!'

Sheridan laughed at her expression. 'I can see it's a new experience for you, ma'am.'

'Too damned right. And one which I don't intend to experience for too long. So, I'd better visit the bank manager, we can't have the rabbits and deer eating our potential profits,' said Diana. 'Oh, if only Norman Leadbetter would give me the final figures concerning my own financial standing, but he only hints that there isn't much left.' She sighed. 'For the life of me I can't think why not. I always earned a good salary.'

'Perhaps you spent a lot,' ventured Sheridan, who'd never had much money, but knew there was only one way it disappeared, by being spent.

'Yes, I suppose Hugh and I must have lived up to the utmost limit of our income all the time. My fault as much as his. I was only too willing to have all the very best things in life. Or rather,' she stood still, and sniffed at the crisp morning air, 'I thought then they were the best things in life.'

Now she thought differently. But one of the blots on her new found happiness, apart from lack of money, was the fact that she had not yet been able to persuade Hugh to move down to Mottisley permanently. He came every weekend, and hadn't really objected to any of her plans, but always had a valid reason for not selling the apartment and moving down. Diana was certain that once he came and stayed, then he too would be captivated by the change in lifestyle.

The other blot was May and Bert's continued ill health. May, was a little better and showing signs of her old insouciant attitude to life, but Bert, although cheerful, was growing visibly more frail every day.

He still worked on the farm and because Tony was unwilling to do anything to stop him, Diana had tackled old Dr Evans about it when she'd met him in the village one day. But he was equally uncompromising.

'What do you expect, my dear?' he said. 'That we should tell him to lie down and wait to be loaded into his box!'

'You know I don't mean that. But don't you think he ought to be careful?'

'No point in being careful when you get to eighty-two years of age. Let him do whatever makes him happy. Nature will tell him when to stop.'

'But he might die.'

As soon as she'd said it Diana knew it was ridiculous. He was old. He was eighty-two. But all the same she couldn't bear the thought of him dying.

'Exactly. That's when nature tells you to stop.' Edward Evans peered short-sightedly at Diana. 'Upsets you, eh, the thought of dying? Well, don't let it. It's the only one damned thing you can be certain of in this world. And Bert Slocombe has had a good innings, I don't think he'll be complaining when he's finally bowled out.'

Diana knew it to be true. Bert wouldn't complain. But all the same, she hoped it wouldn't happen for a long time to come.

Three weeks later a transformation had been wrought at Abbey House. Mr Mortimer, the local bank manager, had been lukewarm when presented with Diana's ideas at first. But her enthusiasm and dynamic energy had finally persuaded him that under her leadership Abbey Vineyard would not only survive, it would flourish.

'Just think,' Diana told him. 'You'll be able to say you helped fly the flag of English Wine.' The final *coup de grâce* came when she persuaded the catering establishment in the House of Commons to buy Abbey Vineyard own-label white wine. 'If the government is drinking it,' Diana told Mr Mortimer, 'it must be good.'

Mr Mortimer succumbed and sanctioned a big loan.

The loan enabled wire fencing to be bought to reinforce the vineyard fences, thus keeping out the deer and rabbits, which kept Sheridan happy. The older of the two barns adjacent to Abbey House was converted into a craft shop. The children, now finished school for the rest of the summer, were enthusiastic helpers. As were the villagers when they discovered that they stood to gain too.

On the day before the official opening the general store was humming with speculation and gossip.

'Of course I always knew when Mrs Stratton engaged that Sheridan Porter that fresh blood into the village would bring in fresh ideas.' Mrs Graystock, stalwart of the Mothers' Union and Women's Institute, preened with self-satisfaction. 'Mrs Stratton told me that it was his idea that the Women's Institute should provide home-made preserves for the craft shop, and that we should split the profit fifty-fifty.'

'You've got me to thank for that.' The Reverend Pincher's wife was not to be outdone. 'It was me who told him how short of funds the WI was. We often have a nice little chat at choir practice.'

'Wasn't long ago I heard you saying that he'd never fit in.' Mrs Lomax wasn't ready to be won over yet. And anyway she wasn't at all keen on the idea of the craft shop. Already the sales of wine had suffered a serious setback. People were developing a taste for Abbey Vineyard wine. 'He's a foreigner. It doesn't seem right to see a black face in Mottisley.'

'He's not a foreigner.' Mrs Pincher was indignant.

'Sheridan is an American, that's almost as good as being British.'

'He's not a proper American. He's a darkie.'

Mrs Graystock rushed to Sheridan's defence. She had never liked chapel-going Mrs Lomax's sanctimonious attitude. 'I find that word very offensive,' she said sternly. 'What you must remember, Mrs Lomax, is that we now live in a multicultural society. The *true* Christian attitude is a tolerant attitude, not one of bigoted prejudice.'

'Well said, Mrs Graystock. I agree one hundred per cent.' Mrs Pincher recognized the text from her husband's sermon the previous week.

'That will be five pounds and twenty pence, Mrs Graystock,' said Mrs Lomax sourly, knowing she'd lost the argument.

'Don't go down there this weekend.' Nancy straddled Hugh. Her usually pale face was flushed with triumph. Since they'd made their 'drops' as Nico called them, they were flush with coke and Hugh had just given his best sexual performance ever. 'I want to ride you the whole weekend, darling,' she purred. 'I don't want you to be with Diana. I want you with me.'

'I ought to go. She's opening that damned craft shop this Saturday and it's Clemmy's thirteenth birthday.'

'Thirteen, an unlucky number. Stay here with me,' Nancy commanded. 'I promise you that you'll have a lot more fun. And after all, we both did our duty last weekend. You were nice to Diana, and I was nice to May and that disgusting old Bert.'

Hugh looked up at Nancy. Her dark eyes glittering with lust sent a renewed power surging through his loins. She made him feel strong, as if he could conquer the earth. 'With you I can fuck for ever,' he whispered.

Nancy laughed, 'I know, darling. I know.' Sliding down his body she took his glistening organ in her mouth. Hugh shuddered, the pleasure was almost unbearable. Sliding her hands beneath his thighs, Nancy grasped his testicles, massaging them in her long fingers. Then stopping a moment she raised her head. 'Still want to spend the weekend with Diana?' she asked.

'No,' groaned Hugh. 'No.'

Nancy wrapped her predatory mouth once more around his shuddering organ. She had Hugh where she wanted him; within her power. Smiling slowly, she renewed her sucking, knowing that when the time came to put her plan into action he would be unable to refuse her anything.

Chapter Twenty-four

'One thousand, seven hundred pounds on the first day. I can hardly believe it,' said Diana, collapsing into an exhausted heap on a chair and staring at assembled friends and family.

'Believe it,' said Joe who had appointed himself official cashier for the craft shop on opening day. April had nagged him into it. Not that he'd needed much persuading, only too anxious to appease for his bloody-minded behaviour on the day Diana came to Mottisley to stay, he would have agreed to anything. Not that he let April or Tony know that.

Clemmy leaned over the kitchen table and fingered the piles of notes. She picked up a wad fastened with an elastic band. 'Is this really a hundred pounds?' she asked.

'Yes.' Joe took it back and placed it in the cash box.

'Couldn't I have one for my birthday?'

'You've already had that horrible dress from Laura Ashley,' said Simon. 'You can't have money as well.'

'Why not?' Getting up, Clemmy twirled round so that the full skirt of her pale pink dress swirled out.

'You look like a ballet dancer,' said Miffy. Clemmy smiled, pleased. 'Except for your funny legs.'

'There's nothing wrong with her legs,' said April quickly before there was a row. 'Come on everyone. Let's clear the table. Millicent has nearly got the birthday dinner ready. It's time to eat.'

'What is it?' Miffy was immediately distracted at the thought of food. 'Is it something special?'

Millicent came in from the pantry, waving a large piece of paper with black writing on. 'The menu,' she announced. 'To start with, baked artichokes with pine nuts, parsley, and lemon.'

'I want soup,' growled Bert, 'none of your fancy stuff.'

'And soup for Bert,' added Millicent. 'To follow, braised lamb with white wine and soured cream sauce, buttered baby carrots, courgettes and new potatoes. Bert's will be with gravy not wine sauce,' she added hastily before he could interrupt. 'And for dessert, gratinated pears with sauternes and praline.'

'Sounds all right,' said Miffy.

'Sounds wonderful,' said Diana, glad that she'd kept Millicent on.

'Better than I could ever do.' Griselda sounded despondent.

'Ah, but you did all the hard work.' Millicent was generous, she liked Griselda and hoped they would both be allowed to stay at Abbey House. 'Without you, none of it would be ready now.'

When dinner was finished, and they'd all sung *Happy Birthday dear Clemmy* for the third and last time, Sheridan summed up the general consensus.

'Man, that was one fantastic meal.'

It was long past midnight, before Joe took May and Bert back to Willow Farm. April decided to walk back to the manor house with the dogs, Sam and Seamus for company. 'I'll send Seamus back when we get down the bottom vineyard,' she said.

The children staggered upstairs without being told to go. 'Do you think they've had too much wine?' Diana asked Tony anxiously. 'They don't usually want to go to bed.'

'Of course not. It's damned late, they're just tired. I'm tired as well.'

'Me too.' Diana yawned. Millicent and Griselda started clearing the dishes away. 'No, don't do that. Let's be thoroughly decadent and leave all the mess until the morning.'

The two women didn't need telling twice. Millicent

scuttled upstairs ahead of Griselda, who made slower progress with her plastered leg and crutches.

Tony watched Diana. 'Pity Hugh couldn't come.'

'Yes.' Opening the fridge Diana extracted another bottle. 'Fancy some more Schonburger?'

She didn't want to talk about Hugh, telling herself that she was bitterly disappointed because he hadn't bothered to come down. The excuse he'd given had been so feeble, extra case work indeed, she knew it to be untrue. But the real trouble is, she thought, I've enjoyed myself without him. And it's a relief not to be going to bed with him, pretending that I love him passionately, when all the time I'm feeling more and more lukewarm towards him. There, she'd admitted it to herself at last. Her love for Hugh was slowly but surely diminishing. But if that was the case, why did she have this awful empty feeling inside? Suddenly, in spite of her happiness at Mottisley, Diana found she could put a name to the feeling. It was loneliness.

Tony looked at the green bottle glistening with condensation. 'Why not,' he said.

Diana obviously didn't want to talk about Hugh, so he did not pursue the subject. She probably felt like him, lonely and miserable. Life wasn't fair, and people weren't sensible. Why couldn't April see that Joe didn't love her? He liked her, but he didn't love her. But of course, she didn't want to see. People were very good at ignoring things they didn't want to acknowledge.

'Come on.' Diana opened the bottle, put two glasses on a tray and led the way outside towards the garden hammock. The moon was in its first quarter so the light was dim, but the air was as warm and dry as a midsummer's day.

An hour later, Tony who had consumed almost the entire bottle, was sloshed and sentimental. 'We should get together,' he said, putting his arms around Diana. 'We both need someone to love.'

Joe bringing back Seamus, who'd refused to obey

orders to return on his own, stopped at the wicket gate at the bottom of the garden. Diana and Tony looked as if they would not welcome a third person. He put his hand on Seamus's collar to restrain him, and watched as they walked back into Abbey House, their arms wound around each other. Tony was saying something in a low voice, and Diana was laughing. Joe turned away. So they were lovers. But it was nothing to do with him. Nothing at all. Then suddenly he felt a blind, raging fury. How dare Diana berate him for his two wives and several girlfriends, when she was being unfaithful herself. The hypocrisy of it all was sickening.

'I think I'm going to fall over,' Tony enunciated with all the solemnity of a drunk.

Diana surprised herself by dissolving into a fit of helpless giggling. Abbey House wine, stronger than she'd thought, induced a mood of fatalism. Hugh was unimportant. Everything would sort itself out. 'If we're not careful, we're both going to fall over,' she said between hiccups of laughter, wrapping her arms around Tony to help him stand.

'Have I ever told you that I love you?' Tony hung on to Diana, his lopsided weight making her stagger.

'No, and don't bother to now, because I wouldn't believe you.'

'Nobody believes me.'

Tony looked comically sorrowful. His fine brown hair had flopped down over his forehead, and his soulful brown eyes bore a close resemblance to those of the dog, Seamus. He looked about twelve, and suddenly Diana was reminded of the studious small boy who had sometimes helped Susan with her maths. He'd been kind then, and was now. The memory softened her voice.

'I've got a rule, Tony. Never believe anything a drunken man says.'

'I'm not . . . oh yes, perhaps I am. Just a little.' He

sagged even more, aimed a kiss at her cheek, missed, and ended up nibbling her ear. 'I want to go to bed.'

'The most suitable place for you. But understand this, I'm not coming with you.'

'A hard woman, that's what you are, Diana Stratton,' Tony grumbled.

Getting Tony up the stairs was no easy task, but somehow Diana managed without having to call for the assistance of Millicent. Once flat on his back, Tony revived a little, wanting to talk.

'I love her you know.'

'Who?'

'April, of course. Who else?'

The urge to giggle wore off. Tony's deep unhappiness was tangible, and Diana realized it was not just maudlin sentimentality caused by drink, but real and strong.

'Oh, don't tell me I'm stupid, Diana. I know it doesn't make sense. But as soon as I met April, I knew she was something special. At first I thought I just liked her. She made me laugh, she's sophisticated, and has a wicked sense of humour. But now I know there's much more to April than that. She's kind and caring, and would make the perfect wife.'

'And I thought you were sweet on Susan,' said Diana slowly, remembering the weekend she'd come to Mottisley in answer to Susan's summons. It seemed like years ago now, not just a few months. Then she'd thought how well Tony had fitted in with Susan and the children, and recalled thinking that he was in love with her sister.

'Of course I loved Susan. But it was a different kind of love. She was a cross between a sister and a mother to me. It's April I've always wanted to marry.'

'And April is going to marry Joe. At least I assume they'll marry. Joe seems to go in for weddings, if his other marriages are anything to go by.'

Excess alcohol filled Tony with a sudden atypical rage. 'That's just it,' he spluttered. 'I wouldn't mind so much if

327

I knew Joe was going to make her happy, damn it! But he won't. He's a bastard, he'll destroy her. Trample her underfoot, like a delicate wild violet.'

Diana restrained an impulse to smile. April as a wild violet! The picture didn't fit. It was the wine speaking, but Tony's sentiment was sincere enough. She tried to be calm and sensible. 'April is far tougher than you give her credit for. If anyone can manage Joe, she can. And surely, even you must admit that they do seem very happy together. So if they do marry perhaps it will work for both of them.' The thought of Joe and April's happiness grated irrationally.

Tony was scornful. 'Joe will never marry again. He's told me so himself. He's had his fingers burned once too often. And anyway, quite apart from that, he hasn't a clue what he really wants from life. He's not a man for planning ahead.'

'He never was,' said Diana.

The memory popped up, unbidden, of the days when she and Joe had been lovers. He had never planned ahead then. Stubborn as a mule he'd been, refusing to even contemplate the future, while she'd had everything mapped out, planned down to the last detail. If he'd been different, perhaps then. But no, she snapped the lid shut tight on such errant thoughts. Practical application to the problem of the moment was the priority, and that was Tony. Goodness knows where the meanderings of an undisciplined mind would lead.

'Have you told April that you love her?' Concentrate on now, Diana told herself. Tony has the problem, not you.

'Of course I've told her. Lots of times, but she doesn't believe me. Says she's too old for me, and anyway she thinks she loves Joe. She's wrong of course, she doesn't really love him. She just thinks it.'

'How can you be so sure? Perhaps you are wrong.' Diana felt annoyed. Men were always so damned certain. Even Tony, abject in his rejection, was stubbornly confident he was right. Then she stopped, biting her lip, not wanting to hurt him any more than necessary. He was hurting quite enough already with unrequited love. An emotion outside her own experience. Suddenly she wondered. Was that how Hugh felt? Did he know she was having doubts? Was he unrequited? Oh damn! She didn't want to think about *that*. There was no point in going round and round in aimless circles, not now. It could all be sorted out later. 'People can, and do, often love the most unsuitable people,' she said.

'You mean like you and Hugh,' said Tony, inebriety encouraging him to blurt out what had been in his mind for months.

'No I do not mean that,' snapped Diana. 'Hugh and I are perfectly well suited.'

'Well, if you want my opinion . . .' Tony sat up ready to expand vociferously, then groaned and fell back against the pillows. 'Oh God, I feel awful.'

'Go to sleep,' said Diana, slapping a cold wet flannel on his forehead, glad of his inability to deliver an opinion she had no wish to hear. Someone else's analysis of her relationship with Hugh was the last thing she needed.

'Thank you, nurse,' Tony muttered, and to Diana's relief promptly fell asleep.

Apart from taking off his shoes, and covering him with a lightweight cotton blanket, there wasn't much else she could do. So Diana tiptoed from the bedroom. In the dark she tripped over the Windsor chair near the door. The chair, Victorian, and made from heavy yew wood, thundered over with an almighty crash but Tony slept on, emitting a long drawn out snuffling snore. Once downstairs in the kitchen Diana made herself a cup of cocoa, and curled up on the lumpy old settee beneath the window. Seamus manoeuvred his lanky, long-legged frame up beside her, sighed, and laid his head on her lap, leaving little room for Shakespeare who was equally determined to share her favours. It was comforting feeling the warmth of the two furry bodies pressed close to hers.

Diana sipped the cocoa and wondered how much Tony would remember in the morning.

'I'm not much use as an Agony Aunt,' she confessed to the inert, snoring shapes of Seamus and Shakespeare. 'I'd like to be able to give Tony some good advice, but I can't think of any. Come to that, I could do with some good advice myself. If Hugh and I are so well suited, as I said, why is it I feel so indifferent to him these days? I *want* to love him. In fact, a year ago I thought I was passionately in love. No,' she corrected herself sternly, 'I didn't just think it, I *was* passionately in love.' Lifting up Seamus's ear she asked his opinion. 'What do you think?' Seamus's nose twitched, his whiskers worked violently and he puffled in his sleep, dreaming of chasing rabbits. 'Oh, you're no use,' said Diana, and tipping both animals from her lap went upstairs to make up the spare bed.

There are enough problems in the world without me imagining extra ones, she told herself firmly. This is a difficult time for Hugh and me, we'll be all right. Of course we will, nothing has ever defeated me yet, and it won't now. Are you sure? People aren't so easy to plan as projects. Damn that perverse little gremlin inside her head. Bed made, she climbed in, pulled the sheets up under her chin, switched off the light, and settled down. The slender crescent moon had completely disappeared now, and it was pitch dark. The thick impenetrable darkness of the countryside; quite different in substance to the darkness of a town. Country darkness was a black curtain enfolding the sleeping world, and in it only the creatures of the night moved. From beyond the abbey tower an owl hooted. A long, drawn out, quivering cry. Such a lonely, lonely sound. From somewhere deep inside her, Diana felt an answering cry of loneliness, and in spite of the warmth of the summer night, she shivered.

Chapter Twenty-five

It seemed to Diana that she had only closed her eyes for five short minutes before an agitated Millicent was waking her the next morning. 'Your Aunt May is on the 'phone. She's in a terrible state. I can't get any sense out of her. You'd better come.'

Stumbling sleepily downstairs, struggling into her dressing gown, Diana grabbed the 'phone.

'Come at once.' May's voice cracked, as if she was crying. 'Please, *please*, Diana, come at once.'

'Yes, of course I'll come. But tell me first what is the matter?'

'It's Bert. He's not dead, I'm sure he's not. Please God, he's not. But I can't get him to wake up.'

'I'll be with you in five minutes.' Diana turned back to Millicent. 'Bert's ill, maybe dead. Come on, we've got to wake Tony, and get him over to Willow Farm.'

'That might be easier said than done, Miss.' For some reason best known to herself, Millicent always insisted on calling Diana, Miss. 'When I took your tea up and found him, he still seemed drunk to me. I take it that's why you let him sleep in your bed.' Millicent probed curiously. She'd reported Tony's presence to Griselda and they'd decided that Diana and Tony must be having an affair.

'He can't still be drunk. Not now. He's *got* to wake up,' Diana sprinted back up the stairs.

In her bedroom Tony was still sleeping. He hadn't moved an inch from the way he'd been laying when she'd left him the night before.

Millicent stood behind her in the doorway. 'There you are,' she said. 'Still drunk.'

331

'Rubbish, he's just asleep. Come on, help me wake him.' Grabbing his shoulders, Diana shook him roughly. 'Wake up, Tony. Wake up. You're needed.'

'What? Where? Oh God.' He groaned, sat up, then clutching his head, tried to lie down again.

'I'll get him round.' Millicent was suddenly business-like. 'You get some clothes on, Miss. By the time you're ready, he'll be ready too.'

In view of Tony's ghastly colour, Diana had her doubts about that, but there was no time to argue. May had sounded desperate. Absolutely desperate, poor old darling. Whether Tony was ready or not, she had to get over to Willow Farm.

The ten minute drive had never seemed so long. Diana drove the ancient Volvo estate, Abbey Vineyard's only means of motorized transport, and Tony sat, grey-faced, at her side. 'She should have called an ambulance straight away, not waited for us,' he kept muttering. He had called the ambulance himself on his mobile 'phone as soon as he'd staggered downstairs.

'She didn't sound capable of thinking rationally about anything like that.'

Diana negotiated a right hand bend with all the speed and verve of a formula one racing driver. Tony shut his eyes in terror. 'Jesus! You certainly take after your aunt as far as driving is concerned.'

Diana wasn't listening. Changing up through the gears and gathering speed, she continued worrying about May. 'Poor old thing. All she could think of was turning to the nearest people for help.'

'And dearest,' said Tony with a wan smile, warily watching the road again through half closed eyes. 'Don't forget that.'

Suddenly Diana turned and stared at him. 'You mean me? The dearest?' In spite of her fear at what they might find at Willow Farm, an unexpected warm glow washed over her.

'Yes, of course, the dearest. She loves you. *For Christ's*

sake watch the road!' A tractor chugged out through a field gate straight into their path and Diana, missing it by inches, lost not a moment of speed.

'Don't worry, I saw it.'

Tony didn't answer, he was feeling too sick. Sticking his head out of the window he gulped in breaths of fresh air. Bloody fine doctor I am, he thought. Hung over to the point of being useless, and arriving at an emergency without any equipment. He wished he'd rung his father as well as the ambulance. But it was too late now, Willow Farm was in sight.

The ambulance arrived in the farmyard just as Diana and Tony were scrambling from the car.

'Thank God,' said Tony to the crew. 'Bring all your re-sus equipment. I think we're going to need it. Oh, and shove in all the drugs you've got. I haven't got my medical bag with me.'

'Bloody fine turn up for the books this is,' grumbled one of the paramedics. 'What use is a doctor without his bloody bag?'

'Off duty perhaps,' suggested the other charitably as they pulled down the trolley and loaded it with gear. Once loaded up, they followed the figures of Diana and Tony and ran into the farmhouse.

They were too late.

Tony came downstairs with Diana. 'Make May a cup of tea, that's what she needs,' he said. Then he turned and climbed back up the stairs.

Diana busied herself boiling the kettle on the evergoing kitchen range and made the tea. A crisis in England and we drink tea? Absentmindedly she wondered why. Bert was dead, and May wanted tea.

Tony helped May down into the kitchen. Diana found it difficult to reconcile the broken, shuffling ghost of an old woman to the May she'd always known. Still in her dressing gown, a dark brown fluffy garment, grown bedraggled with the years, May, clinging to Tony's arm reminded Diana of a tiny sparrow. But then she

333

remembered sparrows in storms; battered, and lashed by the elements, still they would cling on to their twigs. The thought was comforting. May was a fighter, she'd weather the storm.

'Here you are.' Gently she sat May down and gave her the tea.

Gnarled hands closed around the cup, and dark eyes, no longer bright and sparkling, but misty with sorrow and old age, looked into Diana's. 'I loved him, you know. There was never another man for me. Only my Bert.' She sipped her tea, staring into the glowing coals of the range. 'I fell in love with him the first day he came to work for my father. He was our new shepherd. Nineteen he was then, and I was sixteen.'

'Sixty-three years ago,' whispered Diana. 'A long time to love someone.'

Edward Evans had said that death was the only certainty in life, and there was nothing to fear. But he was wrong. Fear was the inheritance of the people left behind. Diana could see it clearly mirrored in May's eyes, and the name of the fear was loneliness.

'Yes, a long, long time,' said May slowly. 'So long that you are fooled into thinking that it will all go on and on for ever, and never change. But of course it doesn't. Everything stops in the end.' She sighed, and added, 'we should have married and had children. Once I've gone, there'll be nothing left to show that Bert and I have ever passed this way.'

'Why didn't you marry and have a family?'

The dark eyes resting on Diana sparkled with sudden angry rancour at a long distant memory. 'Snobbery and pride, and a fear of breaking with convention. Bert was from a different class from me. My family were moneyed, middle class farmers, and Bert was a manual worker. I was brave enough to risk sleeping with him, but not brave enough to defy my parents and marry him. Seems so stupid now. And later, after my parents' deaths,' she shrugged philosophically, 'well later it didn't matter whether we married or not, because it was too late anyway.'

'Too late for what?'

'For me to have children, of course.' Giving the empty teacup back to Diana, she leaned back in her chair and closed her eyes. 'Make sure you don't leave it too late, Diana.' she said. 'Make sure you don't end up like me. An empty old woman.'

'Just because you don't have children doesn't make you empty,' said Diana sharply.

May's words became a sharp knife, scoring open an old wound she'd thought long sealed. But it *is* too late. The thought was there before she could stop it. I'm sterile. Bad luck, the doctors had said, a chance in a million of getting a pelvic infection, and even worse luck that it had affected both fallopian tubes. But Diana had told herself then that it didn't matter, and pushed it firmly to the back of her mind. She'd never wanted children. And she definitely didn't want Hugh's children. The thought flickered uneasily before being blinked away. She must concentrate on May.

Tony, overhearing May's words, came to her side. 'There's been nothing empty in your life May, or that of Bert's. And Bert wouldn't like to hear you saying so, and you know it.' He squatted down beside the old lady. 'Nothing is perfect in this life. That was something Bert himself taught me. He was a fatalist, always believing that you made the best of whatever life happened to throw at you. And you two certainly made the best of your lives together.'

'Perhaps you're right.' May sounded tired. 'But I do feel empty now that Bert's gone. There's nothing left for me here.'

Diana stroked her hand, desperately wanting to comfort, but unsure of the right words. 'There's us,' she said. 'Me and the children, we're still here.'

'Ah, but will you stay? I don't think so. Soon Hugh will

335

persuade you back to London, and you'll send the children away.'

'No, no I won't do that. Hugh's coming down to live in Mottisley too. Just as soon as he can.'

'And do you want him to?' Suddenly May opened her eyes and stared straight at Diana. 'Will that make you happy?'

'Of course,' said Diana with more conviction than she felt. May's piercing stare was disconcerting. 'I want us to be together, so that we can make a proper family for the children. And Hugh wants that too.' Does he? her conscience asked. Is that what he really wants? Can you see him acting out the role of a father figure? She couldn't accept that the answer was a positive 'no.' 'Yes, I do want Hugh here,' she said firmly.

May closed her eyes again and grasped Diana's hand tightly. 'Of course, dear, I shouldn't have asked. I'm just a silly old woman whose brain is addled, and at the moment is feeling sorry for herself.'

To Diana's horror, tears began to squeeze past May's closed eyelids, trickling slowly down the wrinkled furrows of her skin. She had never in her life seen May cry. Not even when her beloved Susan had died. That day May's eyes had been bright with tears, but she'd grieved and railed vigorously against the unjust God who had taken her favourite niece from her. Her grief then was a spirited grief. Not like this. Not this soft, hopeless, melancholy weeping.

Diana bent her head, to hide her own tears. They pricked hot and burning behind her eyelids. But who was she crying for? For Bert? For May? in whose life a light had been extinguished which could never be re-kindled. Or for that part of herself, which more and more she was realizing had been lost, and could never be recovered.

On the Sunday morning of Bert's death, Hugh and Nancy were wrangling in her Hampstead home. 'But supposing someone should see us. How would I explain your presence to Diana?'

'Easy,' said Nancy airily. 'I'm your cousin-in-law. I've come over to cook you lunch. Very kindly making sure you survive while Diana is away.'

'I still don't think it's a good idea.'

'All right then. Go back on your own. But go you certainly must. Diana is sure to ring, and you've got to be there in your own apartment to answer the 'phone. We don't want her getting suspicious.'

Eventually Hugh capitulated, and took Nancy with him to the Chelsea apartment on the Sunday morning. Almost as soon as they arrived the telephone rang. It was Diana. Nancy sat cross-legged on the sofa, giving a thumbs up sign, and smiling at Hugh. A clever, feline smile. Diana had telephoned, just as she had predicted.

'Darling? Did you ring before? I've been out. I ran out of milk and popped down to that grotty little shop near the Pimlico tube.' Remembering Nancy's words, Hugh hastily thought up an excuse covering for the eventuality of Diana ringing before he'd got back from Hampstead.

'No.' Diana sounded distracted. 'I've been too busy. I'm afraid I've got bad news. Bert died this morning.'

'Bert? Dead?'

Nancy sat bolt upright, black eyes attentive. Hugh signalled towards the extension in the bedroom, and Nancy picked it up.

'Hugh, I know you're busy. But can you come down? Now, today.' As she spoke Diana wondered why she was asking Hugh. He would hate it. He hated deep emotion of any sort. He liked life to glide along on well-oiled wheels. He wouldn't fit in with the sorrow at Mottisley. But – her chin jutted aggressively – he belongs here, she thought. He is my husband. 'Please,' she said.

'What now?' Hugh didn't want to go. 'Well, I . . .' Nancy nodded her head vigorously, mouthing *you must go.* Hugh, who'd been about to refuse, obeyed. 'All right, darling,' he said meekly. 'I'll be there as soon as I can, and don't worry about letting Nancy know the sad news. I'll give her a quick ring.' Putting down the 'phone he turned to Nancy. 'Why the hell do you want me to go down there? I can't do anything.'

'Oh, yes you can. You can be a supportive, caring husband.' She held up two fingers, and giggled wickedly. 'One down, only one more to go. And that's May. She won't live for long now that Bert's gone. And then there'll be the inheritance. Don't forget whatever Diana inherits, you inherit too.'

Hugh sniffed. 'All she's got at the moment is that bloody vineyard.'

'There'll be more,' said Nancy confidently. 'So go down there, and for God's sake be nice to May. I'll ring her later today and ask if there is anything I can do.'

'There won't be.'

Nancy's white teeth sparkled gleefully. 'Of course not, darling. I wouldn't offer if there was. You ought to know that.'

They left Chelsea. Nancy in a taxi to return to Hampstead, and Hugh in his Porsche for Mottisley, to play the role of caring husband, uncle, and great-nephew.

Chapter Twenty-six

It rained in the night. A torrential, almost tropical down-pour, but by morning, on the day of Bert Slocombe's funeral, the downpour had given way to the soft summer rain of southern England. A fine, warm, misty rain, penetrating everything and blurring the landscape so that it resembled a Seurat painting.

May sat alone with Bert in the front parlour waiting for the undertakers to arrive and seal the coffin. The rest of the family waited in the kitchen.

'Bloody ridiculous, this lying in state,' said Hugh.

'An old woman's foible,' said Nancy. 'You must allow her that indulgence.'

Hugh glowered. He knew damned well why Nancy was being so sweet and understanding, she was counting her inheritance. One look at May's, now quite apparent, frailty, and he could see her mentally filing and valuing everything, and transferring at least half of it into her own bank account. More than half, if she could fiddle it.

'It's the old-fashioned country way,' said Joe. 'Nothing ridiculous about it. I rather like it. While he's here, Bert is still a member of the family.'

'Which is more than you are,' said Hugh nastily.

'May regards Joe as part of the family. You know that, Hugh,' said Diana.

She felt exasperated. All her determination to merge Hugh into life at Mottisley had so far failed. He was polite, helpful in a limited way, friendly, but very distant, giving her the feeling that he thought all the activity at Mottisley superfluous to his own, more important, life in London. And he'd made it quite clear that he wasn't the slightest bit interested in the vineyard, failing to understand how important it was to her plans. She had to get it up and running, it *had* to make money. After last night's heavy rain, she was fretting about possible damage to the vines, wishing she'd been able to get a report from Sheridan before they'd left for Willow Farm and the funeral.

May came to the door of the parlour. 'The undertakers are arriving. Their cars are in the yard. Joe, will you get those guns for me please?'

'Are you sure, May?'

'Quite sure.' May went back into the parlour and shut the door.

'What is she talking about?' Tony walked over to Joe.

Diana joined him. 'Yes, what does she mean? Get the guns.'

'May wants Bert's guns buried with him.'

'What, in the coffin?' April was incredulous.

'Of course. You can't just chuck them in the grave. They'd get ruined.'

'Being buried six feet under isn't going to do them a whole lot of good,' observed Tony.

'Why didn't you tell me about this, Joe?' Diana felt illogically jealous that May had taken Joe into her confidence, and not herself.

'Because I knew your reaction would be the same as everyone else's, including mine. And don't think I haven't tried to persuade her against it. Because I have. But she's adamant, and there's nothing anyone can do about it.'

'Is it legal?' asked Tony dubiously. 'I mean, burying guns. Surely the police will have something to say.'

'I've asked them,' said Joe. 'They're not happy, and advise against it. But as it isn't illegal, there is nothing they can do.' He went across to the gun cupboard, unlocked it, and took out two pairs of guns. Pausing a moment, he touched the highly polished barrels lovingly. 'Purdey, and Holland and Holland, eighty years old, both pairs,' he said. 'Been in May's family since they were made. Pity to bury them, but May doesn't want anyone else to fire them, and I can understand that. They were Bert's pride and joy.'

Diana swallowed her hurt pride at May's exclusion; it was natural she should turn to Joe on a matter concerning guns. 'I can understand her wanting Bert to take them with him,' she said softly. 'They were part of him.'

'I see,' said Simon, nodding his head knowingly. 'It's like when the Pharoahs were buried in ancient Egypt. They took their hunting things with them, and lots of other things as well.'

'Is Bert going to have a pyramid then?' asked Miffy.

'Of course not, silly,' said Clemmy scornfully. 'How could you fit a pyramid into Mottisley churchyard? Honestly, some kids!'

'What it means is that the things Bert loved most are going to be buried with him,' said Diana, putting her arm around Miffy.

'Not May as well,' squeaked Miffy, his blue eyes enormous.

'No, just the guns, darling.'

'More's the pity,' said Nancy under her breath.

'Jesus Christ!' Hugh had difficulty in restraining the disbelieving anger in his voice. He'd never been shooting, but he knew the value of such ancient shot-guns. 'Do you know how much those guns are worth, Diana?'

'No, and I don't care.'

Hugh told her anyway. 'They're worth at least thirty-thousand pounds a pair. That's sixty-thousand pounds being buried.'

'Sixty thousand!' Nancy's black eyes glinted thoughtfully. 'Wouldn't you like to have that in your pocket, Diana?'

Diana shrugged philosophically. 'You're right, I would. But the guns are not mine. They are May's, and her wishes should prevail. It's only right. You'd better take them in to her, Joe. The undertakers are here.' Going out into the hall, she opened the large front door and let the sombre looking men in black suits into the farmhouse.

An hour and a half later the funeral was over. The whole family party, plus a dozen or more villagers and the Reverend Pincher, were back at Willow Farm; soaked to the skin and more than ready for the drinks and sandwiches which Millicent and Griselda had prepared in their absence.

'Tony,' Nancy grabbed him. 'Can I ask a favour? May I use your car 'phone for a moment. It's difficult to make a private 'phone call here. So many people.' She waved at the crowd thronging the kitchen.

'Of course.' Tony wondered what could be so important that she had to telephone right at that moment.

Hugh watching her disappear wondered too.

Diana standing beside Hugh watched the children. They were very subdued. Perhaps Joe had been right. All the while Bert had remained in the house he was still with them, but once lowered into the grave he was gone. The clods of wet earth traditionally dropped down on to the coffin had sounded the final note.

'Perhaps I ought not to have let the children go,' she said.

'Go where?' asked Hugh, still thinking of Nancy.

'To the funeral. It's depressed them.'

'For God's sake don't start getting all motherly, I couldn't bear it. Anyway, I don't believe those kids feel anything.'

'They've learned how to cover up their feelings,' said April, who'd overheard. 'It's the one lesson we adults are good at teaching. Never, never show your true feelings.'

'Today has reminded them of their mother.' Diana fretted about the children. 'I shouldn't have let them go.'

'They'll be all right. You can't protect them from life. So long as you're here, they'll be all right.' April gave Diana's arm a quick squeeze. 'Don't worry about them. I'll go and make sure they've got something to eat. You know Miffy. Once he's tucking into food, he forgets everything.' She laughed and pointed. 'Look, what did I tell you?'

342

Diana smiled. Millicent had come in with a tray of gingerbread men, and Miffy, beaming seraphically, held one up in the air before biting off its head.

'Perhaps I do worry too much.' She turned to Hugh. 'But I can't help the way I am. If I'm to look after the children, I've got to be a little bit motherly.'

Hugh picked up a plate and helped himself to sausage rolls and sandwiches. 'I don't want you back in London being motherly.'

'But I'm not coming back to London. I've told you that. Don't you believe me?'

'I thought staying down here was a temporary measure. Until you found someone suitable to take over.'

Diana stared at him in amazement. How could he say that? 'Haven't you listened to anything I've said these last few weeks. I'm staying. I'm staying for good. I'm being a mother to the kids, as best I can, and I'm going to make the vineyard a profitable operation. I aim to make enough money to enable us to live in relative comfort. And as soon as Norman Leadbetter gives me the final figures of the money I've got invested, I intend to plough most of it into Abbey Wines. I'm planning on expanding.' Hugh was silent. 'Is that why you've put off coming down?' asked Diana. 'You've been waiting for me to change my mind?'

'Yes,' admitted Hugh.

'Well, I'm not going to. So you'd better reconsider.'

'I can see that.' Hugh, momentarily thrown, cursed his carelessness for having boxed himself into a corner through his own bad temper. Then he slipped a casual arm around Diana's shoulders. Mustn't alienate her. 'I suppose I could get used to living in Mottisley,' he said. 'In fact, I can see that I'm going to have to.' He kissed the tip of her nose. 'How foolish I was thinking I could persuade you to change your mind. I've been married to you long enough to know that a strong-minded woman like you doesn't change her mind. Well then, there's nothing for it. You'll have to help me turn into a country gentleman.'

'Oh, I will, I *will*,' said Diana, smiling happily. At last her plans were coming to fruition. 'Once you get used to it, I know you'll love it. We can be a proper family. You, me and the children. Promise me you'll come as soon as you possibly can.'

'I promise,' said Hugh.

'Stop here. At that pub, the Blacksmith's Arms.'

'Stop? Already? We're only just through Cowdray Park.' Hugh turned and stared at Nancy who was smiling. An excited, self-satisfied smile.

'I know that. But this is as far as we're going for the moment. Go on, stop, and go over and book us a room. We might as well make good use of the time. We have to wait until it's dark anyway.' Nancy pushed an acquisitive hand inside Hugh's flies. 'I feel in need of sex.'

'You always do.' Hugh pushed her hand away. There was something about her smile which made him strangely nervous. 'But can't you wait until we get back to London? It's cheaper than renting a room.' Quite apart from Nancy's smile, the thought of Diana's next meeting with Normal Leadbetter, and the imminent disclosure of her true financial position took the edge off his sexual appetite. If only he could lay his hands on some ready cash.

'We're not going back to London,' said Nancy. 'We're waiting here until it's dark, then we're going back to Mottisley.'

'We are what! What the hell are you playing at?'

'It's no game,' said Nancy softly. 'It's serious business. Collecting what is rightfully mine. You can have your half too, if you help me.'

Hugh parked the car and turned to Nancy. Usually able to follow her devious thinking, this time she had him completely foxed. 'What are you talking about?'

'Sixty-thousand pounds.'

'The guns?'

'Yes.'

344

'But they're buried.'

'So we dig them up.'

'But they're in the coffin.'

'So we open it,' said Nancy. She laughed, excited at the prospect. 'Sometimes Hugh, you are awfully dense.'

'But you can't . . . I mean, I can't. The coffin is six feet down, how do you expect to get it out? It would take all night to move that earth. No, Nancy, we can't do it.'

'Can't, can't, can't.' Nancy pouted. 'Is that the only bloody word you know? I hate negative men.' She got out and slammed the car door, and Hugh hastily followed suit. 'Just as well I telephoned Nico. He's coming down with his brother Rick, and bringing some spades and protective overalls to use. *He* didn't raise one single word of objection. In fact, he thought it a brilliant idea and rather exciting into the bargain. He's never robbed a grave before. Unlike you, Nico is always ready to try something new, especially if there's a nice little hand-out at the end of it.'

'You've contacted Nico?' Hugh was beset with even greater apprehension.

'Yes, I phoned him on Tony's car 'phone.'

'You know I don't like you having too much to do with that crook.'

'Darling, I deal with whoever *I* want to, not who *you* want me to. I'm going into the pub and booking myself a room. You can go back to London and forget what I've told you. You can also forget the thirty-thousand quid you might have had, because, believe me, I won't part with it unless you help me get it.'

Thirty-thousand pounds. Hugh thought of Norman Leadbetter. With that amount of money at his disposal he could have a quick flutter on the stock market, recoup everything he'd spent with Nico if his luck held, maybe even more. Then he could hand over the money and say that he'd taken it to reinvest it more profitably. That would get him off the hook financially. Then all he'd have to do would be to keep in with Diana until May finally kicked the bucket. Once she had inherited half of Willow Farm and its contents he could start divorce proceedings and get half the proceeds. Put into perspective like that it was a simple answer to what he'd previously thought of as a complex problem.

'All right, you win,' he said. 'I need the money. Can't say I'm happy about opening a coffin though.'

'It'll be an experience,' said Nancy with an excited laugh. 'Nothing like opening up a coffin after a few good orgasms. Come on, I can't wait to feel a prick inside me.'

And not too fussy about who it belongs to, thought Hugh moodily. The thought of teaming up with Nico and his brother depressed him. He would never have admitted it to Nancy but they scared him. Like Nancy they got their thrills in life from sailing close to the wind. And Nancy was much too friendly with Nico.

By midnight it had stopped raining, but the clouds still hung, burdened with rain, low in the sky. A wind had sprung up, a southwesterly, blowing up from the sea, laden with brine. It gave a sharp tang to the damp air, and to Hugh, added an extra feeling of menace.

'It'll be an experience,' Nancy had said, and she was damned right there, thought Hugh, wielding his shovel alongside Nico and Rick. But not an experience he'd be wanting to repeat in a hurry.

'Bloody hard work,' he grumbled, pausing to rest on the shovel handle.

'Don't waste time,' hissed Nancy. 'We want to get it over and done with and be out of here as soon as possible.'

'Shut your mouth, smart arse,' snarled Nico, who was also finding it heavy going. 'You're not the one moving this earth. How much farther down do you think we need to go?' he asked Hugh.

'About another foot.'

'It's hard 'cause it's wet. The earth's wet. That's right, isn't it Nico? The earth's wet,' said Rick with a loud guffaw of laughter. He was large, loud, and rather slow on the uptake.

Mentally retarded bugger, thought Hugh, stabbing his shovel into the earth viciously. They could do without him making a racket.

Nico thought so too. 'Keep your voice down, bruv. We don't want to get caught, do we.'

'We most certainly do not,' said Nancy tartly. 'Otherwise you will have used all your energy for nothing.'

The next twenty minutes passed in silence, except for the sound of shovels clinking against flints in the soil now and then, and the rhythmic sound of wet earth being thrown on the evergrowing mound behind them. Then there was another, sudden, loud sound. Metal against wood.

'We've reached the coffin,' grunted Nico. 'Bring the torch over,' he called to Nancy, 'and bring the pickaxe as well.'

Nancy leaned over the edge of the excavated grave, dangling the torch with one hand and handing down the pickaxe with the other. The three men looked at each other. Hugh shivered at the sight the uneven torchlight revealed. Covered with black, wet earth, the three men looked like strange subterranean creatures.

'You look as if you've just emerged from the bowels of the earth,' said Nancy breathlessly, relishing the scene. 'Quite wonderful.'

'We haven't emerged, we've just dug our bloody way down here,' said Nico, and swung the pickaxe above his head. Although short, he was a powerful man, and one blow from the pickaxe shattered the coffin lid. 'Go to it Rick,' he said.

Hugh watched in fascinated horror as Rick tore aside the broken coffin lid with his bare hands to reveal Bert lying there in his Sunday best suit, his hands crossed piously on his breast, clasping a prayer book. The guns lay, as they'd been placed by May, one pair each side of him.

'Get the guns,' said Nancy, greed rasping in her voice.

Although he wanted the money, Hugh couldn't bring himself to reach down into the coffin, afraid that he might touch the body of Bert. But Nico had no such qualms. Picking up one pair he tossed them to Hugh. 'Get out of the grave,' he said.

Not needing a second bidding Hugh slithered and scrambled his way to the surface, clasping the guns to his side. At the top he turned and looked back. Rick had hold of the other pair of guns. 'Let's get out of here,' he said, knowing that if he didn't leave soon he'd throw up.

A car drove past the churchyard and the guilty quartet froze into silence. But it drove on, and all was silent save for the wind soughing through the branches of the ancient yews. They started breathing again.

'God knows what we'd have done if someone had come over here,' whispered Hugh. Glad that it was dark and no-one could see him shaking.

'We'd have thumped them over the head, of course,' said Nico.

'Well, we didn't have to. So let's get out of here before anyone else passes by. Put the guns in the boot of Hugh's car,' Nancy was in a hurry.

'When do we get paid?' Nico wanted his money.

'As soon as we get back to London.' Nancy laid a placating hand on Nico's arm. 'I promise.'

'All right. I'll be round sometime tomorrow. See you.' Nico and his brother went off in the direction of his car, well hidden behind a field gate.

'Have you got the money to pay him?' Hugh unlocked the Porsche and he and Nancy climbed in.

'Yes, it's only two thousand. He doesn't know how much the guns are really worth. They did it for the kicks as much as anything.' Nancy lit a cigarette and laughed. 'Fun, wasn't it?'

Hugh didn't answer. There was a flash of silver and a roar of a powerful exhaust. Nico had driven off in his silver Jaguar. 'He'll wake the entire village with that racket,' he grumbled.

'Do stop moaning, darling. And let's get back to civilization.'

Driving back to London, Hugh glanced sideways at Nancy. Sitting in the seat beside him, slowly smoking a cigarette, she was humming happily and hopelessly out of tune. With a rare flash of insight Hugh realized that his own life was hopelessly out of tune. Remembering the scene at the grave he felt sick again. He'd been a fool, letting Nancy dominate him; and for the first time since he'd met her he acknowledged to himself that not only did she wield an unhealthy amount of power over him, but that, in truth, he was afraid of her. I must do something, he thought. I must reinstate my own authority over my life.

Chapter Twenty-seven

The sound of a squeaking recorder awoke Diana. It was Miffy struggling to play Frère Jacques.

'Frère Jacques, Frère Jacques,
    Dormez . . . Dormez . . . Dormez . . . Dormez vous?'

Diana winced. Four attempts to find the right notes for 'dormez'! Never mind he was trying hard. She smiled, thinking of the three children. In practice she was scrupulously fair in her dealings with them, at least, she hoped she was, but in her heart of hearts she had to admit that Miffy was her favourite, and not just because he was the youngest. In theory, as the youngest, he should have been the easiest to manage, most malleable, but, as Diana was beginning to learn, family life never conformed to theory. The practice was always quite different. Far from being malleable, Miffy was difficult. He was awkward, stubborn as a mule, and utterly charming. Just when she was on the point of feeling she could wring his neck, he'd turn to her, blue eyes glinting with affectionate mischief, and she'd feel her knees turn to water. And every time that happened she was struck afresh by wonder. She, who had never wanted children, had always thought them an encumbrance, loved Miffy more than she had ever believed it possible to love another human being. Of course, I love all the children, she frequently told herself, but there was no denying that Miffy was her best beloved.

Frère Jacques finally ended on a particularly strident squeak, and there was silence in the house. Diana yawned and stretched, it was six-thirty in the morning and she knew she ought to get up. Outside her open window the sun already shone, and the house-martins swooped, dived, and darted, gathering insects to feed their ever hungry young. There was a nest under the eaves outside her window, and she could hear the babies chittering and scuffling about as they waited for the parent birds to return. Across the yard she heard the tractor start up in the shed. Sheridan was off to collect a load of pig manure from George Jones's farm on the other side of Mottisley.

She sat up. Today was the day of Mottisley Abbey's Summer Fete and she had promised to help. A delectable smell of baking drifted up the stairs and into her bedroom. Millicent must already be up and baking for the fete.

By the time Diana entered the kitchen, the wide windowsills of the room were the resting place for trays full of fairy cakes. All neatly iced and each one adorned with a cherry.

'They look delicious, Millicent. You must have been up at the crack of dawn.'

'Yes, Miss, I was. I couldn't sleep. Kept thinking about yesterday. So I thought I might as well get up and get on with the baking.'

Yesterday; Diana shivered. Suddenly it was as if a chill cloud had passed over the warm sun, darkening the golden summer day. Yesterday they had buried Bert for the second time, four days after his original funeral. The Reverend Pincher had performed another service, which Diana had not allowed the children to attend. In fact, she had kept the whole horrible episode of the grave robbing from them as much as possible. Hugh hadn't been able to attend, he'd been in the middle of a case in Court, and Nancy hadn't come either. In a way Diana was pleased, the quieter the affair the better. To her relief everyone in the village seemed reluctant to talk about it too, as if by talking too much they would be tainted by the evil which had occurred. The horror of the event had shocked everyone rigid. The police had been wonderful, very circumspect. May was well known and liked, and no-one, including the police, wished to cause her any more grief than necessary.

'Yes, yesterday,' said Diana slowly, putting the kettle

351

on for a cup of tea, and feeling guilty that she'd slept like a log. But she had been so exhausted. Apart from attending the burial service, she had weeded three rows of vines by hand. 'Perhaps it's just as well there is the Fete today, it will take everyone's mind off the whole horrible business.' She sighed, 'Although what I'd really like to do is get on with the weeding. There's still such a lot to do.'

'Why don't you spray as Sheridan suggested?'

'Millicent, I am trying to be as environmentally friendly as possible. Spraying kills so much, and not just in the area you spray.'

Millicent tut-tutted. 'You're as bad as Miss Clemmy. You'll be turning bright green next.'

Diana smiled, it was a tough job persuading Millicent not to eradicate everything that crawled or flew, and to prevent her from pouring gallons of bleach down the drains. 'I will not. I'm just trying to be sensible in the way we do things. Don't tell me you wouldn't miss the purple vetch in the hedgerows, or the harebells or the foxgloves, because I wouldn't believe you.'

Millicent looked unconvinced. 'All this rubbish about destroying the world and a hole in the ozone layer. I don't believe it. Everything looks the same to me.' It irritated her that Diana had banned bleaches and insect sprays.

Griselda stomped into the kitchen. In a half plaster now, she was able to get around with surprising agility. 'Aah! Good, tea,' she said as the kettle began to whistle. 'I'll do the toast.'

'No need. I've made some croissants,' said Millicent. 'Sheridan loved them. He ate four as soon as they came out of the oven.'

'You spoil us.' Diana frowned suddenly. 'But can we afford them? We spent an awful lot of money on Clemmy's birthday dinner, and we're giving the cakes to the Abbey Fete. So can we really afford the ingredients for croissants? You *are* keeping within the budget I hope, Millicent.'

'Yes, Miss, I am,' said Millicent crossly. 'Croissants cost next to nothing. They're only flour, yeast, eggs, milk and butter. And now we've got Daisy, we've got milk and butter coming out of our ears.'

'It was good of Joe to buy her for us,' said Griselda, eyes gleaming cheerfully behind her pebble lenses. She was much more self-confident these days. 'Having a cow makes all the difference.'

'We've still got to feed her,' Diana reminded them a trifle sharply. It *had* been good of Joe to give them a cow, but Diana doubted that he'd thought the whole project through. And anyway she wasn't all that happy about accepting presents from Joe. It made her feel beholden. Although he'd told her in no uncertain terms that Daisy was for the children's benefit, not hers. But was it really cheaper getting milk, butter and cheese from a cow? She wondered, and worried.

For no matter what she did, she couldn't escape her ever-present concern over money. The vineyard shop was bringing in some money. Not as much as it had on the opening day, but at least it was a steady source of income which more or less kept the house running. The main worry was the enormous loan she'd taken out. Maybe she shouldn't have bought that new filtration system for the winery. But Sheridan had assured her that the revolutionary new equipment would result in a clearer, better flavoured wine.

'With a better quality wine, we'll be able to charge more,' he'd said.

Diana hoped so; constantly prayed for an abundant, good quality harvest, and kept her fingers crossed that the interest rate on the loan would not rise.

'Daisy doesn't cost much to feed in the summer.' Griselda was quite protective about the cow whom she milked herself. 'Today, for instance, she's grazing at the side of the main vineyard. Keeping the grass down, so you needn't mow it, and feeding at the same time. Don't worry, she's tethered,' she added hastily, seeing Diana's

353

anxious expression. Griselda hadn't forgotten Diana's threat to turn Daisy into steak and kidney pies after she'd munched her way through a quantity of grapes in the lower vineyard. 'And I've got four dozen pots of live yoghourt made from her milk to sell at the Fete. All the profit coming back to Abbey House.'

'I'm glad to hear it,' said Diana, slightly mollified at the thought of some additional income.

The Fete was well under way. Mottisley brass band arranged themselves in a semi-circle in the middle of the field, and struck up a spirited rendition of tunes from *West Side Story*.

'I can't help feeling they should have chosen something. less ambitious,' said April as the trombones got hopelessly out of time with the cornets. 'Everything is definitely *not* good in America!'

Diana grinned. She and April were running the 'bowl for a piglet' competition, and to her surprise, in spite of everything that had happened in the previous few days, she was enjoying herself. 'You wait until you hear Miffy and his schoolmates playing their recorders. I'm praying that the rest of the class will drown all his wrong notes. By the way, where is he? And the others, where are they?'

April pointed to the far side of the field. 'With Joe at the lucky dip.' Shading her eyes with her hand she watched them. 'Maybe if I got pregnant Joe would want to marry me,' she said. 'He loves kids.'

Diana looked up quickly. 'A slightly desperate measure, don't you think?' The thought of Joe and April having children bothered her. What about Tony? Remembering his confidences the night of Clemmy's birthday party, she knew he'd be heartbroken if April married Joe *and* got pregnant as well. But she firmly stamped on the thought that it would bother her too. Why should it? She didn't care what Joe and April did, it was Tony she worried about.

'Desperate situations call for desperate measures,' said

April gloomily, still watching the children and Joe. Then she said, 'Funny how alike Miffy and Joe are. Have you noticed?'

'No,' lied Diana quickly, 'I've never noticed.' She looked towards the group. 'He isn't a bit like him, similar colouring perhaps, that's all.' She remembered the first time she had noticed the similarity. It had been the day Miffy had started the fire. The day which had changed her life. She could see them now. Joe and Miffy standing side by side in the doorway. Smiling at her with the same, slightly lopsided, wicked grin, the same piercing blue eyes. Since that night she had wondered whether Susan had had an affair with Joe, and Miffy had been the result. Common sense told her the thought was ridiculous. Susan had been devoted to Tom. She would never have been unfaithful.

'Are you two going to stand there all afternoon gossiping, or can I have a bowl for the pig?'

Diana and April turned in surprise. 'May!' they both said together.

'Whatever are you doing here?' said Diana.

May peered up at them from beneath the brim of a large, beige, floppy sunhat, and leant on her walking stick. It was Bert's stick, Diana noticed, the one with the bone handle carved in the shape of a badger's head.

'What does it look like?' she said. 'I've come to enjoy the Fete. No point sitting on my own in Willow Farm thinking bad thoughts. I've done enough of that these last few days. And Bert wouldn't want me to vegetate. Anyway, the Reverend Pincher and Emily insisted, so I came.'

'Do you good,' said April.

The subject of Miffy was forgotten. Although not entirely by Diana. It lingered, uncomfortable, disconcerting. Suppose Susan had had a liaison with Joe, and Miffy was his son. Could he lay claim to him? Take him away from her? Never! she thought fiercely. All the children are mine. Given into my care by Susan. For the first time in her life Diana knew what it was like to be riven through and through with a sudden, gut-tearing jealousy. I'll adopt them, she resolved. Make all three of them, and Miffy most of all, *really* mine. Then they will be *my* children, Joe will never be able to lay any sort of claim to Miffy.

The sound of clapping jerked Diana's turbulent thoughts back to the Fete. A large crowd was watching May bowl. 'She's got the highest score so far,' said April, 'and still one ball to bowl.'

'There!' All nine skittles tumbled over, and May dusted off her hands triumphantly before taking her stick back from April. 'A strike. Knew I hadn't lost my touch.'

'Well done,' said Emily Pincher joining them. Her large figure was clad in a white dress patterned with enormous sunflowers.

'Looks like a walking advert for margarine,' whispered April irreverently.

Tony and Joe materialized alongside May with the children.

Miffy poked an exploratory finger through the wire meshing of the cage, and the pig snapped at it.

Diana snatched Miffy away.

'It's all right. Pigs aren't carnivorous,' said Clemmy airily, 'and they only bite sometimes.'

'He won't bite me, he's only a baby.' Miffy looked up at May. 'If you do win, you can give him to us.'

'We haven't got a sty,' said Diana hastily, not wishing to add a pig to their already expanding menagerie.

'I'll make you one,' said Tony, putting his arm around her waist. 'Give me something to do in my spare time.'

'What spare time?' said Joe grumpily. 'I should think you could find something better to do than to spend what little time you do get off with Diana.'

'We keep one another company,' said Diana, annoyed by Joe's censorious manner. 'What's the matter with you?'

May, watching the four of them through narrowed eyes,

356

snorted with laughter. 'What are you quarrelling about?' she asked slyly.

'We're not quarrelling at all,' said Diana.

'Ah, Mrs Stratton. We've been looking everywhere for you.'

Diana turned to find Tara Cotton, and Dorothy Stoodley standing beside her. They looked just as forbidding as the previous time she'd seen them, and were even wearing the same dresses. 'What do you want?' she asked warily. Tony had told her that they were likely to come, unannounced, and inspect her. To see how she was coping with the children. But surely they hadn't picked this afternoon to do that?

'We didn't realize that you'd be involved with the Fete. But we do need a private talk.' Tara Cotton took charge.

'Come on.' Emily Pincher whisked May away. 'Let's go and find the white elephant stall.'

'Why not. I could do with a white elephant,' said May.

'Who is that strange woman?' Dorothy Stoodley planted her fat legs firmly apart and stared after May, bobbing along looking like an animated mushroom, almost extinguished by the size of her floppy sunhat.

'That is my aunt, and there's nothing strange about her,' said Diana sharply.

'We're going to get toffee apples.' Clemmy and Simon clung on to Joe's hand, who looked at Diana, and raised his eyebrows helplessly as he was dragged off.

'Bring me one back,' shouted Miffy, 'I'm staying here and talking to the pig.'

Diana looked around. Even Tony and April seemed to have deserted her. They'd wandered up to the far end of the bowling alley and seemed to be replacing the skittles very, very slowly; and now no-one was bowling the rest of the crowd had drifted away to other sideshows and stalls.

'This is about as private as it's ever going to be,' said Diana. 'We can talk now.'

'It's about the children,' said Tara Cotton.

'What about them? And why now?'

'This grave robbing business is extremely serious. It could be very emotionally disturbing. So we are thinking it might be better for them to be moved away for a bit. To a good foster home.'

'Keep your voice down,' hissed Diana, aware that Miffy was still there. He was on all fours, snorting and playing at being a pig. 'The children know very little about it. I've taken great care to keep it from them.'

'Easier said than done,' said Dorothy Stoodley ponderously.

Diana looked at her pink, perspiring face, and longed to hit it. 'It *was* easy until you turned up,' she said icily. 'You have no good reason even to consider taking the children away from me.'

'On the contrary. You may be their aunt, but you have no experience of children, and now we hear that you have an aged aunt to care for as well we feel it will be too much for you.'

'Absolute nonsense.' Diana was furious. 'My aunt May might be aged, but believe me she does not need looking after. That was her you met just now. Good heavens, she runs her own farm.'

'Oh,' said Tara Cotton. 'the one who wanted to buy a white elephant.' She made a note on her clipboard. 'A little strange,' she murmured, then said. 'How old is she?'

'Strange,' shrieked Diana. There was something unnerving about the two women and she lost her temper, consequently throwing all caution to the winds. 'Strange!' she repeated. 'Not nearly as strange as you two. And as for her age, it's none of your bloody business.'

'What's going on?' At the sound of Diana's shouting Tony and April hurried up.

'Aaah!' Dorothy Stoodley screamed, and staggered backwards. 'I've been bitten. That child,' she pointed at Miffy, 'has bitten me.'

'I am not a child. I am a pig,' said Miffy. 'But don't worry I shan't eat you, I'm not,' he hesitated, 'coniferous.'

Then spitting noisily he looked up at Diana. 'She tastes horrible,' he said.

'My friend might get blood poisoning.' Tara Cotton put an arm round her fat colleague. 'I've read that human bites can be dangerous.'

'Rubbish,' said Diana. 'Much more likely that Miffy will suffer an upset stomach. There must be hundreds of germs on that leg.' She looked distastefully at the leg in question. Miffy's teeth marks were plainly visible, and there were two pinpricks of blood.

'There's a St John Ambulance station near the vicarage. I'll take you there,' said April.

'He's a doctor. Why can't he help?' Both social workers pointed at Tony, who had walked back towards the skittles shaking with silent laughter.

'He hasn't got any equipment,' said April hastily. 'Much better we go to the St John Ambulance man.'

'We'll see you at the case conference next week.' Tara Cotton shouted at Tony. 'We'll be recommending that the children be taken away from this inept, single woman, and placed with a proper family.'

'But I'm not single,' said Diana. 'I'm married.'

'Ah, but your husband is never here. So you might just as well be single.' Tara Cotton made the pronouncement with malicious satisfaction.

'You are wrong. I am here.' Hugh suddenly materialized beside Diana. 'And I'm staying. So what is all this nonsense about my wife being single? I can assure you she's very much a married lady.' He gave Tara Cotton the benefit of one of his most charming smiles, and taking her hand said, 'May I introduce myself. I'm Hugh Stratton.'

Hugh's sudden appearance, and his pronouncement that he was staying surprised Diana, but she immediately saw it was good ammunition to use against the two social workers.

'So there's no need for a case conference on the children now,' she said.

'I wouldn't say that.' Tara Cotton glowered at Miffy. 'That child is definitely in need of some very firm discipline, he's a horrible child. Look at Dorothy's leg. Look at the blood.'

'Not enough to cover a bee's knee,' said April briskly. 'She's got plenty more, about eight pints in fact. Come on, we'll go to the First Aid tent.' She dragged Dorothy Stoodley away.

'Now that I'm here,' said Hugh, directing another charming smile at Tara, 'I promise that there'll be no more problems with discipline. Misdemeanours will be dealt with accordingly.'

Diana opened her mouth to object, then closed it. If Hugh could get the social workers off her back then it was all to the good. She smiled at Miffy who beamed back at her.

'Well, if you say so, Mr Stratton.' The charm of Hugh's smile was beginning to work. She sounded indecisive. 'Perhaps we'll postpone the case conference for the moment, and review the situation later.'

'No we won't.' Tony rejoined the group. 'We'll have it on Monday as you planned, and we'll settle the case on this family once and for all. We'll make a decision, and close the case. Don't worry,' he said to Diana, before following the Misses Cotton and Stoodley towards the First Aid tent, 'I'll make damned certain the children stay here.'

'Thanks.' Diana breathed a sigh of relief. She turned towards Hugh. 'And thanks to you too.'

'What for?' asked Hugh, who only had the haziest of notions of what the conversation had really been about.

'For turning up at exactly the right moment, of course. Are you really staying, or did you just say it to shut up those two ghastly women?'

'I'm really staying. I've put the Chelsea apartment on the market and moved myself down here.' Something in Diana's expression made him pause. 'It's what you wanted, isn't it?'

'Yes,' said Diana. 'It's what I wanted.'

But why was it the sun suddenly seemed to have lost some of its warmth? She looked around at the crowded field. A moment ago she'd felt an integral part of the traditional village scene, now, with Hugh standing at her side, she felt like an outsider. A moment ago she'd felt secure and confident with Mottisley and its people the centre of her new universe; things could, and did, go wrong, but at the back of her mind she was always sure that eventually everything would sort itself out. But now Hugh had arrived, it seemed to Diana that her world was out of balance, tipping slightly on its axis.

'You don't seem very pleased.'

'Oh, I am. It's just the suddenness. I wasn't expecting you yet. This time last week you didn't know when you'd be able to move.'

Yes, of course, that was it. Once Hugh had slotted into his natural place in the order of things, it would be different. We need time, she thought. That's all, time.

'As soon as I knew that you had absolutely no intention of returning to London, I came. It's as simple as that,' said Hugh. 'I did not want us to be apart any longer.'

He couldn't tell her the truth. That he'd fled London and Nancy. The grave robbery had terrified and sickened him. He was afraid of Nancy, and afraid of what she might do next, afraid of what she might persuade him to do. With Diana he reckoned he would be safe.

Chapter Twenty-eight

Joe gazed moodily at the parkland surrounding the manor house. A herd of muntjak deer silently cropped the grass beneath the towering horse chestnut trees spaced out at regular intervals throughout the park; the work of some long dead landscape gardener. The deer had been a good acquisition, he thought idly; they looked attractive and kept the grass down.

Late evenings in August on the edge of the South Downs at the end of a long, hot, summer's day, had a peculiar magic all of their own. The golden crimson glory of the sinking sun had a special warmth at this time of year. Firing the sweeping boughs of the horse chestnut trees with a savage beauty. Each leaf, tipped with fiery gold, threw into greater relief the dense darkness of the interior of the ancient trees. As Joe watched, the deer, with one accord, turned to face the setting sun, as if in an act of primitive worship. It was a scene of timeless beauty, enough to soothe the most troubled mind.

But it failed to soothe Joe. He remained bad-tempered, and what made his temper worse was that he didn't really know why he should feel so restless, grouchy and, Oh God! what did he feel? He didn't know. A woman would have known. She would have been able to define such emotion without any difficulty at all. It was depression. But Joe, not being a woman, couldn't bring himself to face his emotions. He sheered away from attempting to tackle them head on, putting the blame on other things. Things outside his control. It's the bloody stockmarket he thought, flinging his Tokyo Portfolio across the study. If my shares lose any more value when the Nikkei opens tonight, I might as well kiss goodbye to all the money I've invested there.

For a moment he wished he was back in the old days, when he hadn't any money to invest or lose. Viewed through the lens of nostalgia, being poor seemed preferable to the comfort he enjoyed today. Then he'd earned his living by restoring scrapped cars, and physically occupied, there'd been no time to moon idly about, worrying about money, or people. No time to admit to himself that a young girl had irrevocably changed him by walking out of his life. That same young girl, now a woman, who'd come back and taken up residence with her husband at Abbey House. He grinned suddenly. Ironic really, it was she who'd made him work, she who'd made him rich. Angry, and wanting to forget, he'd worked every hour of the day, and made the money he earned work for him. Before he realized it, he was rich. Perhaps I should have moved away from Mottisley then, he thought, on this rare moment of introspection. I should have been like the rolling stone, and gathered no moss. But on reflection, he realized that although he had stayed put, still he'd gathered no moss; still he felt no real sense of permanence. Before he could stop, his thoughts switched to April. Permanence – that is April's ambition. She wants to stay here, be cosy, and gather moss until she is like an old lichen-covered rock, indistinguishable from the place itself. He shook the thoughts away. This was delving deep, much too deep into his subconscious for his liking.

'I'm going out,' he called to April who was in the kitchen.

'But dinner is nearly ready.'

'I'm not hungry.' Conscience made him pause, and call back. 'Maybe I'll eat later. At the moment I need some exercise.'

April didn't reply. Instead she switched off the gas oven and watched through the glass door as the cauliflower and stilton soufflé, she'd prepared so carefully, slowly collapsed into an unappetizing looking mess at the bottom of the dish.

'That just about sums up our relationship,' she said out loud. 'Deflated. No life in it. Fit only for the scrap heap.' Then she began to weep.

Joe automatically turned towards Abbey Vineyard as he walked. There would be company there. He knew Sheridan, along with Ronald Pugh and Isaac Skelton would still be working on the vines. In August the grapes were well developed and needed as much sunlight and air as they could get, so the leaves around the fruit had to be removed. This could only be done by hand, and was time consuming. Knowing Sheridan and his helpers would work as long as there was enough light for them to see, Joe thought he might as well join them. Not as good as taking a car to pieces and reassembling it, but at least it was some form of activity. Pushing through the boundary hedge that divided his property from that of Abbey House, he found them in the lower vineyard.

'Hi, man,' said Sheridan cheerfully as Joe appeared.

'Hi.' Joe sounded anything but cheerful. 'Want a hand?'

'Well,' Sheridan paused, and straightening himself rubbed the small of his back with one hand. 'Only if you're not as miserable as you sound. I've had enough of bad temper today. Diana has snapped my head off every five minutes. Come to think of it, even Tony seemed edgy when he called in today. I don't know what's the matter with everyone.'

' 'Tis the evil spirit hanging over this place,' said Isaac Skelton in a sepulchral voice. 'I've felt it in my bones ever since Bert Slocombe's grave was robbed.'

'Rubbish,' said Sheridan, and Joe agreed. 'As far as Diana's concerned, I think it's that husband of hers.' Sheridan pulled a face as he spoke. 'Doesn't get on with the kids at all. Gave Miffy a clout round the ear this morning. My God, you should have seen Diana, she was furious. The result was that Hugh went off to London in a fine old rage, and she has snapped everyone's heads off all day.'

'It must be difficult for him. Having to adjust to a ready-made family.' Joe tried to be fair, but couldn't help feeling just the tiniest prickle of satisfaction. Diana had been so certain that in no time at all she'd turn the fortunes of the vineyard around, and play at happy families at the same time. All her life she'd had the Midas touch, it would do her no harm at all to find that she was not invincible.

But Isaac was not to be put off. 'Nothin' will go right until that grave robbing is solved. You mark my words.'

Joe stood on the opposite side of a vine to Sheridan, and began deleafing around the succulent bunches of grapes. 'I'd certainly like to see those villains caught,' he said.

'And nothin' will go right either, 'til that Hugh Stratton leaves,' Isaac rambled on. 'Mixed up in it, he is. I knows it.'

'How do you know?' said Joe sharply. 'Or, perhaps more to the point. What do you know?'

'I knows nothin',' said Isaac, 'but I has a feeling.'

'Isaac, how can you have a feeling? Do you know something you haven't told the police?' Joe was worried. Surely Hugh Stratton couldn't be mixed up in something like that. It was too unpleasant even to contemplate.

'I knows nothin',' Isaac repeated stubbornly. 'But I has a feeling.'

'Indigestion,' shouted Ronald Pugh from the adjacent row of vines. 'It's all those pickled onions he eats. Take no notice. He's always getting feelings about one thing or the other.'

Joe relaxed. It was only Isaac being peculiar. He'd always had a reputation in the village for being a bit strange. 'You'd best mind what you say,' he said severely. 'The police want hard evidence. Not feelings. You'd better keep your mouth shut.'

'All right, I will,' Isaac grumbled, 'but that won't stop me getting my feelings.'

Hugh dialled on his personal line. 'Nancy? Hello, I . . .'

'I was wondering when you'd get in touch.' Nancy laughed derisively. 'Stopped shaking yet, darling?'

'That was not the reason I left London, I . . .'

'Oh yes it was. You were shit-scared. One little bit of action and you run away.'

'I had to go to Mottisley. You know that.' Hugh watched his hand trembling as he held the 'phone, and felt the cold chill of sweat on his upper lip. God, but he needed a snort. He had thought he could do without it, but now he knew he couldn't. If he didn't lay his hands on some coke soon he'd be a gibbering wreck. 'Anyway, don't let's argue,' he said, trying to keep his voice calm. 'Have you disposed of the goods yet?'

'You mean the guns? No, darling, I haven't. That's a job for you. I've got some suitable addresses, a nice long distance away from here. You'll have to go as I don't drive. And don't try and chicken out, and suggest that Nico should do it, because I wouldn't trust him to deal straight with his own grandmother.'

Hugh thought rapidly. It had to be done. He desperately needed the money for drugs. The resolve to pay something back to Diana had receded as his need for cocaine increased day by day. 'All right. But I'll need something to help me.'

In her Hampstead home Nancy slowly smiled. She knew very well what he needed. She'd known all along, that Hugh was dependent on cocaine, and that made him dependent on her. Just the scenario she'd had in mind right from the beginning. His break for freedom hadn't lasted long. Just three weeks, in fact. Now she had him back where he belonged, at her beck and call.

'Come over tonight,' she said softly. 'I have what you want. We can discuss all the details after you've had your fix.'

'All right.' Hugh almost cried with relief. She had some coke, thank God. The 'phone practically slipped to the floor, his hand was shaking so much. 'I'll tell Diana that I'm working late on a case and staying overnight in a hotel.'

'Tell her what you bloody well like. Soon you won't be needing to make any excuses. I have a plan which will dispense with that necessity. Come as soon as you can.'

'Yes,' said Hugh. 'Yes, I will.'

Diana had never thought it possible to feel so tired. She felt permanently tired. Unused to manual labour, the work in the vineyard was taking its toll. Everything ached, her arms, her legs and most of all her back. Added to the vineyard work was the inconvenience of the stream of holiday makers looking round the vineyard, since she'd opened it to the public. True they were buying wine, and picnicking in the grounds on sandwiches and other snacks bought from Abbey House kitchen. All were useful sources of revenue, but additionally exhausting.

This evening Sheridan had banished her from the vineyard, where a late dressing of additional fertilizer was being added. The deleafing had all been finished a week ago. 'Go up and do something in the shop, if you must work,' he'd said. 'No point in crippling yourself, and there's only half a row left to do anyway.'

Toiling up the slope towards Abbey House, Diana collected up some loitering visitors. 'We close at six o'clock,' she reminded them, and waited pointedly while they gathered together their picnic things. Under her eagle eye the two children in the party picked up the sweet papers which lay scattered in gay abandon. That was the only problem with letting the public in, some of them were so messy. 'I'll take you to the winery shop,' she said, shepherding them firmly in front of her, 'you can see if there is anything you want before you leave.'

Mrs Graystock was on duty in the shop. The Women's Institute had organized a rota for serving, and Diana was

367

very grateful. Their main interest, she knew, was in selling their own jams and curds, but they did a good job in selling Abbey House honey, wines and vine prunings as well. And since they'd had Daisy, Griselda made farm fresh butter and yoghourt which had proved very popular with the customers.

'Hello, Mrs Stratton.' Mrs Graystock bustled forward and latched on to the visitors. 'Everything well with you?'

'Yes, thank you,' said Diana. She didn't much care for the woman, she was officious, but at least she was a good saleswoman. It was a determined visitor indeed who managed to escape the shop without buying something when Mrs Graystock was there. 'I'll leave these good people with you,' she said, and made her escape.

Everything well, and she'd answered yes. Well, she supposed, her answer was in part true. At least Tony had been as good as his word. The case conference had duly been held and he'd managed to get those two ghastly interfering women off her back. She now had it in writing, that, as far as the Social Services were concerned, she, Diana Stratton, was considered to be a suitable guardian for the children. That was something to be thankful for.

She turned her face towards the sun, unwilling to go into the house yet and face the babble of questions from the children, and walked to the edge of the rose garden at the back of the house overlooking the vineyard. Seamus, always at her side these days, her very own black and white shadow, went with her. Sitting down on the rough stone wall, gently pulling at the dog's silky ears, she stared out across the sea of luxuriant greenery that was Abbey House vines.

In the beginning, when she'd first made the decision to stay, she'd been happy. She'd been certain that her years of managerial experience would enable her to turn Abbey Vineyard around, from the unprofessional mess it had been, to a viable concern within the space of a year at the very least. And then when Hugh had finally moved down, and the Chelsea apartment was on the market, she'd looked forward to using half of the profit from that sale on the vineyard as well.

But now, Diana faced the fact that everything was far from well. Hugh might as well have stayed in London for all the difference it had made to their marriage. Something had gone terribly wrong between them, and Diana knew it wasn't just because of her own doubts. Once he'd joined her at Mottisley, she'd made a determined effort, and thought she'd succeed in extinguishing all the misgivings she'd had about herself and Hugh. Determined to draw him into the family circle, she'd taken care never to exclude him from anything, never to retaliate when he was less than good humoured, and had been a loving, dutiful wife, even to the point of neglecting her work in the vineyard when he returned to Mottisley from London each evening. He'd made an effort to please her by moving down to the country which she knew he disliked, so she had made an even greater effort, knowing how hard it would be for him to adjust.

But right from the beginning something was wrong. Diana sensed that Hugh was unhappy. No, unhappy was the wrong word, disturbed would be a better description. He was edgy, and irritable, and terribly difficult with the children; making no allowances for their youth at all. In the privacy of their bedroom he was a cold stranger. Not once had he even tried to touch her, and several times Diana had awoken in the night to find him lying beside her drenched in perspiration, rigid and trembling. She'd wanted to ask him if he was ill, and suggest that perhaps he should see Tony, but such was the unpredictability of his moods that she'd remained silent.

She sighed. Would that was her only problem. But it was not. Norman Leadbetter had been in touch at last. 'I think it better that I come to see you in person, my dear,' he had said on the 'phone. That had been yesterday.

Pleased to hear from him at last, and totally unsuspecting, Diana had said. 'That's a lovely idea. I'll be able to show you Abbey House and the vineyard. You can't fail but to fall in love with it.'

She'd met him off the train at Chichester, on another perfect summer's day, and drove him up through the winding lanes of the Downs to Mottisley. The hills lay still under their heavy burden of ripe wheat, shimmering in the heat that rose in intensity as they left the sea behind them. Not a breath of wind moved the golden ears of wheat. The flintstone cottages of passing villages slumbered in the sun, the only sign of life the occasional cat curled up on a windowsill. 'You must admit this is better than London,' Diana said happily.

'I admit it,' he replied, allowing himself a tight smile.

Funny old thing, she thought, can't imagine him ever letting himself go. Seamus bounced all over them, turning round and round in circles, always a sign that he was pleased, when they arrived. 'I hope you like dogs,' said Diana, trying to quieten him.

'Love them,' he said, and to Diana's surprise bent down to nuzzle the dog's head. 'When I retire I shall have one for company.'

As the weather was fine and the forecast good, Diana had arranged for them to dine in private in the sunken herb garden at the side of the house. They could talk business over a pleasant lunch.

'Once this was a perfect knot garden,' Diana told him. 'Of course, it's all overgrown now, but one day we shall restore it. In the meantime it's a paradise for bees.'

The table, already set, was partially shaded by a cloud of delicately perfumed jasmine running riot up and over the sheltering wall of the garden. Millicent brought out the soup. Her own recipe, iced courgette and watercress served with floating islands of rose wine sorbet. Diana smiled, judging by his expression, Norman Leadbetter shared her opinion, it was delicious.

But it was a working lunch, the accountant reminded himself. So sitting in the sheltered garden, the soporific hum of the bees going about their business as background music, he began to speak. 'Mrs Stratton, your pecuniary situation is . . . how shall I put it, well the word "impecunious" springs to mind.'

His old-fashioned language set her teeth on edge. If he had something unpleasant to say, she'd prefer it in plain English. 'Mr Leadbetter, do you have to talk as if you have sprung straight from the pages of a Dickens' novel?'

He looked embarrassed. Never happier than working with his books and papers, he found it difficult to convey bad news. Especially when the bad news was undeserved, as he was sure it was in Diana's case. Her husband had spent her money, on what he didn't know, and anyway, it was immaterial. The point was that Hugh Stratton had disposed of his wife's money, but Norman Leadbetter couldn't make a bald statement to that effect. It would be too cruel. He stammered a little with nervousness and said, 'I was trying to break it gently.'

Seeing his embarrassment, Diana regretted speaking sharply. 'I know what impecunious means well enough,' she said on a softer note. 'Are you trying to tell me that I have very little money?'

'Hardly any. In fact, when the outstanding bills on the Chelsea apartment are settled, I would go so far as to say nothing.'

'Nothing?' Diana's voice rose in a disbelieving squeak.

'Nothing. Not even enough to pay me. Not that I shall press you for any sort of payment. So you needn't worry about that, my dear.'

Diana shook her head, trying to clarify her confused thoughts. She felt as if someone had dealt her a heavy blow. I was counting on that money, she thought, suddenly panic stricken. I promised Mr Mortimer I'd pay off some of the loan as soon as I had it. I promised him at least ten thousand as a sign of my good faith. 'But I don't understand,' she said slowly. 'I know I should have a clearer idea, but because I was always so busy, Hugh dealt with all our finances.'

'Perhaps he's not very good at managing money,' said

Mr Leadbetter uncomfortably. It was a tactful way out, she could take that route if she wanted to. 'Some people aren't you know.'

She didn't. In business Diana had always believed in coming straight to the point. The habit remained. 'Hugh has a very keen mind.'

I don't doubt it, thought Norman Leadbetter drily, but he didn't say that. Instead he asked, 'and he has never mentioned to you that your expenses were exceeding your income?'

'No.' A disquieting memory of a bounced cheque flickered through her brain. Now she thought of it, the staff at the bank had seemed embarrassed when she'd raged at their inefficiency. Maybe even then her accounts were almost empty. The peace and tranquillity of the herb garden receded. Diana sat up, her back ramrod straight. She felt as tense as she used to at the hated board meetings with Alan Sinclair, and her instinct was the same. She had to know the bottom line. So, in spite of the fact that she didn't want to ask, she knew she had to. Looking Norman Leadbetter straight in the eyes she said, 'why did you insist that I closed all our joint accounts when you took over my affairs? Was it because you didn't trust my husband?'

'I wanted to make certain that I had control over deposits and withdrawals in the initial stages of my investigation.' He breathed a sigh of relief, congratulating himself on skilfully skating around that one.

'I see.' Diana realized that he had evaded the question.

Millicent arrived with the main course. Pheasant in a rich red wine sauce, decorated with tiny bunches of dessert grapes. Clemmy followed her with a dish of vegetables. 'All from our own garden,' she said proudly as she placed the dish carefully on the table. 'I hope you like roast potatoes. Millicent does the most scrumptious roast potatoes I've ever tasted.'

'I love them,' the accountant assured her. 'And they look absolutely delicious. Was that the eldest of the three children?' he asked when Clemmy had disappeared.

'Yes. Bang goes that private school I had in mind for her.' Diana looked at the food before her. Suddenly her appetite had disappeared. Her mouth felt dry and she had difficulty in swallowing. 'I suppose I've got to talk to Hugh,' she said dully, more to herself than to the man opposite. 'Although in a strange way it hardly seems to matter now. Facts are facts, they can't be changed. Where the money actually went is irrelevant.'

The older man reached across and clasped her hand. 'I've hated doing this,' he said gently. 'Perhaps if you came back and worked in the City for a couple of years, you could recoup your losses.'

'No,' Diana's reply was quick and adamant. 'Whatever happens I'm staying here. I promised the children, and I can't break that promise. Anyway, I don't want to.' She tilted her head determinedly, her grey eyes suddenly darkened, becoming hard as slate. She would succeed. Griselda and Millicent would have to go, plus probably one of the vineyard workers. 'Other people have started out with a lot less than I have here. My financial problems are not insurmountable.'

Now, as she recalled yesterday's conversation a slight breeze wafted the soft perfume of roses mixed with a more pungent aroma of manure; Diana looked down at the roses and smiled. Griselda had been heavy handed with her muck spreading again. I must speak to her about it, she thought, it will put off our visitors. Then the smile faded. Griselda and Millicent were going, although she hadn't told them yet.

My financial problems are not insurmountable. Brave words. Had she really only said that yesterday? Today, after sitting in the library for a couple of hours with the vineyard accounts, she felt less confident. Telling Millicent and Griselda that they were redundant was bad enough. She didn't want to dispense with their services, but there was no way she could afford to go on paying them.

And when, or perhaps more to the point, *how*, was she

373

going to tackle Hugh? He hadn't come back to Mottisley again last night, so the opportunity had been denied her. The second time this week he had stayed up in town because of work, and Diana had guiltily experienced heartfelt relief. He'd become so difficult to live with lately, that his absence provided her with a brief period of longed for tranquillity. Strange, but now she thought about it, she realized that he had seemed slightly less edgy this last week. Diana smiled wryly. She would soon shatter that when she tackled him on the subject of the disappearing money.

That conversation could well be the end of my marriage, she thought, putting into concrete form the slowly crystallizing thoughts which had been hammering inside her head the last few weeks. The manifestation of the failure she'd always dreaded. She, who had always made everything work, finally admitting that her marriage was not functioning. She sat in the garden, waiting for the feeling of humiliation, and Seamus getting restless laid his head in her lap. But the feeling didn't come. Instead she felt as if a door had been opened slightly. Pushed ajar, ready for her to fling it wide open.

She got up and moved towards the house. First things first. Tonight she would tell Millicent and Griselda that they were redundant. As if to reproach her, Daisy suddenly gave a loud and melancholy moo from the lower vineyard where she was tethered. Oh God! thought Diana, I'll have to learn how to milk a cow.

Chapter Twenty-nine

Yesterday she had broken the news to Millicent and Griselda that she could no longer afford them. How she was going to manage without them she didn't even allow herself to begin to think about. One step at a time. Telling them had been bad enough, especially as they'd both been understanding, and had put forward all kinds of helpful suggestions.

'I'll cut down on the housekeeping,' said Millicent. 'We'll turn vegetarian. We've enough vegetables in the garden and deep freeze to last the rest of the year.'

'And I'll use smaller yoghourt pots but charge the same amount in the shop. That way we'll get more money. And I'll put up the price of the cheese and butter as well. People are willing to pay almost anything for really fresh stuff.'

'Thank you both. But that will only make a difference of a few pounds a week. It's *you* I can't afford. I haven't got the money to pay your wages.'

'I suppose you'll be keeping Sheridan,' said Griselda jealously.

Diana sighed. 'I'll have to. I don't know enough about winemaking myself to manage without him. I need him if the vineyard is to make decent wine. But your jobs I *can* do. I can't pretend that I want to, but there's no alternative.'

'What about doing the snacks and cream teas for the visitors?' asked Millicent. 'How will you do that?'

'I shall close down that part of the vineyard activity. Autumn is on the way anyway, and the numbers of visitors will be fewer.'

Once they realized that no argument would prevail, and

that there really was no alternative but for them to leave
Abbey House, they'd become tearful. It was only with
difficulty that Diana had prevented herself from joining
in their tears. But for the sake of the children she knew
she had to be strong. Positive thinking can achieve the
impossible she told herself firmly.

'Can we come and visit?' asked Griselda.

'Of course. And I'll give you both glowing references.
I'm sure you'll have no difficulty in getting other employment.' Diana tried to sound optimistic. It had been a joint
decision that they should leave the next day; no point in
prolonging the agony, and upsetting the children more
than necessary.

So now while Millicent prepared the last supper she
was to cook at Abbey House, Diana waited restlessly for
Hugh to return from London. One unpleasant task out
of the way, another yet to be tackled. The longer she
waited, the more she pondered on the relevance of even
asking Hugh about the missing money. What point was
there? It was gone, and that was that.

But when he roared up the drive in his Porsche, and
shouted at the children to get out of the way, an inner
rage whipped up inside her. It had been *her* money, she
had a right to know. She would ask him, and damn the
consequences. Walking to meet him, she took his arm and
led him away from the house, over the sweet-smelling
grass, down the slope towards the main vineyard.

The south-facing slope trapped the rays of the evening
sun, and it was hot walking down between the vines. Hugh
wrenched off his tie, and, using it as a whip, lashed
irritably at an overhanging tendril. 'The last thing I need
after a tiring day in court is a tramp through the country,'
he said.

'I want to talk to you in private, and thought it best to
get well away from the house.'

Diana eyed him curiously. Looking at him she felt
almost schizophrenic. Half of her saw him as the man she
had married. Tall, dark, strikingly handsome, who when

he smiled could charm the birds from the trees. A charming gentle man, a supportive husband, a man any woman would be proud to be seen with. The other half saw the man who had raped her that Friday night in London. The man whose eyes could become glittering black stones, who was subject to moods and cold rages. A man she did not know, and more and more was coming to the reluctant conclusion, had no wish to know.

Walking with Hugh beneath a sky burnished with the glowing colours of a late August sunset, Diana watched a V-formation of birds flying east into the navy blue of the dusk. The high pitched sound of rushing air from their wings emphasized the emptiness around them. Suddenly she felt as if they were the only two people in the world. Here they were, together, and yet quite separate. A great lassitude swept over her, and Diana felt inconsolably lonely.

'Well,' said Hugh. 'What was it you wanted to say?'

'Norman Leadbetter came to see me yesterday.' She watched him carefully, apart from a muscle twitching in the side of his cheek, Hugh didn't seem unduly worried.

'And?'

'I have no money. It's all been spent. Apparently, even when the Chelsea apartment is sold there is unlikely to be much left over.'

Hugh carefully controlled his breathing. Nico had been right. A shot of heroin in the vein worked wonders. He was glad he'd had a fix before he'd left London. Now, instead of sweating with terror at the prospect of being found out, he felt calm, detached. Everything was in its proper perspective. None of it mattered a damn.

'You surprise me. I should have thought you'd have kept a more careful eye on your money,' he said.

His tone of voice, his disinterested manner, everything about him made Diana long to lash out, scream abuse, and ask him what he'd done with it. But she bit her lip, and maintained her self-control. She would not lose her temper. Their marriage would not end through her

377

ill-chosen words. For in spite of her conclusions the previous day, that it no longer really existed in any true sense, Diana was still reluctant to be the one to pass final sentence. Reluctant to take on the burden of a failed marriage.

'I thought you were looking after it for me,' she said quietly. 'I never checked where the money was going. Not until I took on the responsibility of Abbey House and the vineyard. Then, of course, I had to, and engaged Mr Leadbetter.'

'If you had never come here, everything would still be the same,' said Hugh, believing the lie himself. 'You would be earning money, and we could be living a life of luxury. Instead of pigging it down here.'

'But I still wouldn't have any savings. I haven't spent that much on the vineyard. I've taken out a loan.' She stopped walking and turned to face him. 'Are you telling me, Hugh, that you think we spent everything we earned? That we lived up to and beyond our means all those years in London?'

'Yes,' said Hugh, looking straight back at her. 'I am. *We* spent the money. Both of us.'

He emphasized the 'we', and Diana knew that if she ever did get at the truth it was never going to be with Hugh's help. His dark eyes regarded her unblinkingly, and Diana could see herself reflected. Two tiny Dianas mirrored in his eyes. As usual his eyes were giving nothing away, all they did was to throw her own image back at her. There was nothing more to say.

They walked back to the house in silence. Supper was a subdued affair that evening. Hugh was aloof and cold. The children sniffled miserably, knowing that Millicent and Griselda were departing the next day. Sheridan tried to be cheerful, but eventually gave up the unequal struggle. And the following morning when Hugh announced that he would be staying up in town that night, all Diana could feel was an overwhelming sense of relief.

Today was the beginning of her new multifaceted life.

Millicent was cooking the breakfast and Griselda milking Daisy this morning, but after that she, Diana, was the housekeeper, cook, foster-mother and dairymaid all rolled into one. At least with Hugh away she wouldn't have the added burden of trying to pretend to be a wife. Perhaps he wouldn't come back. Perhaps everything between them would just dissolve away into nothingness. No pain, no guilt, no sense of failure. Just freedom. Perhaps.

Diana tethered the cow to the ring at the end of the milking shed. She felt exhausted but reasonably pleased with herself. The day had gone better than she had expected, the children helping her with the housework, and now, having already prepared the vegetables for the evening meal, all she had to do was to milk Daisy.

Before she'd left at lunch time that day, Griselda had given Diana detailed instructions on how to clean the equipment, how to pasteurize the milk needed for drinking, how to prepare the milk for yoghourt and unpasteurized cheese, and how to milk the cow. There seemed so much to do, Diana wondered if she'd ever have time for anything else, but decided if Griselda could do it, then so could she.

Sitting herself down on the milking stool, she positioned the stainless steel bucket and leaned her head into Daisy's flank the way Griselda had showed her. She felt very nervous. Were all cows this large? and did milking hurt them? Tentatively holding on to two udders she squeezed and pulled downwards. Nothing happened. She tried again. A single drop of milk plopped with a hollow ring into the empty bucket. She squeezed and pulled again, slightly harder this time. Plop. Plop. Two drops of milk. At this rate it would take all night.

Raising her head she looked up. Daisy had stopped chewing the cud and was peering round. Her enormous brown eyes, fringed with lashes long enough to make any film star envious, looked anxious.

'You're not trying,' said Diana severely. 'You're holding it in on purpose.'

She tried once more and was rewarded this time with two plops and a tiny squirt. Good, I'm getting the hang of it now, she thought, moving the stool to get more comfortable. But Daisy was getting impatient, and letting out an anguished bellow, shifted her position and in doing so knocked over the bucket.

Sheridan came in to investigate the noise, and found Diana tearfully kneeling beside the upturned bucket. 'What's the matter?'

'Bloody animal. She's kicked the bucket over and I've lost all the milk.'

'What milk?'

'That, of course.' Diana pointed to a drop, enough to fill a teaspoon, on the floor.

Sheridan began to laugh. 'Is that all you've got?'

'Believe me. Getting that wasn't easy.'

Picking Diana up and moving her unceremoniously out of the way, Sheridan sat down and began to milk Daisy. Squirt, squirt, squirt, a rhythmic flood of milk hit the side of the bucket. The volume began to grow and Daisy, looking contented, started chewing the cud once more.

'How can *you* do it, when I couldn't?'

'You were both nervous. Two uptight females together,' said Sheridan. His white teeth flashing in a smile. 'A recipe for disaster.'

'Oh!' Dignity in tatters, Diana stormed out of the shed. 'I've never thought of you as chauvinistic before,' she said icily. 'Supper will be ready when you've finished.'

'Yes, ma'am.' Sheridan continued to grin, unrepentant. 'I'll be right in.'

The atmosphere in the kitchen was strangely silent. Diana, aware that the three children and Sheridan were watching her closely, opened the oven door in triumph.

'I may not be able to milk a cow,' she said, pushing a mop of dishevelled hair out of her eyes, 'but at least I can cook a meal. Just because Millicent has left does not mean you will be going hungry.'

Oh, but it had been a struggle. Extraordinary how difficult it was to get everything ready at the same time. Even something simple like sausages, gravy, mashed potato and spinach. How was one expected to make sure the gravy thickened, which it refused to do, and mash potatoes at the same time? Eventually she compromised. Instead of serving everything individually in dishes on the table, she'd dished the food up on each plate, poured the gravy, which after the addition of copious amounts of cornflour had finally thickened, over it, and put them all in the oven. Then she'd set the table, raked her fingers through her hair, no time to look in the mirror, and tried to look as if she cooked for five every day of her life.

The plates were passed round. Diana noted with pleasure the delicately browned sausages, fluffy mashed potatoes and bright green spinach. All topped off with glistening, delicious looking gravy. Mrs Beeton herself could not have done better.

'Excuse me,' said Miffy.

'Yes,' said Diana, pulling out her chair and sitting down. 'What is it?'

'Isn't gravy supposed to move about a bit?' He poked the gravy with his fork. It was solid. Absolutely immovable.

Diana poked hers. It was the same, solid as a rock. 'I wanted it thick,' she said.

Clemmy began to giggle. The others followed. At first little snorts of suppressed laughter, spilling over into hiccups, growing louder and louder as they became more and more helpless with laughter. Sheridan rent the air with great guffawing gasps, and they all, including Diana, laughed until the tears ran down their faces, and at last, weak from exhaustion, they could laugh no more.

Then Sheridan got up. 'I'll go down to the village on my bike and get some fish and chips,' he said. 'The treat's

381

on me. Open a bottle of wine to breathe while I'm gone.
I reckon we deserve a drink.'

Griselda and Millicent arrived early the next morning.
Complete with the suitcases they'd taken away only the
day before.

'I think we ought to talk in the Library, Miss,' said
Millicent, taking charge.

'The Library, yes,' echoed Griselda, nodding so vigorously that her glasses almost fell off.

'But the breakfast things . . .' Diana waved at the chaos
in the kitchen. Half-eaten slices of toast, half a dozen pots
of different jams, and every packet of cereal the larder
had contained, were scattered the length and breadth of
the kitchen table.

'We'll clear up,' said Clemmy, sensing that something
good was about to happen.

'Yes.' Simon usually unwilling to do anything in the
house, started stacking up the plates. 'You go and talk in
the Library. We've finished.'

'I haven't,' said Miffy, extricating a greasy paper bag
from his trouser pocket and emptying the contents, cold
chips, on to his plate. 'I've got these to eat first and I want
some tomato sauce.'

'Disgusting little toad,' said Clemmy passing him the
sauce.

'Come on, Miss.' Millicent led the way. 'Don't let's
waste time.'

Griselda followed, out of plaster now, she still limped
slightly, and the effort of lugging her heavy case emphasized it. Diana brought up the rear feeling slightly
bemused.

The moment they were in the privacy of the Library,
Millicent sat Diana down in the chair behind the desk.
'Griselda and me have had a long talk, Miss,' she said,
'and this is what we've decided. We're coming back here
as lodgers. If you'll have us, of course. I will do exactly
what I did before, but you won't have to pay me. As an

382

unemployed person I can claim Income Support, which I'll give you as my rent. It's all quite legal, I've been down to the Social Security office and checked it out. I might even get housing benefit which would mean a bit extra. I'm not worried about not having any money. I've got nothing to spend it on anyway. All I'll cost you is the food I eat.'

'And I,' said Griselda breathlessly, before Diana had time to interrupt, 'will continue renting out my little house. The couple in there at the moment want to stay, so that's all right. The rent from my house will pay for the rent of a room here. And like Millicent, I'll do all the same things that I did before but you won't have to pay me. I'll be paying you.'

'There,' said Millicent triumphantly. 'What do you say to that?'

Diana burst into tears. She ached with a mixture of joy and humility at their offer. But she couldn't accept. Much as she wanted to. It wouldn't be right.

'It's a wonderful offer from you both,' she said shakily. 'But I can't possibly let you do it.'

'Why not?' demanded Millicent.

'I can't take your money, and at the same time allow you to work here. It's . . . it's . . .' she searched for the right words. 'What would people say?'

'It's nobody's business but ours,' said Griselda, sounding unusually positive. 'And don't think we've suggested this because we are sorry for you. We *want* to live here. We *want* to be with you and the children.'

'Oh,' said Diana.

Sensing she was weakening, Millicent moved in for the kill. 'So that's settled then,' she said. 'We'll take our cases upstairs, and get to work straight away. Goodness knows what those children have been up to while we've been talking. And I dare say you'll be wanting to rush off and help Sheridan. He was hauling great bundles of nets out of the barn as we came past.'

'I'll get you the twine and the special needle used for

repairing them,' said Griselda. 'I know where it's all kept. The nets always need repairing. Susan did it every year. And have you milked Daisy yet? because if not I'd better do that right away.'

'No,' said Diana, who had been putting it off and hoping Sheridan would come back and offer. 'I haven't milked Daisy.'

'Well, why won't you accept it?' Joe was offering a loan at nought per cent interest.

Diana looked at him. It was good of him to offer to help. Like almost everyone else in Mottisley, once he'd heard she was short of money he wanted to do something. 'Because I must be sensible. I already owe money to the bank, and God knows how I'm ever going to pay that back. I can't borrow from anyone else, and get even deeper in debt.'

'The loan would be for as long as you want. I wouldn't press you for payment. Surely you know that. I think too much of the children to put their happiness in jeopardy.'

'I know you do. But the answer is still, no, thank you. As May told me in no uncertain terms recently, I've got to learn the hard way. I only hope my character and stamina is resilient enough for whatever lies ahead.'

Joe, sensing it was hopeless, gave up trying to persuade her. 'You have the reputation for being a tough lady,' he said. 'So I suppose you'll survive all right.'

'Well, now we shall see, won't we. I've got to prove that I'm worthy of that reputation.' She pulled on an ancient pair of wellington boots. 'It's time to do the bird patrol for this evening.'

In mid September a heavy dew began to form as soon as the sun started setting, and the grassy tracts between the vines became quite wet. Diana needed the wellington boots. Arming herself with a butterfly net and a long stick, she was ready.

'Bird patrol?' queried Joe.

'Now that the nets are over the vines, someone has to

384

shoo out the birds that have got themselves trapped.
Blackbirds are the worst, absolute simpletons they are.
Usually Sheridan and I do it together, but tonight he's at
choir practice. Do you want to give me a hand?'

'That's the first time you've invited me to do anything,'
said Joe.

'Is it?' Diana thought about it. Why had she been so
hostile? Stupid really. The past was not his fault. He had
no guilty secrets. What was more he loved the children,
and they could do with all the love they could get; they
certainly weren't going to get much from Hugh if the last
three weeks were anything to go on. Children thrived on
love. Where had she read that? Not that it mattered. Joe
was good natured, and so was April. They were her
neighbours. She ought to be friendly. 'Well,' she said,
handing him a butterfly net, 'there's a first time for
everything.'

They walked down the rows beneath the nets, the last
rays of the sun poking inquisitive golden fingers through
gaps in the branches of the vines, and far away on the
still air could be heard the faint honking of geese. Early
visitors on their way to the tidal mudflats of Pagham
harbour. Somewhere in the village an open fire had been
lit, the distinctive, slightly bitter perfume of burning wood
drifted down the slope. All was quiet, as if the whole world
was holding its breath, and in spite of all her troubles
Diana felt the peace soaking into the core of her being.
They would be all right. All of them.

'How different the vineyard looks now,' said Joe.

It was true, it did. Everything appeared to be strangely
solid, because the vines were held in tight blocks by the
nets. No longer were they a lush green. Now the leaves
flamed golden and russet, and many had already fallen,
exposing healthy, evenly formed bunches of grapes.

'It's going to be a good harvest,' said Diana, lovingly
touching a gleaming cluster.

A blackbird fluttered guiltily before them, still holding
a grape in his beak. 'Got you,' said Joe, trapping him with

the net. The bird didn't struggle as Joe gently held him, neither did he let go of his stolen trophy, the grape. 'There you go.' Lifting the netting at the edge of the section he let the bird go and it fluttered off into the gathering purple of the dusk. 'I wonder the children don't want to help you,' he said.

'They do. But they're too noisy. Anyway it's early to bed for them tonight. School starts tomorrow.'

'The summer over already. It hardly seems possible.' He paused and caught a fat mistle-thrush who, hoping to be missed, was playing dead by the root of a vine. It regarded both of them indignantly with a beady brown eye as Joe popped it outside the netting. 'I shall miss having the children around all day,' he said, then added. 'Can't help wishing that I'd had some of my own. But it's too late now.'

Diana felt a familiar coldness assail her senses. Nothing could ever prevent the involuntary reflex reaction whenever someone, or something, triggered off the memory of the long distant abortion. You had a child once, Joe, or at least, the beginning of one, she thought, but it was inconvenient and I disposed of it. She felt a sadness for him, something she'd never felt before. His words had an added poignancy because she had cheated him of a life that had been partly his.

'It's not too late,' she said, wanting to believe it. 'You could marry and have children. You're not old, and anyway age doesn't make any difference to men.'

'I doubt that April is capable of bearing children now.' He attempted a laugh. 'She's always telling me, she's past her sell-by date.'

'So you *are* going to marry April.' Diana suddenly thought of Tony and how heartbroken he'd be.

'I expect so,' replied Joe without enthusiasm. 'Eventually. She's good company, and we rub along well enough.'

'Hardly sounds like a love match,' said Diana.

They reached the end of one block of netting and after fastening the ends as tightly as possible, turned and entered the confines of the next; starting the long walk up the slope towards Abbey House.

'I gave up looking for love years ago.' From above them came the sound of tyres crunching on gravel, Hugh had arrived back from London. 'And is your marriage a love match?' asked Joe.

'I like to think so,' said Diana quickly. Clever words concealing the truth. Whatever that was. Joe had said he'd given up looking for love, and I, thought Diana have given up looking for the truth, because I'm afraid of what I might find.

Chapter Thirty

Hugh lounged on the sofa in Nancy's house. On reflection, he thought that perhaps he'd been a little hasty in rushing down to Diana after the robbery, but at the time he'd been in such a state of abject terror that he'd needed to be with someone strong. Nancy was strong, but hers was a voracious strength feeding on him and sapping his willpower. Hugh had now given up pretending to himself that he was the puppeteer, making her dance to his tune. He knew that through her sexual power and his own weakness for drugs, she had called the shots from their first meeting, and always would. Diana was different, her power lay in the fact that she gave rather than took. Hugh knew he could lean on her. Even though she had changed and was no longer the malleable woman he'd thought he'd married, he was still sure she would always honour her marriage promises. For the time being he still needed Diana and was reluctant to return to London as Nancy was now urging.

Nancy paraded, like a model on a catwalk, down the centre of the beautiful room. She was always complaining about being short of money, but Hugh noticed she had recently bought two enormous matching blue Chinese porcelain jars. Always impulsive, she'd said she couldn't resist them when she saw the pair up for auction at Sotheby's. They stood, ostentatiously flaunting opulence, either side of the marble fireplace. Hugh wondered how much they cost; antique porcelain didn't come cheap. And now, here she was showing off her latest acquisition. A Bruce Oldfield evening dress in red and black, the strapless bodice thickly embroidered in pure gold thread.

Stopping before him, and jutting her shoulders forward

in the time-honoured fashion of models before they turn and make their exit, she said, 'it suits me, doesn't it?'

'Yes.' Hugh lit a cigarette and watched her warily.

Of course it suited her, anything dramatic suited Nancy. With her black hair, ivory skin, and wide pouting red mouth, she looked formidable and absolutely ravishing. Hugh felt the familiar rush of desire, and yet, at the same time, in tandem with the raw lust of desire was a new, but increasingly familiar feeling of fear. She was the dark angel in his life, and he felt helpless. I should never have started back on coke, or let Nico persuade me to try mainlining heroin. The hand holding the cigarette suddenly shook at the thought of how much he was now in debt. I ought to be able to stop. I must stop. But he knew the thought was feeble, sterile wishful thinking. He couldn't stop now. Two shots of heroin, that was all it had taken before he knew he couldn't live without it. Jesus! but he needed some cash.

Nancy came and sat beside Hugh, sliding a caressing hand inside his shirt. 'It's time to sell the guns, darling. This dress costs a bomb, and I haven't paid for it yet.'

Hugh felt his mouth go dry with apprehension at the mere thought. By mutual agreement they'd put off disposing of the guns for another three weeks after Hugh had initially returned to Nancy. The police appeared to have given up looking, but it seemed sensible to wait a little longer. And Nancy had succeeded in persuading Nico to extend Hugh's credit, so that at least he was getting the drugs he now craved. But it couldn't last for ever. Now, in the middle of September the time had come. They both needed the money.

'I don't think I'll be much good. I've never attempted to sell stolen property before.'

'Not stolen, darling, retrieved,' corrected Nancy. 'They'd been buried, remember? No use to anyone where they were.'

Hugh didn't want to remember. He still had difficulty in banishing the sight of that open coffin from his mind.

389

From out of nowhere it would suddenly come, that ghastly black vision, and he'd break out in a cold sweat every time.

'I still don't think I'll be any good,' he stumbled over the words. 'I'll fluff my lines or something. Give the game away.'

'Nonsense, darling,' Nancy purred persuasively. 'You'll be all right. All you need is a little shot to give you courage, just enough to set you off on your mission, and you'll be perfect.' She pushed his sleeve up and peered at the faint pinprick marks on his arm. 'You must be careful though, darling. I'd hate you to spoil your lovely body with the needle.'

Hugh drew a deep breath. 'You told me earlier that you have some addresses. Where are they?' Knowing that it had to be done, Hugh managed to scrape together a few particles of courage and dare not delay. There was no telling when what little courage he had might disappear.

'You'll do it today?' Hugh nodded. 'Great!' Nancy clapped her hands together with excited childish glee. 'I'll change and get the addresses. We'll go together.'

While waiting, Hugh rang Miss Higgins and told her he would not be coming into the office. He had no cases due in court; missing a day in the office was not important.

'Oh, a day's holiday?' queried Miss Higgins.

'No . . . er, yes,' Hugh corrected himself hastily. Nosy old bitch. 'I'm staying down in Mottisley for a rest,' he lied. 'I'll be in tomorrow, on Friday, as usual.'

'Yes, sir. Have a nice day.'

Hugh put the 'phone down, satisfied. A day's holiday in his own home with his wife. Nothing for anyone to get suspicious about in that.

Nancy returned with the addresses. 'I've got half a dozen,' she said, 'scattered through the Cotswolds and Oxfordshire.'

'A hell of a long way to go,' Hugh objected.

'Naturally. We can't sell them near Sussex. And anyway

I've chosen firms that specialize in buying old guns, and are right in the middle of good shooting country. We'll sell one pair in one shop and the other pair somewhere else.' Put like that it sounded very simple, and Hugh's spirits rose at the prospect of some ready cash.

They decided to try the one furthest away from London first, and arrived in the bustling Cotswold town of Stroud just before lunch. Nancy stayed in the car and Hugh went alone to the gunsmiths. He'd given himself a shot of heroin in the car, and by now had the familiar feeling of well being. Striding down the pavement, the guns in a bag beneath his arm, he smiled happily. What had he been worried about? It would be a piece of cake. There was nothing to it.

Hugh let himself into the shop. Greensmith and Sons, Gunsmiths for one hundred and fifty years. Looking around Hugh thought it likely that the interior hadn't changed much in all that time. The shop smelt of polish. Metal polish and burning linseed oil, and had the not unpleasant odour that ancient buildings harbour. Dry timbers impregnated with years of beeswax and wood-stain. An old man in a long green baize overall, tied around the waist with string, came in answer to the old fashioned shop bell which clanged noisily when Hugh opened the door. Hugh unwrapped his parcel and lay the pair of Purdeys on the counter.

'I'd like to sell these,' he said. 'How much would you offer me?'

'Ah,' the old man's face lit up with reverent appreciation. 'A fine old pair you've got there.' He took each gun in turn and inspected it. 'Where did you get 'em?' he peered up at Hugh from above his half-moon glasses.

'They belonged to my uncle who is now deceased. He had them all his life, but I don't shoot myself, so I thought I might as well sell them.' Hugh was pleased with himself. Very smooth, he thought.

'Got the certificates?'

'What certificates?' Hugh felt the first faint stirrings of unease.

'Everyone who owns a shot-gun has a certificate with a photo on it. Your uncle must have had one. They're valid for five years.'

'Oh,' Hugh seized on this piece of information. 'Well, he died more than five years ago, and I've had them for ages. I've always been meaning to sell them, but never have. You know how it is.'

'No,' said the old man abruptly, 'I don't. I wouldn't have let these lie around unused for years.' He sniffed the barrel. 'Doesn't smell that unused.'

The palms of Hugh's hands began to sweat. This wasn't going quite to plan. 'I can assure you that I have no idea when they were last used,' he said. That at least was the truth. 'But if you're not interested . . .' he reached across to take the guns.

'I didn't say that. Of course I am. Only a fool would turn down the chance to buy a fine pair of guns like this.'

Hugh relaxed. He'd been over-reacting. 'How much are they worth? Mr, er . . . ?'

'Greensmith, of Greensmith and Sons. Worth? Oh, I say between forty and forty-five thousand. I'd be prepared to give you forty. That'd be fair.'

Hugh almost leapt over the counter in excitement. It was more, much more than he'd thought. 'I accept,' he said quickly.

The old man was interminably slow. Inspecting the guns again with painstaking thoroughness, when all Hugh wanted him to do was to write a cheque. He and Nancy had already decided it would be in her name. Unlike Hugh, she didn't mind taking the risk of being traced.

'Ah, here it is.' Mr Greenfield fished a pencil and paper from the deep pocket of his green overall. 'I'll just note the numbers and check with Purdeys.'

'What numbers?'

'These, here on the side of the barrels, see? Purdeys have a record of every gun they have ever made, and

392

usually who they belong to. If your uncle had them all his life, he'll be registered. What did you say his name was?'

'I've changed my mind,' said Hugh, snatching the guns back from a startled Mr Greensmith. 'I'm not going to sell them after all. They're much too valuable.' Hastily rewrapping them into a clumsy bundle, he made a hurried exit from the shop.

'Shit,' said Nancy when Hugh told her about the register. 'An old firm like Holland and Holland probably have a register too, so that rules out selling the other pair on the open market. There's nothing for it, we'll have to use Nico. He's got plenty of contacts who won't ask questions. Bloody nuisance though, it means we'll probably get less than a third of their value.'

'Jesus Christ! Hugh blasphemed. 'What the hell are we going to do about money?'

'I'll think of something.' Nancy smiled mysteriously. 'Don't worry.'

After dropping Nancy back at Hampstead, Hugh arrived at Abbey House earlier than usual, just as Diana and the children returned to the kitchen, tired and happy, their baskets full of blackberries gathered from the hedges. Diana had met them from school and they'd had a lovely few hours in the sunshine, and had taken a picnic with them. Seamus bounced along beside them, his long white muzzle stained purple where he'd been eating the blackberries from the lower branches.

'Look,' said Simon, showing Hugh his basket. 'We've got pounds and pounds. Millicent is going to make loads of blackberry and apple jam. We picked up all the fallen apples yesterday. This way we'll save loads of money because we won't have to buy any jam at all.'

Of the three children, Simon was the only one who always made a conscious effort to include Hugh. But Simon's friendly overture was ignored. The only word that really registered with Hugh was the word, money.

Money, bloody money. The disappointment of the day swept over him again with full force. 'For God's sake stay away from me. All of you. You're all filthy,' he snapped. Seamus wandered past Hugh towards his water bowl. 'And keep that bloody dog away. His hairs get all over my clothes.'

As if he understood what Hugh had said, Seamus turned and wrinkled his muzzle back, showing his teeth. He didn't like Hugh either.

Millicent said nothing. She was standing at the sink preparing vegetables for the supper. But the stance of her back showed rigid disapproval.

Determined to ignore his obvious bad temper, Diana went across to Hugh and kissed him on the cheek. He looked awful. His face was ashen, and his eyes had the hard cold look she'd come to dread. 'You've had a bad day,' she said quietly.

'You could say that.' Hugh thought again of the money he'd been counting on and now wouldn't get. 'I'll get changed.'

Diana followed him up the stairs to their bedroom. 'Did you lose a case in court?'

'I wasn't in court today.'

'Well, what then?'

'Christ, you wouldn't understand. For God's sake spare me the third degree.'

Diana kept her temper with difficulty. 'What do you mean, Hugh? I wouldn't understand. I haven't become a simpleton merely because I've moved away from London. You always talked to me about your cases before. Why can't you now?'

'Oh, fuck off,' Hugh snarled.

'Don't you dare use that language to me.' Diana's temper suddenly spilled over into the open. 'I won't have it.'

Hugh sat down on the bed, realizing he'd gone too far. 'Sorry,' he muttered. He shivered. What wouldn't he give for a shot of something now. Coke, heroin, anything to make him feel better able to cope. But it was all in London. All at Nancy's house, and he was here in Mottisley, and somehow had to survive without it until tomorrow.

Diana watched him. The anger slipped away to be replaced by pity. Something was wrong, very wrong. But what? And how could she help if he wouldn't talk to her? It hadn't always been like this. Surely something of what they'd had in those first years together had been real? And surely somehow, together, they could rekindle a small spark of those original emotions. Walking across to him, she put a hand softly on his shoulder. 'Hugh,' she said. 'Is there something you want to tell me? Something you *ought* to tell me?'

For a moment Hugh was tempted. Diana would help him if he admitted his addiction. It was not too late to get off drugs. Never too late, so they said. There were clinics. She would organize it, and then he wouldn't feel like this, a washed out, vulnerable wreck. But then almost immediately he thought of Nancy. When he was with her he didn't feel this way. OK, so he needed the drugs, but when he had them life was fine. Besides, admitting his addiction would only be the beginning. Everything else would then be revealed. His debts, the robbing of Bert's grave, his long-term affair with Nancy. No, he couldn't tell Diana. Besides he didn't want to. He liked his life with Nancy, it was like riding a rollercoaster, full of highs and lows, but never dull.

'I don't know what the hell you're talking about,' he said, shrugging her hand from his shoulder.

'Diana,' Clemmy called up the stairs. 'Millicent says have you had the scales, she can't find them.'

'Coming.'

For a moment, just a brief moment, Diana had seen the conflicting emotions flickering across Hugh's face, and had hoped that he would speak. If he had troubles, and she could share them, then surely that would draw them together. But as soon as the shuttered look came over his face, and his eyes turned the hue of cold stone, she knew it was hopeless.

'They are waiting for you downstairs,' Hugh reminded her. His voice an abrupt dismissal.

'Yes, I must go.' Clattering down the stairs Diana felt a shadowy sense of guilty betrayal. She was almost glad he hadn't confided in her.

The shrill of the alarm awoke her, and Diana climbed wearily out of bed. It was only five-thirty but today the Customs and Excise man was due, and although she'd worked until late last night she still hadn't finished the stock control figures. Looking at the sleeping figure of Hugh, she felt a flash of irritable resentment. He could easily help her with the monthly stock control, but he never offered, being quite happy to divorce himself completely from whatever happened at Abbey House. Why do you stay? she thought, looking down at him, there is nothing to stay for any longer. Our marriage has petered out, withered away into nothing. We are like two dead leaves clinging to a tree. All it needs is one puff of wind and we'll be blown our separate ways. Perhaps he stayed because Abbey House was a convenient roof over his head; but Diana forced herself to put that uncharitable thought away. No, she told herself firmly, more likely he stayed because he too was hoping that by some miracle their marriage could get back on to the old footing. But surely he must see that that would never happen unless they talked. And last night had proved how impossible that was.

It was cold in the bathroom this morning, a foretaste of the winter to come, thought Diana, shivering. But there would be no central heating installed this year, they couldn't afford it. Rubbing a hole in the steamed up mirror, she hastily put on some mascara and lipstick, before brushing her hair and tying it back in a pony tail. The days when she went regularly to the Aphrodite Club for facials and massage, and had her highlights touched up every three weeks, were now a misty dream. I'll be lucky if I manage to get my hair cut this side of Christmas, she thought, clattering downstairs in a pair of Susan's old jeans and a sweater.

'Hi, ma'am.' Sheridan was in the kitchen, and the kettle was boiling. 'Tea or coffee?'

'Coffee please. What are you doing up?'

'Thought I'd help you check the bonded wine. Two people will get the job done quicker.'

'Thanks.' Diana was grateful. Seamus licked her hand in greeting and waited at the kitchen door to be let out, and Shakespeare stretched luxuriously, one leg at a time from his cushion by the Aga, before asking to be let out as well.

'That cat knows when he's well off,' said Sheridan. 'Hardly seen him all summer, but as soon as there's a nip in the air, he's back indoors, on his cushion in the warm.'

They sipped their coffee in companiable silence before crossing to the locked barn which served as Abbey Vineyard's bonded warehouse. The mornings were chilly now, and wisps of mist lingered long after sunrise in the deep hollows of the Downs. The air too had a different perfume these days, more pungent, damp leaves and the special smell of freshly turned earth; the fields surrounding Mottisley had been ploughed ready for winter seeding.

Diana shivered and pulled up the roll collar of her sweater. 'When I took on the vineyard,' she said, 'I didn't realize that the making and selling of wine was not as simple as making and selling other products.'

'Huh! Damned Customs and Excise. Why does it have to be so complicated?' Sheridan grumbled.

Diana agreed. The system generated much time-consuming work. While still in the winery and in the tanks, wine attracted no tax. Neither did bottled wine so long as it remained in a bonded warehouse under bond. But every bottle that stood on a shelf in the shop clocked up excise duty every month whether it was sold or not. Rigorous stock control was essential as the Customs and

Excise Inspector checked both the bottles under bond and the bottles in the shop. Only she or Sheridan were allowed to remove the bottles from the barn.

'For the life of me I don't know how Susan managed to do all this virtually single-handed,' Diana remarked to Sheridan as they began checking over the records.

'The answer is, of course, she didn't. She lost a lot of money through having bottles lying around unsold, and she wasted a lot of wine through not keeping the years moving in strict rotation,' said Sheridan. 'I had to throw some out only the other day. It was five years old, too acid even to be sold as vinegar.'

'Poor Susan, she had a tough time. Nothing went right for her.' Diana sighed, she could never think of Susan without feeling guilty. 'And I wasn't the sister I should have been. When she needed me, I wasn't here.'

Sheridan looked at Diana quizzically. 'From what I've heard, she wouldn't have agreed with you. Everyone in Mottisley tells me she was a happy person. Counted her blessings, not her woes.'

'Yes she did.' Diana's grey eyes lit up with sudden pleasure at the memory of the last weekend she had spent with Susan. Those few days together had been happy. And her last memory of Susan was her laughing face peering in through the car window before she drove back to London. Thank God I came down that weekend, she thought.

But the thought drew her on, back to Hugh, to the real reason she rushed, so impulsively, down to Mottisley that weekend. It was the night he'd violated her body. And quite suddenly she knew. That night had been the beginning of the disintegration of her marriage. She had fought it every inch of the way, and maybe if Hugh had been more sympathetic to the needs of the children, they could still have had some kind of marriage. Or could they? So many other things were wrong too. His coldness, unpredictable moods, unexplained absences, and the matter of the missing money.

Diana closed her eyes, forcing herself to stop thinking. What good was there in prising open one unpalatable casket of episodes after another? Her courage failed her. It was far easier to carry on with the illusion they presented to the world and to each other, preserve the pathetic shell of their marriage until something, or someone happened to shatter it.

Sheridan walking down the rows, ticking off the unopened cases of wine, came face to face with her. 'Diana, are you all right?'

Opening her eyes Diana stared up into his familiar dark face. His big brown eyes, concerned and worried, gazed down into hers. 'I'm tired,' she said, forcing a smile to her lips. 'Let's hurry up and get this finished. There's a lot happening today.'

Diana had decided that the wine shop could open profitably every day only until the end of September. After that it would be open only at weekends. Already, now that the children had gone back to school, custom had dropped off, and visitors during the week were few. 'This Friday,' she told Mrs Graystock, 'we'll do a stocktake. Make sure we haven't got any old pots of things going rotten, tucked away, forgotten, at the back of the shelves.'

'I think that highly unlikely.' Mrs Graystock was slightly huffy.

'Oh, so do I,' said Diana hastily. She always forgot how easy it was to offend the wretched woman. 'But anyway, I need your advice on the best way we can display our Christmas stock.'

Mrs Graystock bloomed noticeably at being asked for advice. So it was agreed. The stocktaking would be done as soon as Diana's business with the Customs and Excise Inspector had finished.

He came almost as soon as Diana and Sheridan had finished the final figures, and while Diana was snatching a hasty breakfast, in between making sure the children had their packed lunches, and arguing with Clemmy over her desire to wear tights rather than ankle socks. To her relief Hugh had already left for London.

'Ten denier tights are just not suitable, dear. You'll ladder them in five minutes. You must change back to socks.'

'But these are much more glamorous.' Clemmy was beginning to fill out a little, and Diana had to admit that her legs did look nice.

'She only wants to show her legs off because she fancies Jimmy Moody,' jeered Simon.

'I do *not*. I'm not interested in boys.'

'Well, whether you are or not. Go upstairs and change,' said Diana firmly. 'Where did you get those tights from anyway?'

'From your drawer,' said Miffy. 'I saw her take them. Can I have an extra sandwich?'

'Oh you little creep! I hate brothers.' Clemmy fled, furious, upstairs.

'Quite a handful.' Mr Smith, the Customs Inspector was amused. 'But you seem to cope very well.'

'Do you think so?' His praise pleased Diana.

Together they checked the figures of the bonded wine, and then the wine out of bond in the shop. 'Your records are excellent,' he said. 'I wish everyone was as meticulous as you.'

Two compliments in the space of twenty minutes. Diana found herself glowing with pride. I'm as bad as Mrs Graystock she thought with amusement. But it was strange how little things had become important, an unexpected source of pleasure to be savoured. A year ago she took any compliment as her due, and it had given no particular pleasure.

After enjoying a cup of coffee and one of Millicent's feathery light scones, Mr Smith went on his way, and Diana began the stocktaking with Mrs Graystock and Griselda, and Seamus who poked an inquisitive nose in wherever he could reach.

'Perfect day for it,' said Griselda. 'I doubt we'll get any customers today.'

The early promise of another fine day had been misleading. Billowing grey rain clouds came buffeting over the Downs from a southwesterly direction, and soon there was a steady downpour. Diana worried about the vines. The bunches of grapes were so heavy now, and she prayed that the rain would not batter them down. The harvest *had* to be good. Only then would Mr Mortimer be likely to extend the loan.

'I do hope this rain doesn't last.'

'Better now than later,' said Griselda. 'The last thing you want is rain when it comes to harvesting. You need to pick on a sunny day, that way the sugar content is higher.'

'Yes, of course, I'd forgotten that.' Diana tried to stop worrying about money, her constant worry these days, and threw herself into giving the shop a good clear out.

The three of them worked all morning. As well as stocktaking they swept and polished, and restocked the old cider jars with fresh lavender and other dried flowers from the garden, already prepared by Griselda. Seamus had stayed with them for a while, but the dust made him sneeze, and he'd retreated to the kitchen.

At half past one, Mrs Graystock departed in her Mini for Chichester and her weekly shop, and Diana and Griselda joined Millicent in the kitchen for a bowl of soup and some crusty bread.

'That damned dog,' grumbled Millicent. 'Ate one of my bread rolls when I wasn't looking; and I need eyes in the back of my head where that cat's concerned. When there's meat about he's an absolute devil.'

'Sorry,' said Diana, wondering why it was she always felt personally responsible for the animals' misdemeanours. Seamus hung his head and looked penitent, but Shakespeare, curled up on his cushion, merely looked smug.

'I'm sure Seamus didn't mean to steal,' said Griselda.

Her initial nervousness of the large dog had now changed to a slavish devotion, almost rivalling that of the children's.

'You're too soft with that animal.' Millicent was not so devoted.

Diana laughed. A morning's hard physical work had left her feeling tired but much more cheerful. 'Don't you worry about Seamus, Millicent,' she said. 'I'll take him with me into Midhurst. I've got some shopping to do.'

By the time Diana had finished her shopping the rain had stopped, so she let Seamus run in the park. But it was cold. The grey clouds which had brought the rain still covered the sun, and the wind was chilly for September. Shivering in her thin summer raincoat, Diana made her way back to Mottisley and Abbey House.

She probably would never have noticed the old couple waiting at the bus stop near the house, had it not been for the fact that the woman was crying. The old lady stood there, damp and bedraggled, in a transparent plastic mac and rain hat, making no attempt to wipe away the tears that were coursing down her cheeks. And the old man, who was shorter than the woman, was standing on tiptoe, ineffectually dabbing at her cheeks with a handkerchief. They looked so pitiful that Diana couldn't just drive past them. She stopped the car and went across to the bus stop.

'Can I help?' It seemed an ineffectual thing to say, but she couldn't think of anything else.

'Mother's a bit upset,' said the old man. 'It's the money you see. We wanted to talk about it, but he wouldn't. But she'll be all right when I get her home. Do you think the bus will come soon?'

'Any minute now,' said Diana, answering the only part of his conversation which made any sense to her.

'I want to go back to Brighton,' the woman sobbed. 'I told you we should never have come.'

'But you wanted to come,' the man reminded her. He looked at Diana with pale watery eyes. 'She's not herself you see,' he explained. 'It's her mind. Senile the doctor says. But she wasn't always like this.' He wiped her cheeks again. 'There, there, don't you worry. We'll sort everything out.' He looked at Diana again. 'Once she was a lovely young woman.'

'I can see that,' said Diana gently, which was the truth. For in spite of the plastic mac and rain hat, she could see that the woman's face had a fine bone structure and her eyes, although tearful and vacant, were dark and deep set beneath delicately arched brows. 'Look why don't you catch the next bus, or even let me give you a lift? Come into my house,' she pointed towards Abbey House, 'and have a cup of tea. Then maybe you'll both feel better.'

But she'd said the wrong thing. The woman shied away from Diana like a startled horse. 'Oh no,' she said, 'I'm not going in there. He wouldn't like it. He'd shout at me again.'

Diana was about to ask who wouldn't like it? who would shout? when the bus arrived. 'Thank you,' said the old man. 'But it's best I get her home. She does worry about money so. And of course, so do I, you can't help it can you? But I'll have to manage somehow. Thank you anyway, dear. It was very kind of you.'

'Hurry up,' shouted the driver. 'I haven't got all day.' And the bus was gone, leaving a fine blue haze of diesel fumes swirling round a very puzzled Diana.

Chapter Thirty-one

'I've just met the strangest old couple, and . . .' Diana burst into the kitchen of Abbey House.

'Hugh's parents,' interrupted Griselda.

Diana stopped mid stride. 'But that's impossible. Hugh's parents are dead.'

'Is that what he told you?' Diana suddenly realized that April was in the kitchen along with Millicent and Griselda. 'I found them wandering in the lane. They asked me where Hugh Stratton lives, so I brought them here,' she explained.

'And that was a mistake,' said Millicent grimly. 'Poor old sods.'

'A pity Hugh was already here,' April told Diana. 'Without him the three of us might have been able to find out what was worrying them so, but as it was . . .' she paused, then shrugged, 'it was impossible.'

'I would never have believed,' said Griselda, 'that anyone could be so cruel to other human beings, especially not to one's *parents.*'

'People are often cruel,' replied April. Turning towards Diana, she jerked her head towards the door. 'He's upstairs. I think he was afraid to stay down here in the kitchen with us three women. Personally, I was near to strangling him, and he damn well knew it.'

Without another word Diana headed towards the stairs and the bedroom she shared with Hugh. He was there, sitting on the bed smoking a cigarette.

Not wasting time with preliminaries, Diana came straight to the point. 'I've just met your parents,' she said. 'The ones you told me were dead.'

'They are dead as far as I'm concerned.'

404

Hugh's face was expressionless, but his thoughts were seething. Money, he was thinking, *money, bloody money*. As if I haven't enough problems, but my fucking parents turn up out of the blue talking about money.

For a moment his totally blank expression threw Diana. Had some terrible trauma caused him to reject his parents? But if so, why hadn't he told her? An image of the pathetic couple at the bus stop flashed before her and gut instinct told her they were not the type to inflict trauma. Quite the reverse. They were the type that the rest of the world walked all over. Anyway, whatever the reason, why had he lied?

'Quite apart from the fact that you lied to me, they . . .'

'I didn't lie. They *are* dead as far as I'm concerned. Anyway, it's no business of yours.'

'Of course it's my business. I'm your wife.'

'More's the pity,' said Hugh, lying back on the bed and crossing his legs. 'A nagging, nosy wife, prying her pointed little nose into affairs which do not concern her.'

A white hot rage exploded inside Diana, momentarily making it difficult to breathe, then the rage was immediately followed by a cold, frightening icy calm. 'You sent them away in great distress,' she said quietly. 'Why?'

The sudden quietness of her voice startled Hugh. He looked at Diana guardedly. 'They were going to ask me for money,' he said. 'Which, I hardly need point out to you, neither you nor I have got.'

Diana thought of the money that had disappeared from her accounts, and for a moment was tempted to pursue it, but then rejected the idea. The weeping woman and her husband were more important. 'How could you turn your back on your own parents? They seemed quite desperate.'

'Rubbish! The old woman's as mad as a hatter, and the old man is not much better. They disgust me.'

'You disgust *me*.' Diana spat the words out, the icy calm

405

deserting her she was unable to disguise her loathing for the man before her. And that man is my husband, she thought, and found the realization quite appalling. She shivered, but then determinedly regained self control, and continued. 'I found them at the bus stop, like a couple of lost children. If I'd known then that they were your parents, I would never have let them get on the bus and leave.'

'All I can say is thank God you didn't know. What would you have done? Brought them back, and have them live here?'

'If necessary, yes,' said Diana. 'And I would have found out why they were so worried, and tried to do something about it. I understand from April that you didn't even give them the chance to explain. Don't you care? Doesn't it worry you?'

'No it bloody doesn't.' Hugh shouted. 'I made the break with my parents when I went to University. I've never seen them since, and have no wish ever to see them again.'

'Why? What did they do to you?'

'Do? They didn't do anything. Just being what they are is enough. Pathetic, working class, small-minded little people.'

'Is that all? Are you telling me that you are ashamed of them? Is that why you said they were dead?'

'Yes.' The expression on Diana's face increased his already foul temper. 'Yes, yes, YES! Oh, it's all right for you. You with your comfortable middle-class background. You never had to count every penny, and live in a council house in Brighton.'

'Oh, Hugh, I just don't understand you.'

Diana went across to the window and leaned against it for support. She looked out at the familiar view, the straight rows of vines, the rolling hills and hedgerows tinged with the mellow colours of autumn. But the scene was obscured now, blurred by the misty rain sweeping in fifteen miles from the south coast. Like my life, she thought suddenly, misty and blurred, nothing is clear cut any more. This man I call my husband. Who is he? Was this really the charming, self-assured man she had married? This man on the bed, whose face was twisted with an ugly hatred for his own parents.

'You are the one who is small-minded,' she said.

But Hugh wasn't listening, he was still talking. 'The last thing I need, is to have them crawling around me asking for money.'

'Did they actually ask you for anything?'

'No, but . . .'

Diana made up her mind. Hugh or no Hugh, she knew what she had to do. 'You'd better give me their address. We can't leave things as they are.'

'I can.' Stabbing out his cigarette with a quick vicious movement, Hugh stood up. 'The conversation is closed.'

'I'm afraid it isn't, I want . . .'

'You want, you want, *you want*.' Hugh lost every last vestige of self-control, and screamed at Diana.

Downstairs in the kitchen the three women looked at each other. 'Oh God,' said April.

'Thank heavens the children aren't back yet,' said Griselda.

Upstairs Hugh continued his tirade. 'Never mind what you want. I'll tell you what I want. I want out. *Out*, do you hear me? Out of this crumbling heap you call a house, out of having three fucking kids around my feet all the time, out of you playing at being a bloody earth mother instead of doing a proper job and earning us some money. I'm going back to London.'

'If you do, it will be the end of us. The end of our marriage.' In contrast to Hugh's gibbering rage, Diana felt quite calm.

'And bloody good riddance as far as I'm concerned. What have you got to offer me? No decent job, no money. You're not even glamorous. All you do now is wear jeans all the time. You've turned into a bloody country bumpkin lumbered with three kids. I married you because you

407

had prospects, and now you have none. You'll be no loss to me.'

The fragile shell had finally splintered into a thousand pieces. Diana knew without a shadow of doubt that her marriage was over. In the end she had had to do nothing. Hugh had done it. He'd taken what remained of their relationship and dashed it to the ground.

No prospects. The irony struck home. Her own words to Joe so many years ago were now being thrown back at her. Diana walked through the open bedroom door. 'Do you realize, Hugh, that you never once mentioned the word love.'

The morning after Hugh's departure, Diana's main emotion was one of overwhelming relief. She didn't even bother to wonder where he would stay when the apartment was sold. That was his problem, not hers.

It was strange that Hugh's parents, people she hadn't known existed, had eventually been the catalyst to end it once and for all. Of course it was an admission of failure, but the failure had been in being attracted to Hugh for all the wrong reasons. To his superficial glamour, to the life they'd led together in which they'd only ever skated on the surface. No deep emotions had been allowed to ripple their glossy veneer. Perhaps Joe had been right when he's accused her of being a cardboard cut-out of a woman. Then she stopped herself thinking. Mustn't think about what Joe had said, he wasn't right all the time. Look at the mess he'd made of his own life.

Before joining Sheridan in the vineyard that morning she telephoned Tony and told him about Hugh and herself splitting up, and about Hugh's parents.

'As a doctor, Tony,' she said, 'you're involved with Social Services and things like that. Is there any way I can trace them? All I know is that they live in Brighton. I've tried Directory Enquiries, but there are an awful lot of Strattons. And anyway, they might not even be on the 'phone.'

'Look, Diana. They're Hugh's parents, not yours. They're not your responsibility.'

'Not technically perhaps, but morally they are. They were really distressed. I've got to help them if I possibly can.'

'But, Diana.'

'Don't "but Diana" me. I must find them. You know what it's like when you see those awful pictures on TV of people starving, or homeless, or dying of some dreadful disease, and it breaks your heart and you want to help. All you can do then is give money because they are so far away. Well, that's the way I feel about Hugh's parents, but they're not so far away, I *should* be able to find them. So, I'm asking you, will you help me?'

'Yes,' said Tony. 'Of course I will. I'll set the wheels in motion through all the agencies I deal with. If they're registered with a doctor in Brighton we should be able to trace them.'

Relieved that something was going to be done, Diana left the house to join Sheridan in the daily vineyard inspection.

'Is Hugh really never coming back?' Clemmy asked at breakfast.

'Never,' said Griselda, smiling.

'Good,' said Simon. 'I never liked him.'

'Why were you always nice to him then?'

' "If thine enemy be hungry, give him bread",' intoned Simon piously. 'That's from the Proverbs. I think,' he added doubtfully.

'Too bloody good to be true. That's what you are.' Clemmy gave him a dig with her pin-sharp elbow.

'Ow!' Simon lunged at Clemmy but was foiled by Griselda stepping smartly between them.

'Don't swear, Clemmy,' she said. 'What would Diana say if she was to hear you?'

'She'd say don't swear,' said Miffy with a giggle. 'But

she isn't here. So we can. Bloody, bloody, bloody, Hugh.' He burst into roars of laughter.

'Stop that.' Millicent could be much more strict than Griselda at times. 'Anyway it isn't strictly true to say that he's *never* coming back, because he is. I'm not quite sure when, but he has to come and collect the rest of his belongings. So just you make sure you are polite if you see him. Or better still keep out of his way.'

Breakfast finished the children went out. The rain of the day before had blown itself out and it was a beautiful warm, autumn day. Simon took his fishing rod and a bag of stale bread for bait, and disappeared towards the stream at the bottom of the village, Clemmy cycled off to visit her current best friend, Peggy Titchfield, and Miffy announced that he was going to find Diana and Sheridan.

Millicent and Griselda watched his small figure, dwarfed by the enormous wellington boots which had been handed down from Simon and were much too large, start off down the slope. Seamus appeared from nowhere and trotted at his side.

'Diana must be somewhere near, then,' said Millicent seeing the dog. 'Can't keep her out of that vineyard these days. So worried about the damned harvest and money. And now that Hugh has gone, I suppose she'll be even more worried.'

'She has no need to be.' Griselda said. 'May told me she's going to make some money and land over to Diana now that Hugh's gone. She'll make sure Abbey House is all right. But it's a secret. You won't tell anyone, will you?'

'Course not. You can rely on me,' said Millicent.

Sheridan had been out in the vineyard with his refractometer long before Diana arrived. As soon as the first rays of sun had started warming the slopes of the vineyard he'd taken some samples and had completed the tests in the small laboratory he had in the winery. When Diana joined him, he was doing his usual rounds of inspecting for damage from weather and animals.

'The sugar reading is coming up,' he told her. 'Another week of weather like this and we'll have a bumper harvest.'

'Oh, please God, let it be a bumper harvest.' Diana raised both hands and crossed her fingers. They reached the end of the row and turned to find April edging her way through the hedge, Joe's labrador Sam squeezing through beside her.

'Whatever!' she exclaimed seeing Diana's raised hands and crossed fingers.

'Praying for a good harvest,' said Diana, making a prayer steeple with her hands. 'Double indemnity, prayer and superstition.'

'I came to see if you were all right. I mean, well . . .' she looked at Sheridan.

'Yes, Sheridan knows Hugh has gone. And, yes, I *am* all right. In fact I have a marvellous sense of freedom. I can concentrate all my energies on solving the problems here now, because there's nothing else to worry about.'

'I understand,' said April slowly. 'Perhaps that's what I need. Freedom to concentrate. See you later.'

'But you've only just come. Aren't you going to come up to the house for a coffee?' April, however, appeared not to hear. She was squeezing back through the hole in the hedge, leaving an irresolute looking Sam standing beside Diana, worried at having his morning walk cut so short. The appearance of Miffy with Seamus at his side made up his mind, he stayed with the party in the vineyard.

'Strange!' Sheridan rolled his eyes expressively, then suddenly went down on one knee. 'Damn and blast them,' he said.

'What is it?' April forgotten, Diana bobbed down beside him.

'Foxes,' said Sheridan, pointing to half a dozen fat bunches of grapes littered along the bottom of the row of

411

vines. 'I wouldn't mind so much if they ate the damned things, but all they do is bite off a bunch, have a chew, and then leave the rest.'

Tony's car crunched to a halt in the gravel outside Abbey House. Parked beside the battered estate car everyone called the 'Vineyard Volvo', was a gleaming white police car.

Inside Tony found a strangely silent kitchen. The three children, and Millicent and Griselda, were all sitting at the table.

'What's going on?' said Tony.

Millicent nodded her head in the direction of the Library, now in use as Diana's permanent office. 'We don't know. Go and see if you can find out.'

Tony knocked. 'Come in,' Diana's voice sounded strangely subdued.

Tony opened the door. Two policemen were with Diana in the Library. Only one of them was a local man. Unsure of whether he'd be allowed to stay or not, Tony said, 'Can I help?'

'I doubt it, Dr Evans.' That was the local policeman. Tony noticed he was putting away a notebook. 'Mrs Stratton has told us all she can.'

'Oh, Tony.' In spite of her determination to keep calm, Diana heard her voice waver. It was all so incredulous she couldn't, no *wouldn't* believe it. 'They say that Hugh has been trying to sell the guns stolen from Bert's grave.'

'No ma'am,' the unknown policeman spoke. 'We're not accusing him. All we've said is that a man answering to your husband's description has been reported as trying to sell guns to a gunsmith in Stroud.'

'How do you know they were the stolen guns?' asked Tony.

'Mr Greensmith, the owner of the shop, has a sharp eye and a good memory. He noted the number on the barrel of one of the guns. It was definitely one of Bert

412

Slocombe's guns. No doubt about it.' The policeman turned back to Diana. 'No need to worry Mrs Stratton. We shall be pursuing our enquiries with Mr Stratton via his office in London.'

Chapter Thirty-two

'Why was those policemen here?'

'Why *were* those policemen here,' Diana corrected Miffy automatically. She looked at Tony for help, realizing too late that she should have worked out some plausible reason for the visit of the police before they left the Library. The last thing she wanted the children to know was the truth.

'They were making routine enquiries about a robbery. But Diana couldn't help them, neither could I,' Tony answered matter of factly.

'Why didn't they ask us?' demanded Simon. 'We might have known something useful.'

'Unlikely. This concerned people Diana and I know in London, not Mottisley. Sorry, young man,' Tony gave Simon a friendly punch, 'but I'm afraid there's no excitement coming your way.' He looked at Diana's worried face. Something had to be done to divert the children's minds from the visit of the police. He remembered seeing banners strung across Midhurst High Street advertising a new McDonald's. 'Who fancies a trip into Midhurst? A McDonald's has opened up, and it's half price Big Macs tonight as an introductory offer.'

'*We would!*' A unanimous chorus of delighted voices greeted his offer, and with much noise and laughter the children began to pile into the car.

'Thanks, Tony,' said Diana. Like everyone else in Mottisley he came up trumps when she needed help. How had she ever existed without people like him around her? But she knew the answer; she'd dwelt in a form of spiritual isolation. Surrounded by people, none of whom either cared for, or meant much to her, not even Hugh. Strange, but now that he'd actually left, Diana realized that Hugh had begun to seem unreal. Even the import of the policeman's questions had a surrealist air.

'By the time they come back they'll have forgotten about the visit by the arm of the law.' Tony's voice interrupted her contemplations. 'And you forget it too. Even if it has got something to do with Hugh, which I doubt, he's not your concern now. Forget all about him. That's an order.'

'Yes, doctor,' said Diana, and waved the excited children off.

'I'm having a cheeseburger with all the trimmings, and a spoonful of every kind of pickle,' announced Miffy as he climbed in the car.

'Huh! and he'll probably be sick on the way home.' Millicent sniffed. She disapproved of American food.

Once the children had gone Diana told the two women the reason for the policemen's visit.

'Oh, my God!' Griselda's mouth dropped open in horror. 'I never really liked Hugh, but to think. Oh, dear.' She shuddered. 'Well, fancy that! Grave robbing!'

'A man answering to his description,' Diana reminded her hastily before Griselda's imagination ran complete riot.

'Exactly,' said Millicent. 'Nothing is proven.' But from the grim set of her mouth Diana knew that Millicent's thoughts were running along the same lines as Griselda's.

But in spite of feeling so remote from Hugh, and knowing that whatever the truth was it had nothing to do with her, the thought still haunted her. And yet, and yet . . . Against her will she remembered the anger in his voice when he knew the guns were to be buried in the coffin along with Bert. She could even remember his exact words. *'Jesus Christ! Do you know how much those guns are worth, Diana? They're worth thirty-thousand pounds a pair. That's sixty-thousand pounds being buried.'* And Hugh did love money. At the time of Bert's funeral she hadn't realized quite how much, but now she knew. Hugh loved money more than anything else. More than her. More than his own parents.

Having finally come to the conclusion that Joe would never marry her, April reluctantly decided to leave Mottisley, and make a fresh life for herself back in London. She told Joe.

Joe's reaction was predictable. He didn't want to talk about it. He was far more worried about the collapse of his Far Eastern investments. Shamrock Enterprises had been built up so easily, and this was the first knock he'd taken. Well, he thought, moodily, not so much of a knock, more of a bloody great bashing actually. Easy come, easy go, had always been his motto. Now the 'easy go' part seemed forebodingly too easy. He'd have to watch out.

'Joe, have you been listening to anything I've said?' April was exasperated. Realistic enough to know he was unlikely to go down on his knees and beg her to stay, she had, nevertheless, expected some reaction.

'Yes. Of course I have.' He glanced at April's angry face. 'Well, to be honest I didn't catch all of it,' he admitted.

'I've been saying, Joe, that I think it will be better for both of us if I moved out.'

'Why?'

'Why not? There's nothing for me here is there?'

'What do you mean, nothing for you here?' Irrational though he knew it was, Joe began to feel angry. Didn't she have everything she wanted? Didn't she live in a beautiful house that she loved? She was always extolling the virtues of the manor house. 'What else do you need?' he asked angrily. The anger fuelled his already simmering resentment at the loss of his Far Eastern portfolio. 'I suppose It's because I'm not as rich as I was. Bloody Japanese, I should never have trusted my money on the Nikkei.'

'What are you talking about?'

'Shamrock Enterprises no longer have a Far Eastern interest. I've lost a bomb.'

April sighed. 'It has nothing to do with money.'

Joe was silent for a moment. He'd been unfair to accuse her of caring about money. Avarice was not one of April's traits. 'Where will you go?' he said at last.

'Back to my own house in Putney, of course. I'm not running off with some other man. Those days are behind me. I'm settling for the life of "spinster of the parish of Putney", it's simpler. I shall be quite happy on my own.'

Joe grunted. *He* wouldn't be happy on his own. He knew that much. But what did he want? He felt confused. He knew April wanted marriage, his confusion didn't blurr that fact, but he didn't. Why was he so against it? Instinct I suppose, he thought, so many mistakes before. Any man would be put off. But April was different. She was intelligent, and kind. Must be, otherwise the Abbey House kids wouldn't like her so much; or Diana either. She got on well with Diana. His thoughts meandered. I get on well with Diana these days too, although there is still something about her which disturbs me. But that was digressing. It was not Diana requiring his attention, it was April. If April left there'd be no-one to run the house. He'd have to get a housekeeper. The thought of sharing his home with some unknown woman was repellent.

'I want you to stay,' he said.

'But, Joe. You don't love me.'

'I'm fond of you.'

'That's not the same thing.'

'I know it isn't.' Joe got up and walking across to April put his hands on her shoulders. 'I could easily profess undying love for you and not mean it. I've said that to plenty of women before. Too many. But I like to think I'm a little more mature now. I don't love you, but I am fond of you. Very fond, and I'd like us to continue living together. Perhaps in a few months' time, we could think about getting married. That is, if you want to stay. I've come to the conclusion that love, the grand passion, is not necessarily a good reason for marrying. But I don't see any reason why two people who get on well together shouldn't make a go of it. What do you say?'

'You want a housekeeper.'

'Yes,' admitted Joe. 'I do, and you're a damned good one. But that's not the only reason. My bed will be lonely without you.'

'You can find someone else to warm it.'

'I don't want to find someone else. I'm happy with what I've got.'

'I don't know what to say.'

'Say yes,' said Joe kissing her. He drew away. 'As I said before, what does grand passion matter, when you're comfortable.'

The two policemen descended the worn stone steps from the building housing Hugh's office into a quiet courtyard of the Inns of Court. The younger man had never been into the Inner Temple courtyards before. The serene air of hallowed and respected tradition impressed him.

'Hardly seems likely, does it, sir. I mean a man coming from a background like this being involved in grave robbing.'

'Stranger things have been known to happen.'

'But you don't think . . .'

'I'm thinking nothing until we've got some facts. The first thing is to interview this Mrs Nancy Morris, and then after that we'll run a few checks on Hugh Stratton's background.'

'Yes, sir.' The junior detective sighed. Sergeant Brown was slow and thorough, old fashioned in his methods. If he wasn't careful they could be stuck with this case for a couple of weeks, and miss something more exciting that happened to come along. But there was nothing for it, he had to do as he was told. 'Where shall I start?'

'You can start by looking into Hugh Stratton's financial affairs. How well off is he? He's split up from his wife. So what financial arrangements have been made there? And find out when he is going to be in court, then go back and interview those two secretaries. Always interesting to get a complete background on someone.'

'You talk as if you think he's guilty.'

'Always guilty until proved innocent.'

'Don't you mean the other way around?'

The older man laughed. 'No, I meant what I said. When you've been around as long as I have, you'll think that too.'

The detective was shocked. 'I hope not. It would go against all my training.'

'Life often does,' was the enigmatic reply. They reached Fleet Street where the police car was parked on the double yellow lines. 'You walk back to the station and get on with your investigations. I'll drive myself over to Hampstead and have a word with Mrs Morris,' said Sergeant Brown.

In the office, Hugh 'phoned Nancy, and told her of his two visitors. 'So you see, darling, I had no alternative but to tell them that I spent that day with you.'

'Don't call me, darling.' Nancy was irritable. 'Why didn't you think up some other alibi? I don't want to be dragged into it.'

'But you *are* in it. The whole thing was your idea in the first place.' Angry, Hugh raised his voice, then remembering Miss Higgins outside hastily lowered it again. 'Anyway, it's the truth. We *were* together. I told him we spent the day in bed at your house. No-one can prove otherwise, and I need someone to vouch for my alibi.'

'Now everyone at Mottisley, including May, will know you're with me. She might cut me out of her will.'

'You don't even know that you are actually in it,' Hugh pointed out.

There was a long silence at the other end of the 'phone, then Nancy said slowly, 'no, you're right. I don't do I? I'm glad you mentioned that. I shall have to do something about it.'

'Such as?'

Nancy's purring laugh reverberated along the 'phone. 'I'll think of something. In the meantime, you stop worrying. I'll back your story up. They can't prove a thing.'

'I hope so. It might be tricky though if they bring the old man from the gunsmiths to identify me.'

'Nonsense.' Nancy sounded confident. 'You said he was old. Well, old people often get confused, don't they? It would be our word against his. They say everyone has a double somewhere. So, it was someone who looked like Hugh Stratton, but it certainly wasn't you. I can vouch for that.'

'Of course.' Hugh felt relieved. Nancy was right. He had nothing to worry about.

Stretching across Nico's prostrate body, Nancy dropped the 'phone back into position and smiled. 'Poor Hugh. He's really got his Y-fronts in a twist. The police have been to see him about the guns.'

'Shit!' Nico sat up in bed, his swarthy face looking worried. 'I hope he can be trusted to keep his mouth shut.'

'He'll be all right. As long as he's kept going on a nice little high with a regular supply of his dope he'll do as he's told.' Nancy stretched, and ran her fingers through the thick dark hair on Nico's back. 'How nice it is to have a chunky, hairy man in my bed, it makes a change from Hugh, he's got so skinny lately.'

'Why don't you dump him?' Nico turned back to Nancy, and cupping her pointed breasts in his two huge hands, sucked ferociously first on one nipple and then the other. 'He's costing me a hell of a lot of money in dope,' he said, coming up for air.

'And I'm paying. Arranging discreet little drops when things are too hot for you. Letting you have far more than your proper share of the gun money when they're sold, and available whenever carnal lust strikes your loins.'

Nico chewed roughly on a nipple. 'Since I've known you that's becoming more and more frequent.' He paused a moment, then sucked at her breast again. 'Say, you know I've been wondering something. Why is it your tits are always cold?'

'Witch's tits,' teased Nancy. Then laughing at his puzzled expression she explained. 'Silicone implants, darling. I like to keep my figure under control.'

'Oh,' Nico fondled her breasts thoughtfully, then grinned. 'You know they'll explode when you're cremated, don't you.'

'I've always planned to go out with a bang,' said Nancy.

Nico began chewing with renewed vigour. 'I wish you'd get rid of that sucker, Hugh,' he grumbled.

'I can't. I still need his services.'

Nico grunted, and suddenly straddled her, savagely pushing her legs apart. 'Don't the services I provide satisfy you?' Nancy's excited laugh was enough to make him come, and without wasting time on preliminaries he plunged into her with powerful thrusts, jerking the breath from her body. 'There,' he said when he'd finished, 'that should satisfy you. You bitch.' Pinning her arms above her head, he looked down at the white, still heaving, body beneath his.

'You didn't give me time to come,' gasped Nancy.

'Work at it,' he growled. 'I'm not going to help you.' A slow grin spread across his face as she writhed beneath him, her gasping breaths growing sharper and shorter as she finally came. By the time she'd finished, he was aroused and began thrusting deep again. 'I'll teach you to need his services,' he said.

Ten minutes later, he rolled off her, and lay on his back. They were both limp and exhausted. For the first time in her life Nancy had found someone with a sexual appetite that excelled her own.

'Nico, you're bloody fantastic,' she gasped.

'So get rid of Hugh.'

'I can't, not yet. When I said I needed him, I meant that I need his legal services.'

'Why?'

'A family matter.'

And with that Nico had to be content. He was just leaving Nancy's Hampstead house when Detective Sergeant Brown drew up in the police car.

'Fucking hell!' Nico scuttled off towards his silver Jaguar, and jumping in, roared off down the hill.

'A friend of yours, Mrs Morris?' Sergeant Morris presented his identity while looking after the rapidly disappearing Nico.

'No,' Nancy lied. 'I lost my handbag in the West End, that man found it and returned it to me. Kind of him, wasn't it?'

'Amazing is the word that springs to mind. The man is an out and out criminal.'

'Oh, Good Heavens!' Nancy clasped her hands dramatically to her chest. 'If I'd known that I would never have invited him in for a coffee.'

'Ah, but you didn't know, did you?' Sergeant Brown smiled. 'Might I come in, Mrs Morris? Just a few questions in connection with your aunt in Mottisley, and the robbery of Bert Slocombe's grave.'

'Come in.' Nancy led the way into the house. 'Although I can't think that anything I shall say will be of the slightest help to you.'

'You'd be surprised. Sometimes one picks up useful information in the strangest ways.'

Nancy smiled, and indicated that he should be seated. What a very dull, monotonous voice Sergeant Brown had. If his character matched his voice, she, Hugh and Nico could play ring-a-ring of roses around him, and he'd never notice.

Chapter Thirty-three

'This is a lovely surprise.' Diana opened the kitchen door to find May and Tony standing outside.

'Well, if the mountain won't come to Mahomet, Mahomet must go to the mountain,' said May, handing Diana a bottle. It was an Aberlour ten-year-old single malt. 'And we've brought our own refreshments as you can see,' she added.

'May, I *have* been over to see you.' Diana looked at the whisky. 'This is lovely, but terribly expensive.'

'I can afford it.'

Which is more than I can, thought Diana, and felt sick at the humiliation of the admission. How times had changed from the days when she'd spent money like water, never once stopping to think whether or not she could afford whatever took her fancy. Her visit to the bank manager that day had been resoundingly unsuccessful. Mr Mortimer had been offhand to the point of rudeness when he'd found that Hugh had left her.

'Hardly wise to dismiss the one person in the family on a regular salary,' had been his acid comment.

'And, anyway,' continued May, interrupting Diana's dismal train of thought, 'it's not a present. What we don't drink I shall take back with me. And as for visiting me, you don't come nearly often enough, and when you do you're always in a rush.'

'True,' Diana admitted. Then asked what had been worrying her from the moment she'd seen May on the doorstep. 'Did you ride your motorcycle over?'

Tony hid a smile. 'No, I brought her.'

'I've decided to go back to four wheels instead of two,' May told Diana. 'I'm driving my old Austin Seven

423

now, not the Rolls. More comfortable for my advanced years.'

'Thank God.' Diana's relief came from the heart.

'Mind you, if I feel like a spin on my bike I shall have one,' said May.

Diana recognized the tone of voice and familiar stubborn jut of May's jaw. 'Of course,' she said hastily, and changed the subject. 'What shall we eat with the whisky? Biscuits and cheese? I've got Cheddar or Stilton.'

'Cheddar, of course.' May dived into the capacious bag from whence had come the whisky and produced a greasy brown paper parcel. 'Some of my own, not that bought rubbish. This is specially matured, extra strong.'

'Nice,' said Tony when they'd settled down around the kitchen table, all munching wholemeal biscuits and May's Cheddar, which was so strong it made the back of the throat tingle. 'It was my idea to come tonight, because I knew you'd be alone now that Millicent's been roped into the church choir for the "Show Boat" concert. They must all be getting nervous now it's near the great day, especially Sheridan.'

'And the Reverend Pincher must be desperate if he's got Millicent in as well,' May grunted disparagingly. She was still a little chary of Millicent since the drinking episode, and that was the reason she intended taking the Aberlour back home with her. Millicent was not going to get drunk on *her* whisky.

Diana laughed. 'On the contrary, she's got a very nice contralto voice, and has been given a solo line to sing. I think Griselda's a bit jealous.' The Aga was alight and the kitchen was hot. Diana got up and opened the window. 'It's very warm tonight for the middle of October,' she said. 'But I'm not complaining. We're going to start picking the grapes on Saturday, unless it rains, of course. Sheridan has organized Isaac and Ronald; they're experienced, and I shall help as well. By Sunday night, with any luck, we'll have the harvest in. And it'll be a good one. The sugar content is high.' Rejoining the others at

424

the table, she took an appreciative sip of the Aberlour, 'that should keep bloody Mr Mortimer happy.'

'Been leaning on you, has he?' Tony glanced at May. Why couldn't she tell Diana not to worry? Why couldn't she say that she'd bail her out if necessary? But May remained stubbornly silent, save for the loud crunching of her biscuits.

'Yes, but I'm not worried.' That isn't true, Diana reflected, wishing the interview with Mr Mortimer had not been so acrimonious. She *was* worried, worried sick. 'Once the harvest is in, I shall invite the damned man here to see for himself just how much wine we're going to have for sale next year. Then he'll change his tune.'

'You should harvest before Saturday,' said May.

'Why? With all this mild sunny weather we're having, the sugar content is rising all the time. I want to make the best quality wine I can.'

'My upper field was chock-a-block with seagulls today,' said May gloomily. 'Always a sign of bad weather when the gulls come inland. There's going to be a storm.'

'Rubbish, young Norman ploughed that field for you today. The seagulls always follow the plough.' Annoyed, Tony poured May another whisky. Couldn't she see that Diana was already worried and try, for once, to be a little tactful? 'Don't be so pessimistic,' he said sharply, and changed the subject. Then felt a guilty scruple. Changing the direction of the conversation was not entirely an altruistic manoeuvre, he was steering it on to a subject much closer to his own heart. 'Seen much of April and Joe?' he asked Diana.

'Joe, yes,' she replied. 'That reminds me, he said he'd help out with the picking at the weekend. But I've not seen April. I gather from Joe that the new book is going great guns, and she's buried away in the study at the manor house typing like a mad thing.'

'Oh,' Tony tried not to sound too interested. 'I wondered why we hadn't seen much of her.'

A hacking, wheezing cough from the doorway

425

interrupted the conversation. Miffy stood, bleary eyed, in his pyjamas. 'Can't sleep,' he said between wheezes.

Diana was on her feet in a flash. Miffy had had only one small asthma attack since she'd been caring for the children, but it had badly frightened her. Now, he was obviously building up to another. His skin was a pale, opaque colour, thrown into greater contrast by his overgrown mop of dark hair, and the dark circles ringing his vivid blue eyes.

'Have you used your inhaler?' She tried to be calm, but heard her voice rise high, and thin with anxiety.

'Can't find it.'

'I've got a new one in my car,' said Tony. 'You take him upstairs, I'll get it and follow you.' He ruffled Miffy's hair. 'Nothing to worry about,' he said reassuringly. 'I'll soon get rid of those wheezes for you.' He looked sternly at Diana on his way out. 'And *you* keep calm,' he said in a low voice. 'The last thing you must do is let him know you are worried.'

Diana took a deep breath, and forced herself to smile. 'Come on, darling,' she said, lifting an unresisting Miffy up into her arms, 'let's get you back into that warm bed.' Tony's right, I mustn't panic, she told herself. But it was difficult. She loved him passionately, with a fiercely protective love. A possessive love, a voice said at the back of her mind. Possessive. Holding Miffy close, and struggling up the stairs, Diana answered the voice back. There was nothing wrong in being possessive. Protection and possession overlapped, it was only natural. The most important fact was that she loved him.

Tony returned with the inhaler almost before Diana had Miffy into bed, and took over. Soon Miffy snuggled sleepily under his duvet, giving Diana a wan smile, before drifting off to sleep.

'His breathing is better now,' said Tony, bending over the bed.

'Do you think so? It sounds awful to me.' Diana was still worried. 'Listen to that whistling.'

'For God's sake, woman. Stop hearing things that aren't there. Of course he's still wheezing a bit, and he'll wheeze tomorrow as well. But we've nipped the full-blown attack in the bud, and that's the main thing.'

'I suppose so.' Diana remained to be convinced.

'It is. Take my word for it. I'm the doctor. Honestly, Diana, you surprise me. I would never have taken you for a panicker. What on earth would you be like with children of your own?'

'They *are* mine,' said Diana fiercely, the depth of her feelings astonishing her yet again. When she'd made the first impulsive decision to stay and become a full-time surrogate mother, their need had been the driving force behind her decision. Affection, of a kind, had been present, but it was not the dominant emotion. I've changed, Diana acknowledged. Before I came here in July I lived in a beautiful, but sterile, bubble. Now I live in permanent chaos, but I have real feelings. Emotions that I'd forgotten existed. Children of my own, indeed! I couldn't love them any more if I'd given birth to them myself.

Tony finished tucking the duvet around Miffy, and straightening up, turned and looked at Diana quizzically. Then he smiled, 'you've got a bad case of mothering,' he said, 'and it suits you.' Putting a gentle hand beneath her elbow he steered her from, the now sleeping, Miffy's room.

'Suits me, huh! That's not what Hugh thought. That was one of the black marks against me.'

'Bugger, Hugh,' said Tony. 'You're not still worrying about him are you?'

'No, not really.' Diana thought for a moment. She might have undergone a transformation in her personality, but her years of marriage to Hugh couldn't be forgotten overnight. 'I am sad though,' she admitted. 'Failure is never easy to come to terms with.'

'Some of us have to come to terms with it more often than others,' said Tony sombrely. 'Anyway, admitting something isn't working, is not failure. It's being realistic.'

'I know. That's what I keep telling myself.' Diana paused at the top of the stairs. 'By the way, any news yet of the whereabouts of Hugh's parents?'

'Not yet. But I'll find them. Don't worry.' Putting out an arm, Tony barred Diana's way down the stairs. 'Can I ask you a favour?' he said.

'Of course.' Puzzled, Diana waited.

'April told me two weeks ago that she was leaving Joe. We went to Chichester for the day, she and I, and she told me then. She promised to let me know when she was leaving, but since that day I haven't heard a word, and from what you say she is still at the manor house with Joe.'

'Tony, you're not still hoping that something will work out between you and April are you?'

'No,' said Tony, then paused. 'Well, yes, to be honest, I was,' he admitted. 'I was thinking that once she'd left Joe, there might be a chance that she'd be able to view me from a different angle. But now she's still here, and I don't know what's going on.'

'And you want me to find out?'

'Please,' said Tony. 'Put me out of my misery. I can't help feeling that they're planning to marry, and that's why April hasn't contacted me. I made a bit of a fool of myself with her that day in Chichester. Wore my heart on my sleeve, so to speak. She's probably too embarrassed to see me.'

Diana looked at Tony. He'd always been such a good friend, and these last few weeks she'd neglected him. Wrapped up with the children and their needs, absorbed with the vineyard and preoccupied with the break-up of her marriage, she'd hardly given Tony and his frustrated love for April a thought. 'Next time I see Joe I'll try and find out.'

'But don't tell him that I want to know.'

'Tony, please! I didn't come up in the last bucket.'

He laughed, and removed the arm barring her way. 'No, but I'm beginning to think I did,' he said.

On Thursday evening Miffy knelt on the couch and stared out of the window. He was still wheezy and Diana had refused to let him go to school that day. Now, sullen grey clouds fanned out from the south-west, filling the sky with the dour prediction of a severe squall. Every now and then the windows rattled.

'Mr Wind is trying to get in, hear his fingers shaking at the house,' said Miffy. He turned to Diana, suddenly worried by his own flight of imagination. 'I can hear the yew tree creaking. Do you think it will fall?'

Diana smiled. 'I doubt it. It's stood beside the abbey, and before that beside the previous Saxon church from which the abbey was built, for nearly a thousand years. A good many southwesterlies must have buffeted it during that time, and it's never fallen. So I don't think it's going to fall down tonight. Besides, I shall not allow it to fall. That is a very special tree to me. It always reminds me of my daddy. Your mummy and I used to watch the moon rise above it when we were little girls. Daddy would tell us the time, and in the summer we would wait, leaning out of the window upstairs, watching and watching until the moon peeped her head above the yew tree. Then I would go to bed happy.'

'Did you?' Miffy eyed her quizzically, screwing up his eyes as if trying to visualize his mother and Diana as small girls. 'And was it windy then?' he asked.

'Of course, darling, sometimes.' Diana joined Miffy at the window and looked out. It *was* windy, much more so than she had at first thought. The vines were bending before the force of the wind sweeping up from the coast.

Sheridan came in, a gust of wind rushing in behind him bringing with it the scent of brine into the kitchen. Slamming the door shut tight, he shrugged himself out of his anorak. 'No need to worry,' he said, seeing Diana looking out of the window. 'I know it's blowing, but the weather forecast is OK and the vineyards are in their own nice little dip in the downs. The house is exposed. We're getting more wind up here. Don't worry.'

'Ah, yes, the wretched microclimate you've told me about. I've read up on it, and understand the theory, but must confess that I'm not completely convinced.'

'Stop worrying,' said Sheridan, a wide grin spreading across his shining brown face. Sheridan was always smiling, and Diana found herself reluctantly smiling back.

Sheridan was always telling her not to worry, but Diana carried right on worrying. A born worrier, Sheridan called her. Now, she looked again down the vineyard slope, anxiously peering for signs of damage, but to her relief the vines seemed to be standing up to the wind very well. Then suddenly the sky darkened even more. An enormous flock of starlings, so thick and close they appeared to be a solid but moving mass, swept past Abbey House. Up they swirled, turning in a vortex away over the roof, disappearing in the distance beyond the horizon, below a hump in the Downs.

'Birds before the storm,' said Sheridan. 'They're not liking this wind. They're searching out a quieter place to ride out the squall.'

'Sensible birds.' Diana remembered May's words. '*You should harvest before Saturday.*' No matter what Sheridan might say, she felt very uneasy.

'Don't fret yourself,' said Sheridan accurately reading the anxious expression on her face. 'Come on, tell me what's for supper.'

'Rabbit casserole,' said Miffy, climbing down from the sofa. 'And dumplings, carrots and beans.'

The wind was forgotten as Millicent said, 'You can call Clemmy and Simon down, it's all ready now.'

'I'll call them,' said Miffy rushing to the bottom of the stairs.

'Amazing how that child's wheezing disappears at the thought of food,' said Griselda.

'He doesn't put it on.' Diana plunged to Miffy's defence.

'Of course not. But when he's distracted it lessens.'

'A happy child is a well child,' said Sheridan. 'That's what my mother always used to say. And luckily Miffy is happy most of the time.' He reached out and grabbed Diana's hand. 'Say, ma'am, what are you looking so dismal about? You look as if you've got the troubles of the world on your shoulders.' He turned Diana's hand over in his, inspecting the slender pale palm lying in his own darker one. 'You've been mending those nets again without wearing gloves,' he accused. 'These are no hands for a lady.'

Diana shrugged and slipping her hand from his, looked at it. Red, and work roughened, they were certainly not the hands of a lady. 'The days when all I worried about was whether or not my nail varnish was chipped are long gone,' she said philosophically.

'Now you have hands with character,' observed Griselda. 'Much nicer than that cousin of yours. I always think Nancy's hands look evil.'

Her percipience surprised Diana. It was something she'd thought herself on the few occasions she'd spent any time with her cousin. Nancy's hands were too white, the fingers too long and her nails always too red. Suddenly, without intending to, she found she was thinking of Hugh. Had those policemen questioned him yet? What were his answers? He must have been furious. He always hated anything to do with Mottisley, and to have his named linked to the grave robbery must have been the final straw. She'd been expecting an irate 'phone call, berating her for directing the police to his London office, but had not heard a word. Strange too, that she'd not heard from the police. It would ease her peace of mind to know that Hugh was definitely not involved. Estranged though they were, grave robbing was a ghastly crime, and she couldn't bear to think that Hugh might be connected to it in some way. Diana pulled herself up with a jerk.

431

What was the matter with her? *Of course*, Hugh was not involved. It was a case of mistaken identity. It had to be.

She looked again at ' :r hands. 'Thank you Griselda. It's nice to have a compliment. Albeit a slightly back-handed one!'

'I'd rather have a dumpling,' said Miffy, bringing the conversation down to a more practical, and important level. That of food.

After supper, and once the children were in bed, Diana settled down in the Library and worked through the accounts for Abbey House and the vineyard, once more. But no matter how many variations on a theme she tried out, the result was always depressingly the same. There was no money to speak of. Unless the bank extended the credit, Abbey Vineyard was in dire trouble. Staring at the ledgers and sheets of papers before her, she wished some inspiration for creative accounting might strike her, but it didn't. According to all the financial magazines it was the vogue at the moment, but to create one needed something to bargain with. That was the problem, she'd mortgaged Abbey House and the vineyard to secure the first loan. There was nothing left, no hidden cards up her sleeve. The only thing she had in her favour was the forthcoming harvest. All her eggs were in one basket, the harvest. It was half past eleven, no point in worrying any more at this time of night. Straightening her tired back, and putting away the papers, she went back into the warm kitchen.

The Library was on the other side of the house, away from the vineyards, the side facing up into the Downs, and sheltered from the south and southwesterly winds. While she'd struggled with the accounts the increasing violence of the storm had passed her by unnoticed. It was only when she entered the kitchen that Diana realized just how strong the wind had become. In addition to the wind, it was raining now. Not the ordinary soft rain of summer and autumn, but a torrential downpour. Driven almost horizontal by the gale, it beat against the windows with a persistent steely rapping, water pouring down the panes like a miniature waterfall.

Millicent and Griselda had already retired for the night, but Sheridan was still up, sitting with Seamus at his side, his feet towards the warmth of the Aga stove. 'Like a tropical downpour out there,' he said, 'only without the heat. Reminds me of the storms before a hurricane in the Carribean.'

'What do you know about hurricanes in the Carribean?' asked Diana.

'I've got relations there. And I always seem to pick the wrong time to visit them.' He laughed, 'I could tell you about some winds that would make this little blow look like a tiny puff.'

His joking didn't fool Diana. He was worried, and she knew it. Crossing the room she pressed her face against the glass, trying to see through the pouring rain into the darkness. She thought about their cow, the poor thing was out in the field. 'I hope Daisy is all right.'

'I brought her in,' said Sheridan. 'When it first started to blow.'

'You did?' Diana was surprised. In this part of the world the cattle very rarely needed to be brought into their winter quarters before the end of November. 'Why?'

Sheridan shrugged. 'Well, if you must know, I had this feeling. In my bones, as May would say, that tonight was going to be rough. So I played safe and brought her into the shed.'

'So much for telling *me* not to worry,' said Diana grimly.

'No point in both of us worrying.' Sheridan got up and joined her at the window. Seamus joined them, pressing in close between them. 'Man, but it's a bad night,' he said.

'Listen!' They both held their breath and listened. Somewhere across the yard a door was banging. 'We'd better go out and make absolutely certain that everything is fastened properly,' said Diana. 'The last thing I need is a bill for repairs. The insurance I have on this place is only the bare minimum.'

Clad in sou'westers, oilskins and wellington boots, they stood by the kitchen door ready to brave the elements. 'Brace yourself,' said Sheridan, 'and for God's sake be careful. There are bound to be falling branches.'

'Seamus, stay in,' said Diana as they opened the door, but Seamus had other ideas. Diana was his mistress and he was going with her.

'He'll be all right,' said Sheridan. 'He'll not go far in this weather. You take that side of the yard and house, and I'll go this way, and do the barn doors. They're too heavy for you to make tight.'

Diana nodded. Once outside in the full force of the wind conversation was impossible. With Seamus at her side, she struggled from one outhouse to another. All the hanging baskets around the vineyard shop had been blown from their wrought iron hooks. She fell over one and grazed her knee, but carried on, wedging doors with the nearest and largest stones she could find, jamming sticks into loose window-frames. The whole bloody place is dropping to pieces, she thought despairingly, as an extra fierce gust snatched at a window, flinging it open. Luckily it didn't break, but it took all her strength to wedge it shut. That finished, she made her way through the rhododendron bushes down to the wicket gate at the side of the garden near to the yew tree. Just as well, it was swinging wildly, back and forth, back and forth, and in danger of disintegrating completely. Struggling to heave a boulder she'd located beneath one of the rhododendron bushes over to the gate, she heard the yew creak, and thought of Miffy's fears. But the creaking didn't stop as she expected, it continued. High pitched, and growing in volume. Then the earth beneath her feet began to shudder. The tree cried out, groaning and weeping aloud in pain, like a living being, and Diana knew the unthinkable was happening. The yew was falling.

'Seamus, come,' she screamed, and began to run away

from the towering blackness that threatened to crush her and the dog. No-one could survive the weight of that mighty tree. Stumbling in the darkness, slipping and sliding in the mud of the garden, she fled, branches slashed at her face, like fingers trying to catch her. It was as if the dying tree was determined that she should die too. But she escaped. The ground shook as it fell to its final resting place, and it was then that she heard the terrible screaming. High pitched, and thin, it penetrated the sound of the wind and rain, and Diana felt a cold knot of fear in her chest. Even before she reached him, she had known what it was. The yew tree had fallen on Seamus.

He stopped screaming as she got to him. For a second her hopes were raised, but then she knew he'd stopped because he was dying. Flinging herself down in the mud beside him, she pushed back the branches, cradling his long, aristocratic, black and white head in her hands. 'Seamus, Seamus, darling, don't die. Please, don't die. I'll get help, I'll . . .'

Seamus moved his head slightly, licking her wet cheek; apologetic to the end for not being obedient. Then with a little puffle of his whiskers, the full weight of his head fell back into her hands, and his mischievous, brown eyes closed for ever.

It was nearly three-quarters of an hour before Joe and Sheridan with Ronald Pugh eventually found Diana. The swinging storm lantern held aloft by Sheridan, illuminated her silent, inert figure, still there, lying amongst the smashed branches of the yew tree cradling Seamus's head in her arms. She was drenched to the skin and icy cold.

Scooping Diana up in his arms, Joe turned to Sheridan. 'Try and dig the dog's body out and get it buried before the morning. I don't want the kids to see him. I'll take her inside.'

Sheridan nodded, his huge brown eyes glistening. 'Man, I loved that dog too.'

'Don't you dare bloody well cry!' Joe said.

'It's an omen,' said Diana wearily, holding on to Joe with cold, numb hands. 'Everything I touch is a disaster. The yew tree falling, and Seamus dying just proves it.'

The falling yew was like having her father and Susan die all over again, but more than that she felt it symbolized her own life. She was crashing down, totally out of control, unable to help those she loved. She felt tired and utterly helpless, and began to weep.

Chapter Thirty-four

'Are you sure you are all right?' Griselda, Millicent and Sheridan chorused in trio.

'Yes,' said Diana fiercely. 'Of course I am. I'm not going to go to pieces over a dog.' Then her eyes filled with tears, and she sat down suddenly. 'Oh dear, I don't know how I'm going to tell the children.'

'I've already told them,' said Griselda in a surprisingly authoritarian tone of voice. 'I've explained about the storm, and what happened. I told them he didn't suffer at all.'

'And I've shown them where he is buried,' added Sheridan. 'They've had a little weep, put flowers on his grave and then I took them over to Willow Farm. They can stay with May for the day, while we get on and see what we can salvage from the vineyard.'

'Thanks,' said Diana gratefully, 'although I ought to have done it myself. You shouldn't have let me duck out of a difficult task.' She took the tea Griselda passed her, and fished a bottle of aspirin out of her pocket.

Her head was buzzing. Quite apart from trying to block out the harrowing memory of the previous night, there was so much else to think of. Outside, the countryside, what little she had seen of it from the window, was devastated. There was no electricity, no telephone, and on Simon's little transistor radio she'd heard that the 'Great Storm' as the Media were calling it, had swept across southern and south-eastern England, and Abbey Vineyard had been right in its path. The region of most damage, roughly south of a line from Southampton to Ipswich, had suffered hurricane-force winds, the worst being between 3.00 a.m. and 6.00 a.m. in the morning. At least twelve people had been killed, possibly more. London was in total chaos, without electricity and telephones and the whole of the southern coastline was littered with wrecks of ships, large and small. The broadcast made Diana realize how lucky they were at Abbey House. Apart from Seamus there had been no casualties, and at least, they had heat, hot water and cooking facilities from the Aga in the kitchen, which was much more than many other people.

'Nonsense, of course it's not a case of ducking out of anything.' Griselda sounded quite bossy. 'We had a conference this morning and decided that this was for the best. You've got quite enough on your plate.'

'Yes, we'll need all hands in the vineyard today,' said Sheridan. 'The last thing we need is to worry about the safety of the children. That yew wasn't the only tree to fall last night.'

'I know, I've seen.' Diana got up and wandered listlessly over to the window sipping her tea. It seemed so strange without Seamus's head pressed against her side, as if she had lost part of herself. She looked out again at the scene of utter desolation. Trees were down all over the place as far as the eye could see. The smaller ones had survived, but the large ones lay like great giants tipped over on their sides, all facing the same direction; their roots, which had once drawn life from the earth, assuming an eerie beauty of their own as they pointed despairingly skywards instead of into the earth.

'And half of the trees that *are* still standing are unsafe,' said Sheridan, 'that's why I wanted the children out of the way. 'We don't want any more accidents. We'll all need to be very careful.'

Diana was tempted to despair, to ask what was the point in even going out into the vineyard? But strangely enough the despair spurred her on. Something *had* to be harvested. Nothing would be gained by weeping and doing nothing.

'How many people do you think we shall need?'

'As many as we can lay our hands on. It's not going to be easy,' replied Sheridan.

Diana gave a grim smile. 'Don't rub it in. But I'm damned if I'm going to be beaten by a bit of a gale. I know all our careful plans have gone out of the window, but the new filtration system which I've put myself into so much hock for, is now about to be tested to its limit. We'll pick every damned grape we can, and we *will* make wine.'

'Diana, you do realize that the grapes aren't actually on the vines, they've all been blown off and mixed up? Muller-Thurgau, Reichsteiner, Pinot Noir, Schonburger, plus the others, it's one huge grape cocktail. We'll never be able to make an individual wine.'

'We'll throw the lot in together, sit back and pray, and call the eventual produce *Hurricane Wine*.' Diana forced herself to sound confident. They needed a boost, all except Griselda, who had already risen to the occasion.

'That's what I like to hear. I knew the woman who prided herself on making the impossible happen would come up with something.' Joe and April suddenly burst in through the kitchen door. Seeing Joe reminded Diana of Seamus and she felt the tears threatening yet again. And once, if he'd made a remark like that she'd have thought it was a sarcastic dig, but now she knew better. It was a compliment, of sorts. 'How are you?' he asked more gently. 'Got over last night?'

The gentleness was her undoing, a tear slid down her cheek. 'All right,' she said, turning away, hoping no-one had seen her weakness.

'Good,' said Joe, and changed the subject quickly. 'I saw Isaac and Ronald walking up the lane, they'll be here in a minute. You'd better get us organized.'

'Right,' said Sheridan, putting on wellington boots and an anorak.

Griselda struggled into her outdoor clothes. 'I'm coming too. Just tell me what to do.'

'I'll stay here, do the housework, and prepare a

warming lunch for the workers,' said Millicent.

'Diana.' April crossed the kitchen and put her arms around Diana. 'I know how you feel,' she whispered, and hugged her. 'Come on, once you start working, it will help. And let's thank God it wasn't one of the children.'

'Oh yes,' Diana closed her eyes momentarily. She hadn't thought of that. One of the children. The thought was too terrible to contemplate.

Aware of all eyes on her, she pulled herself together. There was work to be done. It was not only the children who relied on her, but Millicent, Griselda and Sheridan. They worked for her it was true, but they'd become part of her family, and without Abbey House and the vineyard none of them would have a home. But strangely enough, now she thought about it, far from being an extra burden to bear, their presence seemed to lighten her load. They were in it together. Strength in numbers, she thought resolutely. We'll survive. But before they started work she had to ask Joe something which had been puzzling her since the previous night.

'What on earth were you doing here in the middle of the night? I vaguely remember you picking me up, but not much after that.'

'It was midnight by the time I got here. By then the 'phones were out, all the cables were down. As I couldn't 'phone, I came up to see if Sheridan needed a hand battening down the hatches.'

'We'd already got all the deer into the old stables for the night,' explained April. 'They'd been behaving so strangely all afternoon, almost as if they had some premonition of the weather. So with the help of Albert Carter, we rounded them up and shut them away for the night.'

'You shouldn't have let Joe come up. It was dangerous,' said Diana.

April pulled a face and smiled. 'Since when have I had any say in what Joe does! But I must admit I did heave a sigh of relief when he eventually got back.'

Once word got around the village that the people from Abbey House were out in the vineyards, crawling along on their hands and knees, literally picking up the single grapes by hand, in order to salvage some sort of harvest, they came. The Reverend and Mrs Pincher, Mrs Graystock and some of her more able-bodied ladies, the teenagers who should have been at school but who couldn't get there because of blocked roads into Chichester. Everyone who could come, came.

The morning passed quickly, and to her surprise Diana actually found herself beginning to feel quite cheerful, as long as she didn't think about Seamus. She stopped for a moment, straightening her aching back, rubbing her wet and frozen knees, and listened. The wind-battered slope of the vineyard was humming with voices, punctuated every now and then with bursts of laughter. Even Mrs Graystock seemed to be enjoying herself. Diana could hear her great booming laugh echoing down in the bottom vineyard, followed by what sounded like a string of instructions. The Women's Institute ladies were being drilled into a crack platoon of workers. Their baskets were filling more quickly than anyone else's.

Lunch was a boisterous affair, enjoyed by everyone. They came tramping in, stiff and damp, fingers red raw from scrabbling amongst the fallen leaves for grapes. Millicent had made pans and pans of pasta and they fell upon it like ravening wolves.

'Very cheap,' Millicent whispered to Diana, seeing her apprehensive glance at all the pots. 'Pasta, borlotti beans, garlic and bacon; very filling and costs next to nothing. And mushroom risotto. What about a little wine to go with it?'

'No,' said Diana, thinking of the cost.

'Just one glass each?'

'No.'

'Just to show how grateful you are.'

Put like that it made Diana feel mean, so she relented. Bottles were opened and it was a very jolly party that spilled out of the kitchen into the cold, wet afternoon to finish off the harvesting. But finish it they did, and by that Friday evening the pressing was under way.

The electricity supply had still not been restored, and from reports on the radio it seemed likely that they'd have to wait at least another twenty-four hours before it was. With Joe's help, Sheridan had lugged an old generator from the barn. Diana had been threatening to consign it to the scrap heap all summer, but Sheridan had resisted, saying that it might come in useful. Now, watching Joe and Sheridan tinkering with it, Diana was glad she hadn't dumped it. She was beginning to realize why farmers never threw anything away. Cannibalization from spare bits and pieces kept many a piece of ancient machinery going. The generator was going to be a lifesaver. Once it was working, Joe volunteered to pick up the children from Willow Farm, and Sheridan started work. Now, the winery came alive, quite literally humming with activity as the stainless steel presses got to work. Diana and April stayed to watch for a while.

April sniffed appreciatievly. 'It certainly smells alcoholic in here. What happens next?'

'This is all Sheridan's province at the moment. I've read up on it, but I've never done it, so I'm leaving it to him.'

'But you know,' April pressed. 'Tell me.'

'Well, to put it simply, Sheridan knew before beginning to press the grapes what the sugar and acidity levels were, and therefore he knows the correct amount of sugar and calcium carbonate to add. This must be done before pressing. Once pressed, the juice is called "must" and should not be exposed to the air otherwise there could be oxidation problems, hence all these tubes.' Diana waved at the miles of stainless steel.

'Sounds complicated,' said April.

'It is.' Diana looked at her watch. 'I wonder how long Joe will be before he gets back with the children?' Now was the perfect time to find out from April what was going on between her and Joe. She cleared her throat, and tried to think of an appropriate question to kick off with. It was awkward, but she had promised Tony.

'Another half an hour at least,' said April. 'May is sure to want a blow-by-blow account of what went on here today.'

'Yes.' Diana decided to take the bull by the horns. 'April I need to ask you something.'

'Yes?'

'Are you and Joe getting married?' The moment the words were out she regretted them. It sounded such a bald question. 'Look, I might as well be honest, April. Tony asked me to find out. He seemed to think that you were leaving Mottisley, and was surprised because you hadn't gone.'

'Oh dear.' April sighed and looked shamefaced. 'I knew I should have got in touch with him.'

'Well?' demanded Diana, encouraged by April's reply. 'What is going on? Are you going to marry?'

April laughed slightly ruefully. 'I wouldn't go so far as to say that. Joe hasn't popped the question, and shows no sign of doing so in the foreseeable future, but we have come to an agreement.'

'An agreement?' Diana raised her eyebrows.

'Yes. I'm his housekeeper and bedwarmer. The arrangement is convenient and suits us both, so I decided to stay.'

'I see.'

'You sound disapproving.'

'Of course I'm not. I was thinking,' Diana hesitated, surely April must know how much Tony loved her, and that he would marry her tomorrow if given the opportunity. And surely April must know that life with Tony would be better than any 'agreement' with Joe. She nearly said so, but stopped herself just in time. It wasn't her place to say. That was something only Tony had the right to say, and he ought to, he really ought to be bold and declare his love unequivocally once and for all. 'I

443

was thinking what an eminently sensible arrangement,' she continued rather stiltedly, knowing she had to say something and unable to think of anything better. 'You're both happy, and yet your lives are not cluttered up with unnecessary emotion.'

'Bloody hell, Diana, put like that it makes us both sound absolutely sterile, like a couple of emotional robots.'

'I didn't mean it that way. It just surprises me.' Both Joe and April were fiery people, surely they couldn't really be content with such a humdrum business arrangement?

The sound of Joe's car crunching in the gravel outside the winery, and the voices of excited children abruptly terminated the conversation. 'I'll ring Tony tomorrow,' promised April. 'I know I owe him an explanation. He was very kind to me, letting me cry on his shoulder whenever I needed sympathy.'

'Tony is a kind man.'

'Yes, maybe you should marry him.'

'I've still got a husband. But if and when I'm free, that is the way I intend to stay.'

Diana suddenly felt bad-tempered. Speaking of husbands reminded her that Hugh hadn't been back to collect his clothes. She felt trapped. She wasn't really free, she *was* still married, and would remain so until they divorced. For one brief moment she considered going to a solicitor, then dismissed the idea as impracticable. Solicitors cost money, and that was something she didn't have. Unless Hugh paid the costs, which was highly unlikely, she'd have to stay married for the time being.

Detective Constable Terry Watkins was ambitious. He was also bored. Looking into Hugh Stratton's financial background, as Sergeant Brown had instructed, was proving to be easier said than done. Hugh Stratton was a respected barrister, even if his mistress did know small-time criminals like Nico Guanello. Terry couldn't help wondering if his solid and respectable sergeant had suffered a momentary hallucination. Had Guanello really been at Nancy Morris's house? He could find no scandal attached to Hugh Stratton; leaving his wife was no big deal, everyone did that nowadays.

He'd gone back to the Chambers in The Temple one morning, and hung around chatting, but everyone was very tightlipped, and the old secretary, Miss Higgins, was so nervous one would think he'd come along to arrest her not just to talk! But he prided himself on his astute assessment of character, and where Miss Higgins was concerned he had a suspicion that she did know something but was afraid to tell him. That little youngster who'd been in the office the first day he'd come, now she wouldn't be afraid. He asked where she was.

'Oh, you mean Debbie, the post girl,' said Miss Higgins, moving a pile of buff coloured files tied in pink ribbons from one tray to another, and then back again. Thank goodness Debbie had already brought the post in and disappeared. 'She's on holiday today.'

The words came out in a rush, as if she had just made them up, thought Constable Watkins. Which indeed Miss Higgins had. She dare not let him talk to Debbie, she would tell all. And not only all. She would almost certainly give the police the benefit of her theories, which Miss Higgins had just managed to convince herself could not possibly be true. It was beyond credence that Mr Stratton could be mixed up in drugs and guns. After all he was a barrister, an upholder of the law of the land. There must be some other, quite logical, explanation.

'Back tomorrow?' Terry Watkins persisted.

'No, another day off, I think. I'll ask her to ring you as soon as she's back. Now if you will excuse me, I *am* very busy.' She moved the files again, this time nervously distributing them between the three baskets on her desk, In, Out and Pending.

'Strange filing system you've got.' Terry Watkins

445

looked pointedly at the pink ribboned files before leaving the office.

The first person Debbie saw that morning, when she was sent out at ten-thirty to get the office doughnuts from the sandwich bar on Ludgate Hill, was DC Watkins waiting in the courtyard outside the office.

'Can I buy you a coffee?' he asked, falling into step beside her.

'Well, I shouldn't really.' Debbie was flattered. 'But all right. Only ten minutes though, that's all I can spare. They'll have my guts for garters if I'm too late back.'

'Ten minutes should be enough.'

And it was. With a cup of coffee in front of her, and Terry Watkins's undivided attention, making copious notes as she spoke, Debbie told all. Right from the beginning when Miss Higgins started getting worried about the safe.

Terry Watkins put his notebook away. 'You've been most helpful Debbie, which is more than I can say for that old secretary who works for Mr Stratton.'

Debbie stood up. 'Must fly now, they'll all be waiting for their doughnuts.' Then she was off along Fleet Street as fast as her high heels would allow.

Terry, pleased with his morning's work had reported back to Sergeant Brown. That had been two weeks ago. Now, after the momentary excitement of the gale chaos in London, Terry was bored again. Sergeant Brown had digested the information given him, and then let him be seconded to another detective looking into car thefts from the garages beneath a block of council flats. Depressing, unrewarding work. He wondered what, if anything, Sergeant Brown was doing about Hugh Stratton.

The Tuesday morning after the hurricane of the previous week Diana was alone in Abbey House, except for Miffy who was asleep upstairs. He'd had another bad night of wheezing and coughing. Sheridan was in the winery working, and Millicent and Griselda, having finished the

446

housework, had answered a summons from Mrs Pincher and gone off to the vicarage to help with the sewing of costumes for the concert. The third weekend in October, the weekend of the concert, was rapidly approaching, and Mrs Pincher was panicking about the arrangements. Clemmy and Simon were, very reluctantly, back at school, all the blocked lanes and roads having now been cleared of debris from the storm; they'd been hoping for at least another three days off.

From the kitchen window Diana watched the antics of two young cock blackbirds; they were squabbling about the borderlands of their winter quarters, with much fluttering and aggressive scurrying from bush to bush. In spite of the devastation of the rolling downland, the countryside looked cheerful today. It was mild, and there was a sparkle of sunshine, causing red admiral and tortoiseshell butterflies to venture out. They fluttered across the bronzed carpet of leaves in the vineyard, seeking out the now rotting and fermenting grapes lying on the ground. In the distance, oaks and elms still left standing, were splashed with bronze and pale gold, and in the hedgerows the hawthorn berries glinted ruby red.

As she watched, she saw the small figure of a man making his way up the slope towards Abbey House. Slowly it grew into the tall, unique figure of Joe, and at his side she could see the rotund figure of Sam, the labrador, trundling along. The sight of Sam brought back the loss of Seamus. It still seemed strange to be at the window without his warm head pressed against her thigh. Shakespeare the cat, was still with them and was in the kitchen, but he was a cat, and did as he pleased, only coming to humans when it suited him. Seamus had been her shadow.

Moving across to the Aga she put the kettle on to boil, and got out the jar of coffee beans. Of course she'd known it was Joe from the moment the indistinct speck had appeared at the bottom of the vineyard. There was something singular about the way he moved; he'd never lost the graceful, boyish lope of youth.

The kitchen door opened and Joe and Sam entered. 'Wonderful smell, ground coffee,' said Joe, kicking off his wellingtons and slumping down on the lumpy sofa beneath the window.

'And ground by hand,' said Diana still working at the wooden handle of the ancient grinder. 'I'll be glad when we're reconnected to electricity. I never realized before how many pants and socks those children get through.' She got out a tin of Millicent's flapjacks and set it on the table. 'I might not be able to cook, but I make a mean cup of coffee and always know where to lay my hands on the best biscuits in Sussex.'

'Yes,' Joe sounded gloomy and seemed preoccupied.

Diana glanced at him. Was there some problem between him and April? She hoped not. They'd become good friends lately. It was as if the wall between them had slowly been dismantled, brick by brick, until the undeniable truth was that at last they were friends. Not the kind of friendship that could lead to their ever becoming lovers, but true friends, and more comfortable for being just that. It had begun to blossom since the end of September when he'd offered her the loan which she'd refused. A foolish move she was now beginning to realize, and wondered if she should swallow her pride and tell him she'd changed her mind and would like the loan.

She poured out a coffee and pushed it towards the edge of the table. 'It's ready.'

'I'm not sure coffee is appropriate. Haven't got any cyanide have you? I've read somewhere that ending it all that way is very quick.'

'What the hell are you talking about?' Looking at him properly for the first time since he'd come in, Diana suddenly realized that he looked ill. His face was grey, his lips almost bloodless. Her first thought was a heart attack. What did one do? Oh God, I have no idea, I know nothing about first aid. Tony would know. 'I'll ring Tony,' she said.

'What the hell for? There's nothing *he* can do.'

Diana noted with relief that he sounded irritable. Too irritable to be ill. 'But, then . . . what?' She spread her hands wide in question.

'I'm not ill, damn you,' Joe shouted, and was immediately sorry. 'I'm sorry. I shouldn't have shouted. I shouldn't even have come. You've got enough troubles of your own, without needing to listen to mine.'

In fact when he'd left the manor to walk that morning, it was not his intention to come to Abbey House. But while walking, thinking, trying to formulate a plan to salvage something from the wreckage, he had found himself at Abbey House.

'Joe, please. I hate playing guessing games. What *is* wrong?'

'You've not been listening to the radio.' It was a statement rather than a question. 'And you don't take any papers.' Diana shook her head. 'So you don't know.'

'Know what for God's sake?'

'Yesterday,' said Joe slowly, as if he still could not believe it himself, 'Fifty billion pounds was wiped off the value of publicly quoted companies in a Stock Market crash. Not only have most of my investment shares evaporated, but Shamrock Enterprises is virtually worthless. You are looking at an ex-millionnaire.'

Chapter Thirty-five

Gulping back a mouthful of coffee, and scalding her throat in the process, Diana sat down abruptly. She shivered, the uncomfortable feeling that someone or something beyond all of their control was pulling the strings, manipulating their lives, returned in full force. And absurd though she knew it was, she still felt as she had on the night of the hurricane, that somehow it was her fault.

'I told you I was a disaster, Joe. It seems I'm everyone's bad luck charm. You should keep away from me.' She leant her head on her arms. So now Joe had no money either. That scuppered any chance of taking up the loan she'd once refused. Then guilt swamped her for even thinking about it. 'I'm sorry,' she said, as much to herself as to Joe.

'Don't be so bloody stupid, or conceited,' snapped Joe. 'What is the matter with you? It has nothing to do with you, it's a world-wide crash. The Dow Jones went down by 22.5 per cent, there was heavy selling in Tokyo and the Hong Kong market is closing for the rest of the week. It's a kind of financial meltdown.'

His snappiness jolted Diana out of her slough of despond, and back to reality. He was right. What *was* the matter with her? No-one was pulling her strings except the bank and the rising interest rates. 'I suppose it's being blamed on the US budget and trade deficits,' she said. Although it had little relevance now to her life in Mottisley, force of habit kept her more or less up to date with the world of high powered commerce and politics.

'*And* interest rates, *and* computer-controlled "program trading",' said Joe gloomily. 'Not that it matters what caused it. I'm ruined.'

'Will you lose the house?' He'd never actually said so, but Diana had always suspected that the manor house meant more than just a big country house to Joe. It embodied the tangible proof of his transformation from pauper to prince.

'It's not mortgaged to my company, if that's what you mean. But I'll not be able to continue living there in the style to which I've become accustomed. But that doesn't particularly worry me, it's only a house, that's all. Bricks and mortar.' Diana thought he didn't sound very convincing, but said nothing. Joe was silent, then said, 'April may not be so keen to stay now.'

'Joe Kelly, how dare you say that! April will never leave you just because you've run out of money.' Pity gone, Diana leapt up and standing in front of him, faced him angrily. Men! They made her sick. Always thinking women were as obvious as they were themselves, never able to see beyond the words. Not for one moment did the irony strike her. All her life she'd acted and thought like a man, pushing the feminine side of her character into the background; only now was that facet reasserting itself. 'You don't deserve a woman like her. Come to that, you don't deserve a woman at all.'

Her passion startled Joe. How much she'd changed these past few weeks. Gone was the cool, calm, calculating Diana. In her place was an entirely different woman; unpredictable of mood, animated, and altogether a much more human being. Suddenly he roared with laughter, and leaping to his feet put his hands on her shoulders. 'Well said, Diana Stratton. I like a woman who stands up for her friends.'

Suddenly the world seemed a lighter place. His change of mood was infectious. When Joe laughed, it was hard not to be touched by a warm glow. Anger evaporating, Diana found herself laughing with him.

'Nice to know my wife isn't missing me.' Hugh's sarcastic voice cut across the laughter. He was carrying two suitcases and walked past them towards the door

451

leading to the stairs. 'I've come to collect the rest of my things.'

'I persuaded him. You don't mind do you?' Nancy entered the kitchen. Her black and red flared jacket, and tight black skirt stood out razor sharp against the untidy mellow comfort of Abbey House. She lit a cigarette without asking, and inhaled slowly. 'Hugh had no court cases today, it seemed an excellent opportunity.'

'Why have you come as well?' asked Joe.

'I came with Hugh.' Nancy walked slowly across to a silent Diana. 'He is living with me now. Although perhaps you already knew that.'

'I know now,' said Diana. Suddenly everything began to click into place. Hugh's extra workload, working late, unexplained absences from the Chelsea apartment. All those events had happened after he'd met Nancy again. He must have been seeing her all that time. 'And it's not a recent phenemenon is it?'

'No,' Nancy smiled slowly. 'I always wondered how long it would take the brilliant Diana to find out that her perfect husband was less than perfect.'

'Too long, evidently.'

Nancy laughed. 'For a clever woman you are remarkably gullible.'

'Look here . . .' Joe made to move towards Nancy, but Diana put out a hand and stopped him.

She smiled. Joe reminded her of his own dog, Sam. Whenever the children squabbled in Sam's presence, he always lumbered towards them, wanting to do something but never quite sure exactly what.

'It doesn't matter, Joe,' she said softly. She turned back to Nancy. 'You're right. I was gullible. But now I *do* know, I realize that I've had a lucky escape.'

Hugh returned, suitcases bulging. He had obviously just bundled his belongings inside. 'Escape from what?'

'From you.' She turned towards Hugh. 'I married you for all the wrong reasons. Style, glamour, those qualities wrongly attracted me, but more than that I made the mistake of thinking you were like my father. He was always so proud of me, and I thought you were too. I *wanted* to please him, and in a strange way, I felt the same about you. But I was wrong again. You're not a bit like my father. He may not have been perfect, but he never deceived anyone.'

'How wrong you are, Diana.' Nancy's voice, maliciously triumphant, slithered into the silent kitchen. 'Hugh is *very* like your father. Deceivers both of them I'm afraid. Neither were able to resist my bodily charms. It seems I have a special fascination for men belonging to the Leigh women.'

'What the bloody hell do you mean?' Joe's voice was rough.

'I should have thought it was quite clear.'

'But you were only a child.' Diana's voice faltered, she wanted to shy away from the obvious, but long-submerged memories fought their way to the surface. Rows, tension, and most of all the sudden, precipitous disappearance of Nancy from Mottisley, and the subsequent tightlipped silence of her parents. All these years she'd shut her mind to the months which had followed Nancy's disappearance, but now those days resurfaced with a raw clarity, and she remembered the terrible atmosphere which had permeated the house in those distant days. Diana found herself wondering if Susan had also shut out that memory; certainly, they'd never discussed it.

'A child yes, but very advanced for my years.' Nancy's scarlet lips parted as she laughed, revealing her small white teeth. 'Poor Uncle Geoff. He never stood a chance. He was quite a good fuck though.' A swirl of the red and black cloak and she was gone.

Diana sat down heavily. Nancy's parting laugh seemed to reverberate round and round the kitchen, filling her head and tearing at the very fabric of her existence. Her father and Nancy. She no longer wondered, shied away, or even tried to deny the truth. Nancy had verified what she now realized she had known all the time. Not at the

453

time, of course, then such things had been beyond her childish comprehension. But later she had guessed, just as she now realized Susan must have done. But whereas Susan's attitude to her father had been a realistic mixture of cynicism, sadness and affection, she, Diana, had resolutely put the knowledge away, not wanting to tarnish the man she held most dear. For a second it seemed the hurricane of the previous week had returned, she could hear the yew tree creaking and groaning, and the great screaming sigh as it fell. It seemed, in her imagination, that it had put the final nail in her father's coffin.

'She's probably making it up. She's bitch enough,' said Joe unconvincingly.

'No,' said Diana sadly, 'she's not.'

'You can't blame him, though. Knowing Nancy she probably seduced him.'

'He was an adult. She was a child. He knew it was wrong.' Diana's voice hardened, suddenly she felt angry, unforgiving. Her father had betrayed her trust. 'I thought he was something special. But I was wrong.'

'He was a *man*, for God's sake. With all the frailties of a man. And Nancy was fourteen, a woman, with all the powers of a woman.'

'Wonderful, all the evils of this world can be laid at the feet of women. Men don't seduce, but women do. Men don't indulge in under age sex willingly, a fourteen-year-old girl begs him to. So you are trying to tell me that makes it all right.'

'Don't put words in my mouth. And for God's sake don't be so bloody hypocritical. You put your father on a pedestal, and obstinately refused to see that he was just an ordinary man. And do you know why?'

'No, but I expect you're going to tell me.' Diana was angry with Joe now.

'Because you needed an excuse to do what you wanted. You needed to pretend that everything you did in your life was not for yourself, but for darling daddy. Diana didn't ride roughshod over other people, or discard those she'd grown tired of for herself. Oh dear no, her motives were much too noble. She did it because she couldn't bear to disappoint daddy, and, of course, that made everything all right, so she just went on doing it.' Joe stopped abruptly.

'Shut up.'

'I've finished.'

'Thank God for that. If there's one thing I can't bear it's homespun philosophy.'

But of course Diana knew he was right. Too bloody right, damn him! But it hadn't started off that way. When she was very young the adoration had been real, but little by little as her own ruthlessness and ambition grew, she *had* needed excuses. An excuse for the money spent on *her* education rather than on Susan's who had needed it more. True she'd loved Susan and felt sorry for her, but that had never stopped her grabbing every opportunity that came along, even if it had to be at Susan's expense. She'd always told herself that she needed to do well. That she needed to please her father. And then when she was pregnant, and had wanted an abortion, she'd even persuaded herself that her parents, particularly her father, had wanted the abortion more than she. A lie. She had never intended to have the baby. Just as she had never intended to live at Mottisley. She'd always want more, much more. And now, the wheel had turned full circle, and here she was living in Mottisley, with three children to care for, no money to speak of, and Joe, the father of that discarded foetus, sitting at the kitchen table beside her. While her father, the man she'd pushed high on to an imaginary pedestal and stubbornly kept there, had just toppled off. Crashing down like the mighty yew in the storm.

'I'd better go,' said Joe.

'You needn't. I've got over it now, the worst of it anyway. Surprising what a few moments of retrospection will do.' She looked at Joe. 'You were right, of course, damn you.'

'I'm sure it wasn't all his fault.'

'I suppose not. I wonder what my mother thought.' For the first time in her life Diana found herself thinking of her mother with a degree of sympathy. Nancy's revelation explained a lot of things. They popped up in her mind, little frozen cameos of family episodes; incomprehensible until now.

'I don't suppose it made her very happy.'

'An understatement I should think.' Diana smiled wryly. 'I wonder how many other skeletons there are in the family cupboard?'

'Why didn't you tell me Joe was here?' Miffy made one of his regular appearances in the doorway in his dressing gown, clutching the perennial bottle of cough mixture. Holding the bottle up he took a large gulp.

Leaping up, Joe went across and picking him up hugged him. 'That rotten woman, Diana, didn't tell me you were here either. What's in that bottle, whisky?'

Miffy looked doubtfully at the cough mixture. 'I don't think so.'

'How many times have I told you, Miffy, that you are supposed to take it by the spoonful, not drink it from the bottle.' Diana took the bottle away. It was ridiculous, she knew, to feel such an inexplicable surge of jealousy. But she couldn't help it. There was something about the way Joe and Miffy treated one another, an ease, which she didn't have. But, of course, Joe had known Miffy much longer and much more intimately than she. All those years when she'd never bothered to make more than a fleeting visit down to Mottisley, Joe had been there. Miffy had grown up knowing and loving him. Joe had been part of Susan's family, even when Tom had still been alive. She could hear Susan saying now, *'when I need a shoulder to cry on, I go to Joe Kelly. He always makes me laugh.'* Yes, Joe had been around a long time. Before Miffy was born. It was foolish to be jealous.

*   *   *

'Get everything?' Nancy settled in the car comfortably, re-arranging the woollen cloak to prevent it creasing.

'No, I couldn't find two pairs of my most expensive shoes.' Hugh felt bad tempered. Inevitable though he knew it was that Diana should find out about himself and Nancy, he had, nevertheless, harboured a vague hope that she would not, and that if things went disastrously wrong with Nancy, then Mottisley could still be his bolt hole. Before this morning he'd been sure that he would have been able to persuade Diana to have him back. Now, Nancy had changed all that. 'Was it true what you said about you and her father?'

'Of course, darling. When I was younger I liked older men. That's why I married Joseph.'

'You didn't have to tell her, though.'

'I did,' said Nancy sharply. 'I hate her. Too damned good to be true. I hated both those sisters, and the mother. But I've always had the last laugh. Then and now.'

The car reached the end of the curving drive past the rows of battered vines just as Millicent and Griselda cycled in from the lane.

Hugh stopped the car. 'I'll ask them where those shoes are. They must have put them somewhere.'

The reply did not please him. 'Miss Diana said to give them for the church bazaar,' said Millicent with ill-concealed glee.

'But,' spluttered Hugh, furious, 'they weren't hers to give.'

'She thought you weren't coming back. We all did. She couldn't afford to give anything else, so it seemed sensible to give the shoes. The Reverend Pincher was very pleased. They went on to the *nearly new* stall and raised ten pounds towards the stage lighting being fitted in the church hall.'

'So Diana couldn't afford anything else.' Nancy climbed out of the car. 'If she was hard up a few weeks ago, she must be in a worse state now. I imagine she lost all the harvest.'

'Not quite,' said Millicent. 'We salvaged some.'

'About two thousand bottles, so Sheridan says,' added Griselda.

'Two thousand bottles! Is that all?' Nancy laughed, not bothering to hide her smug satisfaction. 'My God! She'll have to sell up. There'll be no alternative, and then you two will be out of a job,' she added spitefully.

'Oh no we won't.' Furious, Millicent forgot about her promise of silence. 'May Marsham is going to make over part of her estate to Diana now, while she's still alive, and has promised money as well. So, you are wrong, Mrs Morris, Abbey Vineyard will be carrying on because Diana won't have to sell.'

'I see.' Nancy's voice was sharp. 'And has this miracle already come about?'

'Not yet. But it will any day now. As soon as May knows the full extent of the damage to the vineyard. Come on, Griselda.' Remounting her bicycle, she pedalled furiously away up the drive.

Griselda followed her. Millicent had told the truth, but was it wise letting Nancy and Hugh know before it was a *fait accompli*? Puffing, she caught up with Millicent. 'You shouldn't have said that. You promised you'd keep it a secret.'

'I know. But I couldn't stand that sneer of hers any longer.'

'Well,' Griselda tried to dispel her unease. 'I suppose it doesn't matter. There is nothing Nancy can do about it. But you'd better not say anything to Diana. It's only fair that May tells her what she is planning herself. After all, it is her money.'

'You know you can trust me,' said Millicent. 'I shall not say anything.'

Griselda was cross. 'That's just it, I can't trust you. Haven't you just blabbed it out to Nancy?'

Millicent didn't answer, merely pedalled faster and left Griselda behind.

* * *

Nancy pushed the button and wound up the electric window. 'Maybe we should pop in and see May before we leave Mottisley.'

'Why?' said Hugh.

He was thinking. Perhaps he shouldn't have been in such a rush to leave Diana. Now it seemed she was not going to be so poor as he thought it put a different complexion on everything. It would be nice to be independent of Nico, and not have to be a pusher to get what he needed. The requests for drops were becoming more and more frequent, and Hugh's fear grew with every packet he delivered. A fact he took care to hide from Nancy who thrived on the element of danger involved.

'Why?' Nancy's impatient voice dragged him back to the present. 'Because I want to find out just what the silly old woman has been up to, if anything. Turn left here, towards Willow Farm.'

Hugh obediently turned. 'You can't do anything. She can do what she likes with her own possessions.'

'I know that, darling. But if she hasn't already done anything, then . . .' She tapped her front teeth thoughtfully. The long red nails flashing in the weak October sunlight.

'Then what?'

'Then we'll see, darling. We'll see.'

Chapter Thirty-six

'Well, what are you going to do now you do know?' asked Tony.

Diana put the folded paper in the pocket of her jeans; on it was the address of Hugh's parents. 'I'll write to them tonight.'

'And say what?'

Diana thought of the weeping woman with the dark, vacant eyes, and her husband, trying to comfort her. But most of all she remembered their worry over money, and knew she had to do something. She was young, strong, and capable, and surrounded by supportive friends, yet was still worrying herself sick over lack of funds; so what must it be like to be old, helpless and alone, as well as being poor? 'I shall tell them not to worry,' she said, 'and say that they can come and live here. It's the least I can do.'

'Two extra mouths to feed,' warned Tony.

Diana shrugged. 'I doubt that they'll eat much, and we've plenty of spare rooms. Goodness knows Abbey House is large enough. In fact I was thinking that next summer I could take in paying guests to help with the finances.'

'And end up giving yourself a mental and physical breakdown,' grumbled Tony.

'Rubbish, of course I won't have a breakdown,' said Diana. 'I don't work all that hard. I've got Millicent and Griselda who are marvellous, and now they pay me! Ridiculous isn't it? I feel guilty about it, but I take their money. And as far as Hugh's parents are concerned, they may, of course, say no.' She pulled a sweater over her head, and got ready to go out. 'Now, if you've come to see Miffy, you're out of luck. I let Joe take him back to the manor for the rest of the day. He's dropping him back this evening.'

'How is his chest?'

'Much better. I wouldn't have let him go out otherwise.'

'And how's April?'

Diana paused. She had completely forgotten that she'd promised to tell Tony whatever she managed to find out, and regretted that promise now. How on earth could she explain the strange arrangement at the manor house? But better do it now, and get it over with.

Finishing at last, she heaved a sigh of relief. 'Well, that's it. All I can say is that they do seem to be happy.'

'Slightly bizarre, don't you think?' Tony was not happy.

'Bizarre or not, Tony, that's the way it is, and you'd better accept it. And there's another thing to remember. Now Joe has lost a fortune in the stock market crash, April is bound to stand by him. Out of loyalty, if nothing else.'

'Yes, she'll be loyal.' Tony agreed. He went towards the door. 'How badly has Joe been hit?'

'He says he's an ex-millionaire. In fact, seems pretty depressed about the whole thing.'

'A lot of people are,' said Tony. 'The papers are talking about suicides in the City. Wycombe and Yatton shares held up though.'

'Shit!' said Diana inelegantly. 'Nasty of me, I know, but I wouldn't have minded them disappearing down a black hole.'

'They say the Devil looks after his own,' said Tony.

Diana followed Tony to the door. 'Leave it open, I'm coming out. Sheridan and I are going walkabout to do our sums. See how many vines we shall need to replace.'

Tony looked down the rolling vineyards, golden now with calm autumn sunlight. 'Replace? They all look intact to me. A little battered, but intact.'

'Intact and burnt. Sheridan tells me that many have been so badly damaged by the sea salt blown inland by

461

the storm that we'd best replace them. Thank God we've got a good nursery of strong young vines. At least we'll be able to replace them without my having to go and visit that bloody bank manager again.'

Tony climbing into his car, managed a wan smile. 'I have a feeling you don't care for Mr Mortimer.'

'Your feeling is entirely correct. By the way, shall we be seeing you tomorrow night at the harvest supper?'

'No, I didn't help you with the harvest, and I'm not sure I want to see April.'

'You've got to come. You're invited, and anyway, as you and April will probably be living in the same village for years to come, you might as well get used to bumping into her in a friendly fashion. A party is just the place to start practising.'

Millicent was in her element, and went to town with the food for the harvest supper. Catering for a crowd always brought out her best culinary instincts.

'All very cheap, I hardly spent a thing,' she said hastily, seeing Diana's slightly glazed expression when she saw the enormous spread.

Plate after plate, all ablaze with radish roses and tomato waterlilies nestling between sprigs of parsley and watercress, covered the scrubbed kitchen table top and worksurfaces of the cupboards.

'Absolutely true,' Griselda was quick to corroborate, and took Diana on a tour. 'See, spinach and cheese pie, *our* spinach and cheese, paprika cream cheese in nasturtium leaves, *our* cheese, our nasturtiums, *our* vine leaves for the vine leaf parcels, home-made garlic bread, fruit pies and . . .'

'I believe you, I believe you,' said Diana putting her hands over her ears to stop Griselda reeling off the list of food. 'But don't tell me those are free!' She pointed to a mountain of baked sausages and chicken legs.'

'All free, quite free,' said Griselda triumphantly. 'Mr Shepherd, the butcher donated them to Abbey House for '*being so plucky*', he said. Besides, he did very well this summer with his home-made sausages. Apparently most of the visitors to the vineyard stopped in the village and bought some. I've invited him to the party.'

'He's a widower,' said Millicent out of the side of her mouth. 'Griselda has designs on his sausages!'

Cyclamen pink to the roots of her wild grey hair, Griselda glared at Millicent, then turned to Diana. 'I hope it's all right if he comes.'

'What can I say?' said Diana, smiling at the pink Griselda, 'apart from I hope he enjoys himself.'

Everyone came and everyone enjoyed themselves. Bugger Mr Mortimer and the bank loan, thought Diana, helping Sheridan carry in yet another crate of wine. We'll eat, drink and be merry. Tomorrow is another day.

The wine loosened tongues, and new friendships were formed. 'Of course, I always knew that Nancy was a nymphomaniac,' Mrs Graystock said to Joe, after he had told her, in confidence of course, that Hugh had left Diana for Nancy. 'Quite shocking it was, the affair with poor Diana's father. Naturally, it was all hushed up, but everyone knew.'

'I never heard anything about it.'

'Of course not, you were too young. And anyway, you're not a member of the Women's Institute.'

'What has that got to do with it?'

'We don't just discuss jam and knitting patterns, young man.' Mrs Graystock poured herself another generous glass of wine. 'I must say this is delicious. I've never tasted it before. I shall buy two bottles before I go home.'

'I always knew there was more to country life than meets the eye,' said April wryly.

'You ought to write a book about us.' The wine was beginning to go to Mrs Graystock's head. 'Plenty of sex and scandal if you know where to look, my dear.'

Mr Shepherd, the butcher, buttonholed Diana about a space in the vineyard shop. Remembering Millicent's comment earlier in the evening, Diana found it difficult to concentrate at first. Did Griselda really fancy this elderly man with grey hair sprouting from his ear lobes? But Mr Shepherd was very serious, and it was soon clear that frozen meat was on his mind, to the exclusion of everything else including Griselda. 'I'd pay you a fair rent and put in a little deep freeze. Then people could buy my sausages and local pork and lamb straight from the freezer. That way I'd have access to all your visitors. We local traders should stick together, don't you think?'

'Oh, absolutely. It's a good idea.' Diana began to feel that at last she really belonged. Mottisley and the butcher had accepted her.

Joe brought May but after a short while she said it was too noisy and wanted to go. Tony ill at ease and acutely aware of April on the other side of the room was glad of an excuse to escape, and offered to take her home in his car.

'Coward,' Diana whispered while May was getting her coat. 'You haven't said one word to April.'

'If I had, it would probably have been the wrong word,' said Tony crossly. 'Anyway she's been avoiding me.'

Joe had brought a case of champagne to the party and April made herself a champagne cocktail, lacing it with enough brandy to launch a rocket. By the time the party finished, Joe practically had to carry her out to his Land-Rover.

'Absolutely terrific party,' April kissed Diana.

'She's pissed,' said Joe.

'She's not the only one. In fact, I think I'm the only one who's sober,' said Diana. 'I dread to think what might have happened if I had let the kids stay up any longer.'

'Who is going to clear up that lot?' Joe glanced back through the open door. The kitchen looked as if a bomb had just dropped.

Diana slammed the Land-Rover door shut on April's side. 'I'll make a start on it myself tonight, and hope Millicent and Griselda surface in time to finish it before lunch time tomorrow.' Waving them off she turned back into the chaos of the kitchen.

The old house seemed abnormally quiet after so much noise. But it was a comfortable quietness and Diana felt at ease. Working systematically she washed her way through the glasses, and then started on the dishes; gradually some sort of order was restored as stacks of gleaming china and glass replaced the mess. She'd just finished tying the rubbish bags, and was about to start on another sink full of plates when she heard the gravel crunch under the tyre wheels of a car. The wooden clock on the wall told her it was two o' clock in the morning. She panicked, there must be something wrong. No-one would come calling otherwise. Rushing to the door she flung it open and practically catapulted into Joe.

'I've put April to bed, she's out for the count, and now I've come to help,' he said, picking up a tea towel. 'Well, don't just stand there.' Diana was regarding him with open-mouthed amazement. 'Get on with it. And don't try telling me Griselda and Millicent will do it in the morning. I saw those two staggering up the stairs. You'll be lucky if they regain consciousness before midday.'

'I've never thought of you as domesticated.'

'I'm surprised you've thought of me at all.'

Diana was silent. Little did he know that until recently whenever she had thought of him it was always connected with the nightmare of the abortion. Joe seemed disinclined to talk, so they continued the task in silence. Diana washing, Joe drying, until at last every single plate, and a mountain of cutlery, lay clean and gleaming under the lights of the kitchen.

'It's done, thank God.' Throwing off her rubber gloves, Diana let the water run out of the ancient stone sink and stood holding the edge. Her back was stiff and she felt almost too tired to stand. Hunching her shoulders she rolled her head from side to side to release the tension.

'Here, let me.' Joe came behind her, and placing his strong hands on her shoulders began to massage.

'Utter bliss,' said Diana, and leaned back against him.

How it happened neither of them was quite sure. But suddenly she was in his arms, Joe was stroking her hair, and then his mouth sought and found hers. The years slipped away into the darkness, leaving them with each other, and the sweet tangled web of desire. Diana wondered how they got to her bed, she supposed they walked together, but couldn't remember it. The only reality was a timeless happiness. They were made for each other, their bodies moved in tender harmony, a symphonic poem of love. Nothing carnal, lustful or savage, just a gentle, tender fulfilment, the feeling of coming home after such a long, long time. They clung to each other, afraid to let go, and Diana felt a wetness on Joe's cheeks, his tears mingling with her own.

'I love you,' said Joe softly. 'I know now that I've never stopped.'

'And I love you.' Diana whispered, afraid to break the spell, hardly able to believe that this man who held her in his arms was Joe. What had happened between them was quite different from how it had been in their youth. This lovemaking had been very different from anything she had ever experienced before, and from the expression on Joe's face she knew it had been the same for him.

'Nothing matters now,' said Joe. 'Not the past, not anything. Not now that we've found each other again. Say that you'll never leave me.'

'I don't want to, but there's April.'

'I'll explain. She'll understand, I know she will.' Joe was confident. 'She knows that I've always been seeking an elusive something, a shadowy concept without a name. But it has a name now. It is Diana.'

Fitting herself more closely into the curve of his body, Diana sighed contentedly. 'Strange,' she said dreamily, 'it's only now that I realize just how unreal everything was which I called life before. My marriage to Hugh was a hollow thing.'

'So were mine,' said Joe. 'Both of them. Can you forgive me for those? And for all the other women?'

'Of course. As you said, nothing matters now. We'll start our lives together from scratch. Forget the past.'

Diana knew that now was the perfect time to confess about the abortion. Joe could give her the absolution she needed, and she'd gain the peace of mind she longed for. But her courage failed her and she remained silent.

Joe left her warm bed and dressed. 'I'd like to stay with you now, and never leave,' he said, 'but I must return to April. Make my peace with her and explain.'

'I understand.' Reluctant to part, Diana clung to him.

Gently Joe disentangled her arms. 'I'll talk to her as soon as she's awake. I'll be quite honest. I have to be. I'll tell her about us, all of it, right from the beginning.'

'I hope she will understand.

Diana worried, she was fond of April, unwilling to hurt her. Yet maybe this was meant to happen. Maybe this would open up the way for April and Tony. Perhaps they too could find out where their true happiness lay, as she and Joe had done.

She followed Joe downstairs. At the kitchen door they paused for one last, long, lingering kiss. 'I'll see you later tomorrow.' Then he smiled, 'I mean later today,' he corrected himself, kissing her gently once more. 'I'll speak to April as soon as I can, and after that we can plan for the future, if you don't mind a future with a poor man.'

'I love you. Rich or poor, it makes no difference.'

'Until later then.' Joe drove off. Diana floated back upstairs and falling into bed, spread herself out luxuriously in the hollow where Joe had been lying, sinking immediately into a deep and dreamless sleep.

Chapter Thirty-seven

'He's in London,' said Mrs Beckett, who with her daughter, came in to 'do' the manor house once a week every Saturday. 'Went rushing off in a terrible panic on Thursday morning. April's gone with him. Should be back sometime today. Do you want me to take a message?'

'No.' Diana started to put the 'phone down then picked it up hastily, 'thank you,' she added.

At Abbey House, Diana walked slowly from the hall into the kitchen. Those magical few hours with Joe were already assuming the substance of a shadow. She'd been so sure, so certain. So had he. Or had he? *'I love you,'* he'd said. *'I know now that I've never stopped loving you.'* Oh, Joe, where are you?

Clemmy bumped into her as she entered the kitchen. All three children were in a heightened state of excitement. 'Can we go now? Griselda has done us some sandwiches and we'll buy some Coke from Lomax's.'

'Go?' Diana dragged her wandering thoughts back to the present with difficulty. 'Go where?'

'To the church hall, of course. Millicent and Griselda are taking us.' Clemmy was impatient. 'We're helping put out the chairs for tonight's concert, and then Simon and I are going to help finish painting the backcloth.'

'And I'm going to watch,' said Miffy. 'You said I could.'

'The concert. Of course, oh yes.'

'You didn't forget did you, Miss?' Millicent was reproachful. 'You are coming aren't you?'

'Of course. Off you go then, all of you.'

'I've put a slow casserole in the oven,' Millicent shouted back as they departed. 'We'll all have a quick supper before the concert tonight.'

The house was quiet and empty. On the other side of the courtyard, in the barn, Diana could hear Sheridan practising with a full blooded version of 'Ol' Man River'. He'd just got to the words 'you lands in gaol' when the police car drew to a halt outside the kitchen door.

'So in spite of the fact that he spent all your money you had no idea that your husband might be taking drugs?'

Diana shook her head. 'I can't believe it, I just can't.'

'Can't, or don't want to,' said Sergeant Brown sternly. 'I'm asking you, Mrs Stratton, has there never been a time when he has acted strangely, seemed over excited, or very morose and depressed?'

'No more than other people.' But as soon as she had said it Diana knew it wasn't true. Against her will she found herself remembering the time Hugh had come home that Friday night and raped her. But she couldn't tell the police that. Hugh had certainly been strange that night, a different man from the one she'd married. There were other times too when his temper was on such a short fuse, that she'd been careful to keep their conversation totally neutral; and then there was the missing money. If he'd spent it on drugs, that would account for its disappearance. She looked at Sergeant Brown. 'What I said before is not quite true,' she said. 'Hugh did act strangely at times, but the thought that he might be taking drugs just never entered my head. It's true he must have spent my money, but I have no idea what he spent it on. I'm afraid I can't help you prove anything.'

'Never mind, Mrs Stratton. I didn't really think you'd be able to help, but it was worth a try. We'll be off now, and thank you for the coffee.'

Diana followed them to the door. 'How much money would Hugh have needed for his drugs?' she asked.

Detective Watkins, pleased that at last they were following up his information, had the figures at his finger tips. 'We're pretty sure he's on coke. Just one sniff a day at the current price would cost him £36,000 a year. But the dealer he's paying, deals in heroin as well as coke, so we doubt that he's just on coke. I dare say he's spending between £150,000 and £200,000 a year on drugs.'

'He doesn't earn that kind of money.'

'We know he doesn't. He's probably in debt up to his ears.' Sergeant Brown decided to say nothing about the drops they were certain Hugh and Nancy were making. Diana Stratton looked shaken enough as it was. No point in burdening her unnecessarily. He shook Diana's hand. 'Don't worry, Mrs Stratton. We shan't be bothering you again. We know you are not involved in any way.'

'You mean, you think I'm innocent?'

Sergeant Brown smiled, and put a fatherly hand on Diana's shoulder. 'Of course. It never entered our heads that you were ever anything else, my dear. Now, you get on with your life and forget about this for the time being. Sorting out this mess is our job. We'll try to involve you as little as possible.'

Forget about it, thought Diana, watching them drive off. Fat chance of that! How can I? Whether I like it or not I'm still married to Hugh, and it now seems I have a drug-addicted grave-robber for a husband. And as for getting on with my life, what about Joe? How can I get on with anything when I don't know what has happened. But that couldn't be blamed on Sergeant Brown. He had his problems. Joe Kelly was hers.

She started cleaning the house in a desultory fashion. Millicent and Griselda would never get around to it today, they were too wrapped up and too excited in the preparations for tonight's concert. But tidying and vacuuming proved no recipe for tranquillity, she couldn't stop thinking first about Hugh, and then about Joe.

Finally she took herself in hand and gave herself a good talking to. Hugh wasn't her problem, as Sergeant Brown had said, that was a matter for the police. As for Joe, stop behaving like some moonstruck teenager she lectured herself, and behave your proper age. Of course Joe would have had to go to London, his firm was in trouble. Dashing off to the head office was only natural. He'd probably been summoned by his bankers because of the state of Shamrock Enterprises. Banks were notoriously quick to leap in and salvage what they could for themselves from any disaster; and April had a house in London. She would have gone back there once she knew there was no alternative but to leave the manor house. Tonight, Diana told herself, I'll see him when he comes to the concert, and he'll tell me everything.

After the concert the entire village of Mottisley spilled out of the church hall into the street at the side of the abbey all talking at once.

'Well, I never. Didn't know that dark fellow, what's his name?'

'Sheridan Porter.'

'Yes, Sheridan, had such a marvellous voice.'

'He should go on the stage proper. Not waste his time messing around with grapes.'

'Don't say that,' Diana overheard. 'I'd be lost without him.'

'Well done, Reverend.' A crowd gathered around, a pinker faced than usual, Reverend Pincher. 'A marvellous performance from everyone.' There was much back-slapping and kissing.

'Even the string quartet kept in time, if not in tune,' said May.

'Shut up,' Diana gave her a dig and kissed Millicent. 'Your solo line was wonderful, Millicent, you've a lovely strong voice. And Griselda,' she kissed Griselda too, 'I could hear your voice even in the chorus. The best soprano there, so clear and true.'

'All this kissing,' said May looking around at the excited crowd. 'I don't approve of it. You'd think we were foreigners!'

'Wonderful, darlings, wonderful the lot of you.' April swooped in and joined the party from Abbey House. 'I was right at the back, and I could hear every word.'

Diana stared. April looked so happy; surely she ought to be just a little upset? Anyway, what was she doing here? She heard herself asking, 'is Joe here?'

'No, still in London. But he'll be back soon. He sent his love to everyone.'

'There's a baked potato van in the square. It's selling jacket potatoes stuffed with cheese, only £1.20 each. Can we have one?' Simon and Miffy pushed into the group.

'Yes.' With difficulty Diana hauled her thoughts away from Joe. *He sent his love to everyone.* April spoke as if she had been with him all the time. 'Yes, of course you can. Here's five pounds, enough for the three of you.' She realized Clemmy was not there. 'Where is Clemmy?'

'Over there, flirting with those boys.' Simon sounded disgusted.

'Clem!' Miffy's piercing voice shrieked across to where Clemmy was swinging self-consciously around a lamppost, tagging on to the periphery of a group of teenagers. 'Do you want a jacket potato stuffed with cheese?'

The jacket potato proved irresistible. 'Yes, please.' Clemmy flew across, Laura Ashley dress billowing out behind her. In a split second she reverted from a gauche young girl trying to be grown-up, to a small girl interested only in food.

'Come and have a drink,' said April.

May shook her head and pecked Diana and April on the cheeks. 'I'm driving back to Willow Farm now. I prefer my drop of malt in the peace and quiet of my own kitchen. You go Diana.'

'Hey, kids,' April called after the trio making a bee-line for the potato van. 'Diana and I will be in "The Ruddled Ram", come and get us when you're ready. Come on,' she said, dragging a reluctant Diana with her. 'I've got something to tell you.'

'The Ruddled Ram' was crowded, but with Diana in tow, April ruthlessly battled her way to the bar counter. 'Two ham rolls, I'm ravenous, one orange juice and . . .' she turned to Diana.

'A lager.'

April clinked her glass against Diana's. 'Here's to me. See, I'm on the wagon.' She raised the orange juice, and bit into the roll. 'Temperance Ladies of the Women's Institute here I come,' she said through a mouthful of ham and bread.

'Is that what you wanted to tell me? That you've stopped drinking?'

April glowed. Yes that's the word thought Diana, *glowed*. 'No,' she said, 'something much better than that.'

'Well, what?' Diana suddenly smiled, half guessing, and started eating her roll. Tony must have been swift off the mark, and now April knew where her true future lay. That was the reason she was so happy, and that was why she was back in Mottisley. Everything had worked out fine for all of them after all. 'Come on,' she said. 'Don't keep me in suspense any longer.'

'I'm pregnant,' said April. 'Joe and I are going to have a baby. Well, what do you think of that?'

The ham and bread turned to sawdust in Diana's mouth. She willed herself to smile brightly, and heard a voice, some other woman's voice saying, 'congratulations'.

'We haven't set a date yet for the wedding,' April rambled on happily, oblivious to Diana, 'but Joe doesn't want a child born out of wedlock. Neither do I. I'm old fashioned enough to believe it's important for a child to bear its father's name from the first day of life. Gives them a psychological sense of security. Don't you agree?'

'Absolutely,' said Diana mechanically.

'Don't you want that?' April nodded towards Diana's uneaten ham roll. Diana shook her head. 'I'll have it then. I've been ravenous ever since I knew. It must be because I'm eating for two now.'

Clemmy popped her head around the bar door. 'We're ready to go home now.'

Diana, hurrying to make her escape, caught her handbag strap around the chair leg. Struggling to free it, she prayed April wouldn't notice the brightness of her eyes.

The unshed tears were stinging, if she didn't get out soon she'd disgrace herself by bursting into tears. Handbag free at last, she bolted for the door. 'See you soon.'

'Yes,' said April, munching her way through the roll and noticing nothing. 'Joe is sure to be up to Abbey House as soon as he gets back.'

In the early hours of the following morning Diana was still awake. All was still and quiet now. A slip of a new moon hung in the sky, a wafer thin crescent. Diana, leaning on the windowsill of her bedroom with the window open, stared out into the darkness, and shivered. What a year. Susan's death, her own change of lifestyle. Hugh probably a drug addict, and a thief as well as having been unfaithful for months. And her father. Where did he now fit into her life? A man who'd had an incestuous relationship with his niece young enough to be his daughter. Then finally, finding and losing Joe in the space of a few hours, surely a record for an affair! And now he and April were to be married and had already started a family. That was the biggest hurt of all; April could give Joe children, she could not.

Somewhere in the village a dog howled at the moon. Diana shivered. Country lore said a howling dog meant an imminent death. She didn't believe it, but all the same the melancholy sound was the last straw. Diana leant her head on her hands and wept.

Chapter Thirty-eight

The Sunday morning directly after the concert Joe arrived at Abbey House.

'You missed the concert,' Millicent, Griselda and the children chorused in disapproval.

'I'm sorry. I got stuck in London, but I heard about it. April told me it was fantastic.' He looked around the kitchen and back out into the yard between the house and barn. 'Is Diana about?'

'Still in bed,' said Griselda. 'Overslept. Unlike her. I'm just taking her up a cup of tea.'

'I'll take it.'

'You can't. She's still in bed.' Ignoring her protestations Joe took the tea. 'Her room is on the right, third door along,' shouted Griselda as he went up the stairs.

'I know,' said Joe grimly.

Dredging herself from the depths of unconsciousness, Diana struggled to awake. 'Your tea,' said Joe, and sat down heavily on the edge of the bed. 'I thought we should talk.'

'Are you all right, Diana?' Griselda shrieked up the stairs.

'She's worried about your virtue,' said Joe with the faintest trace of a wry smile. The sight of Diana in bed reminded him unbearably of their hours together, when all had been right with their world, or rather, he had mistakenly thought he could put it right. He stood up. 'I'll wait for you downstairs.'

No asking me if I *wanted* to talk, thought Diana, trying to feel angry as she sipped her tea. Anger was an easy emotion. With anger you could build a barricade and less easily get hurt. But she found it an impossibility to muster such an emotion. Joe was right. They did have to talk. But no amount of talking, she thought sadly, would ever get them back to where they had been on Thursday morning. The time they'd both thought they'd witnessed the dawning of a new era.

'Got to talk business with Joe,' she said, hurrying through the kitchen, and praying no-one asked what business.

Outside the morning world was still. There was a feeling of waiting in the autumn air. The rush and struggle of harvest time was over, and now the land was preparing for sleep. Diana felt the hush, as if the world was listening, waiting for the last leaf to fall before hibernating for the winter, and remembered loving the autumn as a child, looking forward to cosy evenings spent in front of log fires with Susan. Now she found it sad, everything was coming to an end, including her world. No money, no husband, no lover, just a growing pile of debts and responsibilities.

But I have the children, she told herself, as she walked towards the waiting Joe. I must be positive, I *will* be positive, and I bloody well *will* succeed, with or without the damned bank manager. The future belongs to the children and I'm going to make it good for them. They love me, and I love them, her fierce expression softened, especially Miffy she thought. Still thinking of Miffy, she realized that she had superimposed his face on that of Joe's as she walked towards him. That's how Joe must have looked when he was little, she thought, rather like Miffy. A strange thought which increased the pain of knowing they were about to say goodbye. From now on they would be neighbours, nothing more.

Sam same running up to meet her. He still looked for Seamus, always puzzled that she hadn't brought him. Rubbing Sam's silky ears, Diana fell into step beside Joe and they walked down the slope between the vines.

'I know about April,' said Diana, breaking the awkward silence.

'Believe me, I didn't. Not that night. If I had, I . . .'

'Wouldn't have compromised yourself.' said Diana.

'Compromise isn't the word. I wouldn't have . . .'

'It doesn't matter.' Diana felt weary. The sooner they said what they had to say the better. 'No-one knows about us, either in the present or the past, and I think it's essential to keep it that way.'

'Yes,' said Joe.

'I know that you are going to marry April.'

'I have to.'

'Of course. I'd be disappointed if you said anything else. I hope you'll be happy. I mean it. April is nice, she'll be a good wife and mother.' Diana stopped walking and turned to face Joe. 'I've been thinking,' she said. 'I think we were mistaken to believe it was love which drew us together the other night. It wasn't. It was a mixture of emotions. Nostalgia for things which might have been, but which never can be. Tiredness, and plain old-fashioned physical attraction. Thinking we were in love was a myth, a nice one, but a myth none the less, it had no substance.'

'It wasn't a myth for me.'

'It has to be, Joe. Surely you can see that.'

'I suppose so.' He sounded reluctant. 'We'll stay friends?'

'Of course. We'll just forget about the other night.' Diana forced her voice to sound cheerfully breezy and turned away. She had no intention of seeing Joe too often, and risking the danger that her mask might slip letting her pain show. Strange how the real pain was realizing, after a decade, that she'd wasted most of her adult life chasing after inconsequential material things, while the real prospect of happiness had lain all the time slumbering in Mottisley. But it was too late now, there was nothing either she or Joe could do but accept the inevitable. 'I must go. There's a lot to do. Mr Shepherd is coming to see me today about the deep freeze for the vineyard shop.'

Feet slipping on the fallen leaves, she hurried back up the slope. As she hastened away the irony struck Diana forcibly. This time it was she who was running away from Joe, and the cause, yet again, was a tiny spark of life. Only this time the spark would live and thrive.

Edward Evans made one of his rare visits to May. 'Old bag,' he told Tony later. 'Taunted me, said I was too old and ought to retire and let you run the practice properly.'

'Quite right,' said Tony. 'If I had a younger partner, we could apply for recognition to the Royal College and take on a full-time junior doctor as a trainee instead of a part-time one. With all these new rules and regulations coming into force, we really ought to set up a proper health centre, and then perhaps I'd make some decent money and could start thinking of a wife and perhaps a family.'

'Not still sweet on April Harte I hope.'

'Why not? Don't you like April?'

His father looked at him pityingly. 'So you *are* still sweet on her. Well, my son, even if I do retire, you can forget about sharing your life with April, because she's pregnant. She and Joe are getting married.'

Tony gasped. 'I don't believe you.'

'It's true. May Marsham told me. April gave May the news herself, and Diana has confirmed it. She must have gone to some London clinic, because she hasn't been to see me, and she obviously hasn't been to see you.'

'No,' said Tony faintly, 'she hasn't.' A wild flight of mixed emotions chased through his brain. Anger, distress, fear and then utter wretchedness. A child would cement Joe and April's relationship permanently, there was no chance for him now.

'Oh, and another thing,' said his father. 'Old May was very mysterious. Said she wanted to see you and Diana together. It was, to quote her, "*of the utmost importance*".'

It took several reminders from his father, a telephone call from May, and finally one from Diana, before Tony obeyed the summons.

'I can't think what it is that can be so important,' he grumbled as he drove Diana to Willow Farm.

'I don't know either. Knowing May, it's probably nothing.'

Diana hadn't discussed April's pregnancy with Tony because since her talk with Joe on Sunday morning she'd made up her mind not to think of it. A decision made easier by the fact that the manual labour involved helping Sheridan replace the damaged vines with new stock, had proved to be so exhausting that she worked all day, and fell asleep each night in the kitchen after supper, only to be awoken by Millicent or Griselda and packed off to bed. Besides, she guessed that Tony must be heartbroken to have his dreams shattered with such brutal finality, and was unlikely to want to talk about it either.

They arrived to find May had gone to the trouble of laying out afternoon tea. 'Ada did the sandwiches for me,' she said, 'and I made the fruit cake.'

'This is terribly formal,' said Tony.

'Part of it is formal,' said May, making the tea. 'Sit down both of you. Up at the table, I want you to be able to lean on something.' When they both had their tea, she sat down, and said, 'first things first,' and extracted a large manilla envelope from the enormous handbag which went everywhere with her. 'My will,' she said, and passed one copy to Tony and one to Diana. 'Read it, and then you, Tony, sign it. I want you to be a witness.'

'Good, you've left everything to Diana and the children,' said Tony, scanning it quickly.

'Yes. I know, Diana, that as it stands, it's not much use to you at present, so next week I'm having a legal document drawn up which will enable you to have some of my money now. It will help you keep going until the next harvest, or my death, whichever comes first.'

'Oh, May.' Overwhelmed with relief at the thought of some money to pay the ever-increasing bills, Diana found herself near to tears. 'You've made my day.'

'I haven't finished yet,' said May. 'You'd best wait

before you say that, because there's something else I have
to tell you, and it may well ruin your day. It's about Miffy.'
She looked at Tony. 'As his doctor, I thought you ought
to know as well as Diana.'

'About Miffy?' Diana's heart began to thud. 'What
about Miffy?'

The telephone interrupted their conversation. May
picked it up. 'Hello, Nancy. What's that? You might come
down on Saturday. Well, I'm going to be busy I'm afraid.
Mottisley is having a Halloween party.'

'Heavens I'd forgotten that,' Diana whispered to Tony.

'The children haven't. They've picked my father's
largest pumpkins and have been hollowing them out, in
secret, all last week in his garage.'

'I'm lending one of my fields, the one with the big barn
on the edge,' May continued loudly. 'There's going to be
fireworks, and a bonfire and the children are having a
pumpkin head competition, and after that we're having a
Halloween supper in the barn. Not your cup of tea really
Nancy, but you're welcome to come if you want. What
am I doing now? Well, dear, actually I'm having a tea
party. What for? To celebrate the signing of my will. It's
about time I got round to making one. Tony Evans is
here, he's a witness, and Diana is here too, because she's
the beneficiary, plus something for the children in trust
of course. No, I haven't included you, dear. That ex-
husband of yours has left you well provided for, and
you've no children to worry about. You do understand
don't you?' There was a long pause while May listened.
Then she said, 'Good, I'm glad there's no hard feelings.
See you on Saturday.' Another long pause. 'Yes, all right,
the following Saturday then.'

'I'm surprised she's coming down at all,' said Tony
signing the will with a flourish. 'I thought she was after
your money.'

'Of course she was,' said May. 'Because I'm old and
live in the country she thought I was stupid, although
perhaps now she is having second thoughts.' May took

the signed will and slipped it, and the copy, back in the manilla envelope. 'Old Mr Grimble is collecting it later today, before he flies off to visit his daughter in Australia,' she said. 'I know you don't think he's very efficient, Diana, and he is semi-retired. But I trust him and want him to deal with it.'

'What about Miffy?' asked Diana, more concerned with that than the will.

'First things first,' said May infuriatingly. 'Now, if it wasn't for Ma Kelly I wouldn't be telling you this. But Molly Kelly doesn't approve at all of April and Joe's baby, so she and her husband are going back to Ireland.'

'Going back to Ireland? Because Joe is going to be a father? That's a bit drastic isn't it?' Tony was astonished. Thinking he was the only one disapproving of April's pregnancy, he was surprised to hear about the Kellys.

'Yes. Well, in part. The real truth is that Joe's father has never really liked the respectable life. He hasn't been able to annoy anyone since they've lived on the manor land. So now that Joe might have to sell the house and the land, it's given him a heaven-sent opportunity to go back on the road. But as Molly says, there is no point in leading the gypsy life in England. No peace here any more. Too much traffic whizzing about and no place to graze the horse at night. So they've packed up, lock, stock and menagerie, and taken the car ferry back to Rosslare.'

'Very interesting. But what has this got to do with Miffy?' Diana tried not to show her impatience.

But May was not to be hurried. 'As Molly Kelly said, it didn't seem right, her going away and leaving me here the only one to know, so we decided you two should be told. She's not so young any more, and when she dies, which will probably be before old man Kelly because he's drunk so much alcohol his body is pickled. He'll live for ever, permanently preserved as you might say.'

'May! Do get on with it.'

'When she dies, it will be in some God-forsaken bog in

481

a remote corner of Ireland, and neither of us will ever know.'

'Know what?' asked Tony, who had completely lost the thread of the conversation.

'That the other one of us is dead, of course.'

Diana felt like screaming 'get on with it' but said instead, 'May, what has all this to do with Miffy?'

'Ah yes, Miffy,' said May, as if she had only just remembered him. 'Well you see, dear, Ma and Pa Kelly are Miffy's grandparents.'

'But that means . . .'

'Yes, it does. It means that Joe is his father.' Tony and Diana both opened their mouths to speak, but May raised a hand to silence them. 'The reason I am telling you both, is because, in different ways, you are responsible for the welfare of Miffy. No-one, other than myself and Molly Kelly know of Miffy's parentage. Susan did, of course, but she's no longer with us. But Joe has never known, and never need know if that is what you decide, Diana. But someone has to carry the secret, and as Ma Kelly said, my days, like hers, are limited in number now.'

'I don't see why I had to know. I wish you hadn't told me,' said Diana.' Slimy fingers of jealousy gripped her heart, squeezing it until she felt sick. I should have known, she told herself, the likeness to Joe, the fact that Tom was already so disabled when Susan conceived. I should have guessed. And Susan, what of Susan? Always held up to be a paragon of virtue, and now I find out that even she was not what she seemed. Even *she* had her secrets. A double dose of jealousy assailed Diana. Susan had an affair with Joe and conceived his child, but unlike herself, she had kept it, and the result was Miffy.

'Why have you told us?' asked Tony quietly.

'Because perhaps one day you might think that Joe ought to know. Who can tell what the future holds. One day it might be important that Joe *should* know.'

'I shall never tell him,' said Diana fiercely. '*Never!*'

Why should Joe know that he already had a son? A

child he'd seen grow up and whom he loved dearly. April was expecting his child, that should be enough for him. Why should I gift him the child I love best of all? Miffy may not be mine, but I love him as if he were. Diana knew she was being unreasonable, but she couldn't help herself. Love and jealousy combined to twist her judgement. She wanted Miffy for herself.

'Never is a long time,' said May.

'Forget it,' said Tony as he drove Diana back to Abbey House. 'I can't foresee any reason why Joe should need to know; and it would only be disturbing to Miffy if he knew. Make him feel different from the other children.'

'I wish May had kept her mouth shut.' Diana was miserably aware that her anger was unjustified, but couldn't help it. She felt hurt, deceived and, most worrying of all, vulnerable. She turned to Tony. 'And Susan. How could she? I've always admired her, but now I find she cheated too. Cheated on her husband *and* Joe.'

'No, it wasn't cheating. She obviously told May and Molly Kelly, and they told her to keep quiet. If you think of it sensibly, that course of action was for the best.'

'How could she have an affair with Joe when she always professed to love Tom? I know Joe thought he was in love with Susan once, he told me. But he said she turned him down because she loved Tom.'

'She did.'

'And Miffy? How did he come about?'

'Loneliness, I guess,' said Tony. 'Tom was very difficult towards the end of his illness and Susan had a lot to put up with. I suppose she needed a shoulder to cry on, and Joe was there. I doubt that it was anything more than that.'

'I suppose so.' The jealousy was still there. Sticking like a hard lump in her throat.

'It won't stop you loving Miffy, I hope,' said Tony.

'Stop loving Miffy! Of course not. But I'm damned if I'm going to share him with Joe. He's mine.'

'As I said before, there's no need for Joe to know. But

don't you think you ought to be keeping quiet for Miffy's sake, not your own?'

'Yes,' admitted Diana, 'but can I help it if I'm less than perfect?'

Tony laughed, for the first time that afternoon. 'Join the club,' he said.

When Nancy put the 'phone down after speaking to May, two bright spots of rage burned in her normally pale cheeks. Lighting a cigarette, she drew on it fiercely, then tapped out the number for Hugh's private line.

'Hugh?' Her voice was harsh, abrupt. 'Have you got that will typed out yet?'

'Nearly.'

'Only nearly?'

'I'm doing it myself. I have to wait until Miss Higgins has gone. You know that.'

'Well, make certain that it's finished by Friday, because on Saturday we are going down to Mottisley to get it signed.'

'But how are you going to persuade . . . ?'

'Never mind. Just make sure it's ready.'

Nancy put her finger on the button and cut Hugh off. Then looked up Nico's number.

On the Friday afternoon before Halloween, Diana saw Mr Mortimer yet again in the bank at Midhurst. She'd gone to see him after receiving a curt little note demanding her presence.

'I didn't realize, until one of the staff told me, quite how disastrous the storm was to your vineyard. You told me you were counting on a good harvest. And now, I understand that there isn't one.'

'There is. Albeit a small one,' said Diana. 'We shall make approximately two thousand bottles of extremely good quality wine.' Damn the man, she wasn't going to admit that the quality was dubious, that in fact the stuff might not even be drinkable. 'But, yes you are right. The storm was disastrous, not only to me, but to many others. Surely I'm not your only customer to have suffered.'

Mr Mortimer looked up over the top of his half-moon spectacles in the supercilious manner which always infuriated Diana. 'Of course not. But my other customers took wise precautions. They insured themselves. Do you have insurance against harvest loss?'

You know damn well I don't, thought Diana, but merely said, 'no, I couldn't afford it,' in what she hoped was a suitably humble voice. It was essential to keep in his good books for the time being. How surprised he'd be when she got her windfall from May.

'As I thought.' Mr Mortimer closed the file, leaned his elbows on his desk, and putting his hands together made a steeple with his fingertips. 'Mrs Stratton, it is my unpleasant duty to inform you that the bank is calling in its loan. I feel it is only right that I should tell you this in person.'

'Why, because it gives you a thrill?' Diana gave up trying to be humble or polite. She didn't need the odious little man because she'd be all right once May had been into her bank in Chichester next week.

'There's no need to take that attitude, Mrs Stratton. I could have just posted a letter to you. As it is, I will give it to you now.' He took a long white envelope from a drawer in his desk and passed it across to Diana. 'You have one month to clear the loan.'

'It will be cleared,' said Diana, snatching at the envelope and getting up. 'And when it is I shall close my account and move to another bank.'

'That is your privilege.' Mr Mortimer smiled disbelievingly.

Reckoning that this was no time for false pride, Diana detoured on the way back from Midhurst, and going to Willow Farm showed May the letter.

'Don't worry, dear,' said May. 'We'll fix him. I've an appointment in Chichester next Wednesday. It would have been sooner, but Mr Smithson, the manager, couldn't make it before, and I do hate dealing with the under-manager.'

Diana wished it could have been sooner, but there was nothing she could do except wait. There was no need to worry now, but still she did. Supposing something went wrong and May never made it to the bank. Supposing, supposing, endless scenarios flashed before her anxious mind until finally she told herself to stop. I'm becoming neurotic, she thought. But with good reason. So much had happened during October, so much trauma, so many revelations, that she knew she would draw one big sigh of relief once 31 October was over and done with. Maybe next month, things would settle down.

May went to the tea caddy, opened it and took out a fifty-pound note. 'Take that for now. It's all I have in the house at the moment.'

'No I don't want . . .'

'Go on, take it. You're giving some food for the Halloween party, you can spend it on that.' She sniffed. 'I told them they should have let me leave more money here. But after Bert died, Joe and Tony made me empty my hiding places and put the rest of the money in the bank.'

'All right, I will. Thanks.' Diana stuffed the note into her purse. 'Now Millicent can get on with that enormous cheesecake she's been dying to make. I'll make sure we save you a piece, as you are paying for it.'

May chuckled and kissed her goodbye. 'I'm looking forward to tomorrow,' she said. 'We haven't had a Halloween party in the village for years.' Her enthusiasm was infectious, and Diana felt happier as she went back to Abbey House.

On the Saturday morning, Griselda and Diana were making trifles for the party, and Millicent was busy whisking mountains of cream cheese for the cheesecake, when the children brought their hollowed out pumpkins to Abbey House.

'I thought you were going to surprise us,' said Diana.

'We couldn't wait.' Miffy squeaked, jumping up and down with excitement.

'You mean, *you* couldn't wait, so we all had to bring them,' said Simon, scrabbling in the cupboard by the side of the dresser. 'Where are the candles, Diana? Oh never mind, I've found them.' Flushed with excitement he dragged out a large box of night lights.

Millicent helped them fix a night light each in the bottom of the pumpkins, then the curtains were drawn and the candles lit. Three eerily grinning faces flickered on the kitchen table.

The kitchen door opened and closed. 'My God, it's enough to scare the living daylights out of anyone.'

'What are you doing here?' Diana didn't mean to sound so shrill, but the shock of Joe's unannounced arrival unnerved her.

'Joe!' Miffy shrieked, and flung himself into Joe's arms. Simon and Clemmy clambered around him too, although were more restrained, and Diana, watching, told herself sternly not to feel jealous. Miffy doesn't like Joe any more than the other two, it just seems like it to me, because of my heightened senses, and feeling of guilt. Although what have I got to be guilty about where Miffy is concerned? Joe is the one who should feel guilty, except, of course, that he doesn't know. She felt cross at letting the knowledge bother her, and wished once more that May had kept the secret to herself.

'I've brought two apple pies, April's contribution to the party. Can you take them up to the field with your stuff? I've got to supervise the building of the bonfire and setting up of the fireworks.'

'Yes, of course.' Griselda darted forward. 'I'll take them.'

Joe departed, to Diana's relief, and at Abbey House the rest of the day passed in a buzz of activity and excitement.

* * *

In his consulting room at the Surgery in the village, Edward Evans pondered on a problem.

'A knock on his door heralded the entrance of Tony. 'Dad, I've come to remind you that you are on duty tonight. I'm going to the Halloween do, up at Willow Farm.'

'I know, I know. No need to remind me,' grumbled his father testily.

'Well, it so happens that I know there's an archaeology meeting down in Chichester tonight, and it wouldn't be the first time you've had a lapse of memory and gone off and left me in the lurch.'

'You're getting to be a real slave driver.'

Tony looked at the pathology slips on his father's desk. 'Problems?' he asked.

'What would you say to a woman who has two consecutive pregnancy tests reading negative, and who, on internal examination shows no sign of pregnancy, but is utterly convinced that she is pregnant.'

'What a question. I'd tell her she wasn't pregnant, of course. Who's your problem patient?'

'April Harte.'

'April, not pregnant!' His father nodded. 'Are you sure?'

'Positive.'

'Have you told her?'

'Not yet. Damned woman's gone rushing off to London to see her editor. Said she'd come and see me when she got back. I'm expecting her about six-thirty this evening.'

Chapter Thirty-nine

'No. Absolutely not.'

For the first time since he'd met Nancy, Hugh rebelled. When she'd imperiously ordered him to stop in the lane at the side of the Mottisley Abbey churchyard he'd had no idea why. Now he did know, and refused to do it.

'But it's Halloween,' Nancy hissed in a fury. 'I want to make love in a churchyard.'

'What the hell for?' Even the sense of well-being, induced by a shot of heroin before they'd left London, couldn't stop Hugh shuddering. He felt as if he was in the middle of a nightmare from which there was no escape.

'Don't you believe in black magic?' Nancy's dark eyes glittered angrily.

'I think you're mad,' said Hugh slowly in a horrified whisper. 'And get this straight. I'm not going to fuck you in the churchyard now, or any other night. So forget it.'

He tried to hide the fact that by now he was physically shaking in fear. He'd prepared May's will as instructed by Nancy; and in it May left everything to Nancy. At the time he'd thought it a waste of time, wondering how Nancy would persuade May to sign it. Now he was beginning to realize that she would do anything. Anything at all.

Hugh did not believe in black magic, but a dark, troublesome core of doubt remained in his mind. Much as he hated admitting it, he could not escape the fact that he was in Nancy's power, because she controlled his supply of drugs. I'll kick the habit, Hugh vowed to himself. Once tonight is over I'll give it up completely. I'll leave Nancy. I'll even go to a clinic if necessary. I am going to take control of my life once more.

'All right, damn you! Drive on to Willow Farm.' Nancy's seething rage was palpable.

When they got to the farm May was out. Hugh was relieved. 'Let's leave signing the will to another time,' he said.

But Nancy had a key, and unlocking the front door, opened it. 'I'm not leaving anything to another time. It has to be tonight. One, because it's Halloween and I'm superstitious even if you're not, and two, because she is not expecting us. I told her I'd be coming down next Saturday. Diana and Tony were in the room at the time, so they will know, and that's our alibi. We'll wait. She'll be back.'

Hugh's sense of alarm increased. 'Supposing somebody comes back with her. And what do we need an alibi for?'

'You never know,' said Nancy sharply. 'And if there is anyone with her, then we'll wait in another room until she's alone. One way or another this will is going to be signed tonight.' She turned and stared at Hugh fiercely. 'Since you're so scared,' she said scornfully, 'you can go. I can manage perfectly well on my own.'

'No, I'll stay,' said Hugh.

Nancy was insane. Now there was no longer any doubt in his mind. What puzzled him was why he had not seen it sooner. Now he could see her clearly in the light of May's kitchen it was so obvious. Her eyes glistened feverishly, and two spots of scarlet burned in her pale cheeks. Suddenly he feared for May's safety, and knew that he had to stay with Nancy. But the sense of impending doom was so strong that he almost changed his mind. The impulse to run away from Nancy and everything she represented was overwhelming. But he did not. He gritted his teeth and stayed. I'm in it now, up to my neck, he thought, I've no choice but to follow it through. Whatever 'it' might be.

Diana was the last to leave Abbey House for the bonfire festivities. The children had gone on ahead, clutching their pumpkins carefully, eager to put them on the competitors' display table. Millicent and Griselda, after loading the food into the Volvo, had left with Sheridan driving. Diana remaining behind, fastened the door to Daisy's stall. Not that any fireworks were likely to land near Abbey House, but she wasn't taking any chances. She also caught Shakespeare, much to his annoyance as he'd been happily mousing, and dumping him on his cushion by the Aga, shut him in. On the point of leaving, she heard the bell on the front door.

'You said we could come.'

'And I meant it.' Diana hoped she managed to conceal her surprise and dismay at seeing Hugh's parents on the doorstep. 'Come in.'

'We don't want to be any bother.'

'You're not,' lied Diana. Writing and inviting them to stay was one thing, but she hadn't bargained on them turning up without warning, and tonight of all nights.

They wanted nothing to eat, and seemed very tired. So after explaining about the bonfire party, Diana hastily made up the big double bed in the spare room on the side of the house, and installed them in it, with a hot water bottle each, a mug of hot milk, and a promise that they would all have a long talk in the morning.

'You are kind,' said old Mr Stratton. 'Me and the wife, we're very, very grateful.'

'It's the least I can do,' said Diana.

'So there you are,' she told May, when she eventually made it up to the field at Willow Farm. 'Hugh's parents are here.'

'I'm not sure that I approve of your turning Abbey House into a home for waifs and strays,' said May, adding practically, 'you'd better make sure they contribute something towards their keep.'

'I will. But I don't want them to have to *worry* about money. And I couldn't just turn my back on them. I'd never have lived with myself.'

May snorted. 'I'll say one thing. Your heart's in the right place, even if your head is a little skew-whiff. You're getting more like your sister every day.'

The pumpkin competition was won by Cyril Lomax of the general stores, his pumpkin was twice the size of anyone else's.

'It's not fair,' wailed Miffy. 'Mrs Lomax fed that pumpkin every day with half a pint of milk. Cyril told me. I wanted to feed ours but Dr Evans wouldn't let me. He said water was good enough for pumpkins, and milk was for people.'

'And quite right too,' said Diana. 'When you think of all the starving children in the world, it seems wrong to feed a pumpkin.'

'But we haven't got any starving children in Mottisley. And it was *old* milk.'

There was no answer to that, and Diana was glad his attention was diverted by an announcement over the loudspeaker that supper was being served and Joe Kelly was about to light the bonfire. The fireworks would start in about three-quarters of an hour. The children raced away jostling with all the other competitors to be first in the queue for the chicken legs and sausages. May and Diana followed at a more leisurely pace.

'I'll have a bite to eat, say hello to a few people, then go back to the farm,' said May.

Tony joined them. 'Seen April?' he asked.

'No, she's probably with Joe.'

'She's not. I've been with him.'

'I'd hoped you'd given up chasing her,' Diana said quietly.

Tony seemed distracted, and didn't answer. After a while he wandered off, mingling with the crowd around the bonfire.

'Shall I walk back with you?'

'Certainly not,' said May. 'I'm safe enough in my own field, crossing to my own farmhouse. No, you stay here, and make sure those children don't go too near that bonfire. We don't want anyone getting burned. I'll come back out for a while when the fireworks start.'

Diana watched May until she saw her open the gate leading into Willow Farm garden on the far side of the field, before turning back to look for the children. As she walked towards the bonfire, she saw April and Tony out of the corner of her eye. April was dabbing at her eyes with a handkerchief, and for a moment Diana thought she was crying. But seeing Diana looking in their direction, both she and Tony waved, and April cried out, 'See you in a moment,' so Diana supposed it was smoke from the bonfire bothering her.

The scene in the immediate proximity of the bonfire resembled a medieval painting. The children of the village pranced like small, excited dervishes around the roaring fire, and Diana told herself not to be a fusspot, restraining an overwhelming urge to rush up and drag her three, especially Miffy the most excited dervish of the lot, away from the bonfire. Pleased when Miffy came away from the fire and ran to her, she readily agreed that he should go and fetch May in time for the fireworks. He had a torch, and she watched him cross the field and saw him safely through the white painted garden gate of Willow Farm. He'd be safe enough coming back with May for company.

May poured out her customary malt whisky, and settled down by the fire. Buggins poked his whiskery nose over the top of the stable door, blowing noisily through his nostrils. 'Go to bed, boy,' she said. 'I'll come and give you your bedtime carrot in a moment.'

Knowing, from the tone of her voice, he was not going to get any biscuits, the big horse clopped back across the yard.

'Now,' hissed Nancy, and walked from the front parlour, where she and Hugh had been waiting, into the kitchen. 'Hello, May.' Without waiting for a reply she went across to the kitchen window, opening and closing the curtains twice.'

'What are you doing? I thought you were coming next Saturday.' May was not pleased.

'I changed my mind,' said Nancy.

Hugh lurked uneasily in the background. Unsure of what to do. Unsure of that Nancy was doing. Why had she twitched the curtains? He soon knew. Nico and his oafish brother, Rick, walked into the kitchen leaving the stable door swinging open behind them.

'What on earth . . .' May began.

'Shut up,' said Nancy. She fished the will from her handbag and placed it on the small table at the side of May's armchair. 'Just sign this and then we'll all leave you in peace.'

'What are they doing here?' Hugh tried to control the frissons of alarm spreading through him.

'My insurance,' said Nancy briefly. 'I knew you wouldn't have the stomach for anything rough.'

'But . . .'

'Belt up.' Nico stood behind May. 'Sign, old woman.'

May had put on her glasses and was reading the will. Hugh admired her calm, and wished he could be the same. 'I'm not signing this,' she said, throwing it to the floor. 'I've already made a will.'

'But now you're going to make another,' said Nancy, and nodded at Nico.

Quick as a flash he grasped May's left arm and pinned it behind her back. She shrieked in pain, and Hugh lunged forward.

'Oh no you don't,' Rick grabbed Hugh and held him back.

'Sign,' snarled Nico pressing May's arm hard up against her back. Nancy picked up the will and put a pen in May's right hand.

'Sign it,' gasped Hugh, knowing Nico would break the old woman's arm if he had to. 'Just sign it.'

'So you are on our side after all,' said Nancy

494

sarcastically. 'Don't break his arms, Rick. We may need them.'

Rick guffawed, and slackened his hold a little.

May screamed again, then whispered, 'All right.'

'Release her,' said Nancy.

Hugh saw May sign, and heaved a sigh of relief. He thought of nothing beyond the fact that now they could go. Forcing the old lady to sign a will was one thing, sheer brutality was another. He didn't want to see any more of that. The sooner he got Nancy and those evil brothers away from Willow Farm the better. The thought had barely flashed through his mind when May snatched at the will and attempted to tear it, simultaneously Nico grabbed her and she screamed. A kaleidoscope of single events began to merge into a chaos of screaming, scuffling, and then there was fire.

As May screamed so Buggins charged in through the open stable door. Panicked by the sound of his mistress in pain, he kicked out. His hoofs clattered against the fire grate, knocking down burning coals. Split seconds later flames whooshed up from the old-fashioned rag matting on the floor.

'Get that bloody horse out of . . .'

Nico's words were drowned as Buggins flailed round in terror. The big horse, panic-stricken at the flames, turned round twice before charging out through the door. His bulk sent a chair flying, toppling it into the grate. It started to burn, and more hot coals scattered across the room.

'Take it.' Nancy thrust the signed will into Hugh's hands. 'Take it and go. I'll come back to London with Nico.'

'But . . .'

'We'll get May out. You go. Put the will in your office. Keep it safe.'

The heat was searing Hugh's eyelids, his clothes clinging to his body were soaked with perspiration, and he knew that he had to get out. He ran, the will still grasped in his hand. Outside, the chill of the night air brought him to a stop. Looking back, he hesitated a moment, then walked on. Of course Nancy would get May out. Mad she might be, but a murderess she was not.

He crossed to the barn where his car was hidden, and swung the door back. It was then that he heard Miffy. Turning back he saw the small boy was peering in through the kitchen window, and must have seen the fire because Hugh heard him cry out before he dashed into the farmhouse. The very next second Hugh heard the powerful roar of a car, there was a flash of silver as Nico backed the Jaguar out of the other barn, a squeal of tyres on the cobbled yard, and then it was gone.

Appalled, Hugh suddenly realized what the three of them had done. They had left May in the burning house, and now Miffy was in there too. For a moment he stood rooted to the spot, then he began to run. *I can't let them die, I can't let them die.* The words pounded through his brain, driving him on. Regardless now of his own life, he ran straight back into the blazing farmhouse.

'I can't hang on much longer. Where are they?' Joe, waiting to start the fireworks, was impatient.

'Miffy has gone to get May.' Bouncing up and down with impatience themselves, Simon and Clemmy swung on Diana's arms.

'Perhaps I'd better go myself.' Diana turned towards Willow Farm in time to see a brilliant finger of orange flame lick up the side of the chimney breast. 'Oh my God.' In the split second before she started to run, Joe turned and saw the flames, as did half the crowd.

Suddenly the whole roof was blazing, and then there was a deafening series of cracking explosions. 'It's those bloody bullets above the stove,' said Joe.

Willow Farm was providing its own terrifying firework display as the cartridges caught fire and exploded, whistling up through the darkness like so many miniature rockets.

'Fire, fire.' The cry went up. The crowd surged forward. But Diana didn't hear them. Already, she and Joe were halfway across the field.

April held on to Simon and Clemmy as Diana ran past. 'I'll keep them safe.' Diana heard the screamed words and ran on. April restrained the frightened pair of children. 'No, darlings, stay here. This is work for grown-ups.'

'But Miffy . . . Aunt May.'

'They'll be all right,' said April with more confidence than she felt.

Joe got to the doorway first, but Diana was there a moment later. Hugh had an unconscious Miffy in his arms. In the split second before he threw him to Joe, Diana saw that the windows had shattered with the heat and that Miffy was cut. Blood was pouring from his wrist, even in the brilliant orange of the flames his face looked blue.

Tony was there too, and took Miffy from Joe. 'Give me your handkerchief,' he shouted to Diana. She did as she was told, and Tony made a tourniquet around Miffy's arm, at the same time she was aware of Hugh and Joe dragging an unconscious May over towards the door. They were nearly there when, with a thundering roar, and a blasting belch of heat, the roof caved in. Joe darted forward, dragging May to safety with him, but Hugh, not so quick to move, was trapped. An ancient beam, half a tree trunk, had fallen, pinning him to the floor.

'Oh my God.' Joe tried to go in but was beaten back by the heat and smoke.

'Hugh!' Diana heard herself screaming.

Hugh looked up. Through the smoke and flames his eyes met hers, and he smiled. Perhaps it was the flames, but Diana could have sworn that she could see, really see into Hugh's eyes. She saw regret and resignation combined with a curious tranquillity. One of his hands was free, and in it Diana could see some folded paper.

'He doesn't stand a chance,' Joe whispered. But Diana didn't hear him. Transfixed with horror she watched as

Hugh held the paper towards the flames. As the last piece of the paper curled and blackened into ash he smiled at her again. It was the last thing she remembered. Then the firemen dragged her away.

Diana couldn't recall the journey to the hospital. She supposed she must have done whatever was necessary, because now she was here in the intensive care unit. Miffy and May were both there too, hitched up to machines and surrounded, it seemed, by dozens of people in white coats.

'Come on. Come into the office and have a cup of tea.'

'I don't want . . .' Diana didn't want to leave either of them.

'We'll leave the office door open. They'll call us if you are needed. It is better that you wait there.' The nurse was firm.

Tony appeared. Seeing him, Diana had some idea of what she must look like. White faced, smeared with soot and ash, and clothes filthy. She remembered now. They'd been showered with burning debris when the roof fell in.

'Miffy will be all right, won't he?'

'Yes.' No point in saying otherwise thought Tony. One bridge at a time.

'And May? She'll be all right as well?'

'I think so. By the way, April is staying at Abbey House with the children and the rest of them until you get home. So you are not to worry.'

'Thank you.'

The night, so busy for the medical staff, passed slowly for Diana. It was a white nightmare. White lights, white coats, white beds and two inert lily-white patients. Joe and Tony were at her side but they didn't talk. Diana was glad, she didn't want to talk. What had Hugh been doing at May's farmhouse? He was dead. She knew that. No-one had told her, but she knew. He could never have survived that inferno. Later, as his next of kin, she would have to identify his body, she knew that too. But first things first, as May was always saying, and the first thing was that May and Miffy should recover. Diana sat there concentrating her mind, *willing* them both not to die. Not once did she allow herself to think otherwise. They would recover. They *had* to recover.

The flintstone church next to Chichester hospital was tolling its bell for matins when the specialist in charge of the unit came out to the waiting three and smiled. Squatting down on his haunches he took Diana's two cold hands into his. 'Young Timothy is going to be fine,' he said, 'and Miss Marsham is conscious now.'

'Timothy?' For a moment nothing registered.

'Miffy,' said Tony.

'You can go in,' said the doctor. 'But not too much talking. Especially not to Miss Marsham. She is still rather agitated.'

A grimy trio trooped into the kitchen of Abbey House at Sunday lunch time. The big kitchen table was covered in food, two roast legs of lamb, baked potatoes, cauliflower, peas, and gravy, but the usual lively chatter of the communal meal was absent. The helpings on the plates were small, and looked as if they would remain uneaten.

'They are going to be all right,' said Joe. 'Both of them.'

A small ragged cheer, that grew in strength and confidence, ricochetted around the room.

'Praise be to God,' said Millicent, and crossed herself.

'I didn't know you were religious,' said Griselda.

'I'm not. But I like to keep on the right side of whoever is up there.'

It broke the tension, and everyone began asking questions at once. Through the bedlam of explanations of what, and who, and how, Diana saw two pale wraiths hovering the other side of the kitchen table. She had completely forgotten about Hugh's parents. Panic-stricken she turned to Tony.

'We'll tell them in the Library,' he said.

In the event it wasn't the ordeal Diana had feared. Both Mr and Mrs Stratton took the news of their son's death calmly. The fact that Diana told them, that in spite of what had happened, they could stay at Abbey House for as long as they wanted, seemed to be much more important. Pleased and reassured, they nodded like a couple of mandarins.

'We'll talk about the money later,' said Mr Stratton.

'Of course,' said Diana, supposing he meant their contribution to the household expenses. Poor old things. Fancy worrying about that at a time like this.

'That's a good idea, isn't it mother?' Mrs Stratton nodded. 'There, you can see it's taken a load off her mind already,' he said. Then taking his wife's hand, they slipped silently back into the kitchen and began to eat their lunch quite happily.

'I wish I knew what they were talking about. Do you think they really understood?' Diana asked Tony.

'Yes, I think they understood about Hugh, and just accepted it. But there is something else worrying them.'

'I didn't tell them about me and Hugh splitting up. It seems unnecessary now that he's dead.'

'I agree,' said Tony. 'No point in distressing them further. That part of your life is water under the bridge.'

'Yes,' said Diana slowly. For the first time the realization that she was now a widow struck home. 'It is, isn't it.' Then, immediately, guilt swamped her because she couldn't help thinking how much more simple life would be without Hugh. Now there would be no divorce to go through. She was free.

'You won't need a divorce now,' said Tony, accurately reading her mind. Then he said, 'but what's still puzzling me, is what the hell was Hugh doing at Willow Farm in the first place. Do *you* know?'

Diana shook her head. 'May will tell us when she's better. She must know.' Looking around the Library she remembered the sunshine on the day in April when Mr Grimble had read out Susan's will. That was when it all began. 'So much has happened since,' she said to herself.

'What?' Tony didn't hear.

'I said, so much has happened since Susan died. And

so much of it seems to have been crammed into this last month. Only yesterday I was thinking that I'd be glad when the end of the month arrived, because enough had happened to me in one month to last a year. But I never dreamed the ending would come in such an awful and dramatic way.'

'Thank God young Miffy and Aunt May both survived. That's the important thing,' said Tony. 'By the way, talking of things happening, there's something else you should know.'

The Library door burst open and Griselda charged in. 'It's the hospital on the telephone, Diana. They want you to go back at once.'

'Miffy,' gasped Diana.

'No, he's all right. It's May.'

'I'm really very reluctant to do this,' the doctor told Diana, 'because she's in atrial fibrillation. But the old lady is so agitated we decided that it would be best if you spoke to her. Maybe you can set her mind at rest.' He led the way into a side room.

'May, it's me.' Diana grasped May's hands. How dry, and paper thin they felt, as if she were a shadow, not a real person at all.

'The will,' May whispered.

Tony sat the other side of the bed. 'Don't worry about it, May. The will is safe. You gave it to Mr Grimble, remember?'

'No. He didn't come.' Tony and Diana leaned close, trying to hear the faint voice. 'I left it in the rolltop desk in the kitchen, and the desk was on fire.'

'Relax, May. You can make another when you are well,' said Tony.

'And don't you worry about making that money over to me. I'm going to tell Mr Mortimer to take a running jump, and tell him that you said so. We will manage very well, we're not destitute.' Diana hoped that she sounded as confident as her words. The truth was they *were* very nearly destitute. She'd stopped thinking about the out-standing bills, and was not allowing herself even to begin to think about when May might be well enough to go to the bank and transfer the money as she had planned. Getting her and Miffy well and back home was the priority now. Financial matters would have to wait.

'Another will. There is another will.' May's voice was getting weaker and weaker.

'I can't let you stay too long,' the doctor came back into the room.

May waved her arms feebly, waving him away. 'Nancy and Hugh came . . .'

Tony edged closer. 'So that's why Hugh was there.'

'A will. Nancy had a will. Everything to her. I signed it. A man Nico. Held my arm, it hurt.' May paused, gasping for breath.

'Never mind, darling. Tell us later.' Near to tears, Diana wanted her to stop. 'Look, May, I don't care what you signed. All I want is for you to be well.'

But May had no intention of stopping. With a sudden surge of strength she pushed herself up on to her elbows. 'Buggins tried to help. He kicked, started the fire. Is he all right?'

'Yes, yes, Buggins is safe. Mr Shepherd, the butcher from the village, has taken him and stabled him with his old mare for company. My father organized it,' said Tony.

May sank back on the pillow. 'About time your father earned his keep,' she whispered. Then she said. 'Get that will back from Nancy. I want to see it destroyed.'

'We will,' said Tony, a grim note to his voice. 'We will do that for you, May. And now stop worrying.'

'Yes.' May closed her eyes.

'She seems more relaxed,' Diana whispered to Tony.

'I am,' said May, her eyes still closed. 'I'll make a new will tomorrow. And put everything back as it should be.'

Chapter Forty

The weather men were saying it was the coldest mid November since records began, and the straggling group emerging from Chichester's Law Courts after the inquests on May and Hugh were wrapped up against the cold. When Diana saw the posse of press men, she was glad she had her coat collar turned up to the brim of her large black hat.

The press men swooped. 'Mrs Stratton, Mrs Stratton.'

'Take no notice,' said Sergeant Brown. 'Say nothing, that way you can't be misquoted.'

'Bloody nuisance all these people,' grumbled Joe bad-temperedly, following them down the steps of the Law Courts.

'There's no point in being bad-tempered, Joe,' April said. 'We'll talk to Diana later. Today is not the right day.' Two press men lunged in their path, cameras clicking, and April aimed a discreet kick at their ankles. 'So sorry,' she said, sweeping past, leaving a cameraman hopping on one foot.

'Bloody vultures.' Sergeant Brown wasn't feeling the cold. He was hot with rage, as he elbowed the press corps out of the way, and put Diana in the taxi to take her back to Abbey House. 'Why couldn't that kid have got there a few minutes earlier, then he might have seen something. As it was he saw nothing except the fire. All we've got that implicates Nancy Morris and Nico Guanello is a dead woman's word, and that's secondhand.'

Terry Watkins feared for his superior's blood pressure. 'You know, sir, the verdict, death by misadventure, would have been the same whatever that child had seen. He's only five, you'd never have got a conviction with him as a witness. The Coroner wouldn't even allow him to come to the inquest. But we'll nail Nico and Nancy Morris sooner or later.'

'I know, I know. Don't try teaching your grandmother to suck eggs,' said Sergeant Brown irritably. 'It's just that I would have preferred it to be sooner rather than later. What's more, I'd like to know why Nancy Morris hasn't turned up with that will in her favour? The will Mrs Stratton thinks she has. Why has she taken a sudden holiday in Miami? If she thinks she's in the clear, you'd think she'd be here to claim her inheritance.'

'May Marsham was an old woman, maybe she made a mistake and didn't sign any will. Or perhaps she did, and it got burned in the fire. Or maybe Nancy Morris saw the child and thinks he saw her.'

'And decided to cut and run. You might be right there.'

Terry Watkins sighed. He was as annoyed as his sergeant at not being able to tie the case up neatly. 'Even with no will, half of May Marsham's estate is legally hers anyway.'

'When the legal beagles have sorted it out. I understand the estate is anything but straightforward. I've spoken to Diana Stratton's solicitor, he reckons it will take two to three years to sort out the mess. So much money and property is involved. The only good thing is that Nancy Morris won't get the money she so obviously wanted, immediately. She'll have to wait.'

'But if Nancy Morris has to wait, then so will Diana Stratton. She's the only other close relative.' Terry Watkins felt sorry for Diana. From what Tony Evans had told him, he knew that Diana had had more than her fair share of bad luck recently. 'Did you know that the bank are still calling in her loan because they say they can't wait two years for her to collect her inheritance? And her aunt's bank won't help, because its not part of their national policy to loan on the strength of prospective legacies.'

'Bloody banks. They're all the same. That's what the

computer age does for you. No feelings involved, just bloody numbers on a screen. Diana Stratton is fighting a losing battle there.'

'Maybe we should go to Miami,' suggested Terry. 'See what we can pick up on Nancy Morris there. You never know, we might win our battle.'

'I'd never get the budget sanctioned. There's not enough evidence to make it worthwhile. No, we'll have to wait. But don't worry, give Mrs Morris long enough, and I'm sure she'll eventually provide enough rope to hang herself. I can be patient.'

'I wish I could.' But Sergeant Brown didn't hear Terry. He had already opened the door of the police car and was climbing in.

'You know,' said Miffy seriously, one week after May's funeral. 'I think May enjoyed the way she died.'

'You do?' Diana looked at him in astonishment. 'That's a strange thing to say.'

'Yes. It wasn't dull or ordinary like other people. The hospital part doesn't count, because I think May really died in the flames. I think she shot up to heaven like a big firework.' He warmed to his theme. 'Of course, everyone else thought that those were bullets shooting up through the roof into the sky, but I knew all the time it was May. It was her soul shooting up to join Bert in the stars. She didn't want to wait and be really old. Aunt May never liked waiting for anything.' He spread a piece of bread with Marmite and took a bite. 'That's what I think. And I know about souls, because the Reverend Pincher talked to us about them in Sunday School. He said that souls are the lights inside us. That's why I know it was May being a firework.'

'It's quite nice when you think of it like that,' said Clemmy. 'Imagine May, whizzing up to heaven.'

'Yes dear. I suppose it is.'

The children, as usual, had proved remarkably resilient, especially Miffy. They never stopped amazing Diana. In some ways they were very wise, they learned to cope in the best way they could, and if they wanted to think of May skyrocketing towards heaven, well, what harm was there in that? She looked at her watch. Nearly time to take the Strattons down into Chichester to catch their train. She had tried to dissuade them, feeling, when they announced after Hugh's funeral that they were leaving, that she must have failed them in some way. But they'd been adamant.

'Mother is quite happy now, she wants to go back to Brighton,' old Mr Stratton had said. He'd patted Diana on the hand, adding vaguely, 'and you are not to worry, my dear. Life is full of surprises.'

Diana began to wonder if it was only Mrs Stratton who was senile. She hadn't a clue what he was talking about, and doubted that he did either. But he was right about one thing. Life certainly was full of surprises, and lately most of them had been unpleasant. Not that the envelope she'd opened that morning had been a surprise. It was merely from Mr Mortimer, reminding her that the loan was due for repayment by the end of the November.

'Declare yourself bankrupt,' Norman Leadbetter had said when she'd sought his advice. But Diana couldn't bring herself to do that. Not yet.

The three children, Millicent and Griselda said goodbye to Mr and Mrs Stratton. 'You were the best behaved guests we've ever had,' said Millicent.

'And we're sorry to see you go,' added Simon politely.

'Thank you,' said Mr Stratton, and his wife bobbed her head in a silent goodbye.

The winter had arrived early. As Diana drove the Strattons through the winding lanes of the Downs towards Chichester, she noticed that, although it was early afternoon, the curves and hollows were already wreathed in mist, and in sheltered places the previous night's frost clung on with tenacious fingers. The balmy days of summer, when she'd walked through the vineyard with Sheridan, seemed years away rather than only weeks.

Thinking of Sheridan brought her mind back to the subject of money. After December there was no way she could continue to pay him, but by then the first racking of the wine would have been done, and she would know how to do the second herself. The fermentation process was going well, according to Sheridan, and he was confident of producing two and a half thousand bottles of good quality 'hurricane' wine. I'll miss him, Diana had to acknowledge, he'd been an absolute tower of strength. But more than that, everyone else would miss him. His dark brown face had become a familiar, welcome sight in the village, and since the concert, he'd been asked to do guest singing at various concerts throughout Sussex. 'The Marvellous Bass/Baritone from Mottisley' the *West Sussex Gazette* called him. And the inhabitants of Mottisley were proud, regarding him as their own home-grown property. A far cry from the first days when he'd been regarded with suspicion. But all that would soon be history. He'd be leaving because she couldn't afford to keep him, and although common sense told her that it was not her fault, Diana felt guilty because she'd be putting him out of work.

At the station she decanted Mr and Mrs Stratton. Normally almost totally silent, Mrs Stratton seemed quite vivacious at the thought of going home. She turned to Diana. 'I'm glad we found you,' she said. 'It was wrong of Hugh to have kept us apart.' Her dark eyes were no longer so vacant, although they were still melancholy.

'She's in for one of her good turns,' hissed Mr Stratton as he ushered his wife through the train door, 'and it's all due to you, Diana.' Then screwing up his face, he suddenly darted forward and planted a shy kiss on the side of Diana's cheek. 'You will keep in touch, won't you.'

'Of course. And you must come to stay again in the summer when the vineyard is at its best,' said Diana automatically. *If you are still there*, she could almost here Mr Mortimer's supercilious voice saying the words. Damn, the bloody bank manager! There had to be some alternative to selling the place.

On the way back to Mottisley Diana stopped in Midhurst, and went into the supermarket. Once she'd have paid Mrs Lomax's exorbitant prices without a thought, but not any more. These days every penny counted. At the checkout she literally ran her trolley into Tony and April.

'What are you doing here?' Diana, surprised at seeing them together, suddenly realized that she hadn't seen Joe, April or Tony to talk to properly since the funerals.

'Just the opportunity we've been looking for,' said Tony not answering her question. 'You can come and have a quick cup of tea with us. We have a bit of explaining to do.'

Crossing the road to 'Ye Olde Tea Shoppe' they nearly got mown down by a bright yellow Council lorry trundling up the High Street, its mechanical arm looping the electrical Christmas decorations from one lamppost to another.

'Oh my God, Christmas!' said Diana. 'I'd forgotten all about it.' Depression cascaded over her like black, sticky glue. Christmas, and everything that went with it. Presents, food, Christmas cards, decorations, the list was endless, and every single thing cost money.

As if to reinforce her gloom, the tea shop was dripping with red and green decorations and 'Jingle Bells' was playing as background music.

'This is nice,' said April, beaming from ear to ear.

Tony ordered tea and scones then turned to Diana. 'April and I are going to be married,' he said.

Diana stared at him, dumbstruck.

'It's because I'm not pregnant,' explained April beaming more than ever. 'I tested myself, and made a mistake. I never was.'

'Easily done,' said Tony. 'Especially when you've been tanked up the night before, as April was the night of the harvest supper.'

'So there's no reason for me to stay with Joe any longer.'

'And no reason for musical beds either,' said Diana sharply, feeling irritated. What right had they to look so blissfully happy when her world was falling down around her ears. 'What on earth will people in the village say?'

'For God's sake, You sound like a younger version of Mrs Lomax.' Tony drew a deep breath. 'They'll talk about it for a week or two,' he continued in a calmer vein, 'and then they will forget all about it.' He was suddenly very serious. 'This isn't a game, Diana. This is for keeps. You know I've always loved April.'

'But April loved Joe,' said Diana. 'And I wrongly told him that she'd stick with him even though he'd lost his fortune, which just shows that I was wrong yet again.'

'I would have stuck with him if he'd wanted me to. But he didn't. He was only marrying me because he thought I was pregnant. I knew he didn't really want to.'

'And it was really me she loved all the time,' said Tony. 'Hell, where is that tea I ordered?' He got up. 'I'm going to hurry them up. I've got surgery in three-quarters of an hour.'

April looked at Diana and shook her head. 'That's not true. I haven't been nurturing a secret love for Tony and he knows it, although he insists that I am mistaken. Says it was there all the time in my subconscious.'

'Very convenient.' Knowing she was being irrational didn't stop Diana from still feeling put out.

'But I have always been very fond of him,' added April defensively, challenging Diana's bad-tempered glare. 'Look, I know what you're thinking, and I suppose in a way, you're right. It *is* convenient. But I always knew Joe didn't love me. He just liked me, and at the time I thought that was enough.' She put up a hand to silence Diana. 'I'm older than you, Diana. I'm thirty-eight, nearly thirty-nine, and I'm tired of rocketing around the world with different partners. The one thing I've longed for more than anything else this past couple of years is to put down some roots and stay put. Mistakenly I thought Joe was the answer. But he wasn't.'

'And Tony is?'

'Yes,' April's voice softened. 'I really do think he is. He does love me, Diana. Probably you find that as difficult to believe as I did at first, but . . .'

'No,' interrupted Diana, regaining her common sense and compassion. 'I've known it for a long time. What I couldn't understand was why you could never see it.'

'Oh, Diana,' April reached across the table and clasped Diana's hands. 'I can't tell you how good it feels to have someone as kind and good as Tony love me for myself. Warts and all.'

'That's what loving is all about,' said Diana slowly. 'The warts and all bit.'

'He'll never, ever regret it. I'll make him a good wife. I'll really cherish him.'

Diana smiled for the first time. 'I know you will, and what's more you sound as if you are beginning to love him already.'

'Yes, I do, don't I?' April blushed.

Tony came back with the waitress and the tea things. 'One pace, this place,' he grumbled. 'Dead slow!'

Diana was silent. So Joe was free now. But she had conditioned herself these last few weeks to viewing the years ahead on her own. Just her and the children. They formed a tight, close-knit little circle, just the four of them. She didn't need anyone else, besides, she'd proved herself to be a hopeless judge of character with Hugh, how could she trust her feelings for any other man? And remembering her utter desolation the night she had thought April was pregnant with Joe's child, Diana wondered whether she even wanted to get back on an emotional rollercoaster.

'If you're wondering why we haven't mentioned it to you before,' said Tony, as soon as the waitress had gone, 'it's because, after May's death, we all thought you had quite enough to handle at the time. But as you had to know sooner or later, now seemed the ideal chance to tell you.'

'Actually, Joe was more disappointed about there being no baby, than about there being no me in his future,' said April with a wry smile. 'He's always wanted a son.'

'But of course, he might have a son, later.' Tony looked at Diana and she knew he was thinking of Miffy.

Suddenly she felt angry. Tony was trying to manoeuvre her into telling Joe about Miffy. He wanted everything neatly sorted out to salve his conscience. Never mind *her* feelings. Those few brief hours with Joe when she had thought there was a future for them together, had been before she had known about Miffy. The fact that Joe was Miffy's father changed everything. If she stayed alone, Joe would never know. It was no use, she couldn't purge herself of the possessive jealousy she felt whenever she thought about it. And anyway, it was better that way. Better for Miffy, and for Clemmy and Simon too. Drinking down her tea without tasting it, Diana pushed the cup back and stood up.

'I hope you'll both be very happy,' she said, and hurried towards the door.

Tony caught up with her outside and barred her way. 'Secrets are a terrible burden,' he said.

Diana knew that he'd accurately guessed her thoughts, but her stubborn streak rose to the fore. 'Not to me,' she said.

'Look, for God's sake, tell Joe the truth about Miffy, and take it from there. Who knows, it might work out very well for both of you.'

'I told you once that I'd never tell him,' said Diana obstinately, 'and I see no reason to change my mind. He'll only know if you tell him.'

Joe's Land-Rover was standing outside Abbey House when Diana returned.

Miffy came running to meet her as soon as he heard her car stop. 'Look what Joe has brought us.' He held out a tiny, quivering puppy. Brindle and rough haired, it had a clumsy head, long spindly legs, and cuddled into Miffy's hands.

'She's fifty per cent lurcher and a fifty per cent unknown,' said Joe, following Miffy out into the gravelled yard. 'I thought you'd like another dog for company.'

Miffy put the dog down on the ground and tried to get her to run. After a few tentative steps the puppy sank down in a frightened heap, afraid of the big outdoors. 'Poor girlie,' said Miffy, picking her up again and making crooning noises.

Diana looked at the puppy. She felt ill at ease, and more than a little guilty as she remembered her last words to Tony. Joe must have come up to tell her about April, not knowing that she already knew. Apprehensive, she wondered what he expected her reaction to be.

'I met April and Tony in Midhurst,' she said quickly, wanting to make the first move.

'Thank heavens. I was wondering how the hell to broach the subject. I've practised saying, I am not an expectant father, and it sounded so bloody strange.'

'I'm going to take May inside now,' said Miffy.

'May!' Diana and Joe spoke in unison.

'Yes.' He kissed the puppy on the tip of her pale pink, freckled nose. 'I've named her after Auntie May. Simon and Clemmy think it's a good idea.'

'He's not what you might call orthodox in his thinking, is he,' said Joe, smiling.

A smile broke through her careful reserve. 'No,' Diana admitted. She found the words *he takes after his father* were on the tip of her tongue, and had difficulty in restraining herself from speaking them out loud. 'He's a one-off,' she ended up saying.

'Yes,' said Joe staring after Miffy's retreating back. 'He is.'

There was something about the way he said, *he is*, that made Diana look up. Their eyes met, and without a word being exchanged Diana understood that Joe knew exactly whose son Miffy was, and that he'd always known. Suddenly she felt afraid. 'You know,' she said accusingly.

'Since the day he was born.'

'Then why?'

'Didn't I say anything?' Joe thought for a moment, then said, 'because he was an accident of nature. I slept with Susan only once.'

'Once too often,' said Diana acidly. Then hated herself for being bitchy. 'I'm sorry. I shouldn't have said that.'

Joe didn't reply. He carried on as if she hadn't spoken. 'It was quite obvious that Susan thought I didn't know, and that she didn't want Miffy to be different from the other children. She wanted him to be wholly within the family she and Tom had created, and that was right. It would have been quite wrong of me to have tried to lay claim to him. What did I have to offer? Certainly not the family stability Susan and Tom had. So I kept quiet, and eventually Susan relaxed, sure that I didn't know, and I let her think it.'

'And now?' asked Diana. She waited, heart in her mouth. What would Joe say? I want him to remain silent for Miffy's sake she told herself fiercely. Not for mine. But she was, as she had once admitted to Tony, less than perfect, and knew that she wanted to cling on to Miffy for herself.

'And now?' Joe looked at Diana, his clear blue eyes surprised at her question. 'Nothing has changed. I'm not going to upset a small child's life by turning all his known values upside down. As far as he is concerned his mother and father were Susan and Tom, and that's the way it's going to stay. I've loved him from a distance, as an adopted uncle all these years, and I shall go on doing so.'

Diana flushed, ashamed of her own possessive thoughts. True love was giving, not holding on, and Joe had passed the test with flying colours, whereas she had failed. 'I shouldn't have asked.'

Reaching out, he touched her arm gently. 'You thought I was about to claim him?' Diana nodded, mutely. Joe put a finger under her chin, tilting her head so that she was forced to look at him. 'Then you don't know me very well,' he said softly.

Looking into his eyes, the colour of the sea in summer, Diana suddenly realized that she didn't know him. Didn't know this man, this mass of contradictions, at all. But neither did she truly know herself, because she'd always been too busy, or too afraid to look. 'No, I don't think I do,' she said unsteadily, 'but then, you don't know me either, Joe.'

'I'd like to find out more.'

'You may not like everything you find.'

'Probably not,' he said cheerfully. Then his expression changed, becoming serious. 'Look, I know this is a bit precipitate, but on the night of the harvest supper we decided that we could make a go of our lives together. Remember?'

'Yes.' Diana did remember, although now she was no longer certain it had been such a good idea. Joe didn't know that she had cheated him, and as Tony had said, secrets were a terrible burden.

'Well, since I've known that I no longer have to go through a shot-gun wedding with April.'

'Oh, Joe, really!' Diana was forced to laugh. 'You were hardly being forced to the altar by an irate father.'

'By an irate conscience – mine. That's almost as bad. Anyway, since then, I've been thinking. At first I'd planned to turn the manor house into a hotel, build a swimming pool and so on, but . . .'

'What has this got to do with me?' Diana was beginning to feel confused.

'I said at first. I've since discarded that idea, because I've had a better one. If I sell the manor house, I can put the money from the sale into the Abbey Vineyard, make it solvent again.'

'And come and live with me at Abbey House?'

'Of course,' said Joe. 'What did you think?'

'I think you're trying to bribe your way in.'

'Of course,' said Joe again, his eyes crinkling into a slow smile. 'What else?'

'Everyone will think we are terribly immoral. I've only been a widow for a few weeks.'

'Damn everyone,' said Joe.

'And you have only just broken off your engagement to the woman you've lived with for the past year.'

'A mere detail. Besides, what the hell does it matter what other people think? It's what *we* think that matters. So tell me, what do you think?'

'I think it's a good idea,' said Diana, suddenly realizing that it was. 'But I'm afraid I might be saying that because it would get me off the hook, financially speaking. I no longer have any faith in my own judgement where relationships with men are concerned. My record so far is not very good.'

'What has changed since the night of the harvest supper?'

'Me,' said Diana. 'You are not the only one who has had time to think. Thinking has made me doubt.'

'OK. So let's lay our cards on the table. I've made a mess of my life. I think we'd both agree on that. None of my relationships has lasted because I suppose, if I'm to be honest, I really didn't care too much whether they lasted or not. Not a record which deserves to be rewarded. But the fates have been kind, they've put me in the position of being able to help you and the children, and doing myself a good turn at the same time; given me the chance of a proper family life, something I've always wanted. Just because I've screwed up the first half of my life, is no good reason for screwing up the second half as well. I'll work bloody hard at making it work, because I know this is my last chance of real happiness.'

It makes sense, thought Diana. It's not only Joe who is being given a last chance, it's me too. But a fresh start wouldn't stand a chance, unless she was honest too.

'You said you've always wanted to be part of a family,' she said carefully. 'So while we're laying our cards on the

515

table, there's something you ought to know. I can never give you children. I'm sterile.' That was the easy part. The next part was more difficult and Diana hesitated a moment, but then went on. Time now, to disperse that unhappy ghost from the past once and for all. 'I was pregnant when I was eighteen.'

'Mine?'

'Yes. I had an abortion.'

'I see,' said Joe slowly.

'The clinic where I had the termination was chosen because of its secrecy, not efficiency. I left the afternoon of the day I had it done, and was admitted into hospital with a pelvic infection two days later. If I hadn't been so anxious to pretend that there had never been a baby at all, I'd have taken more care, and would probably not have contracted the infection which has made me sterile. But it all backfired, and instead of being able to forget, the guilt of it has haunted me ever since. I suppose, in a way, I've never stopped mourning the child that never was.'

There, Diana thought, taking a deep breath, I've said it. I've admitted at last that I regret letting that child be destroyed. A sense of real grief swept through her, as fresh and poignant as if it had all happened only yesterday.

Joe turned slowly so that he was facing her, and Diana looked carefully at her feet, afraid of what she might see in his face. After what seemed a lifetime, he spoke.

'It's time you stopped mourning,' he said gently. 'You can't undo what has been done any more than I can. Like me, you've screwed up part of your life. But there's a lot left. We can go on together and play it straight from now on. If you want to.'

Diana looked up. There was no reproach in his blue eyes, only sadness, the same sadness she too felt. 'I do,' she said. 'As long as you don't mind my not being able to have your children.'

'What the hell,' said Joe, putting his arms around her.

'You've inherited three. I'll share those. Three are enough.'

Yes, he was right, three were enough. Diana smiled. Strange how the burden already seemed light. The residual pain would always be there, that small core of regret, but that would have to be borne. After all, people were but the sum total of their past, and as Joe had said, no-one could undo what had been done. All they could do was learn to live with the past. For the first time in years she felt truly free. It was as if someone had opened a door into a sunlit room, and she had stepped through into the warmth. She slipped her arms around Joe's waist. 'How are we going to tell the children?'

'We'll start off with the sale of the manor house, and work up to us getting married, and my moving in here.'

Millicent's head popped out of the kitchen door. 'Joe,' she shrieked, 'there's a man on the 'phone from London. He wants to speak to you.'

'Good,' said Joe. 'That'll be Archie, my accountant. I told him to look into the possibility of selling the manor house and transferring the money to you. Come on.' Dragging Diana behind him he raced into the house.

'Shit!' Joe slammed the 'phone down.

'That's a bad word,' said Simon disapprovingly as he passed by to go up the stairs.

'Sorry, but I feel bad.' He turned to Diana. She was leaning back against the wall, dreamily planning how to invest the spare money they would have once she'd paid off Mr Mortimer. It would be nice to have the winery walls tiled, and new red flagstones for the floor with a proper drainage system, instead of the haphazard mop and bucket method they used at the moment. She'd just progressed to deciding what colours the wall tiles should be when Joe's voice penetrated her rosy day-dream. 'There won't be any money.'

'What?' Diana had difficulty extracting herself from the plans for the new winery.

'There won't be any money. If I sell the manor house and land Archie says my creditors are sure to demand a share. So either I hang on to it and have no money to speak of, or sell it and still have virtually nothing.'

'It doesn't matter.' Diana put her arms around his waist. 'We'll manage.'

Together they walked back into the kitchen, where Shakespeare, resembling a tabby lavatory brush, was sitting in outrage on the windowsill.

'That wretched puppy! It's no good, I just can't bring myself to call it May,' said Griselda. 'Anyway it has pinched the cat's place by the Aga. Oh, and before I forget. There's message for you from old Mr Grimble. He rang while you were out. He's coming round tomorrow at four o' clock in the afternoon. Something to do with the elderly Strattons' finances.'

'Oh heavens,' said Diana. 'I do hope they don't owe too much.'

'Never mind, we'll just add it on to our list of bills to be paid.'

Diana laughed. 'You're right. In for a penny, in for a pound as they say.'

Epilogue

Mr Grimble cleared his throat ceremoniously then looked around. 'Is everyone here?' he asked, peering short-sightedly through his metal rimmed spectacles.

'Everyone who lives in Abbey House,' confirmed Diana. 'Just as you asked, even the children. Although I don't think it fair to bother them with the Strattons' financial affairs.'

'I'll be the judge of that,' Mr Grimble replied rather pompously.

Joe squeezed her hand. 'Perhaps they've robbed a bank,' he whispered, 'and are going to give you the proceeds.'

'Bang, bang,' said Miffy, aiming an imaginary gun at Mr Grimble.

'Shut up,' said Diana and Joe in unison.

Mr Grimble looked in Joe's direction, and twinkled. Yes, thought Diana, that's the word for it, he's *twinkling*. Suddenly she began to feel more hopeful.

'Not so far off the mark, Joe,' said Mr Grimble, and took an envelope out of his pocket.

'Get on with it, Cuthbert,' said Griselda sharply. She'd known him since he was in short trousers with muddy knees, and so wasn't in the least bit awed by Mottisley's senior solicitor.

'Yes, yes, Griselda.' Mr Grimble huffed and puffed a little then got down to business. 'On the instructions of Mr and Mrs Norman Stratton, it is my pleasure to pass over to you, Diana Stratton, a cheque to the value of five hundred and sixty-three thousand pounds and eighty-six pence.'

Outside the kitchen a chill November wind blew

through the skeletal vines, and rattled the door. Inside the kitchen there was silence, save for the snores of the puppy asleep on Shakespeare's cushion.

'What did you say?' whispered Diana.

'I think he said half a million,' said Joe.

'I did.'

'But I thought they were poor.' Diana was still whispering.

'They were,' said Mr Grimble. 'Poor and happy, until they won the football pools six months ago. Since then they haven't had a moment's peace. Being rich was a responsibility they didn't want, and couldn't cope with. So they tracked down their son, and tried to give it to him. But he refused to listen.'

'Hugh always thought that they *wanted* money.' Diana remembered Hugh cruelly brushing them aside. 'He never guessed that they were trying to give him some.'

'Well, now he's dead,' said Mr Grimble matter of factly, 'and they want to give it to you.'

'I can't believe it,' said Diana slowly.

'Well, my dear. Here is the proof.' Mr Grimble pushed the cheque across the table.

Supper that night was a riotous affair. Griselda made a centrepiece of pinecones for the table, pinning the Strattons' cheque to the top so that it flew like a triumphant banner. And for once Diana let Millicent have the key to the bonded barn and use as much wine in the cooking and for the table as she wanted. The whole evening passed in a daze as far as Diana was concerned. She was hardly aware of what she was eating and drinking, only knowing that everything tasted like ambrosia.

'Are you and Joe really going to be married?' demanded Clemmy and Simon.

'And are you going to adopt us properly so that we'll be a real family?' Miffy wanted to know.

'Yes, yes,' Joe and Diana chorused in unison.

'And live here?' Simon wanted every last detail spelled out.

'Yes, and live here,' said Diana.

'What about the manor house?' asked Griselda.

'I've been thinking about that,' said Joe. He turned to Diana, 'would you object if I leased it to a charity at a peppercorn rent?'

She shook her head. 'Of course not.'

'The Saint Cecilia Trust approached me last year wanting to buy it, and at the time I said no. They run a home for retired, and impoverished musicians, and one of the reasons they wanted the manor house was because of the old ballroom. They wanted that as a concert hall. If I lease it, it will be cheaper for the Trust and will mean that I still own it although someone else will have the use of it.'

'That's a marvellous idea,' enthused Millicent.

'Maybe the retired professionals would be willing to coach Mottisley Brass Band,' said Sheridan.

'It seems the perfect solution,' Diana agreed.

'And will you still need us?' Griselda asked, and suddenly Diana realized that the three of them, Millicent, Griselda and Sheridan were a little uncertain of their own future.

'Of course we'll need you. More than ever. Joe and I aim to turn Abbey Vineyard into the most famous and most successful vineyard in England.

'To Abbey Vineyard,' said Sheridan, raising his glass, his face almost split in half by an enormous grin.

'To Abbey Vineyard.'

'To Joe and Diana.'

'To the family.'

'To the Strattons, bless their hearts and their generosity.'

'Did we leave anyone out?' asked Joe much later. They were alone. It was late and everyone had finally staggered upstairs to bed, tired but very happy.

'I don't think so.' Diana removed the cheque from

Griselda's table decoration, and carefully put it in a folder. 'I can't wait to see Mr Mortimer's face when I deposit this cheque.'

Joe was standing staring out of the window at the vines, now bathed in the cold light of a full moon. 'You will be happy?' It was a question rather than a statement. 'Mottisley, me, the kids and the vineyard, will it be enough?'

'Of course. I've had my share of life in the fast lane, now I want the real thing, where people matter more than things.' Taking his duffle coat from the peg on the kitchen door Diana threw it at Joe, then slipped her arms into one of Susan's old anoraks. 'Come on,' she said, holding out her hand, 'let's inspect the estate.'

They walked slowly past the rows of black and silver vines. 'I meant to ask,' said Joe. 'What is going to happen to May's farm? We can't just leave it.'

'The Solicitors and the Bank are acting as executors, and they are putting in a manager to keep the farm ticking over until it can be sold. All the antiques from the house are going into storage until it's decided to whom they belong.'

'You, eventually,' said Joe.

'And Nancy,' Diana reminded him.

'No. I don't think we'll ever see Nancy again. She overstepped the mark once too often. I think you've seen the last of your cousin Nancy.'

'Well, that certainly won't worry me,' said Diana.

They reached the end of the vineyards, and turning, walked round the house and finally through the garden to where the yew had once stood. Now there were no dark corners in the garden. Moonlight poured through the gap left by the uprooted tree, flooding the garden with brilliant light. Like my life, thought Diana, no dark corners any more.

Joe, thinking about Seamus, put his arms around Diana. 'Don't be sad,' he said.

'I'm not. Somehow I feel that we've survived this awful

year because we were meant to. Now it's up to us to make the best use of our own time.' Diana stared up at the moon. The plains and shadow on its surface stood out clearly, forming the shape of a face. 'You know, once I needed my father to light the moon for me, but now I know that it will light of its own accord in the fullness of time. Perhaps I've finally grown up.'

'Talking of the fullness of time,' said Joe, 'reminds me that it's high time we got married.'

'Yes.'

'Before the waning of this moon.'

'Definitely.'

Looking over her shoulder as they retraced their steps back to the warmth of the kitchen, Diana could have sworn that the glowing face in the sky was smiling.

THE END